KILLS
WELL
WITH
OTHERS

KILLS WELL WITH OTHERS

Deanna Raybourn

BERKLEY

New York

BERKLEY
An imprint of Penguin Random House LLC
1745 Broadway, New York, NY 10019
penguinrandomhouse.com

Book design by Ashley Tucker

The Edgar® name is a registered service mark of the Mystery Writers of America, Inc.

THE POEMS OF EMILY DICKINSON: VARIORUM EDITION, edited by Ralph
W. Franklin, Cambridge, Mass.: The Belknap Press of Harvard University Press,
Copyright © 1998 by the President and Fellows of Harvard College. Copyright © 1951,
1955 by the President and Fellows of Harvard College. Copyright © renewed 1979, 1983
by the President and Fellows of Harvard College. Copyright © 1914, 1918, 1919, 1924,
1929, 1930, 1932, 1935, 1937, 1942 by Martha Dickinson Bianchi. Copyright © 1952,
1957, 1958, 1963, 1965 by Mary L. Hampson. Used by permission. All rights reserved.

Export edition ISBN: 9780593954164

Library of Congress Cataloging-in-Publication Data

Names: Raybourn, Deanna, author.
Title: Kills well with others / Deanna Raybourn.
Description: New York: Berkley, 2025.
Identifiers: LCCN 2024029076 (print) | LCCN 2024029077 (ebook) |
ISBN 9780593638514 (hardcover) | ISBN 9780593638521 (ebook)
Subjects: LCGFT: Thrillers (Fiction) | Novels.
Classification: LCC PS3618.A983 K56 2025 (print) |
LCC PS3618.A983 (ebook) | DDC 813/.6—dc23/eng/20240628
LC record available at https://lccn.loc.gov/2024029076
LC ebook record available at https://lccn.loc.gov/2024029077

Printed in the United States of America
1st Printing

The authorized representative in the EU for product safety and compliance is Penguin
Random House Ireland, Morrison Chambers, 32 Nassau Street, Dublin D02 YH68,
Ireland, https://eu-contact.penguin.ie.

To all of you who took these killers to your hearts and wanted to see them kill again. Thank you.

KILLS
WELL
WITH
OTHERS

AUTHOR'S NOTE

Authors are liars. Some of what you'll read here is true; some of it isn't. You'll have to figure out which is which for yourself.

CHAPTER ONE

APRIL 1982

"BILLIE, YOU HAVE A RUN IN YOUR STOCKING. AGAIN." HELEN'S VOICE is cool as she hands over an unopened package of fishnets. "Have my spares." Billie has been in this position before and knows better than to argue with Helen's eye for detail.

"Just like the last time," Billie says with a grin.

She changes stockings and shimmies back into her costume. "I think I'm going to have to burn my feminist card when this is done," Billie says as she tweaks her Bunny ears in the mirror. Three months of working undercover at the Playboy Club and her blue satin ears are still a constant source of irritation.

Mary Alice, sitting next to her in the dressing room, purses her mouth as she flicks black eyeliner into a sharp wing. She moves back, admiring the effect. "I kind of like it."

"That's because you don't need to stuff your damned bra," Natalie counters from the other side of the room. The lower half of the corseted costumes are altered to slim the waist, elongating the legs and making the hips appear fuller. But the cups only come in 34 or 36D, forcing most of the Bunnies to augment their curves with whatever is lying around—gym socks, fresh maxi pads. Billie needs only a powder puff of a Bunny tail in each cup, while Helen requires a rolled gym sock and Natalie needs three pairs of pantyhose. Mary Alice, whose resemblance to Marilyn Monroe has been deliberately heightened by lightening her hair with a platinum rinse, is the only one of the four whose seams have had to be reinforced. Makeup finished, she stands, straightening the little starched collar and cuffs that finish off the uniform. Like everything else in the club, the costumes—witty and modern twenty years before—are now seedy and tired. The club has been refurbished in an attempt to make it relevant again, but a long decade has passed since it was anything but tacky. The veneer of forced, flirty fun is wearing thin, and they are tired of smiling at the same jokes, ignoring the same worn-out come-ons.

For three months they have carried drinks and sold cigarettes and checked coats. Every shift they have come prepared, ready to carry out their mission, and every shift they have clocked out with aching feet and a rising rage that they have to repeat the cycle all over again. Billie hardly remembers a time she wasn't schlepping drinks with a perky smile. Their current target is the nephew of a Toronto gangster, heir apparent to his uncle's crew. The gangster is happy with his protection racket and gambling, but the nephew is ambitious, pushing the gang into drugs and underage prostitution. He likes violence for its own sake, and his plan is to expand into Chicago, upsetting the status quo.

The old man visits Chicago every few months and he brings the nephew with him, making the rounds of his connections, renewing contacts, smoothing the way for the succession. In his prime, he was a keyholder, dining at the club every night, harassing the girls and paying off the bouncers to look the other way. He's trained the nephew well. The younger man grins as they make their way to the table and he sees a new server approaching. This one has ash blond hair brushing her shoulders, a mouth with a tiny scar just above the top lip, and an ass he'd like to get to know better. He drops a casual hand to her hip as she takes the drink order and watches her reaction. She's good; she almost masks the flinch but not completely, and this is the part he likes best—when they realize he can touch them and there's nothing they can do about it. He relaxes back into his chair and bobs his head to the music as the server slips out of his grasp and heads to the bar to put in the order. She's got a small smile set on her lips and so he has no idea what she's really thinking.

It's only when she turns her back that the smile drops. Mary Alice slides up to Billie after Billie relates the order to the bartender. "How's our boy?" Mary Alice asks.

"Peachy. He copped a feel and smells like a bottle of Drakkar Noir threw up on him," Billie tells her. "Just once, I'd like to kill a gentleman."

"If they were gentlemen, they probably wouldn't need killing."

Mary Alice puts in her own order and turns to scan the room. It's a slow night, with less than half of the tables occupied. To make it seem like the place is swinging, the music has been turned up and the lights down. Olivia Newton-John is blaring from the speakers, wanting to get physical.

Near the entrance, Helen is working the coat check. Her job is to remove the EpiPen that the nephew's bodyguard carries in his overcoat, substituting it with the one they've prepared specially. According to the dossier they've received, the nephew is highly allergic to peanuts. The plan is to induce an allergy attack, mild enough not to kill, but severe enough to require the EpiPen.

Instead of epinephrine, the pen he will use has been loaded with a mixture of Versed and potassium chloride, a cocktail that will stop his heart almost instantly, mimicking the heart attack that could follow severe anaphylactic shock. Traces of peanut oil will be present in his stomach, and the death will be certified as natural causes after accidental ingestion of an allergen. The plan is elegant in its simplicity, but it requires perfect preparation and timing from every member of the team.

Both trays of drinks land at the same time, and Mary Alice takes hers. As she leaves, Billie catches Helen's eye at the coat check counter. With her dark hair and Jackie O posture, Helen is the most patrician of the group. On her, the satin costume looks almost classy, and it occurs to Billie the nephew would never have dared to grab Helen's ass. Helen touches her left cheek with a fingertip, the signal that the switch has happened. Billie turns back just as Natalie joins her at the bar.

Without taking her eyes off the bartender as she relates

her order, Natalie passes a hand over Billie's tray, pouring the contents of a tiny vial into one of the drinks—a lurid-looking grasshopper. Her gift for sleight of hand is so good, not even Billie, who is watching closely, sees the moment she adulterates the drink. Billie glances down to see the shreds of dark chocolate that garnish the drink are glistening with unrefined peanut oil.

Billie hoists the tray with a sense of elation, the same sort of buzz actors feel after months of rehearsal, when the curtain is about to rise on opening night. This hit has been too long in the making. They anticipated finishing it in six weeks, but it's been double that. Twice she's had to make a phone call she dreaded, postponing a trip to Bermuda with a man she needs to see again. Taverner. An image of him as she last saw him springs to mind. Sheets bunched around his hips, sleepy smile and open arms beckoning her back to bed for so long she misses her train. She shoves the memory away. She can't afford distractions now. And the sooner she kills this man, the sooner she can get back to that one.

She approaches the table and performs the trademark move of the servers, a dip that calls for her to gracefully bend at the knees instead of the waist. It requires a slight backbend, putting stress on the knees, but the move prevents a wardrobe malfunction. Billie serves the other two gentlemen at the table first. She doesn't recognize them from the dossier, but they are hanging on the nephew's every word as he tells a joke, a filthy one that Billie has heard at least seven times since coming to work at the club. The uncle is beaming at his nephew, a chip off a particularly nasty block. She deliberately leaves the grasshopper for last, as much to enjoy the anticipation as to make sure it is delivered perfectly. Just as she moves to set it in front of the nephew, he reaches the punchline and throws his hands wide, catching her arm. The grasshopper goes flying, the sticky green liquid hitting her squarely in the chest. It drips into her costume and the nephew, initially irritated at the loss of his drink, makes a vulgar suggestion as to how to clean it up.

Billie gives him a tight smile and apologizes, promising to replace the drink. She hurries up to the bar, where the bartender hands her a towel. She's discreetly blotting her chest when Natalie appears. "Bad news," Billie says from the side of her mouth. "He spilled it. I need a refill."

"Worse news," Nat tells her. "I haven't got one."

Billie turns to look directly at Nat. "Are you shitting me?" she hisses.

Natalie shrugs. "Mary Alice only has one vial."

"*One?* We've been prepping for three months and she has one?"

"She made a second one, but it got broken. It's not her fault."

Billie is fairly spitting at this point, and Nat gives her a warning look. Billie darts a glance in the mirror behind the bar and sees the uncle watching her. He signals for the check. Billie presents it and he shoves a few bills inside the leather folder—exact change for the drinks.

The nephew grins as he stands. "Sorry, tits. But if you want a tip, here you go—be a little friendlier." He leaves, snickering with the others. Billie, her costume sticky with crème de menthe, heads for the dressing room, where she grabs a trench coat from her locker. She throws it on over her costume and belts it tightly. Mary Alice appears just as Billie jerks the bunny ears off her head and tosses them into the corner.

"Where are you going?" Mary Alice demands.

"Plan B," Billie tells her.

Before anyone can stop her, she's out on the street. In the regulation club stilettos her feet hurt, but now she doesn't mind the pain. It keeps her sharp, focused, and in ten minutes she is at the front entrance of his hotel. The bellman sweeps open the door and she crosses directly to the registration desk, sliding a hundred-dollar bill towards the clerk as she gives the nephew's name.

"I'm sorry—" he begins.

Billie sighs to herself, but she knows what she has to do. She lets the coat fall open a little, just enough so that the clerk can see the distinctive satin costume, the collar with its trademark bow tie, the shadow at her cleavage. "Look, he's my boyfriend, and we had a fight before he came to Chicago. I just want to surprise him with his favorite fantasy," she tells him in a breathy tone.

His hands are shaking as he looks up the number. "612."

"Thank you," she says, pulling her coat closed. She's broken every rule of their organization. She's gone alone to finish a group mission. She's made herself obvious, memorable. She's guaranteed that if the desk clerk is ever questioned, he will be able to describe her down to the little freckle on her collarbone. But she doesn't care. She is allowing anger to fuel the job, and it feels good.

She rides the elevator up to the sixth floor and heads for the room. She tests the door handle—a shocking number of people forget to lock up when they leave—but it doesn't give. She is just about to pick the lock when a cheerful voice calls out from down the hall.

"Ma'am? Are you locked out?" It's a housekeeper, about twenty, too young to be tired of the job yet. Most hotel maids hurry past with their eyes down, worn down by drudgery, but this one is still shiny and bright as a new penny as she approaches.

Billie gives her a smile and rolls her eyes in mock annoyance. "I forgot my key and my husband must be in the shower. So stupid of me!"

The maid reaches past her and uses the passkey. "No problem."

"You're a doll." Billie blows her a kiss as she slips into the room. She closes the door behind her, careful to lock it again. She's not surprised to find the nephew is a slob. Traces of cut lines powder the coffee table, and empty champagne bottles are upended into a potted tree in the corner. Heaps of discarded clothes litter the floor. She steps over the pile nearest the bed, noting the pair of skid-marked underwear on the top. She kicks them aside and surveys the room. Outside the bathroom door is a small alcove with a vanity and a pair of marble sinks. The complimentary toiletries are all open, some spilling their contents onto the counter. She flicks all the lights off, plunging the room into darkness. She's left the curtains slightly parted, and the only illumination in the room comes from the street outside. She has prepared the trap. There is nothing to do now but wait.

It's only a quarter of an hour later when the door opens. The man who enters fumbles with the light switch but can't manage it, swearing softly. Billie can smell the liquor fumes as he stumbles towards the bathroom, and her eyes, accustomed to the darkness, can just make out his silhouette. Silently, she slips off her shoes and lunges, crossing the space between them in three steps, and gathering just enough speed to vault herself upwards, using his thigh as a launchpad. In one fluid motion she wraps her legs around his neck and twists her entire body, whipping him onto his back as she lands in a crouch over him. The air is knocked out of his lungs, leaving him gasping and disoriented. Before he can recover his breath, she flips him onto his belly, grinding his face into the carpet. With one knee in the small of his back, she brings her arm around his neck, clasping her elbow with her other hand, drawing it tight and cutting off his air. The whole maneuver has been completely silent and executed in almost total darkness. It has taken less than ten seconds. If she had been in a better mood, she would have held him gently in that position until he slipped into unconsciousness, then strangled him.

But Billie is not in a good mood. Just before he loses consciousness, she grabs either side of his head, using his chin for leverage as she jerks her hands in opposite directions. The snap, she always thinks, sounds like cracking a stalk of celery. He goes boneless and soft in her arms and she lets his torso fall to the floor. It will be simple to make it look like a drunken accident, a fall into the coffee table, maybe. She switches on the light, planning where to stage the body. She will have to slam his head into the corner of the coffee table to get a little blood flowing, but that doesn't bother her. She turns him over, and when the light falls on his face, she stares at him for a long minute, realizing just how much trouble she is in.

"Well, shit," she says as she slumps onto the sofa, considering her options.

Billie Webster has just made the biggest mistake a professional assassin can make.

She has killed the wrong man.

CHAPTER TWO

"ISN'T THIS WHERE YOU TOSS THINGS OUT OF MY SUITCASE AND BEG me not to go?" I asked, throwing a pair of boot-cut jeans into my mini-duffel.

"No," Taverner answered calmly. He was propped against the headboard, eating an apricot and letting the juice drip through his fingers. The shutters were closed—it was too early in the spring to let in the sea breezes—but if they'd been open, I could have seen the broad blue spread of the Aegean rippling away below the cliffs. It would have been a hell of an inducement to stay, but the man in my bed was an even better one.

"You don't seem upset that I'm leaving," I said evenly.

"Because I'm not. You'll go, you'll do the job, and while you're away, you'll miss me."

"I'm retired," I reminded him. "This isn't a job."

I said it more for my benefit than his. I'd been summoned

by the head of the organization we'd both worked for as long as either of us could remember. I had taken forcible retirement a few years before, but good training never dies. The summons hadn't been much, just a thin, old-fashioned airmail envelope with no return address. Honestly, I hadn't even known they still made those. I liked the jaunty little blue-and-red stripe around the edge. Inside was a postcard of Colonial Williamsburg with a scribble on the back—*Wish you were here! N.* Clipped to the postcard was a ticket on the next international flight out of Athens and a printout of a reservation from a cheap car rental at Dulles. They'd left it up to me to make my way to Athens. The ferry ran twice a day, and I had about twenty minutes before the morning boat left.

Taverner took another bite, chewing thoughtfully. "But you hope it's a job."

There was a silk blouse in my hands, and I kept folding, but my hands moved a little slower. "Maybe."

I'd known his smiles for forty years. The one he gave me was gentle, pitying even. "Billie."

I sighed and gave up folding, chucking the blouse into the bag after the jeans. "Fine. Maybe I miss it."

"Maybe?" He laughed. "If you'd ever missed me half as much as you miss the job, we'd never have split up."

"We split up because you married someone else." I turned back to my packing, throwing a handful of underwear on top of the blouse.

He chose his next words carefully. The subject of his marriage was a minefield, suitable for tiptoes and whispers only.

"I married her because I wanted things that you didn't. That you still don't."

I opened my mouth to answer, but he shook his head. "Don't. You'll either say something you don't mean or something I don't want to hear. So, I'll talk." He paused and I shrugged, gesturing for him to go ahead. "You like this paradise you found for us. You like living with me. You might even love me. God knows I love you. But that isn't enough, is it?"

"Taverner," I began.

He held up his hand. "Shut up, Billie," he said, but he was smiling. "You need more. It's taken me four decades to understand it, but I do. I'm not enough for you. Oh, don't worry, I don't take it personally. I'm as close as you'll ever find to what you want. And you'll come back to me as long as I don't try to make you stay. So, go." He dropped his apricot pit into the ashtray on the bedside table and came to stand in front of me.

I put my arms around his neck. "You're one in a million, Taverner."

I spent a few minutes showing him my appreciation before he stepped back. He grabbed my bag and zipped it before holding it out to me. "Go on, then. Get out of here and go kill somebody. I'll be waiting when you get back."

NOW, *GO KILL SOMEBODY* MIGHT NOT BE A ROMANTIC PHRASE FOR most couples, but for us it was goddamned poetry. It meant he understood me. Of course, it helped we were in the same line of work. Both of us had been recruited—Taverner after a stint in Her Majesty's Army, me out of college in Austin—to be professional assassins for an organization known as the Museum. Known to outsiders, that is. The real name isn't important, and you wouldn't recognize it if I told you. It's better that way. The fewer people who know who we are and what we do, the safer for everyone. The Museum was born out of the ashes of World War II with a mission to track down Nazis who had escaped justice. If looted art managed to get recovered at the same time, it was a bonus. Hence the nickname. The organization had been created by the disaffected and the lost—former intelligence officers and resistance fighters left without uses for their very specific skills, one or two who'd worked with the Monuments Men to preserve the treasures of Western Europe, some tame psychopaths who liked the idea of killing and not going to jail for it. Every weirdo and misfit found a place at the Museum, hunting Nazis and looted art with equal enthusiasm.

After a few decades, there weren't many Nazis left to hunt, so the Museum turned its efforts to drug smugglers, arms dealers, human traffickers—folks who needed killing, in other words. I'd been part of a group of four known as Project Sphinx, the first all-female squad in the Museum's history. The other three, Mary Alice, Helen, and Natalie, were the closest thing I had to sisters. They annoyed the shit out of me, and I loved them enough to take a bullet for any of them—and I had.

In the few years since our last outing together, we'd drifted. We'd always been like that. Our first missions were conducted as a quartet with strict supervision. After we had proven ourselves, we were let off the leash a little to do jobs with other assassins and the occasional solo mission. Every so often, we'd be assigned a kill that required all four of us, and even if we hadn't spoken since the last time, we picked up right where we left off. Not that there was ever much to tell on my end. I worked steadily at my cover job of translating textbooks and articles while Mary Alice toiled in accounts payable and spent her free time playing viola in an amateur chamber orchestra. Helen was a stay-at-home society wife in D.C. to a husband with a government job, and Natalie . . . well, Natalie was the wild card. Her cover was officially "art teacher" but she dabbled in performance art, a number of failed gallery shows, and the same number of ex-husbands. Together we had had a hell of a run, taking out bad guys all around the world, and when we found ourselves in the crosshairs, marked for termination instead of retirement, it was only by banding together that we survived. We'd lived and worked together for an intense few weeks while we sorted that situation out, and I think we all heaved a sigh of relief when it was time to go our separate ways for a while.

It had only been a couple of years since we'd said goodbye, but when I spotted Helen in the scrum at Dulles, I almost didn't recognize her. She had gained twenty pounds and let her hair go completely white. The last time I'd seen her, she'd been struggling with widowhood and so skinny, I felt like she'd blow away if the wind came in hard. She looked more substantial now. She looked happy.

She came in for a hug and squeezed me tightly. "Let me look at you, Billie," she said, stepping back to give me the once-over from head to toe. She wouldn't find much changed. The head still had the same streaky dishwater blond hair with a handful more silver and the toes were still tucked inside scuffed cowboy boots. "You look good, kid."

"I was thinking the same about you," I said, nodding towards her snowy hair.

She smiled. "I'd been covering the grey for so long, I had no idea what color it actually was. Imagine my surprise when it grew out fully white." She checked the vintage Cartier Tank watch on her wrist. "We have thirty minutes to wait until Mary Alice's plane arrives and another ten after that for Natalie. Let's have a drink."

I expected her to lead me to the nearest airport pub. Instead she made a beeline for a shiny juice bar and ordered up something green and pulpy, taking a deep suck of her straw. She looked up to see me watching her and smiled, waving the cup. "Yes, I've given up cocktails. And wine. And entire bottles of straight gin. I am reformed now."

"I'm glad. I bet your liver is too," I said, taking a sip from my own cup. Something with strawberries and half a dozen other fruits—a few of which I'd never heard of. She didn't say anything else, but I was happy she'd finally climbed on the wagon. Widowhood had walloped her hard, and she'd spent months in bed with a bottle of Bombay Sapphire for company. It had taken our retirement mission to shake her out of it, and it looked like the changes had stuck.

We talked about nothing in particular until Mary Alice showed up in a black jumpsuit topped with a buttonless coat in an abstract pattern of black and purple and taupe. Her hair was a little longer and the bifocals were new, but otherwise she was Mary Alice, curvy and blond with the kind of pouty lips that other women only got by injection. She'd always resembled a pinup, and now she looked like Marilyn Monroe if Marilyn had lived to her sixties and taken up knitting.

We hugged around and said all the usual things until Mary Alice spotted the airmail envelope sticking out of my tote bag. "I see we got the same briefing materials telling us absolutely nothing," she said.

"Naomi plays her cards close to the vest," I reminded her.

The pouty mouth thinned. "And she can keep them there. I only came because I wanted to make sure she's not dragging us into some trouble."

I wasn't surprised Mary Alice was the least enthusiastic about this summoning. She had the most to lose, after all. She'd been the last of us to find true love, and when she had, it had knocked her sideways. She had proposed to Akiko on their second date, and they'd been married within six months. Their fifth wedding anniversary was coming up, and I tried to remember what the traditional gift was. Wood? Maybe I'd get them a cat scratching post.

I grinned. "How is Akiko?"

"At home, taking care of Kevin," Mary Alice said. "And Gary."

Helen sucked at her straw, making a slurping noise as she hit the bottom of her green sludge. "Gary?"

"Akiko decided Kevin needed a friend, so we adopted Gary. He's a Scottish Fold. He weighs four pounds and Kevin is scared shitless of him."

She whipped out her phone to show us her wallpaper. It was a picture of a stunning middle-aged woman with a sharp, asymmetrical black bob cuddling a small grey cat, its ears lying almost flat on its head like a beanie. He was fighting as if to make a getaway, his eyes rolling like a wild horse's. Behind them stood Kevin, an enormous Norwegian Forest cat who was looking at the newcomer with pure hatred.

"They are struggling a little to bond, but aren't they handsome boys?" Mary Alice asked.

Helen and I made all the right noises of admiration and Mary Alice tucked her phone away, pursing her lips. "Is Natalie here yet? I suppose she's missed her plane."

"She most certainly did not."

We turned around to find Natalie, curls hanging halfway to her waist, wearing flared, striped pants and half a dozen fringed silk scarves. She threw her arms wide to hug us all.

"You look like a refugee from Cher's *Dark Lady* era," Mary Alice told her as she pulled back.

Natalie clucked her tongue and pinched a bit of fabric from Mary Alice's jacket. "Something from the Chico's permanent press collection for elderly travelers?"

"This is Talbots, you bitch," Mary Alice began.

I held up my hand. "Not here. And not now," I said. "And no bloodstains in the car either. It's a rental."

WE COLLECTED OUR BAGS AND MADE OUR WAY TO THE CAR WITH ALL the usual squabbles about who was going to sit where and what music we should play. Since I was driving, I decided both of those. I put Mary Alice in the front passenger seat where she was less likely to inflict injury on Natalie, and pulled up some vintage Linda Ronstadt for the playlist. I was just easing into the trip, tapping my fingers to "When Will I Be Loved," and passing a semi on I-95 when Natalie piped up from the back seat.

"So, odds on what Naomi wants from us?"

"It can't be good," Mary Alice muttered.

I glanced over and saw she was slumped in her seat, watching nothing in particular. She and Natalie always scrapped, but they were off to a faster-than-usual start, and I had a pretty good idea why.

I caught Helen's eye in the rearview mirror and she gave the tiniest of nods.

"Well, I have high hopes our pensions have finally been approved," she said. Retirement benefits from the Museum included substantial pensions, but ours had been canceled when the Board of Directors had decided to kill us instead. Naomi, the acting director when the smoke cleared at the end of our retirement mission, had promised to reinstate them, but so far she'd been stonewalling. There had been a single payout—a generous one, if I'm honest—but nothing since.

Mary Alice snorted. "It's been nothing but delays and excuses. There's no reason to think they've suddenly decided to live up to their promises."

"They'd better," Natalie said, rummaging in her bag. "I need some capital. I'm going to open a new Etsy shop and I need some start-up money."

"For what?" Mary Alice demanded.

"For these," Natalie said, pulling out a crocheted pouch. It was striped in lurid shades of blue and orange and embellished with a pair of tiny white pom-poms.

"What is that, dear?" Helen asked.

"A dick warmer," Natalie explained as she waggled her fingers through it. "There's an extra pocket down here for the balls."

"Ingenious," Helen said kindly as she fingered the pom-poms.

"That is the most disturbing thing I have ever seen," Mary Alice said.

"Really?" Natalie's eyebrows rose almost to her hairline. "I once saw you put an ice pick in a woman's eye and *this* is the most disturbing thing you have ever seen?"

"The woman in question was the highest-ranking member of the Nigerian mafia and had personally tortured her own brother to death," Mary Alice pointed out. She gestured towards the penis warmer. "These atrocities will be perpetrated upon the innocent."

"Now, see here, Mary Alice, I have had just about enough of—"

I would have reached out and turned up the radio until Linda's voice was rattling the windows, but Helen was already taking charge.

"I have the briefing packet," she announced. Helen has three voices—debutante, kindergarten teacher, and Girl Scout troop leader handing out demerits. This voice was the last one, and Natalie and Mary Alice knew better than to test her when she was in that particular mood. Helen went on, skimming the pages she had been sent. Her airmail envelope was thicker than mine, including a map of Colonial Williamsburg and a hotel confirmation. "Did anyone else think the travel arrangements were curious?" she asked.

"Coach seats," Natalie said scornfully.

"They were Premium Economy," Mary Alice corrected.

Natalie rolled her eyes skyward, but Helen carried on. "I meant the travel agency. The tickets were not issued through the Museum's travel office. Although Nat is right—they weren't first-class seats, which is odd, especially as Billie and I both flew in from Europe."

One of the perks of working for the Museum was luxury travel unless it would have blown our cover stories. A group of nuns or broke grad students swilling champagne and snacking on caviar might have raised a few eyebrows. For those trips we packed granola into backpacks and slept on yoga mats, dreaming of the return travel when we would be handed martinis and monogrammed slippers. For all other trips it was strictly first class with all the bells and whistles. Chauffeured cars, corner suites, and concierges. It wasn't a bad life.

"Furthermore," Helen went on, "our accommodations are booked at—" She peered through her glasses at the tiny print. "Oh dear. A Best Western."

"Jesus Christ," Mary Alice muttered. "Do we at least have separate rooms?"

"Doubles," Helen told her.

"And this rental is a compact," I pointed out as I dodged around a semi. The trucker had a book propped on the steering wheel and was spooning up cereal out of a bowl as he drove. The last car the Museum had rented for me had been a Maybach. It was enough to make a girl cry.

"So what's with all the penny-pinching?" Mary Alice asked. "Budget cutbacks?"

To my surprise, Natalie agreed with her. "Wouldn't surprise me. Times are uncertain, and everybody is slicing budgets. Why should the Museum be exempt?"

The Museum running out of money was a sobering thought. It had been founded by people with means and a knack for turning what they had into a hell of a lot more. Nothing had ever been done cheaply. They hadn't stinted on training or missions, and through it all they'd kept tabs on any significant threats to international security and humanitarian causes around the globe—extremely thorough and expensive tabs.

I had my own theory about why we were being summoned on the cheap, and I didn't like it one bit. Nobody wants to be a bargain-basement killer.

CHAPTER THREE

NAOMI'S MAP OF COLONIAL WILLIAMSBURG HAD A FAINT STAR penciled on an empty corner across from the Capitol building. At the bottom of the map, there was a list of opening times and a tiny circle had been ringed around ten AM.

We were in place by nine forty-five. I'd set my alarm for five—jet lag be damned—and gotten in a jog around the area. I ran as much to get the lay of the land as to stretch my legs. A long, easy loop of two miles took me down a street of buildings full of ye olde charm and around a cluster of pastures where a few draft horses and some fat sheep nibbled on the dewy grass. After a shower, I'd joined the others for breakfast at the hotel coffee shop where Helen picked at some oatmeal, Mary Alice ordered an egg-white omelet, and Natalie ate her body weight in French toast. I stuck with yogurt and fruit, and we dawdled over a third round of coffee until it was time to leave. It was easy to see why Naomi had chosen the Best Western. It was prime real estate if you wanted to approach the historic district on foot, and we weren't the only tourists making our way over. It was cool but sunny, an early fog burning away in the pink morning light. We walked slowly, carrying our maps and pointing out landmarks to each other like any other visitors. We passed a few workers heading in, and Mary Alice stared after them.

"Can you imagine coming to work in a mobcap and petticoats?"

Before anybody could answer, a gentleman in a frock coat and breeches rode past on a chestnut horse that tossed its head and pranced a little. He tipped his tricorne in our direction. "Good morrow, ladies."

"Good morrow to *you*," Natalie said, peering over the top of her glasses to watch him ride away. She had a point—he did have a particularly nice rising trot.

"Down, girl," said a voice behind us. "He's a prosperous gentleman in colonial times. I smell an enslaver."

We turned to see Naomi Ndiaye bearing down on us, dressed like any suburban mom and pushing a stroller. She grinned, showing off a smile that was either the result of excellent genes or expensive orthodontia.

"Is that a prop baby?" I asked, nodding towards the sleeping child.

"I wish," she said.

"She's beautiful," Helen said as she peered at the serene little face.

"That's because she's asleep," Naomi said. "Awake, she

shrieks like a pterodactyl and takes a bigger crap than her father has ever managed. Y'all keep your voices down if you don't want to wake the beast."

She led us to a group of benches tucked under a spreading oak tree. She eased down onto a bench and I wondered if her hemorrhoids were playing up. The last time we'd seen her she'd been heavily pregnant with the baby before this one and suffering from a host of baby-related ailments.

She pushed her sunglasses up onto her head and looked around. "Y'all look good. Mostly. A little jet-lagged, but you're keeping it tight."

She seemed a little too pleased by the notion. "You've got a job for us." I didn't make it a question because I already knew the answer.

Naomi grinned. "I like a woman who gets right down to business. I've got passes for Busch Gardens this afternoon and I want to get there before all the funnel cakes are gone." She paused and looked around again. "Does the name Lilian Flanders ring a bell?"

Memory is a funny thing, especially as you get older. I can remember all the lyrics to "Bang Bang (My Baby Shot Me Down)" which came out in 1966, but I have forgotten the faces of half the men I've slept with.

It was Mary Alice who suddenly snapped her fingers. "Our first mission. 1979. We posed as stewardesses on a private plane in order to take out Boris Lazarov, a Bulgarian assassin. He had a flair for torture, if I remember. Lilian was the Provenance agent who compiled the dossier on Lazarov."

Our organization was divided into three departments who

took their names from museum nomenclature. Provenance was surveillance and information, collecting data on two kinds of people, the ones we recruited and the ones we killed. Acquisitions folks were in charge of supply and logistics, doing whatever was necessary to make a mission possible. They built everything from fake social media profiles to elegant explosives. Think Q from *James Bond* and you aren't far off. The third department was Exhibitions—the actual assassins in the field. Overseeing each department was a curator and overseeing *them* was a Board of Directors whose votes to recruit or kill had to be unanimous. Pretty simple as far as international crime syndicates go. Naomi had come up through Provenance, and after a conspiracy that ended up with the previous board members dead, she had taken charge as interim director. She had appointed new curators for each department and was still trying to restore the confidence in the organization's leadership that had been badly shaken.

Natalie was staring at Mary Alice in astonishment after her recitation. "How in the name of Satan's balls did you remember that?" Natalie demanded.

Mary Alice shrugged. "The first boy I had a crush on was named Flanders. I remember wondering at the time if Lilian might be related to him." Helen raised a brow at her and Mary Alice rolled her eyes. "I caught the lesbianism in junior high, Helen. After I learned about boy cooties."

Naomi broke in. "Full marks to Mary Alice. Lilian was a longtime and highly decorated member of the Provenance department before her retirement ten years ago. Now she has died at her home on Mount Desert, an island off the coast of Maine."

"So?" Natalie asked. "What was she, late seventies? She probably keeled over watching *The Price Is Right* when she bid closest without going over."

"She was eighty-one," Naomi acknowledged. "But that's not the point. She was extremely active in her local needle-work guild and line-dancing group, and she passed her last physical with flying colors. At first, the medical examiner chalked it up to a heart attack, but somebody decided to poke around and have a closer look. They found fibers in her mouth and nose from a needlepoint pillow. Lilian Flanders was suf-focated."

Mary Alice gave her a narrow look. "What does that have to do with us?"

"Lilian provided all the information for that mission in 1979," Naomi explained. "Nobody knew more about Boris Lazarov than she did. The hit would never have been possible without her. And I think somebody is settling the score."

"After forty-four years?" Natalie asked. "My god, get over it already. Assassinations happen."

"And who would care enough about Boris Lazarov to avenge him?" Helen put in.

"He had kids," Mary Alice said quietly. "I remember that from the briefing. Three?"

"Two," Naomi corrected. "A boy, seventeen. A daughter, aged eleven. The daughter was killed with her mother in a car accident six years later."

"You think Lazarov's son, at the ripe old age of"—Helen paused to do the math—"sixty-one, has finally decided to take revenge on the people responsible for killing his father more than forty years ago?" Helen was frankly skeptical.

Before Naomi could answer, a seven-and-a-half-foot-tall shadow loomed over us. It was a long-legged, muscular man with a toddler perched on his shoulders. He was wearing cargo shorts and a pair of round, tortoiseshell glasses. The girl had cornrows, each tiny braid finished off with a bumble-bee barrette. Her hands were twisted in her father's hair and she was pulling on it while she drummed her little heels into his pecs.

"Babe, I'm taking Layla to the bathroom. You got any fruit snacks for her?" He smiled at us as Naomi rummaged in her bag and tossed him a pack of gummy sharks.

"Only one," she told him. "And only if she does both."

"Potty now, Daddddddddyyyyy," the little person demanded, kicking him like a pony.

"Ladies." He smiled again at us and left at a jog, the child giggling as he ran. We were all quiet for a minute, just enjoying the view as he moved.

"He looks like a nerdy Winston Duke," Natalie said in a reverent voice.

"Mmmmhmmm." Naomi's voice was a purr.

"What does your husband do?" Helen asked politely.

"Dennis is a theoretical physicist," Naomi replied. "I never understand a damned word he says, but I do like to listen to him talk. And he's very good with his hands."

Nobody said a word, but Mary Alice cut her eyes around

to me and I gave a little cough. "The Lazarov mission?" I nudged. "You think Lazarov's son is behind Lilian Flanders's death."

Naomi got right back to business but Natalie kept watching until the cargo shorts turned the corner. "I do. There was something clutched in Lilian's hand when she died—a figure of a black wolf."

Naomi reached down to pull a ziplock snack bag from her diaper bag and handed it over. Inside was a tiny wolf, rudimentary to the point of being crude. But it was clear what the thing was meant to be. "Obsidian," I said, turning it over in my palm.

Mary Alice peered over my shoulder. "What does that have to do with Boris Lazarov?" she asked.

"The name 'Boris' means 'wolf' in Russian," I told her. I turned the wolf over again. There were characters roughly carved into the belly—Cyrillic characters. One looked like a squared-off six, the other looked a little like pi. "Those are Boris Lazarov's initials," I said. I turned to Naomi. "You think the killer left it behind as a message?"

"I do," Naomi said.

"Maybe it's a coincidence," Helen put in. "Maybe it was a little tchotchke Lilian picked up on her travels."

Naomi shook her head. "The neighbor who visited her every day said she'd never seen it, and Lilian's place was neat. We're talking Shaker neat. No knickknacks or clutter of any kind."

"Like Marie Kondo," Natalie said, nodding.

"Who?" Helen asked.

"Marie Kondo," Nat explained. "You know, the woman who declutters? She wrote a whole book about it. She had a Netflix series? She's from Japan?" she prodded.

Mary Alice shrugged. "Never heard of her."

Natalie rolled her eyes. "The point is, if you use her method, you tidy your stuff once and never have to clean again."

"Natalie, that's sociopathic," Mary Alice said. "People who actually live their lives acquire clutter. It's inevitable."

"It's not inevitable," Nat protested. "It's lazy. All it takes is a little discipline and the proper method. You simply go through everything in your house and hold it in your hands and you ask yourself, 'Does this spark joy for me?' If it does, it can stay. If it doesn't, out it goes."

"Like you did with your husbands," Mary Alice replied.

To my surprise, Natalie didn't rise to the bait. She just laughed before turning back to Naomi. "I agree with Billie. There's something more."

"There is," Naomi admitted. "I had a friend in a government agency do a little digging for me. Off the record."

"Government agency? Like the CIA, which happens to be just up the road?" Helen asked, nodding in the general direction of the Farm, the CIA's training ground and Virginia's worst-kept secret.

"You don't need to know what you don't need to know," Naomi said calmly. "Wherever I got the information, you can trust me when I tell you the source is impeccable. And this source tells me Pasha Lazarov is in the U.S."

The baby made a whimpering noise and started to squirm.

Naomi glanced into the stroller. "She's waking up. You've got about thirty seconds before I put her to the boob."

"Supposing all this is true, that Pasha Lazarov is out to avenge his dad, why involve us?" I asked.

"You're already involved, whether you like it or not," Naomi said. "Pasha can't kill the pilots of that flight, they're already dead, thanks to Billie." She paused with a cocked eyebrow, but I refused to feel bad about killing those two, even if they were fellow Museum agents.

"They started it," I muttered.

Naomi ignored me and carried on. "If Pasha is targeting everybody who had a hand in Lazarov Sr.'s death, then you're next on the list—mostly because you're the only ones left alive."

The kid snuffled again, opening wide eyes and blinking furiously. She balled up her hands and let out a shriek that about peeled the paint off the nearest building. In one deft movement, Naomi scooped her up and pulled the neckline of her top down, settling her to nurse.

Helen gave Naomi a curious look. "Does Dennis know what you do for a living? Does he know who we are?"

"Dennis doesn't ask questions he doesn't want answered. I don't really understand his work, and he doesn't understand mine. We like it that way."

"That seems lonely," Helen said.

Naomi shrugged. "There's a lot of room left that isn't about work. That's where we meet." She paused, wiping up a stray drop of milk from the corner of the kid's mouth.

I brought her back to the subject at hand. "It was nice of

you to warn us about Pasha Lazarov, but this isn't official Museum business, is it?"

She shifted, avoiding my eyes. "It might be off the books," she admitted.

"Hence asking a friend who doesn't work for the Museum to confirm that Pasha Lazarov is in the U.S.," Mary Alice surmised.

Naomi's expression was noncommittal.

"Is that why we got such shitty accommodations?" Natalie demanded.

Naomi leveled her gaze at Nat. "Lyndsay worked hard to find that Groupon for the Best Western," she said, invoking the name of her assistant.

"What aren't you telling us?" I pressed.

Naomi put the child up to her shoulder and started smacking her gently on the back, trying to bring up a burp. "I was off for a few months having this one," she said, jiggling the child as she talked. "When I came back, I realized there had been a security breach. A small one," she hurried to clarify. "Almost imperceptible unless you knew what you were looking for."

"How many files were accessed?"

Just then the kid let out a milky belch. "Good job, baby girl," Naomi crooned.

"Better out than in," Helen agreed.

"Naomi," I said in a dangerous voice.

She sighed and put the kid back into the stroller, stuffing a pacifier into her mouth. The baby made sounds that might have been giggles and reached for her toes. Naomi turned back to us. "There were two sets of files accessed. The Lazarov job and one other—a hit two months ago, and nothing to do with Lazarov or you. I've already notified the agent responsible and he's taking a nice long rest in Tahiti until this blows over."

"Who accessed the files?" Mary Alice asked.

Naomi's face shuttered. "I don't know yet. They've covered their tracks pretty well. But I will take care of them myself when I find out."

She stood up, brushing the creases from her linen pants. "Now, I've got a funnel cake with my name on it. Anything else you need to know is in a packet I've left at a dead drop under a porch on the corner of Duke of Gloucester and Nassau Streets."

"That's it?" Natalie demanded. "Why are you handling this privately if it's Museum business?"

"That's all she can do," I said. "Contain the threat and hope word never gets out." I turned to Naomi. "Because otherwise, your leadership is for shit and you won't last ten minutes."

Infighting in any multinational organization can be cutthroat, but when the organization is made up of trained killers, the stakes are incalculably high. I wouldn't have given a thin Eisenhower dime for the chances of whoever decided to pass on information from the Museum files. Naomi was as ruthless as the rest of us when it came to protecting her position as a director. But if she meant to hold her job, she would have to eliminate the mole and make sure Pasha Lazarov didn't act on the information he'd received. The death of

Lilian Flanders wouldn't raise any eyebrows in the Museum; the loss of four former field agents would set alarm bells ringing from Belize to Bucharest.

"I've done everything I can, and I included a number for a burner. That is the only way I want you to contact me until this is over, and only in an emergency," she said sternly. She popped her sunglasses down on her nose. "Good luck."

We watched her walk away to join Dennis, who was just coming back from the bathroom. Layla was still perched on his shoulders, waving a gummy shark in each little fist at her mother and baby sister. They were such a perfect family they could have been in a car ad, something safe and dependable but also sleek and a little sexy. I could have stood there, watching them and thinking about the choices I'd made and the different lives I might have lived. But I didn't. I liked the one I had too well to go regretting anything I'd missed.

So I turned in the opposite direction from the Capitol, looking towards Nassau Street, almost half a mile away. "Come on," I said to the others. "Let's get that packet. We have a Bulgarian to kill."

CHAPTER FOUR

THE PORCH AT THE CORNER OF DUKE OF GLOUCESTER AND NASSAU was brick, built up from the street level, with arches punched into either side—the perfect place to stash a dead drop. We arranged ourselves casually around one side with Mary Alice and Helen poring over the map like curious tourists as Natalie ducked under the porch. We heard her scrabbling around, cursing a little until she finally emerged with a cobweb festooning her hair.

"Spiders," she said, making a face as she dropped the packet she'd retrieved into Helen's Birkin. It was too early for lunch but Helen insisted the Cheese Shop was a must-do, so we stood in a ridiculously long line for sandwiches that we took back to the Best Western. We assembled in the room I shared with Mary Alice, spreading our sandwiches and bottles of water and slices of pound cake over the two beds as Helen extracted the material from the packet.

"A dozen pictures of Pasha at various ages." She divided them up and passed them around. "Followed by a dossier." She kept this and skimmed it as the rest of us studied the photos.

"Dapper," Natalie said. "I like the pinstripes." She flashed a photo of a man who looked to be in his mid-fifties with fading sandy hair. His looks were forgettable, but you'd take a second glance at his clothes. He wore a navy suit with a wide rose-pink pinstripe, the seams perfectly matched. A violet silk pocket square was folded with precision, and he was smiling around a beautiful briar pipe with a mother-of-pearl stem. He had teeth like Richard Branson, large, white, and permanently on display in every photo.

Natalie moved on to the last photo and squealed. "You have got to be kidding." She turned it over to show Lazarov in a straw boater and a gorgeously tailored cream suit—holding a teddy bear. "He's dressed like Anthony Andrews in *Brideshead Revisited.*"

"God, I had such a crush on him," Helen said. "He was so sexy in *The Scarlet Pimpernel.*"

"'Sink me!'" Mary Alice said, waggling her fingers at her eye to suggest a monocle.

Natalie's face fell as she looked again at the picture. "I'm not sure I can kill a man with a teddy bear."

"You killed a man with a dog," Mary Alice reminded her. Boris Lazarov had boarded our private plane with a couple of bodyguards and an asshole of a poodle. Natalie had put her foot down, insisting she couldn't kill a dog, so in the end,

Helen had scooped it into her flight suit and parachuted out with it.

"I saved the dog," Natalie shot back.

"Helen saved the dog," I corrected. "And I promise, no teddy bears will be harmed in the killing of Pasha Lazarov."

"It's not about hurting the teddy bear," Natalie said. "I'm not *insane*, Billie. It's about the fact that he is clearly a sentimental person. And I'm just not sure a person who carries around a teddy bear is capable of trying to murder us."

There was always a point in just about every mission Natalie worked where she got cold feet. She made the mistake of humanizing the target, trying to find a loophole to get out of the killing. It never made sense to me, because once she got her nerve back, she was always the most enthusiastic of the four of us. It invariably took a deep dive into the dossier, turning over the rocks of the target's life to see all the nasty things wiggling around underneath in order to convince her an assassination was a necessity.

I flicked through the pictures as Mary Alice jerked her chin towards the photo in Natalie's hand. "Maybe it's not really his teddy bear. It could have been for a costume party."

"I don't think so," Helen said slowly. "According to the dossier, he's an Anglophile—almost pathologically so—with a particular fondness for Evelyn Waugh. He has all of his clothes custom tailored in London. The actual biographical data is pretty sketchy. Pasha was born Pavel Borisovich Lazarov on April 26, 1962—an Easter baby, hence the nickname of Pasha. He and his younger sister were both born in the south of France. His father, our pal Boris Lazarov, was Bulgarian. His mother, Irina Feodorovna Dashkova, was White Russian, old nobility. Her parents fled St. Petersburg during the revolution in 1917, and Irina and her sister, Evgenia, were born in Paris. Auntie Evgenia is the only surviving member of Pasha's family, living in an expensive old folks' home in Switzerland. There's no mention of wives or significant partners. No children. He dabbles a bit in dealing art, but no real occupation to speak of. He has a town house in Belgravia."

"Nothing about that makes me feel better," Natalie told her.

Helen's brow furrowed. "This might. Two different Russian oligarchs have fallen out of the windows of that town house in Belgravia."

"God, what is it with Russians and defenestration?" Mary Alice asked.

I shrugged. "Maybe they like the splat." I turned to Helen. "So if our guy has been doing murders in London, why haven't the British charged him?"

Helen turned back to the dossier. "Both happened during parties and other witnesses backed up his story that the deaths were accidental. He also apparently deals drugs—designer club gear, strictly for beautiful party people. He specializes in something called red razzies."

"Ooooh, I love those!" Natalie puts in. "They're shaped like little raspberries and they're flavored. Nice buzz, but you have to really hydrate because they'll suck the moisture right out of you."

Helen stared at her a long moment. "Thank you, Natalie. That is very informative." She resumed her narrative. "British

Intelligence had to warn him off when a minor royal almost overdosed, but they hushed it up to avoid the tabloids carrying the story." She fixed Natalie with a firm look. "The bottom line is: we don't need to feel too bad about killing him."

Natalie opened her mouth to argue, but I pulled a photo of Lazarov on the deck of a sleek teak racing yacht. "Look at the side of the boat. Next to the name. See the animal painted there?"

"It's a wolf," she said quietly.

"A black wolf. Exactly like the obsidian one left with Lilian Flanders's body."

Natalie thought this over while Mary Alice studied the rest of the photo. "That's a gorgeous boat. What do we think, fifty feet? And polished within an inch of her life. They don't make boats like that anymore."

Helen tapped the dossier. "It says here he has a phobia of flying—hasn't been on an airplane since 1979."

1979. The year we'd assassinated his father.

"I guess you can blame us for that," I said. "Knowing your father died in an airplane crash probably messes you up for life."

Helen went on. "He stays almost entirely in Europe, traveling by his yacht—named the *Galina* for his dead sister. That's sweet, I guess. Otherwise, he travels by train. When he has to come to the U.S., he crosses on the *Queen Mary 2.* This says he crossed a week ago, ahead of the hit on Lilian."

"Makes sense if he's that much of an Anglophile," Natalie said brightly. "That ship is all cream teas and cricket. I've always wanted to sail on her."

"Well, it looks like you'll get your chance," Helen said, pulling an envelope from inside the packet. It was red, marked with the Cunard logo in gold. On it was a Post-it with a note in Naomi's handwriting. *P. L. confirmed on this crossing.*

"Is that—" Natalie broke off as she grabbed for the envelope. She yanked it open and four tickets spilled onto the bed. She snatched one up and grinned. "Sailing in five days from New York."

Mary Alice turned to her earnestly. "So would Marie Kondo approve? Does this murder now spark joy for you, Natalie?"

Natalie shot her the bird and I ignored them both.

"That gives us less than a week to figure out how to murder a man on the most famous ocean liner in the world and get away with it," I said. "Piece of cake."

CHAPTER FIVE

THE DAY AFTER WE MET WITH NAOMI WE HEADED TO D.C., STOPPING just long enough to turn in the rental car and hop the train for New York. The trip took the better part of a day, but we weren't in a hurry. We had roughed out a plan for handling Pasha Lazarov and needed time to noodle over the details. The dossier Naomi had compiled had been thin to the point of transparency compared to what we usually got when we undertook a mission. In the course of a regular job, we'd be handed fat binders full of information—the target's history, habits, closest contacts, medical records. Everything from shoe size to preferred sexual position, and we'd use those facts to begin a discreet surveillance, planning a way in. Sometimes a job took months, sometimes a long weekend. Everything depended on how security conscious the target was. The people we took out weren't nice, and people who aren't nice often have a sixth sense for danger. Their instincts for self-preservation are far more refined than the average person's. They can smell a trap, sniff out a potential ambush. More than once, we'd made elaborate preparations only to find ourselves making it up as we went along when our arrangements had been wrecked by a last-minute change of plans from a twitchy target. Some folks think being a professional assassin means being a perfect shot or some kind of strangling savant. Those things help but the most important quality is adaptability.

In the case of Pasha Lazarov, adapting meant dealing with the fact that we had almost no real data to build our plans on. We knew he was sailing on *QM2*, but apart from that, nothing. Mary Alice pulled up a series of pictures of the ship on her laptop and we gathered around, clicking and pointing until we had a rough idea of the layout.

"Let's assume he's in one of the two Grand Duplex suites," Mary Alice said, switching over to the gallery of the poshest cabins. "They're the largest and most luxurious, and a man with handmade underwear isn't going to slum it."

"Potentially problematic," Helen said, bringing up a map of the suite's layout. "Those suites have private dining rooms. What if he takes all his meals in his suite?"

"That is a problem for later," I told her. "For now, let's assume that our tickets will at least get us in his general vicinity."

"They will," Natalie volunteered as she studied our booking. "Naomi sprang for Queens Grill suites. Two of them. They're located on the same deck as the Grand Duplex suites." She used the deck map to trace the path from our numbered suites to the ones we suspected Pasha Lazarov might have chosen. "Easy."

In the meantime, Mary Alice had navigated to the price list for the suites and gave a low whistle. "Dammmmmmmmn. Naomi went all out. I feel bad now for bitching about the Best Western."

"She even included passports," I said, turning out the rest of the envelope. "But y'all aren't going to like it," I added with a grin as I handed them around. Museum practice was to issue fake identification using the actual initials of the agent in question. We'd been extensively trained, but the best agents can get tired and that's when slips happen. It's too easy to start to sign a bill with your pseudonym only to find you've let down your guard and started writing your actual name. Using your real initials gives you a quick way to recover. Plus it means you can even carry monogrammed items on a job, a bonus when it comes to making your assumed identity look lived in.

The names Naomi had chosen were a little over the top—mine was Bianca, for god's sake—but that wasn't the part the others would object to. Naomi had had our photos expertly altered to resemble the appearances we'd have to assume, and she'd changed up our ages a little—a reasonable precaution if Pasha Lazarov was targeting four women in their early sixties. Mine and Helen's were aged down to mid-fifties while Mary Alice's and Natalie's went the other direction.

"Sixty-nine?" Natalie shrieked. "What kind of bullshit is this?"

"I'm supposed to be seventy-one," Mary Alice put in dryly.

Helen preened a little. "Fifty-five."

Mary Alice looked daggers at her before turning to me. "Billie?"

"Fifty-three."

"Biiiiiiitch," she said on a sigh.

"At least you get to wear comfy shoes and stretchy cruise wear," Helen pointed out. "Billie and I will have to strap ourselves into Spanx and high heels." But she preened some more when she said it.

WE DEBATED THE ODDS OF PASHA LAZAROV KNOWING WHERE WE were and decided Manhattan was a big enough haystack to hide four discreet needles. We sprang for the Mandarin Oriental—mostly for the chicken confit in the MO Lounge— and spent the next three days shopping and finalizing our plans. We booked wig fittings, assembled cruise wardrobes, and made salon appointments for the services we needed to change up our appearances. Bigelow Surgical and Manhattan Wardrobe Supply filled in the rest.

On the day of our departure, it took a few hours to finish our preparations. First, we took care to make sure our wardrobes looked a little more lived-in. You can always spot someone using a cover identity when everything is new and pristine. So we lightly scuffed the soles of our shoes, tucked dry cleaning tickets and receipts into our wallets, filled our purses with Altoid tins, random ballpoints, and the odd protein bar. Lipsticks were worn down, and the spines of bestselling paperbacks were broken.

Finally, it was time to get dressed. Mary Alice and Natalie had gone in for expensive lace-front wigs and orthopedic shoes along with elastic-waist pantsuits. Mary Alice wore her bifocals on a chain around her neck, and Natalie went all out with a four-prong walking cane. She stuffed small pads into her cheeks while Mary Alice lightly shadowed narrow lines into her wrinkles with theatrical pencil she'd picked up at a makeup warehouse in Brooklyn. (Pro tip: If you're using makeup to alter your appearance, always go for stage-quality stuff. It stays put and the last thing you want is to blow a cover identity because your wrinkles ran down your neck.) She went after Natalie as well, heightening her marionette lines before powdering them down and finishing with setting spray. The final touch for each was a heavy hit of perfume. This was the sort of detail the male field agents never thought of, but scent has a powerful effect on psychology, and we selected our perfumes almost as deliberately as we chose our weapons. Mary Alice opted for Chanel No. 5 while Natalie almost gagged us out of the room with a heavy blast of Youth Dew.

Aging down was just as lengthy a procedure. While Mary Alice had been shopping for dark pencils and setting spray, Helen and I had been loading up on facelift tape and highlighter sticks. We'd each had our hair lightened at an expensive salon in Tribeca, and the brighter hair color called for stronger blush. Strategic contouring, vicious shapewear, and acid-based hand masques did the rest. Helen's suitcases were full of Ralph Lauren while I'd chosen knitwear from St. John.

Together we looked expensive, well-kept, and not a day over fifty. We even smelled young. She'd sprayed herself lavishly with Coco Mademoiselle and I'd chosen something with a tobacco note by Le Labo. Usually, these were the things the Museum would pay for, and without an official budget, my credit card was weeping quietly in my wallet by the time we'd finished.

We left separately. Mary Alice and Natalie arrived at the cruise terminal via Uber Black, Helen took a car service, and I hailed a good old-fashioned yellow cab. No matter how many times I visited New York—and I'd been plenty, both for pleasure and for killing—I always felt like Holly Golightly when I took a yellow cab.

We were stuck in traffic awhile which gave me a chance to stare out the window at New Jersey as we crept along. I was the last to arrive. As I climbed out of the cab, I saw Mary Alice and Natalie tottering after a porter whose cart was loaded with their bags. Helen was on the move after them, thirty or forty people behind. I joined the queue, leaving some distance between Helen and me.

We progressed smoothly through the embarkation procedures, ignoring each other until we met up again in our stateroom. It was on deck nine, and I gave a silent whistle as I entered. A narrow hall featuring closets and a beverage bar opened into a spacious living room with a sofa, coffee table, and desk, along with an easy chair and a couple of occasional tables. Floor-to-ceiling windows gave onto the balcony, and behind the sofa, a pair of twin beds were neatly made up with coverlets stamped with the Cunard logo. On the wall next to the bed, a doorway was hung with a heavy curtain and from behind it, I heard thumping and bumping. Helen stood in front of the curtain, smiling tightly as she greeted me. "Bianca," she said, using my assumed name. "You made it."

I raised a brow at her. "Lovely to see you, Heather." I jerked my head towards the curtain and her smile tightened further.

"Now that you're here, you should meet Stephen. Our butler."

"Shit." I mouthed the word, and Helen nodded. Just then the butler popped his head out from behind the curtain. "Welcome aboard, Ms. Williams! Shall I unpack for you?"

I refused the unpacking, but Stephen wasn't finished. There were offers of tea, champagne, canapés, and chocolates. We fairly shoved him out the door with effusive thanks, bolting it behind him.

"This is a complication we didn't need," Helen said in a low voice. "Somebody hanging around and clocking our comings and goings."

"It'll be nice," I told her. "Someone to wash your delicates."

"I don't think he does that, and I can take care of my own delicates, thank you very much."

I looked at my watch. "Let's get out on deck and see if we can put eyes on Lazarov. At the very least we can toast our departure."

We made our way outside with the other passengers and most of the crew. The decks were heaving with people, and

Natalie and Mary Alice elbowed their way through to stand beside us. We stood sipping champagne, except for Helen who took a glass of fizzy water with lime.

Mary Alice glanced around at the throng of people and shook her head. "2,620 passengers. 1,253 crew, including officers. Probably some assorted other folks as well, like guest lecturers. Round it up to 4,000—4,000 potential witnesses along with security cameras in every public area. We are out of our goddamned minds," she muttered.

I grinned. "We do like a challenge." I tapped her glass to mine and took a sip.

She probably would have argued, but I gave her a nudge. I'd spotted him, a deck above and leaning on the railing, elaborate pipe in his mouth, a glass of champagne shimmering in his hand. Pasha Lazarov, vengeful son, alleged killer of Russian oligarchs, and now a marked man. He was even holding the goddamned teddy bear, waving its paw vaguely in the direction of the dock. He didn't look down, and I turned back to the rail, lifting my glass for another sip.

The ship's horn sounded then, announcing to the world that we were on our way—2,620 passengers setting sail. And only 2,619 would finish the trip.

CHAPTER SIX

JUNE 1982

PEMBERTON NANNIES ARE RENOWNED FOR TWO THINGS: DISCRETION and expense. They are trained for three years at a college in Kent where they learn how to soothe a toothache, potty-train a toddler, and de-escalate adolescent meltdowns. They are also taught how to thwart a would-be kidnapping, to disarm an intruder, and to detect unwanted surveillance. These are the super-nannies, employed by royal families, socialites, and power brokers all over the world. They move quietly behind their employers, discreet, attentive, and perfectly trained. There is no cachet quite like the smooth ride of a Silver Cross pram being pushed by a Pemberton nanny.

"I can't believe we have to wear hats," Natalie moans from the back seat. "I mean, the gloves are bad enough, but these *hats*." She leans forward to peer at herself in the rearview mirror. She tweaks the small porkpie hat to a different angle over the auburn waves of her wig.

In the front seat, Constance Halliday, mentor and trainer, turns her head slightly and looks back.

"Miss Schuyler, Pemberton nannies wear their hats at a very specific angle, which you well know. Please restore yours to its correct position."

Natalie does as she's told, flicking a quick eye roll to where Billie sits next to her. But Billie, her usual partner in irreverence, doesn't meet her eyes.

As the long sedan glides through the leafy London squares, Natalie leans towards Billie, pitching her voice low. "Are you still sulking about Chicago?"

"I'm not sulking," Billie returns under her breath.

"Pouting. Ruminating. Having an existential crisis—whatever you want to call it," Nat says. "Are you still doing that? Because now is a good time to let that go. We have a job to do."

"I know," Billie whispers tightly. "And it's my ass on the line if I fail again, so back off."

Natalie would have flopped back into her seat, but two weeks of intensive training in the ways of the Pemberton nannies have ensured that her back is straight, knees pressing gently together and angled slightly. She, like Billie, has been carefully made up to look as if she were wearing no makeup at all. Her skin has a healthy glow and her eyes are bright. She presents a picture of calm competence, but she is fizzing with anticipation of the kill to come.

Outwardly, Billie looks much the same. She is wearing an identical uniform—navy twill dress with a navy cape piped in forget-me-not blue. Her white gloves are pristine, her black shoes highly polished. But Nat sees the twitch of the tiny muscle at the corner of her mouth and she reaches over to offer consolation.

"Anybody could have made that mistake," she murmurs. "How were you supposed to know he had a cousin who looked like him?"

Billie doesn't bother to answer. Anything she says now will come out as a snap or a snarl and Natalie is only trying to help. The most important weapon for an assassin is confidence, and Billie has lost hers. In the months since Chicago, she has undergone a formal review and been put on probation. Another infraction, no matter how small, will result in her dismissal from the Museum, an end to her career. The possible future stretches out before her like a blank map, and the very emptiness of it is terrifying.

Constance may sense Billie's nerves, but she does not turn around again. Instead, she folds her gloved hands neatly in her lap and poses a question.

"Miss Webster, kindly relate what you know about the mark."

Billie hesitates and Constance guesses the source of her concern. She nods towards the driver. "Theodore is a fully briefed member of Museum staff with the highest security clearance. Furthermore, he was trained at Benscombe by me. Personally. You need have no concerns about discussing the mission in front of him."

Billie clears her throat. "The target is Isabel Tizón de Rivas, the wife of a South American politician. Her father is the former president, Eduardo Tizón, a strongman with a military background and policies modeled on those of Perón in Argentina. He moved his country from a flawed but functioning democracy to a dictatorship, becoming increasingly intolerant of opposition during his time in office. Those viewed as enemies of his administration were frequently targeted with harassment, and many fled. His term ended with his assassination in 1953."

"And how, precisely, was he assassinated?" Constance asks.

"He was gunned down outside the presidential palace as he walked his daughter back from school. *Life* magazine ran a picture of her with her father's blood soaking her uniform, and the photograph became a rallying point for his followers. The country has experienced seven military coups since his death, swinging between reactionary violence and experiments with liberal democracies."

"Correct and succinct, Miss Webster. And our mark?"

"Rather than pursuing influence for herself, she has taken a more circuitous route to power. She married Major Luis de Hoyos, one of her father's most devoted followers. De Hoyos became an advisor and ultimately a cabinet member in the administration of Aurelio Resendez, the president elected in 1971." She makes air quotes around the word "elected."

"Luis de Hoyos served in the position of Minister of Information and was responsible for disseminating news and propaganda. He controlled television, newspaper, and radio. During his tenure, journalists, academics, students—essentially everyone with liberal leanings—were rounded up along with anyone who had been a vocal opponent of his wife's father. They were never heard from again and are presumed dead. The country is strongly patriarchal, so a female appointee to a cabinet position would not be acceptable, but persistent rumors have indicated Isabel Tizón had considerable influence over her husband, directing much of the effort to suppress dissent from the shadows."

Billie pauses for breath, considering the legacy of blood and ruin their target has left behind.

"And?" Constance prompts.

"In 1975, a coup of liberal young officers swept Resendez out of power and he was shot by a firing squad. Luis de Hoyos left for exile with Isabel and was convicted in absentia for treason and sentenced to death. He never returned to his home country and the sentence was never carried out. He died a year later of stomach cancer. Isabel has since remarried, a man named Julián Domingo Rosas. He is considerably younger and resembles her father, both physically and politically."

"Gross," Natalie murmurs.

"What?" Billie asks her. "The emotional necrophilia or the emotional incest?"

"Both," Nat replies with a shudder.

Constance cuts in. "What is the country's current political situation?"

"It has recently elected Gabriela Treviso, a young judge with progressive politics who ran on a platform of anti-corruption and accountability and who is wildly popular with the younger demographic. As a result, Julián Domingo Rosas is planning a coup against this president with an aim to installing himself as a dictator with Isabel's backing."

"What are his prospects?"

"Slim," Billie says. "But with Isabel's money and the nostalgia among the older people for her father, there is a chance he could succeed. Either way, his attempt to bring down a legitimately elected head of state will cost many more lives and destroy the fragile stability they've managed to build."

"And the wider implications?"

"Geopolitical instability for the entire region." Billie edges a discreet finger under her hat to scratch at the dark red wig pinned beneath.

"And what do we know about the target herself?"

"Godchildren," Natalie pipes up. "She has dozens of godchildren."

Constance holds up a finger. "Miss Webster, please."

Billie takes a breath and carries on. "Unlike her idol, Eva Perón, Isabel has preferred to work covertly, presenting a public face of service and dignity, of devotion to her charitable causes and her godchildren. She has dozens of them, largely due to the understanding that asking her to stand as godmother will secure favors from her. At the very least, it ensures she does not become an enemy. On a more practical level, the custom has allowed her to build a substantial collection of jewels. She sends sterling silver spoons engraved with her monogram to each godchild for their christening. In return, the parents are expected to give her a piece of jewelry, preferably classic Van Cleef & Arpels or Cartier."

Billie pauses, thinking of the photographs she has seen of Isabel Tizón de Rivas. She is an angular woman whose brittle figure is the product of rigorous dieting and a punishing schedule of exercise. She wears sharply tailored pantsuits in solid colors, the perfect background for displaying her collection of jewels. She frequently turns up at birthday parties and graduations, making a point of wearing whatever gift the godchild's parents have sent her. Some play it safe with small pieces in the iconic Cartier panther motif. Those who know her well or are particularly interested in substantial favors from her, send more elaborate offerings. Today's hosts sent a brooch and bracelet of vintage tutti-frutti.

"And where is she today?" Constance presses.

"At the home of the Ketcham-Flints. Cassandra Ketcham-Flint is Isabel's goddaughter, and it is her son's birthday party. Cassandra is married to Nigel Ketcham-Flint, an English race car driver, and they make their home in Kew. Julían Domingo Rosas does not care for England and never accompanies his wife when she travels here. Nigel Ketcham-Flint does not like his wife's godmother and refuses to let her security detail in the house, considering it a disruption. As far as the family, the birthday boy is four today and he has a three-month-old sister. The party includes other children from the nursery school and their siblings; friends from play groups and various lessons, such as Mandarin and harpsichord; and mothers and babies from Cassandra's antenatal group. There are seventy-five children on the guest list."

"Anyone who signs up their kid for harpsichord at the age of four deserves to have someone murdered in their house," Natalie puts in.

Billie carries on. "Most of the children will be accompanied by nannies or other childminders, and at least five of these are Pemberton nannies. The theme of the party is old-fashioned circus. There are fire-eaters, jugglers, and contortionists on the lawn, as well as a petting zoo and bouncy castle with a carnival for games at the bottom of the garden and a continuous series of entertainers. Inside the house will be refreshment rooms, baby eurhythmics classes, and a quiet room for napping."

Just as she concludes, the car stops on a side street near the house.

"We are here," Constance tells them. She adjusts her Pemberton cape and alights from the car, making use of her walking stick. Behind them, an identical car parks and two others get out—Mary Alice and Helen in Pemberton uniforms, also with wigs in varying shades of red. In an enormous house with dozens of guests, witnesses will never be able to tell four young redheaded women in matching uniforms apart. Their statements to investigators will contradict and confuse, exactly the effect the Museum is hoping to create.

The drivers, Museum members from the Acquisitions department, wordlessly open the car boots to extract a pair of prams that are expensive, highly polished, and gently worn. New prams might attract attention, and these should go unremarked. They are also empty. Nannies cannot enter a private party without at least the appearance of bringing in a child. After much discussion, it was decided it would be foolish to use mannequin babies and unethical to use real ones. So these prams are Trojan horses, allowing the nannies to enter bearing gifts—actual gifts for the birthday child purchased from Hamleys and Harrods and wrapped in Paddington paper.

As they assemble on the pavement, the others make scant eye contact with Billie. It is her fault they are here, working as support for Constance rather than making a kill of their own. They are nothing more than a piece of theatre, a bit of visual trickery to keep the guests uncertain of what they've seen, and after all the months of training and the success of their first mission, it stings to have failed so badly on their second.

With one final nod, they each depart from the rendezvous point on foot. They will enter through the garden gate, slipping into the party already in full swing. Mary Alice goes first, maneuvering one of the prams, followed by Natalie, then Helen. Only Constance and Billie are left, and as Billie prepares to go, Constance lays a hand on her arm.

"Miss Webster, I know you think it is a punishment that you are here, supporting me in this mission rather than carrying it out yourself. I want you to know that it is."

Billie says nothing. Shame curdles any speech she might have made.

"All of us make mistakes, and you were fortunate that yours was not worse. You killed an unsavory young man, but he was far too insignificant for our purposes. We might have targeted him at some point, or he might have turned his life around and escaped our attention. It was, frankly, a waste of your talents. And I am sorry to think the cause may be distraction."

She pauses, letting the implication sink in. *Taverner.* The subtext is that Billie rushed the job because she was thinking of a man.

She says nothing and Constance continues to speak, certain the barb has pricked just where it should.

"When you were recruited, I had high hopes for you. I still do. But you faltered at the first jump and nearly fell."

Billie remembers the crisis of confidence she suffered during training. The possibility of a life bigger than she had ever imagined had been dangled in front of her, dazzling and almost within reach until Constance, in a smooth and silken voice, offered to take it all away with the suggestion she would be more comfortable in secretarial school. *Perhaps you'd like bookkeeping. That can be rather fulfilling, I'm told.* The possibility that she could fail at the only thing she'd ever really wanted had been enough to push Billie into becoming more than she'd imagined she could. And now it was in jeopardy. Again.

"You took the correction I offered and made something of yourself," Constance went on. "Now you have tripped again, and the question is, Will you find your footing or will you stay down?"

"I want this job," Billie tells her. "You know that."

"And yet something within you is struggling." Constance tips her head and considers Billie with birdy, beady eyes. "Is there a part of you that wants to be normal, Miss Webster? Is that what this dalliance is about? Do you want the proverbial picket fence? Baking lemon drizzle cakes and picking out furniture with someone?"

"No," Billie says emphatically.

"It is perfectly natural if you do," Constance assures her. "Most people are not like us. Most people want those things."

"I don't," Billie insists.

"Good. You cannot reconcile them with our life, not if you are a woman."

Billie's eyes widen. "That's sexist."

"No, it is pragmatic. A man can easily vanish for months on end for work. Women's obligations are different. Such disappearances, away from home and family, would excite too much interest, raise too many questions. We will not interfere in your private life so long as your private life does not interfere in the work. But we are also realists, Miss Webster. We know what the world is."

"So do I."

Constance pauses, the expression on her face almost sympathetic. "Do not grieve for the life you have not chosen. Very many people can reproduce, and they quite frequently do. We have different gifts and we are called to a different path. The world needs us, Miss Webster, to remove what stands between good and decent people and chaos. We are necessary monsters."

And in that moment, the something within Billie that allowed herself to be soft and human and hopeful gets ruthlessly strangled. She will never again allow anything to interfere with the mission.

Constance carries on smoothly. "The job, Miss Webster, is everything. Today you have the chance to rectify the mistakes of your last mission. I will dispatch our target myself, and you will observe. I shall be making a full report to the disciplinary committee when it is finished."

"It isn't fair," Billie says quietly. "I was the one who screwed up. The others—"

"The others were assigned the mission with you and they failed to remove the target. They also failed to harness your impulsiveness. Next time, one hopes they will try a little harder. Now, to work."

Billie swallows down her feelings and collects her pram, following Constance around the corner and through a small gate. If Isabel Tizón de Rivas's security detail had been present, Billie and Constance would never have passed without credentials. As it is, the junior gardener tasked with keeping out gate-crashers looks up from his meticulous clipping of a box hedge, sees the Pemberton blue uniforms, and immediately waves them in.

They have memorized the map of the house and grounds and there is no discussion of where to go. They deliver their wrapped present to the heaving gift table on the lawn and Billie parks the pram behind a rosebush. Anyone who sees them walking around the party will assume they belong, the advantage of a uniform. *A uniform,* Constance reminded them during their initial briefing, *purchases acceptance, and—if one is lucky—invisibility. People who wear uniforms for a living are forgettable and largely anonymous, two qualities essential in our work. And they are underestimated. Use that to your advantage.*

Billie expects to make a quick circuit of the party before finding their target, but almost as soon as they park the pram, they see her, ladling punch for shrieking children. This is where she is often found at parties, dispensing food or beverages since it gives her a chance to see and be seen, to talk to everyone, to preside. She is pouring punch into small glasses, smiling benevolently, aware of being watched, but completely unalive to the fact that she is being hunted. From this moment on, Billie will cease to think of her as Isabel Tizón de Rivas, as the child in the school uniform stained with her father's blood, as the architect of misery to so many in her country. For Billie, she is now only an objective, the reason for the mission. The target.

Her goddaughter, the hostess Cassandra, is moving like a pinball, levered from garden to house and back again as she puts out fires and finesses the finishing touches. Natalie, with her gift for sleight of hand, has been tasked with creating a reason for the target to go inside where Billie and Constance will be waiting. She hovers behind the punch table like a ghost, waiting for her moment.

Constance and Billie slip into the house to find a dozen nannies on the floor, bouncing toddlers in time to music on a videocassette recorded specially for the occasion by the Wombles. Assorted mothers who have desperately dieted themselves back into pre-baby shape circle the buffet tables with eyes like hungry sharks. They do not eat, preferring to sip kirs and smoke in the conservatory. The nannies are too busy to eat, so the only food being consumed is by the children, whose faces are smeared with chocolate sauce, ketchup, and custard. Billie has never been happier to be child-free than she is at that minute.

The space under the main staircase has been fitted with a slab of marble to serve as a counter. Tucked below it are minifridges, each set at a different temperature, perfectly selected for the white wines and champagnes inside. Above are racks of reds and crystal glasses in assorted shapes. Laid out on the counter with the precision of a surgeon's tray are accessories— vacuum corks, foil cutters, and corkscrews of various shapes and dimensions, some with novelty handles. Billie trails her fingers along the tray as they pass.

The downstairs powder room has been set aside for party-goers, but Helen has locked herself inside, feigning digestive trouble. Mary Alice has taken care of the maid's bathroom behind the kitchen, stuffing a hand towel down the pipe and flushing several times until water cascades over the rim and floods the floor. In the ensuing confusion, Constance and Billie make their way upstairs to the guest suite. Under Constance's direction, Billie does a quick sweep of the bedroom, but it is empty. The windows overlook the back garden and Billie glances out just in time to see Natalie tip the punch bowl onto the target.

In fact, Billie sees nothing of the kind. Natalie manages to give the impression that she is feet away during the disturbance, only turning when the target gives an exclamation of surprise and annoyance. Natalie attempts to daub at the punch stains on the white pantsuit, but the target waves her off impatiently. She stomps quickly towards the house, her heels making stabbing motions in the grass.

"Target is en route," Billie tells Constance.

Constance does not reply. Her gaze is fixed on the wall, intent upon nothing more interesting than a few square inches of toile wallpaper.

"Shepherdess?" Billie ventures. It is Constance's code

name, the only one permitted during missions, and one she has answered to for more than forty years.

Constance's mouth opens and closes without sound. She moves nothing except her jaw, open and closed again and again, struggling to find her voice. When it does not come, she swivels her eyes towards Billie, eyes full of an emotion Billie never expected to see in her mentor. Panic.

They have thirty seconds, maybe a minute before the target reaches them. Billie helps Constance to a chair, guiding her to sit, as they hear the target approaching. They do not hear footsteps, the house is too thickly carpeted for that. But her voice is raised as she calls downstairs in irritation and as soon as the target enters, she marks their presence with a look of annoyance.

"Did you not realize this guest room was in use?" she demands.

"I do apologize," Billie says. "My friend needed a little air and the WC downstairs was flooded."

The target flaps an impatient hand and moves straight past them into the bathroom. "If your friend needs air, take her outside," the target calls. She half closes the door as she strips off her jacket.

For an agonizing minute, the target runs the tap, sponging cold water on her ruined jacket as Billie stares at Constance, willing her mentor to move. But Constance simply sits, motionless. She might have been a statue except for the eyes, imploring as they rest on Billie.

Billie's hand slips to her pocket and her fingers curl around the corkscrew she lifted from the wine bar. It had been an impulse, one she would never be able to explain. She takes the corkscrew from her pocket and twists it, ensuring the worm is fully extended. Half a dozen quick, silent steps take her into the bathroom where the target turns, her hands still plunged in the pink-tinged water.

"What—"

Before she can finish the question, Billie plunges the corkscrew into the base of her throat, careful to seat it in the little notch where the clavicles join the sternum. The target's hands rise to Billie's wrists, but she has no strength in them. The shock of what is happening to her paralyzes her reactions, and Billie hooks a foot behind her knee, buckling the joint and causing her to collapse. Billie holds her close as the target falls on her back, landing on a fluffy pink bath mat. She looks up at Billie with imploring eyes. She cannot scream—there is no air to reach her larynx—and her death is almost entirely silent. The only sound is the metallic ratcheting of the corkscrew as Billie turns the worm, securing it in the trachea. Then the terrible gasping suck as she pushes down on the arms of the corkscrew, forcing the trachea up through the hole. The target lies gulping and immobile as a frog ready for dissection as Billie removes the corkscrew. With one deft motion, Billie flicks open the foil blade and plunges it into the subclavian artery. She twists it and pulls it out again. Blood begins to pour over the floor, rivers of it, flooding the pink rug and the channels between the tiles. The flow moves on, spreading outwards as Billie retreats from it, careful to keep her shoes out of the gore.

It will take the target less than three minutes to die, but

Billie does not wait to watch. A rupture of the subclavian artery cannot be mended by first aid. It cannot be reached for compression. Only immediate surgery can save her, and there is no time even for an ambulance to arrive, much less for her to be taken to hospital. Whatever happens, the target is doomed and Billie is looking at a woman who is just barely alive and only on a technicality.

So Billie turns to Constance, who still sits, eyes wide with fear.

"Shepherdess? Can you hear me?"

Something flickers in Constance's gaze, and Billie knows she is in there.

"You've had a turn of some kind. Probably a small stroke. I have to get you out of here."

Constance blinks rapidly and Billie removes a handkerchief from her pocket. She returns to the bathroom where she dabs it daintily in the blood. She holds it to Constance's nose as she helps her to her feet. Constance is able to stand with her help, and Billie guides her to the door. There is a rumbling in Constance's throat, a protest, Billie knows.

Museum protocol states that any member of the Exhibitions team unable to get out of a mission under their own power should be left behind. Other agents must not be compromised.

Billie tightens her grip on her mentor. "I know what you're trying to say. Forget it. I'm not big on rules, remember?"

There is a wheeze from Constance, which Billie only later thinks might have been a laugh. She manages to get Constance downstairs, giving the tiniest sigh of relief as they reach the ground floor. She doesn't dare take her through the garden and the rest of the party, so she makes her way to the front door.

Just as she puts her hand on the knob, she hears a voice.

"Leaving already?"

She turns to see Cassandra Ketcham-Flint, the hostess, smiling in a harried way and hurrying forward with a lavishly wrapped bag.

Billie gestures towards the bloody handkerchief in Constance's hand. "Nosebleed. She gets them often, but this one was a devil," she says in a thick Lancashire accent. "A bit of a lie-down and she'll be right as rain."

"But where is your charge?" Cassandra asks suddenly. "Surely you came with a child."

Without a pram or toddler in tow, it looks as if Billie and Constance are leaving a child behind. Billie smiles.

"Oh, we came with Dorothy," she says, plucking a name out of thin air. "She's in the bouncy house with the children. I am about to take over for her, so I'm shadowing her for a fortnight. Nanny here"—she nods towards Constance—"is technically retired, but she does love to come see the little ones when they have a day out."

"Of course," Cassandra says, already past caring about the domestic arrangements of strangers. She holds out the bag. "Don't forget your favor."

"Thanks very much," Billie murmurs as she reaches for it. A thin line of the target's blood is etched beneath her fingernail, a crescent of scarlet.

"You'll want to wash that," the hostess says, her mouth set

in an expression of faint distaste as she sees the blood. Her gaze goes to the older woman with the gore-stained handkerchief clamped to her face.

"Yes, ma'am," Billie says in a tone of embarrassed deference. "Good afternoon, ma'am."

Cassandra opens the door for them, but doesn't wait to see them down the front steps. She closes the door smartly and returns to the party to harass the caterer about a tray of vol-au-vents that were unsatisfactory and to see if the housekeeper has managed to reach the plumber after hours. When she discovers her godmother's body, an hour will have passed, and the blood on her bathroom floor will have begun to congeal, ruining the grout. She will have forgotten everything of significance about the pair of nannies who left together.

They were only the help, after all.

CHAPTER SEVEN

OVER THE NEXT TWO DAYS ON THE SHIP, WE ESTABLISHED OUR surveillance of Lazarov. Helen and I, in the role of monied divorcées, dressed ourselves in expensive athleisure and took watercolor classes and twisted ourselves into pretzels during deck yoga. Mary Alice and Natalie sat on their asses in the Chart Room, eating, drinking, and chatting with other passengers before heading off to dance class. We caught the planetarium show and Shakespeare lectures and spent too much time in the casino. There were fencing lessons, cooking classes, and a memorable whisky tasting, and by the end of the second day, Mary Alice came to my stateroom for a debrief.

She yanked off her wig and tossed it aside before kicking off her shoes to massage her feet. "Oh god. My bunions. I should never have taken that samba class," she moaned. "I danced for two hours with a retired maître d' from Barcelona and his wife."

"What sort of samba class encourages threesomes?"

"The wife is Brazilian. She likes to lead," she explained. She looked around. "Where's Helen?"

"Sushi-making class," I told her. "Where's Nat?"

"Listening to live jazz in the Carinthia Lounge," she said in her best travel agent voice. She pointed at me to sum up. "What do we know?"

"Lazarov isn't a joiner," I said. "We haven't seen him in any classes or lectures. He's skipped all the entertainment apart from forty-five minutes at the casino last night where he won a few thousand bucks and mostly looked bored. He had a manicure, had his hair cut at the barbershop, and bought three books at the bookstore." She gave me a quizzical look and I knew what she was asking. "Two Agatha Christies and the latest Janice Hallett."

"He likes it twisty," she said. "I saw him talking to a couple from Liverpool. Nat and I chatted with them later and managed to get a little information but nothing useful. Apparently, they talked to him about pears. Or bears. They were both extremely hard of hearing—probably because they were older than Adam's housecat. Like everybody else on this ship."

"Don't be so ageist," I scolded mildly.

"Ageist? I love it," Mary Alice said earnestly. "We are the youngest people on board by a mile. I'm bringing Akiko next time. And I may never vacation with anybody except the elderly again. It's doing wonders for my self-esteem."

I grinned, wondering if Akiko knew what she was in for. Like samba threesomes. "Back to Lazarov. He seems perfectly content to read in the Chart Room or stay in his suite.

That indicates to me that he's not impressed with the ship. We know he's made the crossing before, probably enough that he's seen and done it all."

Mary Alice nodded thoughtfully. "It's like flying transatlantic in first class on Virgin. The first time, you get so excited by all the fun little perks—the popcorn and ice cream and those cute little salt and pepper shakers—and you can hardly wait to change into the jammies they give you. It's a little less exciting the second time. By the third time, you're wondering why they can't give you the right size pajamas and why the serving of ice cream is so small."

She paused a minute and I took the chance to voice something that had been bothering me.

"Something is off about Pasha," I began.

"Off?" She was still scrutinizing her feet. "Damn. I'm starting a blister."

"The whole Anglophilia thing. The teak yacht. The teddy bear. He's not like other Bulgarians we've targeted."

"He's nothing like his father," she agreed absently.

I didn't say anything else and she stopped messing with her blister to look at me closely. "What?"

I shrugged. "I don't know. I can't explain it."

If she'd pushed me then, I would have told her I didn't have anything better than a strange little flicker of intuition, something nagging at me that I couldn't define. It was like hearing a radio playing far away and not being able to tell what the song is but somehow knowing it's familiar.

She didn't push and I let it go. "At least we won't have to chase him all over the ship," I said. "He's only ever in the Chart

Room or smoking out on deck which limits our opportunities," I said. "What's the situation with his security?"

Mary Alice shrugged "Negligible. One bodyguard in a crappy off-the-rack suit. Russian, by the look of him, or maybe Bulgarian. Lodging in a shitty single room down on deck two."

I raised a brow. Lazarov's suite, like our staterooms, was up on deck nine. "That's quite a hike. Lazarov must be feeling relaxed about the security situation."

"Why wouldn't he?" Mary Alice asked. "Like you said, he's familiar with the ship."

"He just committed a murder and left a calling card," I reminded her, thinking of the small carved wolf he'd left at Lilian Flanders's house.

She flapped a hand. "The fact that Lilian was murdered might have very easily been overlooked. He probably figures nobody has made the connection yet between her death and his father's hit. Or that they've informed us and we're on his tail."

"I suppose," I said reluctantly.

"Relax, sister," she said confidently. "Lazarov has no idea we're onto him. And, in spite of my bunions, this is one of the most pleasant missions I've ever had. It's restful. I may make a habit of murders on ships."

I could see her point. There are pros to killing someone at sea—they can't get away from you, there's a whole ocean for disposing of evidence—but there are cons too. The biggest was that we would be stuck in the same place as the body, putting us squarely in the running as suspects. The longer the period between his death and a postmortem, the better for us. In this particular case, we had to be far enough out from New York to make sure they wouldn't try to fly his corpse back. We also had to be far enough from England that they wouldn't send him that way. And, most crucial of all, we needed to be off the ship and with as much distance as possible between us and the body before any suggestion of foul play was raised. Otherwise, we'd become suspects along with the other four thousand or so people on board.

Everything came down to the ship's doctor. That was the person who would examine Lazarov and pronounce him dead. We'd discussed any number of possibilities, but in the end, we settled on Lazarov dying quietly in his suite. A passenger dropping dead in any of the public spaces would bring complications we didn't need—iPhone videos, hysteria, eyewitness accounts. We wanted a nice, uncomplicated corpse in his own room. It would make for an unpleasant experience for the butler who brought his morning tea, but that was better than every tourist from Tallinn to Tierra del Fuego filming his corpse and uploading it to YouTube. From his stateroom, Lazarov would be quietly moved to the morgue. The QM2 had a four-drawer capacity, so unless something drastic happened—like a mass food-poisoning event—he'd have a peaceful trip to Southampton on his own.

We assumed the ship's doctor was less than ambitious. Otherwise why spend your career prescribing antacids and anti-nausea medication to rich people? Sure, there was always the odd ministroke or outbreak of norovirus to deal with, but that was nothing compared to exotic ports of call and a career spent at sea. I suspected the ship's doctor would be just as happy not to go looking for anything suspicious when Lazarov popped his clogs. If nothing else, the paperwork would be a bitch. Besides that, the cruise line wouldn't want any blowback from the rotten publicity of somebody keeling over dead on their ship. The doctor would be under pressure, spoken or otherwise, to keep things simple. Without specific reasons to suspect foul play, like a ransacked room or a violent altercation with another passenger, the doctor would have no reason to do anything other than chalk the death up to natural causes. Heart attacks are always popular with guys Lazarov's age. The ship's doctor probably wouldn't even contact Lazarov's physician to see if he had a heart condition until we docked. By the time the doctor got a response, the four of us would have gone to ground at Benscombe, lying low for a few days until we went our separate ways again.

We were also feeling good about the security situation. A big, oxlike guard was ideal for us. Guys like that are only ever hired for show. Those beefy muscles might punch like a bulldozer, but they've got one gear—slow. Getting around them is child's play. Folks who are serious about security hire agile women who are hypervigilant and trained to assess every detail. Women like us, actually.

I looked to where Mary Alice was relaxing on my sofa. "It's time to start finalizing plans. What are you thinking in terms of method?"

She considered this. "An exit bag," she said finally. It was an unexpected and elegant suggestion. (Exit bags are simply sacks of thick plastic used for suffocation, often in suicides. If you pair one with a canister of helium, you can avoid inducing the panicky feeling that asphyxiation creates. Nitrogen is even better because it leaves no trace in the blood, a handy trick if you don't want anyone to know you've taken your own life. It works perfectly so long as you have someone to discreetly remove the bag for you. We like exit bags because they are far less likely to cause petechiae, those telltale little red marks that are the hallmark of smothering. Exit bags have the further advantage of being quiet and discreet. Any thick plastic bag will do, and when you're finished, you can walk off with your groceries sticking out the top of the murder weapon and nobody will be the wiser.)

"I like it," I told her. "But if we're going to get close enough to use an exit bag, we've got to get into his suite. There's nowhere else on the ship we can make it work."

"We could have done it in the sauna if we were men," she said archly. "But we're not. So either we get him to let us in or we have to be in his room waiting."

"Next point. The bodyguard. Whether we get Lazarov to let us in or we're lying in wait, we have to work around the goon. His assignment is pretty relaxed, but we still have to assume he's a factor."

"Roofie him?" she suggested. "Although I don't happen to have any GHB lying around."

She paused and we grinned at the same time.

"Natalie," I said. "Remind me to ask her tomorrow if she has anything suitable in her fanny pack."

We were silent a long time, listening to the low, comforting hum of the engines and the slap of waves against the hull. After a while, I heard a soft snore and looked over to find her fast asleep. She was twisted up like a Bavarian pretzel, and I gave her a poke.

"Mary Alice, wake up and take yourself to bed."

She blinked furiously and rubbed at her neck. "We haven't finished working out a plan."

"Unless you start talking in your sleep, you're not contributing much. Go on," I told her.

"I'd argue, but I'm dead on my feet," she said as she struggled to stand. "I blame that damned samba class." She patted me on the shoulder as she passed. "Get some sleep, Billie. We'll pick up in the morning and figure it out then."

I made a noncommittal noise and she left, taking her blanket with her. I went out onto the little balcony with mine, wrapping it around my body like a serape. I flicked open my lighter—heavy silver and set with turquoise, the only thing of my mother's I'd kept. I lit a cigarette and watched it spark to life with its friendly little firefly glow. I thought of Taverner, waiting back in Greece for me, and I thought of the man sleeping a few doors down whom I still had to kill.

It had been two years since I'd been on a job, and as I blew smoke into the endless black of that Atlantic night, I realized there was nowhere else I'd rather be.

CHAPTER EIGHT

IT TOOK THE BETTER PART OF THREE HOURS AND I COULDN'T FEEL MY fingers by the time I finished, but when I finally stumbled to bed, I had it. I slept until Helen gave me a light shove and told me that butler Stephen had just brought breakfast. I sat up and she handed me a plate of food. I usually limited my morning meal to Greek yogurt and fruit, but there was enough in front of me to feed a teenage boy with a gland problem.

"Ooh, full English," I said happily. I started with the eggs and bacon. "How did you know I needed stoking?"

Helen nibbled a spoonful of muesli. "I got up to go to the bathroom about three in the morning and saw you sitting outside." She was familiar enough with my methods to know that when I was working out a hit, I would hunker down with a six-pack of Big Red, drinking and chain-smoking Eves until I had it. The *QM2* didn't run to Big Red, but at least the nicotine did the trick. "Did you get it?"

"I got it," I said around a mouthful of baked beans. I shoved a piece of Cunard stationery at her. There were a few rough sketches on the page along with a series of bullet points. She studied the pictures and skimmed the list.

"Risky," she said finally. "But doable."

"If you've got a better idea, I'd love to hear it," I told her honestly.

She shook her head and dropped the paper on the bed next to me. "I think this is as good as any other plan."

I buttered and jammed a piece of toast. "An underwhelming reaction. Are you afraid of cracking your Botox or just unenthusiastic?"

She pitched a pillow at me and I batted it away, protecting my toast. "I have never used Botox," she informed me. "Fillers only."

I scrutinized her face. "Looks good."

Her gaze slid past mine, and she went to check her reflection, smoothing a spot between her brows. "You think?"

"Helen, you are one of the five most beautiful women I've ever seen in person and definitely the least vain. Why are you looking in the mirror like Snow White's stepmother?"

She straightened, her expression surprised. She couldn't have done that with Botox, so I guessed she was telling the truth. "Actually, I always related to the Evil Queen," she said as she turned back to the mirror.

"Why? Unless you have a stepdaughter I don't know about. Or a boy toy. I always suspected the Evil Queen had something dirty going on with the huntsman," I added, crunching into my toast.

I could see her image in the mirror. To my surprise, her reflection went pink from her collarbones to her hairline. I nearly choked on my toast.

"You're kidding."

"He's not a boy toy," she said firmly. "He's only seven years younger than I am. But . . ."

She trailed off and came to sit on the edge of my bed. I felt stupid I hadn't suspected it. During our last mission, Helen had shuffled around like a woman who was running on a battery with half a charge, so bowed down by grief she couldn't even stand upright. But now she was practically glowing.

"He's the first since Kenneth died?"

She nodded, clasping her hands together.

"How long have you been seeing him? Is it serious? Tell me more, tell me more, like does he have a car." I fluttered my lashes at her in my best impression of a Pink Lady.

She grinned. "It's been going on for seven or eight months. And I wouldn't call it serious. Or a relationship. He lives in Brussels and travels a lot, and I'm at Benscombe, so we just get together when we feel like it. We meet up in Paris or Amsterdam. London if he's over on business."

"Helen Randolph, you have a friend with benefits," I said.

"No, that's what you have with Taverner," she corrected. "I just have benefits. I don't consider him a friend."

"You mean you only get together to get laid?"

Her blush deepened. "You've been spending too much time with Natalie. I prefer to think of it as a mutually satisfactory arrangement."

"Satisfactory?" I hooted with laughter. "If it's only satisfactory, you should consider an upgrade."

"Fine, it's more than satisfactory. It's . . . rapturous," she said, grinning suddenly.

I grinned back. "I'm happy for you."

She sobered just as fast as she'd smiled. "It's just that, lately, I've begun to wonder if I wouldn't like something more. Not necessarily from Benoit. Or maybe from Benoit. I don't know."

Her fingers plucked at the bedspread, pleating and unpleating.

"What's holding you back?"

She shrugged, but when she looked up, her eyes were fearful. "What if he doesn't want that? What if I think I want it and I really don't? How do you even start something permanent with someone at our age? I mean, when you get together for—what does Natalie call them? Butt dials?"

"Booty calls," I corrected. "And nobody says that anymore. I think it's 'Netflix and chilling' now."

She flapped a hand. "Whatever the kids are calling it these days. The point is, I know when I'm going to see Benoit. I have time to prepare. I take care of stray hairs and the callus on my big toe. But a relationship is different. Someone who's around all the time is going to notice I wear my glasses on a chain around my neck and spend my morning with the *New York Times* crossword."

I patted her arm. "Any man who loves you is going to love you even when you look like a demented librarian with glasses on a chain and crossword in hand. I don't know what to say about the big toe except maybe book your pedicures a little closer together."

She gave me a gentle shove and I grabbed her shoulder, peering closely at her face. "And don't worry about that mustache. Some men have a kink for that."

"That lip is as smooth as a baby's ass cheek," she told me. "I waxed just last week." She grabbed the last piece of toast, and I was glad to see she was looking more like herself. Helen's widowhood had brought with it a crisis of confidence that had paralyzed her at a particularly inopportune moment. But she'd redeemed herself, and the time since seemed like it had done her a world of good. Throwing herself into a project had been the best possible thing for her grief, although I suspected getting stuck into more than just the Farrow & Ball tins had been the real magic.

She picked up the list again and read it through, over and over again, just like we'd been taught, until she'd got it memorized. "I'll let the others know and then I will get the things on the list that we need from the shops."

"Get them to put everything in a big bag," I called after her. "We're going to need it."

CHAPTER NINE

BY LATE EVENING, WE WERE READY. THE PRELIMINARIES HAD GONE
perfectly. Natalie was still the best at legerdemain, so she was
the one who tipped a bottle of eye drops into the bodyguard's
tea. It's a common misconception that eye drops cause diarrhea,
but tetrahydrozoline generally doesn't upset the stomach—it
goes straight for the heart. First, the rhythm changes. A steady,
regular beat will start to thrum erratically. Then the blood
pressure drops, and sleepiness sets in. That's the sweet spot.
Too much in the system and you get breathing difficulties,
and the last thing we wanted was a bodyguard wheezing his
way into the infirmary. Tetrahydrozoline is unpredictable as a
means of inducing cardiac arrest, but as a makeshift sedative,
it's cheap, easy, and generally effective. In a pinch, I've used it
to take the wind out of a target's sails before getting down to
business. A mark is less likely to fight back when they're half-
conscious. Natalie will argue that Rohypnol is far more reliable,

but she'd used the last of her supply on a final job in Marrakech and hadn't restocked. She's also usually packing molly, a joint or two, and some industrial-grade accelerants in case she needs to burn something down, but then she was a Girl Scout and I suppose that kind of preparedness training sticks with you. In any case, her fanny pack didn't have anything we needed, so we ended up going with eye drops from the ship's gift shop, a more discreet option than a vial of GHB anyway.

I could never admit this to anyone else, but I actually like it when a job goes slightly wrong. There's something exhilarating about walking that razor's edge between success and complete failure and then sticking the landing in spite of the odds. In this case, it meant dealing with the security cameras and coming face-to-face with Lazarov. But security cameras are not as foolproof as everybody thinks, mostly because cameras are only half of the equation—the guards that monitor them are the other half. Every image has to be monitored, and an absent or inattentive guard is just as bad as not having a camera at all. Worse, actually, because many people rely too much on them instead of investing in better training for their guards. Movies love to show people hacking into security systems, but that's like using a sledgehammer to hang a picture nail—too much trouble and potentially disastrous. Most systems have an alert built in to flag somebody trying to gain access through a back door, and even if you manage to get the tech right, there's no guarantee it won't be traced. Far better and much easier to take care of the human element instead. Well-trained observers can penetrate the best disguises, but only if they know they should be looking in that direction

The trick is to get them to look past you. Hide in plain sight and you'll never be seen.

From across the Chart Room, I monitored the bodyguard's condition. He fought the sleepiness hard, pulling himself up with a jerk each time he seemed about to nod off. When his body language indicated he was about to get up, I opened the latest copy of *Harper's*, snapping it slightly. That was the signal for Mary Alice to totter by, stumbling slightly against him as he got to his feet. Under other circumstances, he wouldn't have even felt it. She would have gently bounced off him. But in his current state, he swayed, putting out his hands and grasping Mary Alice's shoulders. She gave a merry little laugh as they untangled themselves, chattering brightly, and unless you were watching carefully, you'd never have seen two fingers dip into his pocket and retrieve his key cards. We figured he'd have two—his own and Pasha's. Rich people are used to people coming and going all the time, and the very last thing they want to do is keep getting up to open doors for their own staff. We needed only Pasha's key, but there was no way to tell without looking at the room number to see which was which. The hardest part of Mary Alice's job was purloining the keys, choosing Pasha's, and slipping the other back into the bodyguard's pocket. We needed to avoid the bodyguard figuring out he'd lost both keys and heading to the purser to have them reissued.

But Mary Alice was a pro. She chattered a moment longer, just enough for her to dart a look at the keys, then slide the extra key into the bodyguard's jacket. The bodyguard, clearly woozy, flopped back into his seat and was staring into the middle distance with a goofy grin on his face. Mary Alice shuffled on to the next seating area, settling herself into an armchair and taking out her knitting. I got up, collecting my tote, and walked in her direction. Just before I reached her, she dropped a ball of yarn. I picked it up and returned it with a smile, pocketing the key card she'd tucked inside. Maneuvers like that are a ballet of sorts, each of us knowing exactly where the others will be and how they will move. With the key in my pocket, I strolled from the room. The bodyguard didn't register me at all.

As soon as I left the Chart Room, I picked up my pace. I was on deck three and I had to get myself up six levels as quickly as possible without making it seem like I was in a hurry. I was also somewhere midship with Lazarov's suite at the very back of the liner. I jumped into an elevator and rode up to deck eight, hopping out long enough to head down the long, narrow central corridor. Across the back of the ship, the Verandah restaurant overlooked the pool terrace, but just before this was a public ladies' room. The vanity area was empty, and I locked myself into a cubicle. I was already wearing black trousers and flats with a sharply tailored white shirt. I exchanged my glittery red cardigan for a cutaway white jacket—a piece of the cabin staff uniform Mary Alice had lifted during a lucky trip to the laundry. Helen had sacrificed a black silk scarf to make a bow tie, and with the addition of a dark wig pulled into a neat ponytail, I looked the part. I added a pair of nondescript tortoiseshell readers from the gift shop and headed out.

Natalie met me in the lift with a tote of her own—this one

stuffed with pillows. I pulled them out and handed over my bag for safekeeping. She had already hit the buttons for decks nine and ten and when we stopped at nine, I got out alone, holding the pillows up on my shoulder to obscure my face from the cameras. To anybody watching, I looked like any other room attendant delivering an order from the pillow menu. I passed two doors before I reached Lazarov's, pausing to tap discreetly. I waited, then swiped the key card to enter.

I stopped inside the door, listening and running a mental inventory of the whereabouts of all the principal players. Helen was surveilling Lazarov as he took his after-dinner drink in the Commodore Club. It was on the same deck as his cabin but the opposite end of the ship. The bodyguard was either still dozing in the Chart Room or had stumbled off to the bed in his sad little cabin on deck two. Either way, Mary Alice would keep an eye on him until she had the all clear. Natalie was hiding out in the ladies' room on deck ten with my bag. Here, Lazarov's suite was quiet, the hum of the engines far below barely detectable. The wi-fi on board was crap, but I'd managed to pull up full floor plans of the suite as well as a video tour on YouTube thanks to CruiseLuvr2251. I'd studied it until I knew the layout so well, I could have made my way around in the dark. Everything in the suite was exactly where I expected. Just inside the main door was a narrow hallway with a shower room on one side and a small kitchenette on the other. It was really more of a glorified wet bar, but Lazarov's butler kept it stocked with all kinds of treats, I noticed. Fruit baskets, packets of Fortnum & Mason tea, bottles of English perry and cider—even some Devonshire fruit wine which in my opinion is taking Anglophilia a step too far.

I passed into the living area which included a dining table and credenza as well as a full entertainment unit. The door to the terrace was closed, the blinds drawn. In the middle of the room was the staircase curving upwards to the second floor. I vaulted up the steps two at a time, my flats silent on the deep pile of the carpet. At the top was a landing with a stationary bike, the area serving as a mini–exercise room. Double doors opened to a bedroom which was furnished with a king-sized bed, pristinely made with the teddy bear taking pride of place in the center.

"I'm sorry you have to see this," I said to the bear.

I dumped the extra pillows at the foot of the bed and paused. I needed to be hidden when Lazarov arrived. On either side of the bed were doors leading to dressing areas. Beyond those were a shower room on one side and a tub room on the other along with a back door from the suite. The shower and tub compartments connected through separate toilet areas, making a semicircle around the bedroom. Handy for my purposes, but not if I guessed wrong as to where Lazarov would head when he arrived.

I studied the two dressing areas. The one leading to the tub held navy pajamas from Turnbull & Asser marked with his monogram in Cyrillic letters along with two silk robes and a pair of needlepoint slippers with a teddy bear pattern.

The other dressing area was full of more Turnbull & Asser—shirts this time—with a selection of exquisitely tailored suits and handmade shoes. No wonder he wasn't a power player with the other oligarchs. He spent the equivalent of the GNP of a small industrial nation just on his wardrobe. I peeked into the area that held the tub. The toiletries on the vanity were, predictably, Penhaligon's. But I wasn't complaining. My sheets smelled like Penhaligon's thanks to Taverner, although he preferred Endymion to Lazarov's choice of Sartorial.

Given that the pajamas were on the bathtub side, it seemed a reasonable gamble that Lazarov would take a bath before bed. If I chose wrong? I didn't want to think about that. It took only a few seconds to make the necessary preparations. First, I spread the bathtub with a thin layer of cuticle oil I'd borrowed from Helen's toiletry bag. I poured the rest into the bottle of bubble bath on the vanity. After I carefully recapped it, I edged into the adjoining shower room and slid the door almost closed, noting the fact that it was noiseless. I left it open just half an inch, enough for me to keep tabs on what was happening in the tub room, and settled down to wait.

I was prepared to hang out for a while until Lazarov showed up, and I was amusing myself by constructing a mental crossword puzzle with the names of my favorite poisons when I heard voices. For one terrible moment I thought Lazarov had brought back a guest, but it was just him singing— something Gilbert and Sullivan which made me rethink giving him a painless death. I suffered through the entirety of "I Am the Very Model of a Modern Major-General" as he got ready for his bath. There was little chance he'd notice the cuticle oil. It had the advantage of being colorless and any faint scent would be masked by the bubble bath. Curls of steam rolled into the shower room where I was hiding, bringing with it the aroma of more Penhaligon's. I listened to him pee and grimaced when he didn't flush. I was crossing my fingers he wasn't about to do worse—the toilet was about two feet away from me with just the thin pocket door protecting my delicate sensibilities—but he was finished. I heard the soft sounds of clothes being shed and dropped to the floor, then the swoosh of a body displacing the water in the bathtub. I slipped both hands through the gap between the door and the jamb. I began to exert pressure, very light and even, coaxing the door open further. From where I stood I could see Lazarov reclining in the tub. The back of his head was facing me, and there were no mirrors opposite, nothing reflective to give me away as I crept nearer. He was the perfect sitting duck.

I moved forward, but just when I would have stepped into the bathroom, there was a soft knock on the door opposite. The butler. I jumped back like a scalded cat as Lazarov called out a reply. There was no time to pull the door into place, so I kept still and hoped he wouldn't be suspicious. From where I crouched, I could see a slice of the bathroom, about half of the bathtub and a patch of floor next to it.

"Your chamomile, sir," the butler said, setting a cup and saucer on the marble surround of the bathtub. It wasn't Stephen; the largest suites had their own attendant, which was good news for me. The last thing I needed was to be spotted by the guy who had unpacked my underwear and carried in my morning tea.

The butler scooped up the discarded clothes. "I will have these laundered directly. Is there anything else, Mr. Lazarov?"

Lazarov murmured something and waved his hand.

The butler exited with the armful of clothes. I slowly counted to five hundred in English. By the time I repeated the exercise in Arabic, I figured Lazarov was probably starting to prune and the coast was clear. I slipped out of the shower room, moving silently towards the tub. I already had the plastic bag in hand. I'd asked Helen for a big one, but she'd had a better idea. She'd bought an assortment of things from the shops, asking for each to be put into a different-sized bag so I'd have several to choose from. You don't want one too small, obviously. The head has to fit inside neatly with plenty of extra to go around the neck. But you don't want one that's too big either. All that plastic just gets in the way and you can't even recycle it when you're done.

Lazarov had just taken a sip of his tea and was moving to set the cup into the saucer when I sprang, dropping the bag over his head and twisting it tightly. His hands came up but I dodged them, pulling the bag tighter still. His feet scrabbled on the oil-slicked tub, sliding uselessly under him. It takes only ten seconds to choke a person into unconsciousness, but as soon as you let go, the airflow is restored. Then they'll pop right back into consciousness, only now they're good and pissed and surging with adrenaline. The trick to preventing that is to put a little extra pressure on the carotid arteries, ensuring a nice, deep blackout. If your goal is to kill them, then you just keep pressing for a good three minutes which is why I make a point of hitting arm day hard at the gym. It takes a lot more time and effort than you'd think to do it right.

But I wasn't out to suffocate Lazarov—just to incapacitate

him. I only had to hold on for about twenty seconds before he was properly blacked out. He'd stopped struggling after eight; I hung on for the other twelve to make sure he wasn't playing possum. But his limbs were limp, his neck soft as his head lolled to the side like a baby's. The bubbles weren't doing much to preserve his modesty, so I scooped a little foam over his groin and finished the job.

First, I slipped off the plastic bag and stuck it into my pocket. Then I pushed him gently under the water and kept my hand resting on top of his head. Slow bubbles rose to the surface for a few minutes, then gradually stopped. I put a hand beneath the water, feeling for his carotid. There was no pulse, and even if he'd been able to fake that, his bowels suddenly relaxed with a gurgle and I yanked my hand away. I stood back to study the scene. It was supposed to look like Lazarov had suffered a massive heart attack and drowned after losing consciousness. The teacup had been a casualty of the struggle, shattering on the floor, but it was reasonable that a man feeling a coronary coming on could have flailed a bit. That could account for the small amount of water that had sloshed onto the floor as well, so I didn't bother to mop up. There were no marks on his neck. I'd removed the plastic bag before I'd broken any blood vessels. I had worried a bit about that because the last thing I wanted was to leave ligature marks but he was clean.

All in all, it had gone well and the scene looked plausible, I decided. And Pasha Lazarov was as dead as he was going to get. I stepped into Lazarov's bedroom to collect my extra pillows. I was halfway out the door when I noticed it. On his bedside table was a pocket diary—navy crocodile with his initials stamped in silver. I flicked through it quickly. The pages were pale blue, thin, and watermarked, each corner perforated to keep track of the current week. The days at sea were marked with a series of simple slashes, but the pages before that were crammed with entries. They were jotted in a tiny, cramped hand, a mixture of English and Bulgarian, not a proper cipher, but the sort of mishmash you write in when you're bilingual. One line featured a string of numbers that looked interesting, but before I could make any sense of it, I heard a noise from downstairs. The butler. *Again.* There was a soft susurration of footsteps on carpet and I realized he was climbing the stairs. Turndown service, no doubt. In about five seconds he'd be up the stairs and cutting off my means of exit. I didn't plan what happened next. Sometimes instinct just takes over and you find yourself acting without thinking about it. I closed the diary and stuffed it into my pocket, grabbing the extra pillows off the foot of the bed as I heard the butler coming closer. I scuttled back through the dressing area and into the shower room. On the other side of the shower room was the back door of the suite, leading directly to deck ten. I held the pillows at shoulder height again as I slipped out the door. There was no way to lock it behind me. The butler might notice the unlocked door—the only sign of my presence I'd left behind—but then again, he might not. And even if he did, there was nothing to connect that with Lazarov's seemingly natural death.

Except that his pocket diary was now missing, I realized. I paused, thinking fast. Lazarov was meant to have died of natural causes which meant all of his possessions should be accounted for. Under normal circumstances, there wouldn't be an inventory made of his things, but Lazarov was the richest, most important passenger on board. To cover their own asses, the cruise line would probably make a detailed list of everything they packed up. And if they didn't, the bodyguard sure as hell would.

A list that would go where? Who was Pasha Lazarov's next of kin? I flicked back through the mental dossier I carried around on him. The only relative left was Aunt Evgenia, and she was ancient, living in an old folks' home in Switzerland. I didn't expect she'd be sharp enough to notice a missing diary, and even if she were, the omission would probably be chalked up to confusion in the wake of Pasha's death. Maybe the bodyguard would even get the blame. It was fine.

A little flicker of guilt tickled the back of my neck. I was slipping. Unless Provenance had made a direct request for retrieval, taking *anything* from a mission was completely forbidden. We didn't kill outside our briefs and we definitely didn't keep trophies. We never took anything from marks, not even a breath mint. It was beneath us, the sort of opportunistic profiteering a common hit man might engage in. We were better than that.

It was almost as bad as killing the wrong mark. I shoved the memory of Chicago away as fast as it came. That had been my worst mistake, the likes of which I'd never made since.

Until now, of course. I considered my options, but returning the planner was out of the question. I'd made my escape and going back now could mean running into the butler during turndown service. And if he saw me, I'd have to kill him—a can of worms I had no intention of opening. Telling the others wasn't high on my list of options either. The last thing I wanted was for them to give me the look we gave others, the ones who'd gotten soft or sloppy or too old for this job. The quick side-eye full of judgment and relief—judgment at the loss of skill and relief it isn't you.

Blowing out a slow breath to steady my nerves, I eased down the staircase to the ladies' room where Natalie waited. Forty seconds later, I'd ditched my uniform jacket, tugged off my wig and glasses, and shoved them along with the pillows into my tote before pulling my sequined cardigan back on. Natalie and I left together, our heads close as if we were gossiping, but it had the effect of keeping our faces averted from the cameras. We took a circuitous route back to the stateroom I shared with Helen, stopping long enough to ditch the plastic bag in one of the trash cans in another ladies' room.

Back in my cabin, I went into the dressing area and stripped off the clothes I'd been wearing. I slipped the planner into the interior pocket of my tote, zipping it out of sight and out of mind. I slipped on a robe, and when I emerged, the others were there, and the champagne was already on ice.

"Well?" Helen asked anxiously.

I grinned. "Done. Pop the cork," I told her. "It's time to celebrate."

CHAPTER TEN

THE REST OF THE CROSSING WAS UNEVENTFUL. THERE WAS A DISCREET
flurry of activity outside Lazarov's suite the next day and
Natalie kept us updated by peering through the peephole of
our door at the various crew members passing by. I'd expected the body to be found the previous night since the butler had still been in the suite, but he must have steered clear
of the bathroom.

"The butler just hurried past with the doctor," she said.
"Oooh, and here comes another officer. He looks stern." She
glanced at us and waggled her eyebrows. "I do love a man in
uniform."

I half expected the captain himself to turn up given Lazarov's prominence, but if he did, he slipped through the back
door of the suite up on deck ten. That must have been how
they took the body out because although a few crew members

trotted past with a collapsible stretcher, they never made the return trip past our door.

"You don't think they just *left* him there, do you?" Helen asked, wide-eyed.

Mary Alice shook her head. "They couldn't. Too warm, even if they turned the air conditioning way down."

"Naomi confirmed there's a morgue on board," I reminded Helen. "In the lowest part of the ship. They'll stash him there until we reach Southampton. And they probably won't take him off until most passengers have disembarked."

An hour later, the butler came back past our room, his expression solemn. Maybe he actually liked Lazarov, or maybe he was mourning the tip he wouldn't get at the voyage's end. I made a note to slip something extra in an envelope for him and leave it with the purser.

For the next few days, we kept our disguises on, our profiles low. We skipped the gala nights and eluded the ship's photographer every time he popped up. Nat and I spent a lot of time reading on our respective balconies while Helen pinned kitchen pics from Smallbone to her Pinterest board and Mary Alice knitted like a fiend.

"What are you making?" I finally asked. "If that's for Akiko, it's going to be a crop top."

She held up the tiny garment with its alternating rows of green and yellow yarn. "Sweaters for Kevin and Gary. I did Fair Isle for Gary, but Kevin needs stripes. They're slimming and he's carrying a little extra winter weight."

I was sorry I'd asked. And I was tired of keeping my head

down. On the last night, I slipped out of the room and headed for the Commodore Club. I slid onto a barstool and ordered a glass of black Shiraz. I had just taken my first sip when someone heaved himself onto the adjoining seat. He lifted an empty glass towards the bartender, who gave him a tight-lipped smile but poured him another.

"Your nightcap, sir," the bartender said as he pushed it towards him. The tone was clear—he was cutting off the man next to me, and I didn't have to look at him to know why. He reeked of booze, and not the expensive stuff.

I raised my glass to take another sip just as the newcomer reached for his. His elbow jostled mine and a little of the dark ruby liquid pooled on the bar.

"I'm sorry," he said humbly. He tried to mop it up but ended up just spreading it around into a sticky puddle. The bartender hurried to clean it up with a towel and refill my wine.

I thanked the bartender and turned to the fellow next to me. I might have guessed. Of course, it was the bodyguard. Still dressed in black with "henchman" written all over him. But he looked truly miserable and against my better judgment, I gave him a sympathetic look.

"Alright there?"

His eyes were bleary and his face was tearstained. "Yes," he said, nodding as if to convince himself. It came out "yesh" and I realized he was far drunker than he seemed. No wonder the bartender was cutting him off.

"Sure about that?" I asked.

"No," he admitted. "My boss just died. It was a very good job, the best I ever had. Now I am unemployed."

"Sorry to hear it," I told him in a consoling tone. "I'm sure you'll find something even better." I slipped off the barstool to find another seat, but he grabbed my wrist. Instinct flared, and I very nearly flipped him onto his back and drove a barstool leg into his eye, but I resisted the impulse. He was no threat to me. He was just sad and drunk and more than a little pathetic. He had no idea who I was, I realized. He just needed somebody to talk to and I was the most convenient ear.

I sighed and remounted the barstool. The bartender gave me a questioning look from down the bar, but I shook my head, waving him off.

"Please stay," the bodyguard pleaded. "Just for a little while. I buy drinks." He gestured towards the bartender, who walked up looking distinctly displeased.

"Water for both of us," I said firmly. "Big glasses. And maybe something to eat."

"Of course, madam," he said. He filled two huge tumblers with water and even a little ice. He set them in front of us and produced a bowl of mixed nuts. He edged away again, but he kept an eye on things, wiping out glasses that were already spotless. It was sweet. I mean, how was he to know I could have smashed a bottle of Grey Goose and slashed both their jugulars in less than ten seconds? He saw a big guy who was on the verge of losing control, pushing his attention on a much smaller, much older woman and drew the logical conclusion that I might need an assist. I had long since given up being frustrated by that. *Being underestimated is your super-power,* the Shepherdess had always told us.

I settled more comfortably onto my stool and waited. It didn't take long.

"My name is Grigory," the bodyguard said, extending his hand. It was meaty and clammy, two of my least favorite things, but I shook it anyway.

"Bianca," I told him.

"That is beautiful name," he said, tearing up again.

"So, how long did you have your job, Grigory?" I asked.

He shrugged. "A few years. Before this, I was a policeman in Sofia." Bulgarian after all, then.

"Why did you leave?" I asked him.

"I did not like the work. Too many drunks."

"Pot, kettle," I murmured into my Shiraz.

He didn't hear me. He was too far gone into his story. "So I went to work in private security instead. I am bodyguard to very rich man," he said, puffing out his chest and thumping it.

A piss-poor one, but far be it from me to criticize. I took another sip. "Your English is very good."

"My boss, he liked to speak English. He was Bulgarian, like me, but he liked the English." He subsided then into a few remarks in his native tongue that seemed tinged with bitterness. My Russian is dead fluent, but I'd never learned Bulgarian. Why bother? Nobody speaks Bulgarian except Bulgarians and most of them know a second language anyway.

"And now he's dead," I prompted.

"Yes." He leaned close, blowing boozy breath into my ear. "On this ship. He is there," he added, pointing down.

"Hell?"

He snorted, but whether out of shock or to cover a laugh, I couldn't tell. "The morgue. Although hell, this is possible too. Who knows what happens after we die." He sobered a second, holding his head sideways as if thinking hard had thrown him off-balance. That should have been my cue to leave, but I realized this tipsy lout was giving me the perfect chance to do a little digging. The crew was keeping Lazarov's death under wraps for now, and as far as we knew, nobody had been questioned. But we had no way of knowing how much they suspected about the cause.

"How did he die?" I asked.

Grigory's face puckered. "He had big heart attack and drowned in the bathtub."

"Wow," I said, raising my brows in a stab at surprise while inside I did a little fist pump. "That's terrible."

He nodded morosely and thumped himself in the general region of his heart. "I blame myself."

"Why?"

"Because I do not know he has a heart condition. The doctor on the ship says these things can be very quiet for many years. My boss never tells me. Maybe if I know, I can do something."

"It's nice that you wanted to save him," I said.

"This is easiest job I ever had," he confided. "Best job. The boss, he liked me to show myself a little, let people see the muscles." He bent his arm and flexed. The muscles were big and taut, but the veins in his throat popped—the sure sign of a dehydrated steroid user. As I had expected, he had been employed for show, and those heavy gym-tortured muscles would be less than useless during a fight. He might look intimidating at first glance, but I'd have wagered cash money that he had clumsy feet and reflexes like molasses on a winter's day.

He nudged his beefy shoulder into mine, nearly knocking me off my barstool. "I was meant to get bonus. Very big bonus. My boss has very large deal almost finished. Now?" He shrugged. "I get nothing. Is very sad, I was going to open shop for bubble tea in Sofia. You like bubble tea?"

"Love it," I lied with a smile. I was only half listening anyway. Bells were ringing too loudly in my head. "You must have been a big help to your boss with his deal if he was going to pay you a huge bonus."

He shrugged. "I watch his back is all." He laid a finger next to his nose—at least he tried. It landed about three inches off and he poked himself gently in the eye. "You cannot be too safe with Montenegrins."

I leaned in and pitched my voice low. "Grigory, you can't say that about people. It's racist."

He stared at me a long minute with a befuddled expression on his face, as if trying to process what the words meant or trying to figure out the square root of a prime number. He must have given up because instead of replying, he changed the subject. He shot his sleeve back and showed me a discreet Patek Philippe—vintage, I'd have wagered, and not bought with his own money. "I took this when I was packing his things. I will not be paid, you know," he added. There was a belligerent expression in his eyes and I think he expected me to take exception to his light-fingered ways.

I tapped the elegant alligator band where it was cutting into the meat of his wrist. "Make sure it doesn't have an inscription if you plan to pawn it. Watches like that are traceable."

His mouth went slack and it took him a whole minute to process what I'd just said. "Oh, you are a clever lady."

I shrugged. "Common sense." I took another sip, wondering if there was anything helpful at all sloshing around in that brain of his. "Too bad about your boss," I ventured. "I'm sure his family are going to miss him."

He shook his head slowly from side to side, like a bear trying to clear away a serious hangover. "These drinks are very good."

"Yes, they are. So your boss was alone on the ship? No wife or girlfriend?" I pressed. There was nothing subtle about my questions at this point, but Grigory didn't seem to notice.

"He has no women. No men either," he added with a leer as he elbowed me in the ribs.

"Careful, Cujo. I bruise easy."

He threw his head back and laughed, a rough and raucous sound that attracted the bartender's attention. I rolled my eyes and the bartender stayed where he was. I turned back to Grigory. "Sounds like your boss had a lonely life."

"He was rich," Grigory countered. "Rich men can buy anything they need."

"But not everything," I said. "'All your money won't another minute buy.'"

He gave me a blank look and I sighed.

"Kansas. 'Dust in the Wind.'" I hummed a few bars and he got excited.

"Yes! I know this song, but I prefer another." Without preamble, he launched himself into the opening of "Carry On Wayward Son." The bartender shut him down immediately by whisking away the glasses and giving us a pointed look.

"I'll handle it," I told him. I put an arm under Grigory's and hefted him off the barstool.

"You are very strong lady, Bianca," Grigory said. The last round must have hit him hard because he was slurring worse than ever. *Sssssshtrong.* And "Bianca" came out sounding like a breath spray.

"Grigory, you have no idea." I helped him to the elevators just outside the club, bundled him in, and hit the button for deck two. "You're on your own now, chief. Sleep it off."

He lurched forward, blocking the door from closing. "You are beautiful woman, Bianca. You are old, but I will overlook this and make love to you anyway. I invite you to my cabin." He threw his arms wide, finishing on a belch.

"I'm going to RSVP 'no' to that gracious invitation," I said. I put a fingertip to his forehead and pushed. He stumbled back and landed against the rear wall of the elevator, mouth gaping open as if he were about to say something. Suddenly his eyes rolled back in his head and he slid to the floor just as the doors closed.

I could have recalled the elevator. I could have followed him down to deck two and wrestled him to his bed. I could have flagged down a passing crew member and alerted them to the drunk passed out in the forward lifts.

Instead, I turned and made my way back to my own cabin, whistling the first few bars of "Carry On Wayward Son" as I went.

THE NEXT MORNING WE STEAMED INTO SOUTHAMPTON. WE WERE IN no hurry to disembark, so we dawdled outside, keeping an eye on the lower decks. Eventually, when the first hubbub of arrival had died down, we noticed a stretcher being discreetly loaded into an ambulance with its lights off. Lazarov. I'd filled in the others that there seemed to be no loose ends left thanks to Grigory's drunken gossiping.

"If anything, he's made himself a suspect by taking the watch," Helen pointed out calmly. "Lazarov was easily wearing twenty-five thousand dollars on his wrist, and for a bodyguard that would be a tidy little motive."

"Grigory did us a favor," I agreed. And he'd done me one as well. Given his preoccupation with his own unemployment, he probably hadn't noticed the missing diary. I'd thought once or twice about chucking it overboard, but in the end, I never did.

We went through all the usual disembarkation business before picking up our hired car. Natalie and Mary Alice had ditched their canes and wigs, and the four of us were in high spirits as we headed to Benscombe, the house where we'd trained. It had belonged to our mentor, Constance Halliday, and hadn't been properly lived in for a couple of decades after her death. Helen and her husband had eventually bought it, and we had used it as a safe house during our last outing. It had been in shitty shape then with crumbling floors and wallpaper hanging off in strips. The shootout and small fire we'd set hadn't helped. Since then Helen had been living at Benscombe, slowly renovating it back into shape, and this was the first time the rest of us were getting to see her progress. The drive from the port wasn't long—less than two hours—but we weren't in a rush. We made several stops. The first was the New Forest so we could stretch our legs properly now that we were on land again and the horizon was no longer bobbing up and down. Helen and I laced up our sneakers and ran for a few miles to loosen up our muscles while Nat and Mary Alice drove to the nearest village to pick up picnic supplies.

After we'd eaten our body weight in sausage rolls and sandwiches, Helen wanted to stop at a raptor center while Nat and Mary Alice argued about the inspiration for the Hundred Acre Wood in the Winnie-the-Pooh stories and whether it was within driving distance.

I turned to Helen. "A raptor? Really?"

She shrugged. "I have a pigeon problem at Benscombe. I've heard keeping an owl or falcon around would scare them off."

Mary Alice finally proved her point to Natalie—thank you, DuckDuckGo—and we headed for the raptor center. By the time we'd consoled Natalie with a very long pub dinner and stocked up on groceries, the sun was setting as we approached Benscombe.

We were listening to Mama Cass—"Make Your Own Kind

of Music" is basically our anthem—and singing along at the top of our lungs when Helen slammed on the brakes and said a couple of words I'd never heard come out of her debutante mouth.

I looked to where she was pointing and said a few choice words myself. Against the soft purple twilight sky, the house we'd trained in—Constance Halliday's childhood home—was silhouetted, the shadow of the façade moving strangely. A pillar of smoke rose from the bricks, and sparks shot skyward.

Benscombe was burning.

CHAPTER ELEVEN

IT WAS ALMOST DAWN WHEN THE FIRE BRIGADE FINALLY GOT THE last of the embers to stop glowing. A pall of smoke hung in the air, veiling the early light. Helen sat on an upturned flowerpot, huddled into her coat, while Natalie shoved cups of tea at her, courtesy of a nosy neighbor. Mary Alice stood a little apart, watching grimly as the hoses were turned off and coiled away. The house was outside a village, so the firefighters were on call only, the equivalent of a volunteer squad in the U.S., with smaller vehicles and less manpower. But even a fully equipped brigade couldn't have saved Benscombe. It was completely engulfed when we called 999, but we held out hope for the first hour—until the roof caved in and took the upper floors with it. Everything collapsed into the cellars with a roar, and that's when we realized the house was a total loss. We continued to watch as the fire flared up again and again, the exhausted brigade forced to chase down each eruption to keep it from spreading to the gardens and outbuildings. Mary Alice had spent most of the time roaming the perimeter of the property, studying the fire from different angles and poking around the shrubbery while Natalie and I stuck close to Helen, making sure she didn't go into shock.

Finally, the fire was well and truly extinguished. The packing up took a little while, but the trucks began to leave, one by one, until only a co-responder's vehicle was left. The owner was a kid who looked barely old enough to have left uni, and he walked the property with a clipboard, making notes to write up a report.

When he was finished, he came to stand by Helen, cocking his head in sympathy.

"I'm very sorry, madam," he said formally.

"Do you know how it started?" she asked in a hollow voice.

He flushed to the tips of his ears, clearly embarrassed at having to lay blame for the fire. "Well, now. It looks as if some paint pots were stacked up, perhaps a bit of redecorating?"

Helen nodded dully. "I was making over the kitchen."

"Ah yes. The problem is that paint pots are highly flammable, of course, especially with turps and oily rags and so forth. When it's all heaped up together, it's really only a matter of time before the worst happens."

Helen jerked up her head. "But I—"

I cut her off, pointing to an item I'd spotted in his hand. It was wrapped in a sooty handkerchief, about the size of his palm. "What is that?"

"Oh yes. I found this on the front doorstep. Rather a

miracle it survived, but I thought you might like it as a memento," he said, offering the small bundle to Helen.

She stared at the bundle, making no effort to accept it. I took it from him and slipped it into my pocket. "Thank you. And we're terribly sorry about the paint pots. So slipshod of us," I told him with a vague smile.

He nodded. "It is difficult to remember everything with a property of this size. Perhaps something a little more manageable? Maybe a nice, small flat in a housing development?"

He probably thought he meant well, but I wasn't taking it that way, and I knew Helen wasn't either. There's a special tone younger people often get when they're talking to anyone past fifty, all saccharine condescension. Some older people don't mind, but it always makes my fingers twitch for a good piece of garrote wire. Helen's reaction was the same. I grabbed her hand and felt the corded fingers tightened into a fist. "We'll certainly discuss it," I promised him.

"Do you ladies have somewhere to go?" he asked.

"We could always try a nice kill shelter since we're clearly past it," Mary Alice muttered.

He flushed again, and Natalie stepped forward with a charming smile. "Thank you so much for your time. Yes, we do have somewhere to go. Please don't let us keep you. You must be absolutely exhausted," she said, gently leading him towards his vehicle.

He walked with her, obviously happy to be finished with us. We could hear him promising to send a copy of the report when it was complete, calling good-bye as he put his car in gear and headed down the drive. We waved, and I had a little trouble keeping Helen's middle finger from going up.

"That little prick," she said as his car turned onto the main road and disappeared from view.

Natalie gave her an admiring look as she joined us. "Did rooming with Billie on the ship expand your vocabulary?"

"No, I just don't swear unless provoked. And he was provoking the shit out of me," Helen said.

"I don't think I can handle this version of Helen," Mary Alice said.

"We've got bigger problems than Helen suddenly becoming fluent in profanity," I said. My hand had been in my pocket, my fingers exploring the contours of the item wrapped in the handkerchief. I pulled out the bundle and opened it for the others. I already knew what I'd see. Lying on my palm was a small, obsidian wolf identical to the one retrieved from Lilian Flanders's house.

"Holy shit," Natalie breathed.

"I knew I hadn't left those paint cans stacked up together," Helen said triumphantly. "They were in the shed," she added, pointing to the outbuilding on the far side of the garden.

"The lock was cut off the shed door," Mary Alice informed us. She had a surprise hiding in her own pocket—a padlock whose hasp had been clipped neatly in two. "Found it in the shrubbery by the footpath."

"But who would do this? Lazarov is dead." Helen turned to me. "He *is* dead, Billie?"

"Jesus, Helen. I think I've been doing this long enough to

know when I've killed somebody. Yes, he's dead. I checked—twice."

"Alright, no need to get testy," she said in a wounded tone.

I reminded myself she'd had a pretty shitty night and waved her off. "Sorry."

"Lazarov could have prearranged it," Natalie ventured.

But I knew better. I shook my head. "He's got somebody watching his back—and they know he's dead." I thought of my initial impressions about Lazarov, the idea that he was soft, maybe too soft to organize Lilian Flanders's death. Grigory had stressed Pasha's loner habits, but he'd been drunk as a cross-eyed skunk. What if there *had* been someone?

I suggested as much to the others.

"Then why burn my house?" Helen demanded. "Why not just kill us outright?"

"They were able to get into the house and pile up the paint cans," Mary Alice agreed. "It would have been even easier to leave a device on a delay and blow us all to atoms. Why torch the house before we'd even gotten here?"

"Because somebody likes games," I said grimly. "And we may not be the only players." I opened my emergency bag and took out a burner. "Time to make the call."

Natalie shrugged. "I don't have anybody I need to warn."

"Minka," I said. "I think she's in Bali, and she's probably safe, but check in with her anyway."

Minka was a Ukrainian hacker a third our age, a bit of collateral damage I'd brought back from an assassination in Kiev. But she was old beyond her years, and I'd sent her off with an around-the-world ticket to have some adventures. So far she had hiked in Patagonia, spent a few months hanging out with surfers in Cape Town, and had tried twice to summit Kilimanjaro. I'd gotten a postcard at Christmas with a Balinese puppet on the front and a scribbled message on the back. I was surprised at how much I missed her. She'd saved our asses during our last mission, her biggest contribution being the creation of an app called Menopaws. She had populated it with animated cats and features for tracking days since our last periods and hot flashes. At least that's what it looked like. In reality it had given us a way to message each other without using any of the usual apps—and no male security detail was going to look twice at a Siamese in a beret who wanted to talk about vaginal dryness. I'd asked her to make a few tweaks before she left, and I'd taken other precautions as well. We had been successful on that mission, but we'd also been damned lucky. Lady Luck didn't always show up when you needed her.

Mary Alice plucked the phone out of Nat's hand. She swore as she hit the "power" button and punched a series of numbers. "Akiko is going to kill me," she muttered. Akiko must have answered then because Mary Alice's voice was practically a purr. "Hey, honey. I'm safe, but I'm going to need you to do something—" She stepped away to finish breaking the news to Akiko that she was going to have to pack up two opinionated cats and head underground.

A few minutes later, Mary Alice returned looking like she'd just gone ten rounds with Holyfield in his prime. She handed me the phone and I keyed in a number. Taverner answered on the first ring, and he was enough of a pro not to bother with the preliminaries. "Where?"

"You know that small painting of an olive tree I hung in the kitchen? Take it down and punch open the plaster behind it. You'll find a smartphone. Turn it on and look at the homepage."

I heard the sound of breaking plaster and after a minute a muffled laugh. "It's an app called Bread Daddy. There's a dough man waving at me."

"Open it," I told him. Bread Daddy had been Minka's brainchild. She'd used Taverner's talents in the kitchen as her inspiration. The little dough figure resembled the Pillsbury one, but with a significant addition.

"Jesus Christ," he muttered. "It's asking if I have trouble getting my loaf to rise. Does this thing have—Billie, is that a dough penis?"

"Yeah, it's an erectile-dysfunction tracker," I told him. "But it has a messaging function. Grab your go-bag and follow the instructions I left in the app. I'll see you soon."

"Understood." There was a second of silence. "You okay?"

"I'm good," I promised. "But things here have gone off the rails. I'll fill you in when I see you."

I hung up without asking how he was. Taverner could have been bleeding out his eyeballs and he wouldn't have admitted it. But I felt better knowing I'd taken the steps to get him out of the potential firing line.

Nat's call to Minka was short and possibly unpleasant from the expression on Nat's face and the muffled squawking I could hear on Minka's end. When Nat hung up, she shoved the phone back at me.

"How's Minka?" I asked her.

"Pissed. She was two dates into following the band Ghost on their world tour. But she's coming."

A tightness had settled in my chest when I'd seen the wolf. Talking to Taverner had loosened it, and knowing Minka was safe eased it even more. I collected our old phones and dumped them in the well along with the burner. From the bottom of my bag, I dug out a new smartphone, already loaded with the Menopaws app. I always traveled with a spare, and it would be our only source of communication until we rendezvoused with the others.

We climbed into the car and took off. It was a thirty-two-minute drive to the Port of Poole, but I made it in seventeen. We ditched the car, leaving it unlocked in an area frequented by angry young men without much to do. The car would disappear within the hour, I had no doubt.

We used our fake passports to buy tickets on the next ferry to Cherbourg. The ferry runs four times a week, departing at 8:30 in the morning, and we got lucky, rolling up the gangway at 8:28. We headed straight for our cabin, a four-berth box where we spent the next few hours combing through our possessions for anything suspicious—trackers, AirTags, bugs, anything that could give away our locations. When we'd established that the bags were clean, we picked through our clothes, whittling everything down to essentials only. Each of us always carried a spare set of papers and a stack of assorted currencies. We transferred these to our smallest bags. We also packed a few items easily pawned in case we ran into trouble in a place where we couldn't use cash. I used to carry a belt made of pahlavis I'd picked up in Iran—solid gold and worth a fortune—but it was heavy as a small child, and I finally decided the backache wasn't worth it. I'd switched to gems instead. I already wore a pair of flawless blue diamond studs, but I'd added a sizable emerald on a long chain that I tucked into my bra.

The one thing we omitted were weapons that might attract attention. No guns or switchblades. Instead, we opted for things that wouldn't draw anybody's notice. Helen carried a Swiss Army knife that had been modified to include a few nifty extras, and I always had my favorite slapjack. A saddlemaker in Dallas had run it up for me. It looked just like a leather Bible bookmark except for the William S. Burroughs quote tooled around the side—"No one owns life, but anyone who can pick up a frying pan owns death." I'd had the saddlemaker fit it with lead shot on one end. It gripped beautifully, and if swung at just the right spot on a temple, it could shatter the skull, driving a piece of bone straight into the middle meningeal artery. Messy, but it made a satisfying crunch. Mary Alice and Helen always carried a few handy odds and ends, and god only knew what was in Natalie's fanny pack of death. She pulled out a handful of ping-pong balls and a pencil.

"Are you finished with that?" She gestured towards the pork pie Mary Alice had bought at the station.

"Natalie, I told you to get your own," Mary Alice protested through a mouthful of crumbs.

"Not the pie. The foil," Natalie said, grabbing it away from her. She borrowed Helen's Swiss Army knife and set to work, cutting a hole in one ping-pong ball and reducing the others to tiny squares.

"What are you doing?" Helen asked.

"You'll see." Natalie was focused, the tip of her tongue caught between her teeth.

She stuck the pencil into the hole she'd made in the first ping-pong ball and shaped the foil carefully around it.

"It's a bong," Mary Alice said with a frown. "And not a particularly good one," she warned Natalie. "You are going to poison yourself smoking anything out of that."

"It is *not* a bong," Natalie corrected.

"Then what is it?" Mary Alice demanded.

"Mind your business. And wipe your mouth. You've got pork pie on your lip."

It did look a little like a bong, I decided, but Natalie was in too foul a mood to ask her again. I shrugged at Helen and we let her get on with it.

There was no need to talk about where we were headed. The first few months after our last mission had been quiet— alarmingly so. I wasn't used to settling down and not looking over my shoulder. Paranoia is a hard habit to break. So I'd made a few arrangements including finding a dilapidated farmhouse in Sardinia. I'd sent the details on to the others in case they ever needed to lie low for a while, but nobody had used it. I hadn't seen it myself in more than a year. Sardinia is not far off the beaten track; it sits squarely in the middle of the Mediterranean, after all. It has good transportation links to France, Spain, Italy, and even North Africa if you don't mind bribing a guy with a fishing boat. And the thing about Sardinia? There is always a bribable guy with a fishing boat.

The trip was uneventful by which I mean nobody bombed, shot at, or otherwise assaulted us. We changed up our appearances with cheap wigs and hats and reversible jackets. We varied how we walked—sometimes in pairs, sometimes singly, so we didn't stand out as a foursome traveling together. From Cherbourg we took the train to Toulon via Paris. It was a risk sticking with the same mode of transportation for eleven hours, but we were banking on the fact that most travelers leaving England for the Continent would pass through London at some point. We hadn't, and we'd avoided airports although it meant staring out at the endless grey landscape as it rained all the way south.

In Toulon we changed our appearances again and hopped a ferry to Porto Torres. Ten hours later, we staggered off into dazzling Sardinian sunshine. I led the way to a beater I'd left parked in an illegal garage in the maze of alleys behind the ferry terminal. In seven minutes the narrow stone streets of the port were behind us and we were headed southwest, into the interior and as far from tourists as we could get. The drive was two hours if you didn't care about being followed. I wound around for twice that amount of time, backtracking and checking for a tail. I stopped once to buy some snacks to throw into the back seat before Natalie started gnawing the upholstery, but apart from that, I kept my foot to the floor. The landscape got progressively more desolate as we made our way south. There are two schools of thought when hiding out: stay in a crowded area and blend in or get to the high country and hold your ground. Both have their uses, but I wanted to see the enemy coming if they managed to find us.

By the time I turned onto the dirt track leading up to the farmhouse, the countryside was deserted as the moon. In the rocky fields, sheep stared balefully at us as we passed. They weren't fat, fluffy sheep like you see in England. These were skinny, wiry animals, tough little survivors who knew what it took to endure. Like us. Counting transfers, we'd been on the move for more than thirty hours since we'd left Benscombe, and we were stiff as new boots as we unfolded ourselves from the dusty car. I'd parked behind the farmhouse to shield the car from the road, and just as we scrambled out, the back door of the farmhouse swung open.

We might have been exhausted, but good training never dies. Helen and Mary Alice were already on the far side of the car, and Nat and I vaulted over it for cover. Helen's Swiss Army knife was in her hand, the corkscrew locked into position. I was gripping my slapjack as Natalie applied a lighter to the bottom of her homemade foil bong until it started smoking.

"Do you really think getting stoned is the best course of action right now?" Mary Alice demanded.

"Bite my ass, Mary Alice," Natalie said cheerfully. She popped her head above the car long enough to hurl the smoking projectile into the open doorway where it sent out a dense black cloud of chemical stench.

A moment later, we heard coughing and a figure emerged from the smoke, waving a white handkerchief. "Jesus Christ, it's *me*."

"Taverner," I said, pocketing the blackjack. I signaled the others to stand down.

"What was in that thing?" he demanded. "Am I going to die?"

"Just some cut-up ping-pong balls," Natalie soothed. "It's mostly for effect."

"*Mostly?*" He choked a little more.

Helen pecked him on the cheek as Mary Alice thumped his back. "How did you get here so quickly?" Mary Alice asked.

"Quick connection through Sicily," he told her. "I got here last night."

Mary Alice stood on tiptoe, peering over his shoulder, and he smiled, understanding what she was really asking.

"Akiko isn't here yet. Her flight is scheduled to arrive this evening."

"How was the trip?" I asked.

He shook his head. "Uneventful. No tail."

I breathed a little easier then in spite of Natalie's smoke bomb.

"Sorry about that," Nat said as she went to hug him.

He shrugged. "It's your own fault if you've ruined lunch."

She lifted her head, sniffing like a dog. "Lunch?"

"Roast lamb. And homemade bread, of course," he finished. "I never travel anywhere without my sourdough starter."

Mary Alice looked like she wanted to cry. "Taverner, if Akiko and I ever decide to open our marriage to a platonic third, you're the one that I want."

CHAPTER TWELVE

WE ATE AND TOOK THE SARDINIAN VERSION OF A SIESTA, WAKING only when the sun was dropping behind the mountains. I joined Mary Alice on the porch to watch the long purple shadows stretch over the landscape, the edges of the mountains turning a softly smudged violet. In the distance, a plume of dust powdered the air in the wake of an approaching car.

"Akiko," I told her.

She cut her eyes around at me. "Can we trust the driver?"

I nodded. "He's the son of the man who owns this house."

She lifted a brow like she had a fishhook in it. "You don't own it? Sloppy." I didn't take offense. Owning a safe house outright was the only guarantee of it being completely secure.

"I'd trust Bernardu with my life. And yours."

"Bernardu?"

"He's a shepherd. The sheep you saw coming in belong to him."

"And how did you meet a Sardinian shepherd?" she asked.

"Where else? On the job," I answered with a shrug. "The target was a judge who was taking a shit-ton of money to let the Sicilian mafia get a foothold on the island. Sardinians don't take kindly to that."

"They don't have mafia here?"

"Nope. They are suspicious of strangers and they're just as likely to shoot you as invite you in for coffee. But they steer well clear of anything like the Cosa Nostra. It was my bad luck that when I took out the judge, I got clipped by a shot from one of his bodyguards before I finished him off. I couldn't make it to the pickup on the coast." For jobs like that one—sensitive and high-profile—we often avoided airports and large port cities. Sardinia's coastline offered a few thousand miles of quiet coastline to hitch a ride to Barcelona or Rome, Monaco or Tunis, or any one of a hundred other destinations. But the pickups were tightly arranged and if you missed one, you were on your own. The presumption was that something had gone badly wrong, and it was up to you to find your own way out.

I went on. "I found this house and holed up here because it was deserted. Bernardu's mother had lived here until her death and he hadn't gotten around to clearing out her stuff yet."

"I noticed the wallpaper," Mary Alice said with a shudder. There was a fashion among the younger Sardinians for gutting the old stone farmhouses that dotted the countryside and finishing them with fresh plaster walls and limestone counters. They kept the stone fireplaces and brought in sofas upholstered in natural duck and scattered goatskin rugs on the chestnut floors and hung copper pots in the kitchen. They pruned the olive trees and shaped the rosemary bushes and made everything tidy until the results were worthy of the cover of *Architectural Digest.*

This farmhouse . . . wasn't. When I had crawled in, bleeding and delirious, it was like falling into a time warp. The house had been wallpapered—probably in the 1950s—in an eye-watering pattern of red and yellow flowers. There was a brown carpet on the floor that smelled like goat, and the refrigerator growled like it needed an exorcism. The towels were more flowers, pink and orange this time, but I hadn't cared. They'd sopped up the blood I'd left puddled around. Bernardu followed the trail of gore to the bathroom where he found me slumped on the green tiles and unconscious with fever. He'd cut the bullet out and stitched the wound back together before I came to, for which we were both grateful.

"How did he know how to do that?" Mary Alice asked.

"Sardinian shepherds are surprisingly resourceful," I told her. "He said once you've performed a caesarean on a sheep, most things are pretty straightforward. Anyway, he'd heard the news about the judge being shot in Cagliari and put two and two together. They don't get many visitors out here."

"You don't say," she put in dryly.

"Don't talk shit about this place, Mary Alice," I warned her. "It may not be the Ritz, but once a Sardinian decides to trust you, they'll kill for you."

She flapped a hand, turning her gaze once more to the approaching car. "Sorry."

She was testy, but I didn't need to ask why. This was the

first time since our last mission that Akiko's tolerance for what we did was being tested. It had been a sore point with her that she'd found out Mary Alice's occupation after they got married—*way* after, and under challenging circumstances. She'd been a trooper, but I figured Mary Alice was worried about pushing her luck.

"How did she sound on the phone?" I asked, nodding towards the car.

"Stressed," she said in a clipped voice. "I just hope—"

She broke off and I nudged her with my elbow. "The driver of her car is Micheli, Bernardu's youngest. He's a good kid—he'll make sure they weren't followed."

I'd made the safe house arrangements with Bernardu before I'd left Sardinia, six weeks after I'd arrived and twenty pounds lighter. Turns out an infection in the bone is a good way to earn yourself a vacation. I'd had nothing better to do than sit around and learn Sard from Bernardu's hundred-year-old uncle. I'd taught him poker and we'd played for bullets. He had cleaned me out a dozen times over, but in the process I had become a member of the family, and when I'd asked Bernardu if I could rent his mother's house, he'd happily agreed. He had arranged the purchase of the car I had left behind the port terminal, and we'd covered every angle of my arrival if I ever called him with the code phrase I'd written down for him. He'd been true to his word. The house was clean, the car had been full of gas, and Micheli and his taxi had been on hand to pick up Akiko from the airport. Bernardu's wife, Filumena, had even filled the demonic refrigerator with food. I would have worried about imposing on them except I knew how much Filumena loved to cook and how desperately Micheli loved *James Bond* movies. He drove his taxi like it was an Aston Martin, and when he pulled in to the farmhouse, he performed an elegant handbrake stop that threw Akiko into the dashboard. She opened the door and staggered out, cat carriers in hand.

Mary Alice was watching her warily, chewing on her lower lip. She stepped forwards. "I'm so sorry," she began.

She might have saved her breath.

Akiko threw her arms wide, causing the cats to screech. "Let's get this murder reunion started!"

"Jesus, Akiko," I said, coming to help her with the carriers. "That's not exactly discreet."

She glanced over her shoulder. "Oh, you mean Micheli? No worries. He's been talking my ear off for the last two hours about how cool he thinks we assassins are."

"We?" Mary Alice asked her in a strangled voice.

Akiko gave her a level look. "Yes, Mary Alice. You are an assassin. I married you. By the transitive property, I too am an assassin."

I started to protest, "That's not how—" but Mary Alice cut me off with a sharp shake of the head.

"I'm just glad you're here safe," she said.

Micheli grabbed Akiko's backpack and tossed it onto the porch. "Adiosu," he called. I waved and he pulled a few doughnuts, showering us with gravel and dust before he peeled out of the farmyard.

I shouldered Akiko's backpack and jerked my thumb to-wards the house. "Come inside and eat. We have a lot to talk about."

TWO HOURS LATER, WE WERE STUFFED AGAIN, THIS TIME WITH MORE of Taverner's bread and roast lamb and a dozen other things like olives and roasted peppers and little goat cheese tarts. Natalie was busy topping up everybody's wine and Mary Alice was mooning over Akiko, choosing the fattest, crispest pastry for her. The cats had been let out of their carriers to roam around, and they had immediately started a mouse hunt. They were diving under rugs and behind furniture to pounce, emerging triumphant almost every time. They bus-ied themselves lining up the tiny corpses in front of the stove.

Taverner shoved a platter of pastries drizzled in honey un-der my nose and I looked up in surprise. "Where did you get these?"

"Filumena brought them."

I stared. "You met Filumena?"

"Oh yeah. She was opening up the house when I arrived. I gave her some of my sourdough starter and she brought up the sweets. It's her own honey. Did you know she keeps bees?"

I shook my head. After all these years, I still hadn't quite grasped Taverner's ability to make friends wherever he went—especially if food was involved. He was a nurturer which didn't make much sense in an assassin. I'd asked him about it during our first trip together. Romantic relationships in the Museum weren't forbidden, but they did call your judgment into question, particularly if you were a woman. It was easier to keep our affair under wraps and Taverner had been willing to oblige. I never did know how Constance Halliday found out about us, because nobody else ever knew until I told Helen, Mary Alice, and Natalie. We'd met for almost a decade in out-of-the-way places, campsites or resorts well off the beaten path. The isolation meant we saw a hundred sunrises in places most other people only read about in *National Geographic*. It also meant there was nowhere to go when conversations got real, so the trips usually ended in a fight with one of us storming off to the nearest train station or airport. That first vacation had been one of the better ones—a rafting excursion in Costa Rica where Taverner did all the cooking from whatever he found each day in the local market. He'd been late back because one of the market grannies had been teaching him how to pat out the perfect tortilla. Over a plate of beans and rice and roasted redfish, I asked him about the urge to feed people. "It's a contradiction to what you do for a living," I'd pointed out. He'd cocked his head to the side and finished a bite of fish before answering.

"It's not a contradiction," he had countered. "It's an affirmation. Food is life." He'd paused to grin. "So is sex."

I knew he was remembering that conversation as he passed me one of Filumena's pastries. We had known each other for almost forty years, but we'd broken things off for nearly thirty of those when he chose marriage and I chose the job. I don't talk shit about his wife. The truth is, I almost never think of her. She gave him exactly what he wanted—the white picket fence, a couple of kids—but she was unlucky enough to die before she got to grow old with him. I looked at his silver hair, at the lines on the face I'd loved more than half my life, and I made a mental note to send flowers to her grave. It wasn't fair that she'd had to leave the show without taking a bow, but nothing about life was fair.

Just as Taverner was passing a platter of sliced fruits along with some strong Sardinian cheese, Micheli turned up with another arrival. She burst into the room like a breath of fresh Kievan air, dropping her bag and hurling herself at me with all the force of a small atom bomb. Minka.

"Billie!" She started chattering in Ukrainian and I hugged her back hard, mostly to shut her up. She felt a little thin, and when she pulled back, I saw that her face had matured. Her jawline was sharper, and I could have sliced the Sardinian cheese on those cheekbones.

"How have you been, kid?"

She peered at me. "Better than you. Nobody tries to kill me. How do you like my hair?"

She preened, showing off the fresh piercing in her philtrum and her new haircut—she'd buzzed it short on the sides and dyed the long Mohawk in a cherry ombre effect.

"It's cute," I told her honestly. "Hungry?"

"Starving! The flight didn't have a vegan option," she said. That was a new development. Half-Ukrainian and half-Polish, the Minka of old could demolish a pork roast in no time flat. New Minka was a tofu queen.

She made the rounds then, hugging everyone else until we settled back around the table. Taverner fixed her a plate of roasted vegetables and bread as she scooped up the smaller cat.

"Who is this?" she asked.

"Gary," Mary Alice told her.

"He is very small," Minka observed. She was the only person I knew who actually pronounced it like the meme. Smol. Gary settled down onto her lap, cuddling up in her sweater. Akiko reached out to pinch the fabric of it between her fingers.

"This is interesting. Cashmere?"

"Seaweed," Minka said, digging a fork into the plate Taverner passed her. "Knitted on a 3D printer. Very eco-friendly, see?" She turned back the sleeve to show the zero-waste seams. "I am all about the environment now."

I decided not to mention the fact that flying around the world to follow a band on tour might damage her eco-warrior street cred.

Now that we were all safe, I allowed myself a minute to be good and pissed. I didn't know if Naomi had lied or just made a mistake in the briefing about Lazarov's lack of attachments, but it was a whopper of a screwup—the kind that can get you killed. I breathed in deeply, all the way to the bottom of my belly, and blew it out as slowly as I could. The anger was justified, but I knew how dangerous it was to let fury take over. I had learned a bit of pranayama could be helpful in these situations, so I focused on my breathing until the heat passed. The others chatted about a lot of nothing, the good kind of nothing. The nothing that had filled our days since the last mission and kept us all alive. If I'm honest, that kind of nothing had been giving me a little itch, just a small feeling of restlessness between my shoulder blades. Greece is gorgeous, don't get me wrong. I lived on an island straight out of Homer, all wine-dark sea and herb-scented hills. The sunsets were the kind that made you believe in the chariot of the gods, winging its way in an arc across the sky. And I had someone to share it with—someone who loved me to my bones and liked to cook. I should have been completely happy.

But as I sat in the safe house, looking around that table at the people I cared most for in the world, trying to figure out who wanted to kill us, I realized that there are some jobs you leave, but they never leave you. I was playing at being retired because the truth was, I would be a killer until the day I died.

CHAPTER THIRTEEN

I TEXTED NAOMI BEFORE I CALLED SINCE I FIGURED SHE WOULD JUST ignore an unknown number. When she answered, I skipped the preliminaries.

"Something you'd like to tell us?" I asked.

"Billie. Good to hear from you. How are things on your end?" She sounded like a woman who was trying hard to be nonchalant. Too hard.

"Fine," I said politely. "And how are *you*?"

"Good, good. Matters here are under control." In the background I could hear a few quick pops. Gunfire or fire-crackers.

"It's a little early for Fourth of July," I said. "Where are you?"

"Nowhere special," she replied. "Hang on a second." She must have put the phone down because things sounded muffled. Another quick pop, then a second, much closer than the first two. When Naomi came back to the line, she was breathing heavy.

"Naomi, is someone shooting at you?"

"A little," she admitted. "It's actually not a great time for me. Maybe we could talk later?"

"Sure. Just find out who is trying to kill us before you call me back, okay?"

I heard running footsteps and the bang of a heavy door slamming shut. She was puffing hard now. "What do you mean? Who's trying to kill you?"

"That's what I need you to find out. They burned down Benscombe."

"Were you in it?"

"No, they torched it before we arrived."

"Then they weren't trying to kill you," she pointed out calmly. More running footsteps and more puffing.

"Have you considered a little cardio? Maybe a mini-trampoline. You could keep it under your desk," I suggested.

"Screw you, Webster," she said before returning a volley of gunfire. "Got him. That's right, you little bitch. Stay down."

"You better be talking to your target," I said mildly.

"Keep your panties on. I have to finish him." A patter of running footsteps, another volley of gunfire, and some muffled whimpers. Naomi gave a grunt and then came back to the phone. "Sorry about that."

"Shootout?" I asked. The sounds were familiar.

"Church league paintball," she said. "We're undefeated. But damn, I'm hungry now. I should have put a Luna bar in my purse. I'm going to treat myself to a bacon cheeseburger on the way home. Double fries."

"Get a milkshake too," I urged. "You earned it."

"Look, I'll chase down anything else I can find on Pasha Lazarov's known associates," she promised. "But the files were pretty thin. The only relative we have on record is his aunt Evgenia, and she's in an old folks' home somewhere. Switzerland, I think."

She sounded a little too offhand for my liking. "Naomi, we're stuck in a safe house with our nearest and dearest and a couple of cats who aren't any happier about the situation than we are. Put this at the top of your basic bitch Rae Dunn to-do list."

I punched the "end call" button but it wasn't nearly satisfying enough. I missed receivers you could slam down. Hell, I even missed flip phones you could snap shut.

I went back to the dining room where the others were waiting.

"She'll look into it," I said.

"That's all?" Mary Alice demanded.

"She had her hands full when I called," I explained.

"So we're just going to sit here?" Nat asked.

"If you've got a better idea, I'd love to hear it," I told her. "Until then, we have no leads on who Pasha's associate might be. There's no point in chasing our tails."

"Maybe we know more than we think we do," Nat pushed.

"Like what?" Helen asked.

"I don't know," Nat replied. "Let's just throw spaghetti at

the wall and see what sticks." She rummaged in her backpack and emerged with a green eyeliner pencil. She uncapped it and cleared a space on the table. Then she started scribbling on the oilcloth roses of the tablecloth. *Pasha Lazarov*, she wrote in block capitals. She drew lines out for his family members and jotted their names. Father, Boris Lazarov. Mother, Irina Dashkova. Sister, Galina. Aunt, Evgenia Dashkova.

Helen plucked the eyeliner from her hand and started crossing people out, starting with Pasha's parents. "Lazarov is an orphan."

"Thanks to us," Natalie pointed out.

Helen went on, slicing lines through the names. "Father, mother, and sister dead. He's been on his own for a long time."

"No wife?" Akiko asked. "Girlfriends? Boyfriends? Partners for furry sexcapades?"

"Funny you should mention furries," Mary Alice said. She started to describe Lazarov's devotion to his teddy bear, but Nat stopped her.

"I can't with the teddy bear, Mary Alice. It's too sad."

"What do you mean?"

"I mean, what happened to him? Did they put him in the coffin with Lazarov? Did they pack him up for the next of kin?"

"God, that *is* sad," Helen put in.

"Speaking of next of kin, what about Aunt Evgenia herself?" Taverner asked.

"I found the facility in Switzerland," Minka piped up. She turned her phone to show pictures of an elegant grey stone building set on sweeping green lawns. "A home for old people. Exclusive and expensive."

"How did you find it?" Mary Alice demanded.

Minka shrugged. "Was easy if you know where to look."

"If she's that old, do we really think she's capable of traveling to England and torching Benscombe?" Natalie asked. Helen winced at the mention of Benscombe.

I shrugged. "She could hire somebody. We don't know if Lazarov pays for the old folks' home or if Auntie Evgenia has money of her own. Either way, there is a slim chance she might know who Pasha would choose to partner with in his little assassination games."

"Or she might be the brains behind the whole thing," Mary Alice suggested. "Old women can be nasty. We should know."

"Preach, sister," Natalie said, raising her glass to clink with Mary Alice's.

Taverner was frowning into his coffee. "So Pasha Lazarov had no other living relatives besides his aunt, no known associates beyond a handful of paid bodyguards, no wife, no kids. That sounds grim."

"That sounds understandable," I corrected. "He was a child when his father died, and his mother and sister were killed just a few years later. Losing your entire family when you're young can mess with your head, make it hard for you to trust in anything. Some people never really recover from that."

Taverner's gaze sharpened. "So I've heard." He stopped

talking then which was good. It gave me a chance to let the little flicker of rage that had risen up die down again.

When I spoke, my voice was level, and the hand that reached for my coffee cup was steady. "I think our next course of action is clear," I said calmly. "Pack your bags, girls. We're heading to Switzerland."

CHAPTER FOURTEEN

BENSCOMBE, 1986

BILLIE'S FLIGHT LANDS EARLY IN THE EVENING, BUT IT'S JUNE AND the sun is just beginning to set when she pulls up to Benscombe. She's flown halfway around the world with nothing but a handbag that holds a change of underwear and a toothbrush. She's wearing what she thinks of as her off-duty uniform—a silk blouse, thin suede jacket, and boot-cut jeans. Her vintage cowboy boots crunch across the gravel as she crosses the drive. She pauses just long enough to breathe in the scent of roses and cut grass and remembers it's Midsummer night. The telegram in her pocket is creased; the message consists of only three words: *It is time.*

She doesn't lift the knocker. Constance is expecting her and has left the door unlocked. She walks through the house, the hallways as familiar to her as her own reflection in the mirror. Constance is in the kitchen, sitting at the table she's covered in oilcloth, a cheerful red patterned with oxeye daisies and fat pink roses. On the table is a pot of tea and a pair of cups, her best Royal Doulton.

Billie sits without speaking and Constance pours for her. "Drink it. You will feel better."

Billie does as she's told, putting the cup back carefully into the saucer when it is empty. "I don't feel better. That was a lie. This isn't going to work if either of us lies."

Constance gives her a long, level look, her ice-blue eyes assessing. "Fine. There is a rather good single malt in the cupboard. I was saving it for a special occasion. I suppose this qualifies."

Billie's laugh is brittle, but she retrieves the bottle and a pair of glasses. She pours two fingers for each of them and pushes a glass towards Constance. She lifts the other, and Constance mirrors the gesture.

"What shall we drink to?" Constance inquires in an arch voice.

"Midsummer night."

"To Midsummer night."

They finish their drinks and Billie quickly pours another. Constance's mouth twitches with amusement.

"You can't put this off, you know."

"I know."

"I've trained assassins for decades—the best who ever worked have passed through these halls," she said, gesturing expansively towards the house. "But I chose you for this."

"Why?" Billie asks.

"Because you are the only one I trust to see it through. You may flinch, but you will not falter." The words are not said with warmth, but Billie feels the affection in them. And she hears the tiniest thread of something she has never heard from Constance before. Fear.

That's when she understands exactly what Constance wants from her. It isn't her expertise or her competence. It's her humanity.

Constance smiles thinly and when she speaks, her tone is arch. "Don't get sentimental on me now, Billie."

Billie drains her second drink. "I wouldn't dream of it," she says, putting the glass down decisively. "Are you afraid?"

Constance tips her head, her expression thoughtful. "A little. I don't much care for pain. But I think it will be alright. And I will do this, with you or without you, you know."

"I know."

Constance's smile is mocking. "I always knew I would die like a Roman."

"Do you have any regrets?"

Constance thinks again. "No. Every death at my door—and there have been many, so very many—was a thing I was called to do." Her expression turns severe. "When you are in my position, I hope you will remember that what we have done, what we do, is a small evil to preserve a much greater good. Humanity is so very fragile, Billie. It is threatened from every side, by greed and wickedness and chaos and a thousand other villainies. Humanity requires champions, like the knights of old, those who are willing to fight and die, bloody themselves so the others may survive."

"You make it sound noble," Billie says.

"It isn't nobility," Constance says calmly. "It is necessity.

We are as nature made us, content to play God and take lives, and who knows what price we will pay for that hubris. But the world needs us. Remember what I told you all those years ago," she adds.

"We are necessary monsters," Billie finishes.

"Just so." Constance sighs, her energy suddenly spent. "Let's go upstairs then. I have everything ready."

They pass the closed door of Constance's study. It has been a long time since the door was open, and if it were open now, Billie knows she would see the portrait of Astraea hanging over the desk. Astraea, the goddess of justice with her scales and sword, to weigh the deeds of men and to administer the reckoning. But the door remains closed and they pass on to the stairs.

Constance leads the way upstairs to her room, slowly, painfully, putting both feet on each step as she climbs. Billie knows better than to try to help, but she maneuvers directly behind Constance to catch her in case she falls. The disease has settled in the aging bones, leaching the calcium and leaving them brittle and prone to breaking. A slip on an icy patch of gravel the previous winter snapped a femur and a wrist. The resulting scans were straightforward and the prognosis brutal. Constance dutifully completed her physical therapy before calling Billie and laying out what she wanted from her.

"It will be some months yet—two or three at least, so you needn't decide right away," she had said briskly. "If you refuse, I quite understand. I can take care of matters myself. I'll just leave a note on the door for the milkman for when it's done and he will fetch the police."

"I'll come," Billie told her.

"Are you certain?" A shadow of doubt in the voice that had always been commanding.

"I'll come."

In the months since, the promise has followed Billie like a shadow, dogging every footstep. Now that the time is here, she feels lighter, almost buoyant. It is nearly over.

The bed is neatly made with a candlewick spread, and Constance climbs under it wearing an old-fashioned white nightgown. She smooths the spread out and settles herself on the pillows. There's the faint crackle of a waterproof cover, a precaution to protect her dignity when the inevitable happens.

"Wait," Constance says suddenly. She gets up, struggling a little. She makes her way to the window, using pieces of furniture as crutches as she crosses the room, her progress slow and breathless. The closed shutters have made the room gloomy, and she wrestles with the catch. Billie comes to help her, and together they fold back the panels and raise the window sash. Fresh air billows into the room, carrying birdsong and the smell of the sea that dashes on the rocks below the cliffs.

"That's better," Constance says firmly. She returns to the bed and arranges herself. She gestures towards the bedside table, indicating a photo frame. It stands beside a worn copy of Angela Carter's *The Bloody Chamber* and a battalion of pill bottles. It is small and the picture inside is faded, a wedding couple stiff in their 1930s finery.

Constance looks at the image for a long moment, then hands it back, closing her eyes. "I am ready."

She keeps her eyes closed while Billie pushes up her sleeve. From the items on the bedside table, Billie selects a narrow Liberty scarf and a silver teaspoon to fashion a makeshift tourniquet. The skin of Constance's forearm is pale but surprisingly smooth, and with a twist of the spoon in the knotted scarf, Billie has the veins rising blue and vivid as rivers on a contour map. Constance has already prepared the mixture to her own specifications, choosing the amounts carefully and filling the syringe. Billie finds the most promising vein, a wide line in the crook of Constance's elbow. The needle is poised just over the skin, and Billie hesitates.

Constance turns her head and opens her eyes. She says nothing, but she gives Billie a nod before turning back. She waits, eyes closed.

Billie doesn't cry. She can't. She owes Constance a good death. So she blinks back tears and sets to work, slipping the needle gently into the vein, angling it precisely and aiming it towards the heart. She pulls back the plunger slightly and blood, red and dark and slow, flows into the syringe. The needle is seated perfectly and she makes her mind a careful blank as she depresses the plunger as smoothly as she can.

Constance gives a little gasp as the lethal cocktail hits her bloodstream. Billie removes the needle and puts a cotton pad in the crook of Constance's elbow because it matters that this death—of all the deaths she has orchestrated—that this death is tidy. She puts the syringe aside and waits.

It isn't a long time. Only a handful of seconds pass before Constance opens her eyes again, tears standing in the corners, bright and unshed. She smiles. "Thank you."

She sighs out the last word as she turns away, and the last thing she sees through her shuttering lids is Billie's face, wavering, shimmering as if life itself were the mirage and the only reality is what lies beyond.

It is several minutes before Billie moves. A compact, vintage silver and engraved with Constance's initials, lies on the bedside table. She could open it and use the mirror to check for a breath, but she has seen enough death to know there's no need. Whatever Constance put into the syringe, it has worked, quickly, painlessly. With dignity.

Billie stands up on legs that feel a hundred years old. The relief that the favor Constance asked of her is finished hasn't come yet. Instead, there's only a cool, numb emptiness. She crosses to the window where the last golden rays of the sun are stretching over the landscape, gilding the trees and the grass and every living thing under its light. Somewhere in the distance, a nightingale sings, and Billie closes her eyes, raising her face to the fading warmth of the sun.

Midsummer night. A beautiful time to die.

CHAPTER FIFTEEN

THE BEST WAY TO GET INTO AN OLD FOLKS' HOME IS TO BE OLD FOLKS.
We were a few years shy of needing assistance with our living,
so we knew at least one of us was going to have to age up by a
decade to get in the door.

"Not it," Natalie hollered. "Mary Alice and I suffered
enough in our incontinence pants on that ship."

I looked at her over the top of my glasses. "Natalie, if you
are not incontinent, then why in the name of all that is holy
and good were you wearing the pants?"

"They pad out your butt," she explained, twitching her
ass from side to side. "Nothing else gives you quite that lumpy
look."

Mary Alice raised her hand. "They make slimmer versions now, but I'd like to point out that I did not, in fact, wear
the pants."

"You should have," Natalie told her. "They make a nice

cushion when you're sitting on a hard chair. Prevents hemorrhoids."

"I shall make a note of that," Mary Alice said solemnly. "But Natalie is right. We had to wear all the old-lady gear last time. We are definitely not it this time."

I looked at Helen and she shrugged. "I'll do it."

"Really?" I was surprised. I'd seen enough social media posts to know that #ageisjustanumber and #sixtyissexy. To be older and stylish meant turbans, crimson lipstick, velvet caftans—everything from Elton John sunglasses to Chinese parasols heavy with fringe. Anything to make you stand out in vivid Technicolor. And Helen had always been the best dressed of us all. Over the years she'd traded her Bobbie Brooks and Oscar de la Renta for more daring pieces. In the last photo she'd sent she'd been wearing a pink boiler suit and turquoise Chuck Taylors because she'd been repainting a stone wall at Benscombe. Her hair had been tied up in an Hermès scarf, and I knew she'd have been wearing her signature Chanel perfume. But the point of disguising yourself as an elderly woman is blending in, nothing but bifocal lenses and elastic waists, and you couldn't smell like anything more alluring than Bengay.

It seemed like a stretch for her, but she lifted her chin and smiled. "Yes," she said, nodding to Mary Alice. "I'll sit in a wheelchair and make Mary Alice push me around as my private secretary."

"Sold," Mary Alice said. She twisted her lavish blond hair into a tight knot and perched her glasses on the end of her nose. "How's this?"

"Sexy as shit," Akiko told her. "Hot librarian suits you."

Mary Alice grinned at her wife as Natalie spoke up. "I can be the devoted niece who comes with to make sure you are getting the best care."

Helen arched a plucked brow at her. "I think sister-in-law would be more believable than niece."

"Bitch," Natalie said, pulling a face. But there wasn't any heat in it, and I was just glad the roles had been assigned without drama. Nat turned to me. "And what exactly will you be doing?"

"Driver," I said succinctly. "I'll poke around as much as I can when I'm 'looking for the bathroom,'" I added, making obnoxious air quotes with my fingers.

Taverner spoke up. "I'd make a more convincing chauffeur."

"That's sexist," Natalie countered.

"No, it's expected," he replied. "More men are professional drivers. I would be less remarkable in the role than Billie."

I held up a hand. "You're both right. Taverner, you would be less noticeable, but the reason for that is sexist, so Natalie scores there. But your points are also moot since Taverner isn't going."

He rolled his neck slowly. "Pardon me?"

"You're not going. Neither is Akiko," I said, spearing her with a look. Minka didn't even glance up from her phone.

Akiko held up her hands. "No arguments here. The view is nice and the food is good. The cats and I will hold down the fort."

"Good," I said, pushing back from the table.

Taverner pushed back too and I stopped him. "We are not fighting about this. You are in a safe house because of me. I'm not going to endanger you further."

"Endanger me?" A note of humor threaded through his voice. "The only thing in danger of getting killed here is my sourdough starter. Billie, you're overreacting."

"Maybe. But it's my call, not yours."

We squared off, facing each other with our arms folded over our chests in identical postures.

"Jesus," Natalie breathed. "Is this what passes for foreplay with you two?"

"If so, Taverner is in for a raging case of blue balls because he's not coming to Switzerland," I answered flatly.

He took a half step closer to me. "So that's how it is."

"That's how it is," I said.

Nobody said anything for a long moment. I don't even think the cats let out a breath. We stood locked in opposition, waiting for the other to blink. Finally, Taverner put his hands up, palms out.

"Fine."

I narrowed my eyes. "You never give in that easily. I don't trust it."

He shrugged, his expression unreadable. "Why would you trust it? You don't trust anything else."

It was a good line, so I didn't blame him for using it as an exit. He didn't even bang the door as he went out. Instead, he closed it quietly, as if shutting something in the past. I'd have liked it a hell of a lot better if he'd slammed it.

THE FOUR OF US LEFT THE NEXT MORNING. MIKELI TAXIED US TO THE ferry port where we took the first boat to Ajaccio. Somewhere on mainland France would have been more logical, so we opted for Corsica instead as the less expected option in case anybody was watching. From there it was a quick hour and a half to Basel by plane. By lunchtime we were in a rented Mercedes, speeding east. We'd stopped at a pharmacy long enough to collect a top-of-the-line wheelchair for Helen and spent the rest of the trip going over everything Minka had dug up online about the facility we were visiting.

"Discreet and expensive," Mary Alice said, reading from her notes. "It's actually two separate wings, one for elder care if you're rich and connected. The other is for recovery, also for the rich and connected."

"What kind of recovery?" Helen asked, peering over her shoulder at the screen of Mary Alice's smartphone.

"It doesn't say, but if you read between the lines, it sounds like everything from plastic surgery to Oxy addiction."

"A full-service facility," Natalie mused. "You know, Helen, you don't have to pretend to be old. We could wrap you up in bandages and tell them your facelift was botched."

"Or we could tell them you need help with a sex addiction," Helen replied coolly. "Your collection of dildos is frankly alarming."

I nearly drove into a hedge. It wasn't like Helen to bite back, and I wasn't entirely sure she was joking. Neither was

Mary Alice. She shot me a surprised look, but Natalie hooted all the way to the facility.

We pulled up to a set of gates that wouldn't have looked out of place at Buckingham Palace. There was an intercom and camera, and I managed to pantomime through a series of apologetic gestures that I didn't speak German. A lie, but they didn't need to know it. I heard the voice on the other side mutter a few choice Teutonic insults—mostly disparaging my mother, but it was nothing I wouldn't have said about her myself. After a second another voice came on, smoother and more diplomatic. "Please follow the signs and park to the right."

The gates opened onto a drive, wide and curving and lined with sternly clipped, geometrically precise hedges. "Damn, the gardener must use a protractor," Natalie remarked.

Beyond the hedges, the grounds were just as tidy—broad expanses of grass punctuated here and there with well-behaved trees. A few benches were scattered around, but the morning was chilly and nobody was using them. The building was a grey stone mansion, old-fashioned but impeccably clean. Just behind it, I could make out a more recent addition of glass, silvery and cold. Stone terraces were set with outdoor furniture in conversation groupings with all the pieces arranged at right angles. Even the potted trees stood at attention.

"You have to love the Swiss," I muttered. The sign directing traffic to the parking lot was discreet, set low to the ground and lettered in tasteful grey. I pulled into a vacant spot and hopped out to set up the wheelchair, taking care to roll it around to Helen's side of the car in case anybody was watching. She settled herself, and Nat draped a cashmere blanket over her knees, tucking it carefully.

"Showtime," Mary Alice said, taking charge of the chair. The front door opened as they approached and a middle-aged woman appeared, smiling the tight, slightly insincere smile of someone who is irritated by an interruption but can't let it show for fear of offending a potential client with a fat checkbook. I waited long enough to hear her greet them and gesture for them to enter before I hotfooted it around the side of the building. The terrace on this side had an occupant—an old fellow tucked into a wheelchair, so swaddled in blankets and quilts that only his face was visible. Even his wrinkles had wrinkles, but the eyes were sharp. He flicked them open as I trotted up.

"Guten Tag," he said, raising a finger out of the bundle of blankets to wave hello. He was wheezing like he'd just run a mile, and I remembered the fashion for sending tubercular patients to the mountains in centuries past. The cold clear air is supposed to be good for lung complaints, but by the sounds coming out of him, it wasn't helping. I'd heard healthier noises from recently castrated cattle.

"Guten Tag, mein Herr," I replied. "Es ist ein schöner Tag."

He shrugged. "Die Tage sind für mich alle gleich." He leaned forward a bit, looking me over from head to toe in a way that was frankly a little gross, even in someone who probably had a cocktail date arranged with death somewhere in the near future. "Du hast schöne Titten."

No matter how many times a strange man tells you that you have nice tits, it's always creepy. I sighed. I wasn't going to kill him—we had rules about that sort of thing—but damn, I was tempted. It wouldn't take much, just a quick release of his brake and a friendly shove towards the edge of the terrace. From there, it was a steep drop-off to a handy ravine with lots of nice sturdy pine trees and some rock outcroppings that wouldn't do him any favors. I glanced up at the eaves of the building. There weren't even cameras mounted outside. It was practically an invitation.

But I was better than that. Instead, I cocked my head, thinking. The facility was old-fashioned with its personal greeter at the front door and lack of obvious security. They would have client information locked up nice and tight, thanks to all their Swiss training. It would be a miracle if the other three managed to learn anything useful about Auntie Evgenia. They'd get a tour and a bundle of brochures, but we had a short amount of time, and I was feeling impatient. I didn't like how I'd left things with Taverner and I didn't trust him to stay put. I knew the sooner I made it back to Sardinia, the better. And that annoyed me even more. I didn't like being responsible for anybody, even somebody I was sleeping with.

Especially someone I was sleeping with. It felt too much like commitment, something I'd always run away from. I suppose I could have gone to therapy, but what was the point? I knew exactly where I'd picked up my issues. Unknown father, abandoned by my mother at age twelve, the rest of my youth spent in an unlicensed foster home. You might think the last part sounds the worst, but at least in that place I had someone making sure I ate my vegetables and did my home-work. I left town the day after my high school graduation and never looked back. Add all of that to the steamer trunk of the job I'd chosen, and I had enough baggage to sink a battleship.

But regardless of why I was feeling irritable, we were un-der pressure. We needed results from this trip so we could figure out who was still targeting us, finish the business, and get back to our lives.

I leaned down a little, giving the old fellow a glimpse at my cleavage. If he was going to die, he'd do it with a smile on his face. "Kennen Sie Evgenia Dashkova?"

He wheezed and bounced a little, and from his excitement, I guessed she had nice tits too. He pointed to the terrace door. "213."

"Danke," I said, moving towards the door. He mumbled something—either an invitation or a come-on, I couldn't hear which—and snaked a hand out to pat my ass as I passed.

"I could break your neck with a toothpick," I told him in English. "Cool it, Adolf."

I slipped through the terrace door into a sort of breakfast room. It was empty, but the smell of coffee and incontinence pants hung in the air, overlaid with the lingering smell of an expensive commercial air freshener. I sniffed deeply. Freesia, I decided. I eased into the hall where the air was cooler. A wide wooden staircase wound upwards. Leading off the hall were half a dozen doors and an old-fashioned elevator cage. From the rattling, I guessed Helen and the others were cur-rently inside the lift, on their way to tour a guest room. I'd just have to take my chances and hope they weren't headed to the same floor.

I took the stairs two at a time since nobody was around. The floors were numbered European style—ground on the level where we'd entered, the first floor above, and the second one higher still. I wasn't surprised that Auntie Evgenia had bagged a room at the top. The views would be best up there.

Number 213 was near the stairs, and as I moved across the wide, carpeted corridor, I heard the lift stopping on the floor below. I could just make out Helen's voice, sharp and a little annoyed as she spoke. Good. A bit of visible irritation out of a potential client would keep their guide focused on making them happy and less likely to notice anything I might get up to.

I paused with my ear to the door. I couldn't hear anything, but the carpets were thick and the door was heavy oak. I pushed it open a crack and peered inside. The room was furnished like a posh hotel, with floral wallpaper and what looked like either very good antiques or *very* expensive reproductions. There was even a fireplace, tiny and unlit, with a mantel of green marble carved into Art Nouveau curves. A long window was framed by chintz curtains and I was right; the view was spectacular—long rolling hills fringed with thick pine forests and in the distance the peak of an alp just to remind you where you were. A bed had been positioned to make the most of it, and that bed was the only odd note in the room. It was a proper piece of hospital equipment, fitted with all the levers and switches, but it had been made up with flowered sheets and a satin quilt. To make it cozier, I guessed.

Propped up against the pillows was a woman in a jade green velvet bed jacket. I nearly had a heart attack when I realized she was staring directly at me.

"Are you coming in?" She addressed me in German, but I had an idea.

"May I?" I inquired in politely old-fashioned Russian.

Her eyes lit up and she gestured. "You are Russian?"

I shrugged as I closed the door behind me. "For today I am. I am visiting my uncle Feodor, and he said there was another Russian here."

She frowned. "Feodor? I do not know him."

Considering the fact that I had just invented him, I was certain she didn't. But the place was big and it was an old folks' home; there was bound to be some turnover.

"He's new," I said, coming near to the bed. On the nightstand was a crystal pitcher of orange juice with a small glass. There was a remote control for a television that must be hidden somewhere—probably behind a painting of a depressed clown that would haunt my dreams—but no other personal effects, no address book or letters. The only other decorative item was a large vase of lilies. Some had dropped their pollen, staining the creamy marble top of the nightstand. It was the sole bit of untidiness I'd seen since I had arrived.

"Those are lovely," I said. Actually, I hated lilies. To me they always smelled like funeral homes, but she smiled.

"From my nephew, Pasha," she said with a little purr. There was no grief there, only pride, and I realized suddenly that she had no idea he was currently reposing in a mortuary somewhere in England.

"Does he visit often?" I asked.

She shook her head. "He is a very important and busy man of international affairs."

International affairs? Either that was code these days for club drugs and art smuggling, or Auntie Evgenia didn't know the illegalities Pasha dabbled in.

"But he sends me flowers. Expensive ones," she added loftily. "He comes every year for my birthday in August." Her face puckered a little. "I wish he would marry. It is not good for a man to be alone." She gestured towards the mantelpiece. "There is a photograph of him. He is a handsome boy. You will see."

I went to look. In pride of place on the mantel was a heavy silver frame, the kind you see only in antiques stores or the most exclusive French flea markets. It was engraved with a Cyrillic monogram in elegant script. The picture inside was Pasha in one of his superbly tailored English suits, an arm around his teddy bear. I wondered if they'd send it to Aunt Evgenia along with his suits.

"Nice bear," I said, returning the frame to its place. There were a few other pictures on the mantelpiece, arranged with military precision in order of size. One was a double portrait of two identical young women facing one another. They were wearing matching full white satin dresses, each holding an armful of creamy roses. Evgenia and Irina, Pasha's mother, I guessed.

"My sister and I at our coming out," Evgenia told me proudly. "There was a ball at the George V in Paris. Very exclusive, you understand."

Next to the debut portrait was another photograph of them together, this time with one dressed in a fluffy cloud of white organza with her sister in green tulle.

"Her wedding," she said in a distinctly cooler tone. I noticed there was no image of Boris Lazarov anywhere in sight. Instead, there were portraits of the two sisters and several of Irina's children, Pasha and his little sister, Galina. Assorted other pictures filled in the spaces between the larger studio portraits—some candid yachting photos, family picnics, even a distinctly tsarist-looking one that seemed to have been taken at an imperial function in St. Petersburg. The good old days for the Dashkovs, I guessed. They must have had a ball, trampling on serfs and organizing pogroms.

I moved on, and the last photo in the line caught my attention. It was one of the pictures taken on a boat, probably Pasha's, given the way he was preening. In the background was a woman, not even a whole woman, just a slender profile. There was something elusive about her, as if the photo had been snapped right as she was turning away from the camera and that she'd done so on purpose. Her hair had whipped across her features, obscuring most of her face, but I thought I detected a resemblance to Pasha. The idea that crept into my mind was one I didn't want to consider, but I had to know.

I carried the frame to Evgenia's bedside. "Who is this?"

She peered. "I don't know her." She looked up at me, blinking hard, her expression suddenly blank. "Who are you?"

The whole time I'd been in her room, she had been curious but not suspicious. Now she looked at me with a little fear, as if she had just awakened in a room full of strangers.

"I am nobody," I told her. "Just a friend passing by." I made sure to keep my voice soft and back up a step so she wouldn't feel threatened.

But I had to know. I held up the frame again. "Are you sure you don't know her?" I pressed.

She shook her head stubbornly, pushing out her lower lip, her tone querulous. "Why do you ask me questions? I want you to go now."

"Sure," I said. But I didn't leave. Instead I poured her a glass of orange juice from the pitcher on the nightstand and handed it over.

She didn't thank me, just drank greedily, a little of the juice running out the side of her mouth. I reached out and wiped the juice from her chin with my fingers.

"Evgenia," I said, pushing gently, "is this Galina?"

Her entire face lit up like the proverbial Christmas tree. "Irina!" she cried happily. She took the frame from me and kissed the glass a few times, leaving damp smudges.

I tried again. "This isn't your sister," I told her. "It's not Irina. Is it her daughter? Is it Galina?"

I could almost hear the gears turning as she stared from me to the photo and back again, thinking hard. After a long moment, she gestured towards the nightstand and I opened the drawer. Inside was a small bakery box, fuchsia pink. A name was scrolled on the top in gilt lettering with a flourish. She gestured again, imperiously this time. I opened the box and inside were half a dozen cookies, dark gold and shaped like diamonds.

Evgenia held out her hand, clicking her fingers impatiently, and I passed her the box. She took one of the pastries before pressing the box back into my grasp. I watched as she took a dainty bite, sighing in contentment. When she looked up at me, some of her sharpness seemed to have returned. "Take one," she ordered. "Very special and very delicious. Galina brings me a box every time she comes."

"Does she now?"

The cookies were speckled with some kind of dark dried fruit—never a favorite of mine—but Evgenia was watching me closely, so I took one and nodded my thanks. I nibbled a tiny bit from the corner. It was sandy with a pronounced taste of butter, and I might have had another bite if I could be sure I wouldn't get a piece of raisin or currant at the same time.

"Lovely, thanks," I told Evgenia, and I meant it. The cookies were fresh which meant Galina had paid a recent visit—before she heard about Pasha's death, I was guessing, since the old woman didn't know he was dead.

Evgenia motioned for me to replace the box and I studied the name lettered across the top—Malvestio. There was nothing to indicate an address or phone number, and I wondered if the bakery was in the Italian-speaking part of Switzerland. While Evgenia finished her cookie, I slipped mine into my pocket.

"Does Galina live near here?" I asked in a casual voice.

But she'd gone vague again. She shook her head as if she didn't understand the question or didn't like it. Instead she smiled blankly and began to hum a tune, a snatch of something operatic. Classical music isn't exactly my forte but just about everybody has heard the "Flower Duet" from *Lakmé* thanks to British Airways and *The Simpsons.*

Evgenia's voice cracked as she warbled higher, but I smiled at her encouragingly, humming along to the end. "That's very pretty. Delibes, right?"

She started the melody over from the beginning, as if she were stuck on a loop. I checked the time. I was pushing my luck staying so long. Some nurse or orderly was bound to show up soon. I tried one more time.

"Evgenia, does that song remind you of Galina?"

She stopped short, her expression turning suddenly sly. "Galina loves opera. She loves opera *singers,*" she added in a malicious whisper.

"Oh, is that right?" I gave her a small, conspiratorial smile. I had her pegged as the kind of woman who loved a good bitchfest, and I was right. Her smile deepened, and she gestured for me to come closer.

"Do you know what she is?" I shook my head and she told me. There are a lot of words in Russian for "slut" and she used one of the nastier ones.

"Why do you say that?" I asked.

"She does not always wear underpants," Evgenia said firmly.

Jesus, if that was all it took to be a slut in Evgenia's book, we were all doomed, I thought. Especially Natalie.

She went on. "She was always a bad seed. Not like my Pasha, such a lovely boy." I could tell she was about to launch into another panegyric about her beloved nephew, and if I had to sit through that, I'd have smothered her with her bed jacket.

"What makes Galina a bad seed?" I asked. A question that direct might have spooked her, but she was too eager to talk shit about her niece.

"She was in a terrible accident with my sister, and my sister did not live. Galina did."

Shit. It was good to have confirmation of my hunch, but the fact that Galina Lazarov was alive was not good news.

I kept up my end of the conversation. "And you blame Galina for surviving the accident that killed your sister? Why?"

She shrugged her bony shoulders. "She is probably the reason for the accident. My sister was a nervous driver, and Galina was always singing and shouting. She was very loud. That is the Bulgarian in her."

"She sounds like a normal kid," I replied.

Evgenia flapped a hand. "Galina was a nuisance. I took her because she was my sister's child, but she was always difficult, always sulking in her room, crying."

"Yeah, grieving children will do that," I said. "What a hardship for you."

The thing about rich narcissists is they almost never smell sarcasm. Evgenia took the remark at face value and simpered under what she mistook for sympathy.

"It was very hard," she said. "Only boarding school made it bearable. I sent her away as soon as I could. It was for the best."

"For you," I shot back before I could stop myself. If

Evgenia kept telling tales from Galina's childhood, she was going to have me feeling sorry for a Lazarov.

"Where is Galina now?"

Her brows snapped together, and she reached out and twitched my arm into a pinch. Those bony old fingers were sharp and I jumped back, rubbing my arm.

"That's going to bruise," I told her irritably. "Why did you do that?"

"You ask too many questions."

And then she was gone again, humming, a vacant expression in her eyes. When she finished her tune, she snapped her fingers and pointed to the pitcher. "Drink."

"I hear your family was White Russian," I said pleasantly. "I'm beginning to sympathize with the Bolsheviks."

I poured another glass of juice and handed it over, neatly extracting the frame from her hand as I did so.

"Enjoy your juice," I told her. I replaced the frame on the mantelpiece on my way out of the room. But now there was a blank square of cardboard where the photograph of Galina Lazarov had been.

I HUSTLED DOWN TO THE CAR THE WAY I'D COME. THE LITTLE PERV ON the terrace was gone and the only person I passed was a mildly surprised orderly carrying a batch of clean linens. He just looked on as I called a friendly greeting and continued on my way. Generally, you can get away with being just about any-where you aren't supposed to be if you carry yourself with confidence and don't stop long enough for anyone to ask you questions. (That's a useful tip in case you're taking notes.)

I got to the car just as the others were arriving. We saved the debrief for the drive back to Basel. "Find anything?" I asked.

Helen waved a brochure. "For starters, the facility charges three hundred thousand euros a year for a private room."

I snorted. "For a place with the security of a public kindergarten?"

Natalie spoke up from the back seat. "I managed to get a peek at Evgenia's file. Her next of kin is Pavel 'Pasha' Lazarov who resides in London. I dialed the phone number they have for him, but it just went to an answering service in the UK. They offered to take a message, so if they know he's dead, they're not talking about it."

"Anything else?"

"They spend a lot of time in enforced crafts," Mary Alice said sourly. "I swear to god, if I ever need that kind of supervision, I'm just going to have Akiko push me off a cliff. Nice and quick."

"A cliff?" Natalie was skeptical. "You might get snagged on a tree on the way down. If that happens, you could survive, only you'd be all banged up. Maybe paralyzed."

"Alright then, what would you choose?" Mary Alice demanded.

Natalie started naming her preferred methods for self-destruction while I took one hand off the wheel and fished in my pocket for the photo. I handed it to Helen. She studied it as Mary Alice began rebutting Natalie's suggestions.

"What am I looking at?" Helen asked.

"Proof that Galina Lazarov is still alive," I said. The bickering in the back seat skidded to a halt.

"The hell did you just say?" Mary Alice asked, reaching for the photo.

"Galina Lazarov, a person with just as much motive to kill us as Pasha, is not dead as we were led to believe," I told her. "She's alive and well, or at least she was a few days ago. She brought Evgenia cookies."

Natalie snatched the picture from Mary Alice. "You have got to be shitting me."

"Nope."

Helen turned to me. "We weren't 'led to believe' anything. Naomi told us straight out that Galina and her mother were killed in the same accident years after we assassinated Boris Lazarov."

I shrugged. "Naomi was doing this off the books which means she had to prepare the report with no help," I reminded her. "She probably saw the story about the accident and took it at face value without checking."

"Sloppy," Helen said with a sniff.

I had been just as furious when I had realized the truth, but I found myself defending Naomi. "She was working on her own, with few resources, on a tight schedule. All while trying to also figure out the identity of the mole who turned over the files in the first place."

"I suppose." Helen still looked sulky, but she'd get over it. She was always fair.

"Do we have any idea where Galina is?" Mary Alice asked.

"Nope. I took a quick peek in the nightstand drawer. Aunt Evgenia doesn't seem to have anything like an address book, and I suspect Galina likes it that way."

In the rearview mirror, I saw Natalie cock her head. "Why?"

"She's been playing dead for thirty years. The obvious conclusion is she likes being a ghost. There was nothing in that room to give away anything about her whereabouts."

"Careless of Galina to let Aunt Evgenia keep a photo up," Natalie observed.

"It's a picture of Pasha," Mary Alice pointed out. "Galina is barely a profile. She probably thought nobody would ever spot it and put the pieces together."

"But if she's monitoring Aunt Evgenia, she'll know someone was there," Helen said suddenly. "It won't take her long to find out there were four of us. She'll be putting some pieces together herself."

I pushed the accelerator towards the floor. "Then it's time we got the hell out of Switzerland."

CHAPTER SIXTEEN

WE MADE IT BACK TO THE FARMHOUSE BY THE NEXT AFTERNOON, having taken a roundabout return trip via Tunisia. Mary Alice picked up a few souvenirs in the Tunis airport, and after we'd eaten a late lunch, she presented Taverner, Minka, and Akiko with leather slippers and packets of dates.

"It was slippers or stuffed camels," she said as she pitted a few dates and tossed them to the cats. They didn't eat them, but batted them around as we talked.

"So," Akiko said, propping her elbows on the table, "what did you learn? Did Pasha Lazarov have a secret wife? A business partner? Is Auntie Evgenia an octogenarian Octopussy and she set her acrobatic minions on you?"

"None of the above," Helen told her. "But Billie discovered proof that the whole Lazarov clan has been keeping a secret." She paused and looked at me, and I retrieved the photograph I'd lifted.

"According to Aunt Evgenia, the woman in the picture is Pasha's sister, Galina."

Akiko blinked. "The dead girl?"

"One and the same," I told her. Taverner was ostentatiously quiet. He just ladled out stew and sliced bread and filled glasses with fizzy water spiked with thimbles of murta arba, the Sardinian liqueur of choice made from myrtle. But there was an alertness about him that meant he was listening to every word and thinking hard.

"But why did your organization tell you Galina died in the car accident with her mother?" Akiko asked.

"It could have been an honest mistake," Helen explained. "Our Provenance department keeps track of thousands—*millions*—of people at a time, and this information would have been logged before the databases were digitized. Back then it was just old-school newspaper clipping and paper filing. The accident happened in the south of France and the details in the local newspaper were probably sketchy, maybe incomplete. Someone in Provenance would have cut out the mention of the accident and filed it away. Simple human error, end of story."

"Or," Natalie said slowly, "the Lazarovs deliberately concealed the fact that Galina survived. Think about it—we killed Boris and even though we did a bang-up job of making it appear to be an accident, there would have always been at least a suspicion of a deliberate assassination when you're talking about a guy like that. Then Irina Lazarov's car goes off a cliff."

"But we didn't do that," Mary Alice pointed out.

Natalie rolled her eyes. "It doesn't matter what we did or didn't do. It only matters what they *think* we did. If they were suspicious about Boris's death, Irina's crash, no matter how accidental, is only going to spook the family further. So if you're Aunt Evgenia, your sister is dead and her kids are possibly in danger. Maybe the local reporter got it wrong or maybe Aunt Evgenia suggested that he get it wrong on purpose. She could have even slipped him some francs to make sure of it, keep Galina off the radar of whoever might have been targeting her family."

"She couldn't have known for sure that Boris had been assassinated or that Irina's crash was just a tragic mistake," Helen mused. "But Russians are nothing if not paranoid. Letting people think Galina was dead was a good way of keeping her safe."

"Why not protect Pasha?" Mary Alice challenged. "If the Lazarovs believed they were being picked off, Pasha would have been just as much a target as Galina."

"He was already almost grown," Akiko put in. "Maybe he wasn't under Aunt Evgenia's thumb. Galina was still a kid."

"A kid who's all grown up and playing games with us," I said, tapping the photograph.

"What did the aunt tell you about her?" Taverner asked quietly.

I shrugged. "Evgenia said she was a bad seed, and maybe she is. That would certainly fit with torching Benscombe. But I don't know. The behavior she described could have just been that of a grieving kid. Galina visits and brings her cookies, but I don't think they're close."

"Any idea where she is?" Akiko asked.

I shook my head. "Auntie Evgenia is not exactly a reliable witness these days."

"She's nuttier than a Christmas fruitcake," Natalie put in helpfully.

"She is struggling with dementia," Mary Alice corrected.

"She did say that Galina loves opera—and opera singers. She used a particularly foul Russian word to describe her. Other than that, no leads," I said.

As the words left my mouth, I realized it was a lie. I stuttered to a stop so quickly, the others stared.

"What is it?" Mary Alice asked.

"Maybe nothing—but, *shit.*" I got up and went for my bag, rummaging for the things I'd thrown in as we were packing on the ferry. I'd been in such a hurry, I hadn't really clocked it at the time, but there it was—the diary I'd taken from Pasha's nightstand. I don't know why it ended up in my tote. Suppressed guilt, maybe? Knowing I'd need to come clean to the others at some point about screwing up the mission by taking it? Or maybe I really was just getting sloppy in my old age. In any case, I flicked it open, looking for anything that might give us a clue. I skimmed entries for all the expected appointments—tailor, dentist, shoemaker, jeweler, hatmaker. His whole life was a series of services designed to make him polished and presentable. All he was missing was a Build-A-Bear checkup for his teddy.

But then I flipped another page and there it was, a chain of symbols Pasha had jotted down the week before, on the date

Lilian Flanders had been murdered. A string of numbers, thirteen of them, beginning with a 7 he'd written backwards.

And then I realized exactly what it was.

I held up the diary as I went back to the table. "There might be something in here."

Helen took the planner and studied it. "Smythson," she said, eyeing the watermark on the Nile blue paper. "Very nice."

"Your day planner?" Nat asked.

"Not mine. Pasha Lazarov's. I lifted it from his stateroom when I did the hit."

Mary Alice stared. "You stole from him?" There was no mistaking the judgment in her voice.

"Yes. I'd just made the hit and was going back through the stateroom when I saw the diary. I thought it might have something useful in it, so I was flipping through when I heard a noise on the stairs. My exit was cut off and I had to move quick."

"That doesn't explain why the diary went with you," Helen said, handing it back to me like it was a piece of dirty laundry.

"Because it was still in my hand and I got spooked," I told her. "At least that's what I thought at the time. But now I think I might have taken it because I knew what these numbers were. Subconsciously, I mean."

"We have rules about that sort of thing for a reason," Helen said coldly.

"I know, Helen."

She looked at me hard for a long moment, and I realized she was truly pissed. But that was not a now problem, I decided.

It was more important to dig out whatever information we could from the planner.

"Look." I flipped the diary to the correct page to show the others. "The day Lilian Flanders was killed in Maine, Pasha has a note in his diary." I pointed to the string of numbers.

Mary Alice peered through her bifocals. "It could be a phone number, but that doesn't make sense. The seven at the start is backwards."

"Because it isn't a seven," I said grimly. "Pasha was Bulgarian which means his first alphabet was Cyrillic."

"Is a *G*," Minka said, pointing her fork at the page for emphasis.

"Exactly," I said. "I think *Galina* killed Lilian Flanders."

They were quiet a minute, and the only sound was one of the cats washing itself.

Nat broke the silence. "It's possible. She would have just as much motive as Pasha."

"And it explains the itchy feeling I had about Pasha's involvement. He didn't feel like the killer because he wasn't," I said.

"Don't get ahead of yourself," Mary Alice counseled. "They could have been in on it together. Otherwise why was Pasha even in the States?"

"Good point," Akiko said.

I shook my head. "I don't know. There are way too many unanswered questions. But look." I pointed to the planner again. "The day after Lilian's death, there's a notation about a flight to London. We know it wasn't for Pasha, he didn't fly."

"Galina," Nat said. "That puts her in the vicinity a week

later when Benscombe was burned." She pointed to the string of numbers behind the Cyrillic *G* in the first notation. "But what are the rest of those numbers for?"

"It's a phone number," Taverner said quietly. "Venetian."

"How do you know that?" Mary Alice asked.

He launched into a story about a blissful year he spent exploring all the bakeries and bacari of the city, just as my phone rang.

"Naomi," I said to the room at large. I slipped onto the front porch and answered. In the background was the shrieking jingle of a kids' show and the sound of a toddler squealing with laughter.

"Where are you now?" I asked. "Chuck E. Cheese?"

"I'm at home and I have exactly two minutes until she gets bored with Peppa Pig and I have to go. You want to spend it arguing or you want to know what I dug up?"

"What do you know?"

"You should probably sit down," she started.

"So you can tell me Galina Lazarov is alive?"

There was silence on her end except for Peppa. "You want to tell me how you know that?"

"We paid Aunt Evgenia a visit. Switzerland is nice this time of year. You should go."

"I'll be damned. You're wasted in Acquisitions. They should have put you in Provenance."

"Do I seem like a desk job kind of person, Naomi?"

"Do I?" she shot back. She sighed. "Look, I'm sorry. We should have caught the information about Galina but it got overlooked."

"Overlooked? Naomi, that's a pretty mild word for a pretty significant fuckup."

She went on as if I hadn't spoken. "The file on Galina was thin—too thin."

"Wait, you keep actual files?"

"There are two sets of files," she explained. "We mostly work from digital databases these days, but on older subjects, some of the material may only be available in hard copy, especially if they died before we got around to digitizing. And yes, those files are real—old-school manila. I went to the physical archives in our deep-storage facility to find Galina's dossier. Like I said, it was sketchy. All it had was the information that she'd been killed in the car accident with her mother. I pulled Irina Dashkova's file too, and there was a copy of her death certificate, but nothing in Galina's, just a newspaper obituary and you can buy those. So I started to wonder if—"

"If Galina survived the crash and that's why there was no death certificate in her file," I finished.

"Exactly. I ran some searches on the big database and found a mention of a 'Galina Dashkova' who would be the right age. That's when I realized that after her mother's death, Galina must have gone to live with her aunt and taken Evgenia's surname. Operating on that theory, I was able to find a few more things—records of a student by that name at a boarding school in the Spanish Pyrenees, one or two property transactions. Nothing that would stand out as suspicious."

"Then why was Galina Dashkova in the database at all?" I asked.

"As a footnote," Naomi said dryly. "When she was younger,

she was occasionally photographed on the arm of a shady businessman or two."

"What business?"

"Nothing we'd be interested in targeting," Naomi replied. "Mostly art dealers who don't mind a little fuzzy provenance on the pieces they move. A small-time coke distributor. A third-tier oligarch who dated her for two weeks and dumped her for a Moldovan supermodel. Nobody who was going to put her on the map, career-wise."

"Sounds like she had her fingers in lots of little pies," I mused. "Tell me, was she ever a footnote in her brother's dossier?"

Naomi cleared her throat. "There may have been a mention of her as a possible business associate."

My fingers tightened around the phone. "And nobody made the connection between Galina Dashkova and Pasha Lazarov, whose dead sister was named Galina and whose mother was a Dashkova?"

"Somehow that detail slipped past whoever was following up on the Lazarov kids. Our mistake."

"The kind of mistake that gets people killed," I reminded her. There was silence for a minute and I sighed into it. "Never mind. Just tell me you know something helpful now. We need to find her."

"She's almost as elusive as her brother," Naomi said. "I can tell you the city where she lives. It's—"

"Venice," I cut in.

"Stop doing that! How—"

There was no point in concealing the truth. "I have Pasha

Lazarov's planner. There's a phone number in it, and we think it's hers. We've identified it as Venetian. That doesn't tell us if she's still there or where to find her if she is."

Naomi's voice was cool. "You have Pasha Lazarov's planner. A planner I assume he didn't just hand you out of the goodness of his heart."

"No, I took it from his nightstand after I killed him."

"You should have sent that directly to us," Naomi said.

"You mean to *you*. This mission is off the books, remember? You can't send us into the field with half-assed intel for a job that doesn't even officially exist and then come at me for not following protocol," I shot back. Then I stopped talking and waited. Technically, Naomi was right. I should never have lifted the planner, and the first thing I should have done after reaching England was arrange for it to be couriered to her. But Naomi had committed her fair share of missteps in this little fandango and I wasn't about to be hung out to dry when mistakes in the Provenance files had nearly gotten us killed.

Naomi must have decided to pick her battles, because she let the subject go. Temporarily, no doubt. I was sure she was just filing the subject of the planner away for a come-to-Jesus meeting down the road.

"I do have something else that might help," Naomi said. "It's not much, but she's an opera fan."

"I know that too," I told her.

"Well, do you know she has a thing for baritones? She works hard to keep her name and photo out of the papers and

press releases, but I found a few discreet mentions. Fundraisers, opening nights. She takes on protégés, usually young
men. Her latest is named Wolfgang Praetorius, a Bavarian
baritone. Say that three times fast." She was clearly trying to
lighten the mood, but I wasn't having it.

"Naomi," I said in a warning tone.

"Sorry. Bottom line is, the baritone is your best lead. Galina likes to pave the way for her little opera babies, so she's
probably got something lined up for this one."

"Thanks for almost nothing," I told her as I hung up. I
was certain I was going to feel bad about being short with her
later. But she was a handy punching bag, and I made a note
to send her something—maybe a muffin basket—as I went to
join the others. I brought them up to speed and Minka started
tapping away on her laptop.

She pulled up a profile of Wolfgang Praetorius and showed
us a photo of a beefy blond youth. "He won a prize in Germany." The piece was from a newspaper in Erlangen, confirming what Naomi had said about him being Bavarian.

"There's no way his name is really Wolfgang Praetorius,"
I said.

"Stage name," Minka confirmed. "His real name is Wal-
ter Krebs." She snickered.

"Definitely not a name you'd want to see up in lights,"
Helen put in.

"There's a Mr. Krabs joke in there somewhere," Nat added.

"Where is he now?" I asked Minka.

She shrugged. "He has not updated his personal website

recently and his social media game is weak. He should work on that if he wants to be famous. Maybe TikTok reels."

Natalie took the phone and squinted at the picture. It was slightly blurred, as if emphasizing how youthful he was, how unformed. "Damn, Galina likes them young." Nat studied the picture some more and raised her brows approvingly. "He's a little Teutonic for my taste, but good for her."

"You're missing the point," I said, plucking the phone out of her hand and giving it back to Minka.

"Which is?"

"We don't have a good lead, just a Bavarian opera singer who might be anywhere and a Venetian phone number," I told Nat.

"Let's try it," she said, pulling out her phone. She tapped the numbers in and put it on speaker. It made a series of odd beeps and clicks before a melodious woman's voice told us in liquid Italian that the number was no longer in service.

"Not a surprise," Mary Alice observed. "We already theorized that she's the one who burned Benscombe and left the wolf for us and that she likely has eyes at the nursing home. She'd cover her tracks and ditch that phone."

"Only if she knew we had the diary," Helen put in. She'd been quiet for the last several minutes, thinking hard, it seemed. "Billie didn't get the number from Aunt Evgenia, she got it from the diary she stole from Pasha Lazarov."

"'Stole' seems a little harsh," Mary Alice said. "She didn't lift it on purpose, and anyway how would Galina know that she'd taken it?"

"Exactly," Nat put in loyally. "It's not Billie's fault."

"Yes, it is," I told them. "Helen's right. Someone would have made an inventory, the butler, the bodyguard. And that inventory could have been sent to Galina from the ship. Pasha was a creature of habit. If the planner was missing from the inventory, it would have told her someone had been in his room."

"But it could have been stolen by anyone," Nat argued.

I held up a hand. "I don't imagine Galina is the kind of woman who gives most folks the benefit of the doubt. She intended this to be some sort of nasty little game from the beginning—that's why she left a calling card at the scene of Lilian's murder. And when Pasha's planner went missing, she would have suspected we were involved, and she'd have been right. I think that's why she burned Benscombe." I leveled my gaze at Helen. "I'm sorry, Helen."

"That doesn't bring my house back," she said.

"No, it doesn't. But we've got a job to do. You can hate me when it's finished, okay?"

"Oh, I'm planning on it," she told me, and there was a little flash of the cobra about her when she said it.

A stillness had settled, as if the room itself had been holding its breath. It wasn't often that we squared off against each other and meant it, but this was one of those times. The silence might have stretched on forever, but Natalie spoke up in an artificially bright tone.

"So the number is out of service, but we have a lead. I say we go to Venice," she said, looking around.

"We just go to Venice," I repeated.

"Italy has opera," Mary Alice said in a thoughtful voice.

"The best in the world. Chances are, if Galina is pulling strings for her little toy, she's gotten him in with a company somewhere like Venice or Milan. Starting our search in Venice isn't the worst idea. If nothing else, it puts us closer to where we know she's been."

There was a chorus of agreement from the others.

"This just got a whole lot more complicated," I said, suddenly tired. I started ticking items off by holding up fingers. "We have to get to Venice. We have to set up a safe house, do surveillance, and figure out how to take out Galina Lazarov—sorry, Dashkova. And I don't have contacts there. Do you?"

I looked around the group but everybody just shrugged or shook their head.

Taverner tipped his chair back, whistling. I whipped my head around. "Do you have something to add, Taverner?"

He took his time, lacing his hands behind his head and drawing out the moment like the drama queen he was. "Oh, I was just thinking of my friend Signora Bevilacqua. Lovely older woman. She owns several properties dotted around the lagoon. She rents them out on VRBO for a bit of extra cash. Did I mention she owes me a favor?"

"How big of a favor?" I asked through clenched teeth.

"Enormous," he said with a shit-eating grin. "Her daughter was married to a Sicilian mafioso and in the course of assassinating him, I made sure her daughter was safely returned to her parents in Venice. I spent a wonderful fortnight skiing with them in Torino. I still have her grandmother's recipe for risotto al nero di seppia. You remember that dish, Billie. I cooked it for you over that one remarkable weekend in 1983."

His eyes were fairly dancing—with malice or mischief I couldn't quite tell. Probably both.

Mary Alice looked to where the cats were still batting the dates around. "Then I suppose we'd better pack up and make tracks. Looks like we're off to Venice, kids."

BY THE TIME TAVERNER REACHED THE SIGNORA—WHO AS IT TURNED out was actually a contessa—and made the necessary arrangements, it was too late to leave that night. We made a plan to head out in time to catch the first ferry from Olbia straight to Livorno. From there it was a four-hour train ride to Venice. If our luck held, we'd all be settled into our lodgings in the Campo Santa Margherita by dinnertime—Minka, Akiko, and Taverner included. Minka stayed up late to forge passports for the cats, but everybody else turned in. I stepped outside to look at the stars. In the distance, a nuraghe, one of the Bronze Age towers that dotted the Sardinian landscape, punctuated the horizon. Overhead, the sky was a peculiar, oily shade of black, sometimes slicked with blue or green or purple. Here and there smudges of white showed the edges of the galaxy and spots of silver hung like Christmas ornaments.

I heard a step behind me and I kept my back turned, rummaging in my pocket for a packet of cigarettes.

"I saw no Way—The Heavens were stitched—
I felt the Columns close—
The Earth reversed her Hemispheres—
I touched the Universe—

And back it slid—and I alone—
A Speck upon a Ball—
Went out upon Circumference—
Beyond the Dip of Bell—"

"Nice," I told Taverner. "Dr. Seuss?"

"Emily Dickinson, you philistine," he said, flicking open his lighter. He didn't smoke, but I did, so he always carried a lighter. I'm sure somebody would find that romantic. He touched the flame to the tip of my cigarette and I pulled in a deep breath.

"Do you plan on sulking the whole trip or just until Venice?"

I blew the smoke out into rings that brushed his face. "I haven't decided yet."

He smiled in the darkness, but it was humorless, a baring of the teeth. "You can't stand it, can you?"

"What?"

"That you, just occasionally, might need someone else."

It was on the tip of my tongue to tell him I didn't need him, but that seemed childish. So I said nothing at all, and that seemed even more juvenile.

"My god, you can't bring yourself to even say it," he said.

"Why should I? You seem to enjoy saying it enough for the both of us." I took another drag on the cigarette, but it didn't taste as good as it usually did.

"And what's wrong with that?" he demanded. "Do you realize how seldom it happens? Relying on someone else doesn't make you weak."

"It's not a sign of strength," I countered.

"You are the strongest woman I have ever known," he said solemnly. "I could live a thousand lifetimes and no one would ever compare to you. And if you just once in a decade or two let me do something for you, the world wouldn't come screeching to a halt."

I stayed silent again, and his shoulders drooped a little.

"We are in a relationship, Billie. At least I thought we were."

"We are," I admitted. "But it's never going to be the kind of relationship you need it to be."

"You don't know what I need," he shot back.

"You need a woman who is helpless enough to let you play the hero," I replied. "And that's not me."

His eyes fairly bugged out of his head and he opened his mouth a few times before shutting it with a snap. I smoked half the cigarette while I waited for him to answer.

"I don't need to play the hero," he said finally, in a calm, resigned voice. "But I can't be with someone who won't ever let her guard down enough to trust me."

"I trust you—" I began, but he reached into his pocket for the lighter.

"You don't. But someday you'll have to decide to start."

He pushed the lighter into my hand and walked away.

As exits went, it was a pretty good one.

CHAPTER SEVENTEEN

MY ANNOYANCE WITH TAVERNER MIGHT HAVE EASED UP BY THE TIME we got to Venice if it hadn't been for the house. I was expecting a typical Venetian property, tall and narrow, with worn brick or sooty ochre plaster—something nondescript that would blend in with the neighbors. Instead, we got a miniature palazzo, or close enough as made no difference. It was three stories and as wide as it was tall, washed in dark rose paint. The ground floor had stout oak doors that looked like they'd been there since Savonarola was pitching bonfires in Florence, but the windows on the floors above were elegantly framed in dark green trim. A set of French doors led onto a tiny balcony that was dripping in vines. Here and there a few early pink blossoms shoved their heads above the window boxes.

I scanned the building for security. No cameras, just the heavy wooden doors and metal bars at the windows. They were laid in a decorative pattern of running squares, but they'd keep intruders out as long as they weren't rusted through. We'd have to station doorbell cameras at strategic spots. No problem—I hadn't expected state-of-the-art security from a VRBO. What I had expected was discretion. The house was easily the prettiest in the Campo Santa Margherita, and I didn't like it. Pretty got you noticed.

The others weren't bothered. Helen was busy throwing open the shutters to let in the afternoon light while Mary Alice was chattering with Signora Bevilacqua as our hostess pointed out the features of the apartment in rapid-fire Italian. She was older than the pyramids, Signora Bevilacqua, with a flame-red wig and a face powdered to a dead white, punctuated by a thick pair of false eyelashes and a slash of cherry pink lipstick. She wore vintage Chanel which she probably bought from Coco herself back in the day, and she had pearls in her ears the size of ripe grapes.

"The wi-fi, sometimes she works, sometimes she does not," the signora said. The Venetian dialect looks like Italian on paper, but to the ear it sounds like a different language. Where Italian is staccato, Venetian is curvy and lyrical. It is musical if you like your music Baroque. Mary Alice seemed to be understanding about one word in twelve, but with hand gestures and facial expressions, she was catching the gist. They discussed the hot water situation—unpredictable at best—and where to buy the best bread. The signora produced a list with her recommendations and turned to plant two cherry kisses on Taverner's cheeks.

I turned away. "Let's get unpacked and set up. It's going to be a long night."

———

MARY ALICE AND AKIKO BAGGED THE LARGEST BEDROOM AT THE BACK
of the house while Nat and Helen took smaller private singles
on the floor above, and Minka grabbed the tiny maid's room
behind the kitchen. That left a double for Taverner and me to
share. It was just above the salon and had the same view of
the campo. Shutters had been thrown open and I could hear
kids knocking around a soccer ball as the afternoon waned.
Taverner was smart enough to make himself scarce while I
unpacked. He headed for the kitchen, banging and chopping
and stirring as I threw my stuff into a wardrobe that looked as
old as the house and went back downstairs with a notebook.

Akiko eyed it. "Keeping it old-school. I approve."

"I think better when I can doodle," I told her. I also think
better when I can smoke, so I took a chair near the open windows and put my lighter to good use. I flicked the ashes into
a handy potted plant until Mary Alice pursed her lips and
brought me a saucer to use as an ashtray. I jotted a few questions for research, then marked them out, feeling an itch I
couldn't scratch.

"What?" Mary Alice asked. She has always been the most
in tune with my moods and the least likely to judge them.

I blew out a mouthful of smoke. "We're on the run again
with no real clue as to how to find the woman who wants us
dead. Helen is barely speaking to me because I got her house
burned down. I am sharing a room with a man I am currently
annoyed with, and I killed a man in front of his teddy bear."

"Which of those things is a now problem?"

"Finding Galina," I said promptly.

"I might have an idea," she replied. I gave her a hopeful look, but she made a vague gesture with her hand. "Later. What's going on with you and Taverner?"

I shrugged. "The same stuff we've been fighting over for forty years. I won't let my guard down, blah blah. Commitment issues. Blah."

"He's not wrong," she says, and it's a testimony to how much I love her that I didn't punch her right in the mouth.

Instead, I gave her a warning look. "Mary Alice."

"Seriously, Billie. I don't understand what your problem is right now. He's been helpful so far. He's kept us fed and he's the one who figured out the clue in Pasha's diary. You should be thanking that man with home cooking and blow jobs, but instead you're pouting like a teenage girl left home on prom night."

"Taverner and I haven't worked together in a long time," I reminded her. "And I don't like mixing business and pleasure. I never did."

"What are you so afraid of?"

She didn't really expect me to answer that. She knew better. Instead, she waited while I took another long drag on my cigarette and stubbed it out carefully on the saucer she'd brought.

I sat back in my chair and looked at her until she cracked with a sigh. "Fine. I'll tell you what I'm thinking. Our hunch to come here was right. I found her boy."

She tapped on her phone before handing it over. I scrolled the site she'd pulled up. It was the official site of the Gran Teatro La Fenice, the tiny jewel box of a theatre that housed Venice's opera company. It was over the top, a pink velvet confection with gilded frosting. I'd been there once, a lifetime ago, when I was scouting a target. I'd sat through an excruciating *Die Meistersinger* but I'd enjoyed the people watching.

"I always thought it looks like a Baroque bordello," I said, passing the phone back. "What did you find out?"

She tapped again. "I have been scrolling the calendar. Next week they are mounting *Faust* by Gounod."

"Never heard it," I told her.

She rolled her eyes. "Of course you haven't. You're still listening to Cher on the original vinyl." Mary Alice played viola in an amateur chamber orchestra and loved anything written before 1900. I preferred Southern swamp rock and Fleetwood Mac. She went on. "It's not a bad work if you like your opera a little on the avant-garde side. But I am bringing it to your attention because I have scoured the cast lists for every performance of every opera, and I found something quite interesting." She paused for dramatic effect. "It's the story of Faust's bargain with the devil. And the role of Valentin, brother of the heroine, Marguerite, is being sung by—drumroll, please—the very baritone we've been looking for. Wolfgang Praetorius."

"Damn," I murmured, impressed.

Mary Alice cocked her head. "Now go make up with your boyfriend. It smells like dinner is ready and I could eat a cactus, I'm so hungry."

BY UNSPOKEN AGREEMENT, WE DIDN'T DISCUSS THE CASE UNTIL DINNER was finished. It would have been a crime to tarnish that meal

KILLS WELL WITH OTHERS

with work talk. Taverner had leaned in hard to the local pro-duce, whipping up a pitch-black squid ink risotto to follow fried sweet and sour sardines and a pot of salt cod pâté with piles of grilled bread he'd rubbed with garlic and green olive oil. He served a heavy Sicilian white wine with it but he wa-tered it to keep us sharp. For dessert there was a bowl of cher-ries bobbing in ice water alongside tiny cups of mint tea. Because he was also an assassin—and a smart-ass—there was also a box of pastries from Malvestio. Just like Auntie Evge-nia liked.

I raised an eyebrow at the box. "You've been busy," I said to Taverner.

He smiled expansively. "I thought a little recon wouldn't go amiss." I didn't say anything, just helped myself to a hand-ful of cherries, popping each one into my mouth and sucking off the flesh before I spit the pit into my hand.

"I think that was a very good idea, Taverner," Helen said in a tone that was a shade too bright. Like family, we had fallen back into our old roles and Helen's was pourer of oil on troubled waters. I didn't miss the fact that she'd chosen Tav-erner's side though.

"Billie doesn't," Natalie said as she grabbed a pastry. Her role was brat.

Even with his mouth shut, Taverner could annoy me. He just smiled over his teacup and kept quiet.

"Smug isn't a pretty color on you," I murmured in his di-rection.

He turned the smile up a notch. "I cooked. You can wash up. I'm going for a walk." He pitched a dish towel in my direction and eased out the door. Silence lay heavy in the room after he went.

"It's been forty years," Natalie said. "Are you still doing this?" She waved her hands to indicate where Taverner had been sitting.

"Do you really want to talk about relationships?" I asked sweetly. "Because if I'm aiming at you, I've got a lot of bullets in my bandolier." She flipped me off, but there wasn't much she could say for herself after three divorces and a string of disastrous love affairs from Hong Kong to Helsinki.

Mary Alice clapped her hands. "Girls. Enough. Now, we have a potential lead on where to find Galina." She explained her hunch about La Fenice to Helen and Natalie who looked suitably impressed.

Minka's phone buzzed and she frowned as she studied it. "Something bad has happened."

I took the phone and scrolled through the article she'd pulled up. Mary Alice came to read over my shoulder.

It was just a few lines from a Swiss newspaper. It had been written in German, but a name jumped out at me. Evgenia Dashkova.

"How did you find this?" Nat asked.

"I set search engine alerts for everybody involved in this business," Minka explained. "That just posted."

I read fast, translating as I went.

"What am I looking at?" Mary Alice asked.

"An obituary," I told her. "Aunt Evgenia is dead."

After we'd passed the phone around and everyone had had a chance to read the obit, we debated the timing of Aunt

Evgenia's death. There wasn't much dissent. We were all pretty much in agreement that it was too coincidental. Besides which, I had seen her just a few days before.

"She was older than Moses's grandmother, but she looked good," I said. "Healthy enough under the circumstances."

"Old people do just drop dead sometimes," Akiko said hopefully. I understood her inclination to chalk it up to natural causes. It was a hell of a lot less scary than the alternative. "I mean, why would Galina kill her own aunt?"

"Because she knew we'd been to see her," I said gently.

Mary Alice filled in the rest. "Galina would have been afraid that Aunt Evgenia gave us information that Galina didn't want us to have."

"Like the fact that she's actually alive," Natalie put in.

"But you still don't *know*," Akiko began.

I held up my hand. "We know." I read aloud from the obituary. "'Evgenia Feodorovna Dashkova is survived by her niece—Lilian Flanders of Mount Desert, Maine, in the United States.'"

"That *bitch*," Mary Alice said.

Akiko looked puzzled. "What's wrong with that?"

"Lilian Flanders is the name of the agent Galina killed before we killed her brother," Nat explained.

"And obituaries are sent to the newspapers by family members," I added. "By making reference to Lilian, Galina is definitely sending a message. We know she's alive and she knows that we know."

"And she wants us to know that she knows that we know," Natalie put in.

"Natalie, this is not the time to be a smart-ass," Mary Alice said shortly.

"I can't think of a better one," I said. Natalie blew me a kiss.

"So, what's the plan?" Helen asked. "Stake out the opera house until Galina shows up?"

"That could take days, maybe weeks," Mary Alice said, looking around the table. "That's a long time—too long." We all knew what she was getting at. The longer we spent surveilling Galina, the likelier it was she'd spot us. If that happened, it was only a matter of time before she managed to kill us—or worse, Akiko or Taverner or Minka. Avoiding collateral damage was the Museum's first rule and one we took seriously.

"We have to draw her out," Helen said. "But how?"

We were silent for a while, each of us ruminating in our own way. Natalie folded her napkin into a series of animals— the rabbit was my particular favorite—while Helen arranged the condiment bowls and salt and pepper into rigid rows. Mary Alice scribbled in her notebook, jotting ideas and scratching them out just as quickly. Akiko busied herself doing the dishes, and Minka headed to her room, probably to play video games. I went to the window to light a cigarette and blow smoke out into the campo. Night had fallen and the little boys with their soccer balls had been summoned to dinner. The bars and restaurants were gently buzzing with customers wrapped up against the chill, settled under glowing heaters and enjoying their Aperol spritzes.

"Wolfgang," I said suddenly. I stubbed out my cigarette and came back to the table.

"I thought of that too," Mary Alice said as Akiko joined us, wiping her hands on a dish towel. "But how?"

"We blackmail him into helping us."

Nat let out a sharp bark of laughter. "We're killers, not blackmailers."

"So?" I raised a brow at her. I never could manage it as well as Taverner, but I'd been practicing.

"We'd have to get information on him in order to blackmail him," Mary Alice said. "How do we even know there are skeletons rattling around in his closet? He might be clean."

"There are two kinds of blackmail," I reminded her. "The kind where you've got something nasty to hide and you pay to keep it secret."

"And the other?" Akiko asked.

"The kind where you're forced to do something because of the consequences if you don't."

"I think that's technically extortion," Natalie said, frowning.

"Don't make me hurt you, Schuyler," I replied.

"It's a step down," Helen said slowly. "It feels grubby."

"It *is* grubby," I told her. "But it's also efficient. Every day we lose waiting around to find Galina is another day we're in danger. All of us," I said with a meaningful nod towards Akiko. She looked startled, and reached for Mary Alice's hand. I went on. "Galina's been calling the shots up until now. I say we take charge and play offense for a while."

"It is better than waiting around," Natalie agreed.

Helen still looked dubious. "I'm not sure I like the idea of threatening a bystander with violence."

"Violence? Jesus, Helen, I'm not talking about pistol-whipping the guy," I told her. "I only meant we should scare him." I held up Natalie's phone with Aunt Evgenia's obituary still front and center. "We show him this and let him know what his girlfriend is capable of."

She considered this. "We would have to find him," Helen said, but I could tell her objections were faltering. "It could still take a while."

"A day or so is all we need," I promised.

"Well, then," Natalie said, raising her glass. "To our first foray into extortion."

CHAPTER EIGHTEEN

IT WAS A PLEASANT DAY, WARMER THAN EXPECTED, AND AS WE climbed the Accademia bridge, the sun made an appearance, glittering on the wide green curve of the Grand Canal.

"God, I love this city," Mary Alice breathed. I would have agreed with her if it hadn't been for the hordes of tourists packing the bridge with their selfie sticks and slices of take-away pizza. Mary Alice and Akiko had honeymooned in Venice, and I had my own pleasant memories of the city. One of my favorite assassinations had taken place there, in the Gritti Palace—touristy, but with a delicious if overpriced Bellini. I always thought it was a nice touch that they served their drinks with little bowls of potato chips.

Over the bridge, we skirted the green space surrounding the Palazzo Cavalli-Franchetti.

"Remind me to stop there on the way back to get Akiko some flowers," Mary Alice said as we passed the tiny florist shop tucked up beside the gates of the palazzo. Buckets of blooms were banked against the front of the shop, spilling onto the pavement. Peonies and lilies of the valley jostled with callas and honeysuckle, sending a riot of perfume into the air. Small potted lemon trees and ferns stood by for the more practical buyers, but even these were glossy green and luscious.

We had no choice but to cross the wide-open length of the Campo Santo Stefano, but we kept our heads down, large sunglasses firmly in place. Mary Alice even wore a hat, a crushable straw thing with a broad brim that threw her face into shadow. A few more turns brought us out in the narrow alley that ran beside the Teatro La Fenice. In the side wall of the theatre, there was a service entrance of wide blue doors embellished with metal bars that looked like spears. Just opposite there was a campiello, a miniature square that housed a taverna, a pair of boutique hotels, and a few private apartment buildings. It was late afternoon, the perfect time to settle in with a drink, so Mary Alice and I chose that as our surveillance cover, diving into a pair of red leather armchairs set outside the taverna just as they became free. We ordered spritzers and a charcuterie plate and settled in to wait, looking like any other women of a certain age enjoying an unseasonably warm Venetian afternoon as we picked at the food and sipped our drinks.

We dragged it out as long as we could before giving up. A succession of builders and decorators had used the side door of the theatre, but everybody who had gone in carried a ladder or a paintbrush.

"I am *starving*," Mary Alice muttered as she reached for the last of the prosciutto.

"You've eaten a pound and a half of pork by yourself," I reminded her.

"Charcuterie calories don't count. Everybody knows that." She wrapped the scrap of prosciutto around a piece of provolone and ate it in two bites.

I looked away briefly from the theatre door. "What else doesn't count?"

"Food eaten standing up, food that takes longer than forty seconds to chew, and anything eaten on Super Bowl Sunday."

"Mary Alice, that is the most insane—" I broke off as the door opened. Mary Alice was too well trained to turn around. Instead, she watched in the reflection of my sunglasses.

"Is that a can of paint he's carrying?" she asked.

"Yep. Still nothing but the scenic crew."

She shrugged and went back to her picking. "You want the last of this?" she asked, nodding towards the plate. There were a few bits of cheese and a sad-looking olive. I shook my head and she helped herself. When she finished, she nodded somewhere vaguely in the direction of the Rialto bridge. "Over that way, there's a pharmacy with a little sign in the window, one of those programmable things with the little red bulbs. It shows a number, just five digits. Do you know what the number is?"

"Should I?"

"It's the current population of the city," she told me. "There's a memo taped up above it that shows Venice had a hundred and forty thousand people living here in 1750."

"How many does it have now?"

"A hell of a lot less. That sign has become a tourist attraction. You know why? Because people are ghouls."

"What's ghoulish about it?" I asked.

"The number is always going down," she explained. "It's not just that the city is sinking, so is the population. Venice is dying." She paused and pointed in the opposite direction. "Out in the lagoon, past Giudecca but before you get to the Lido, is an island called Poveglia. Do you know what it's famous for?"

"Do I want to?"

"It's the most haunted place in Italy. There was a mental asylum where experiments were carried out on the insane, but before that, it was the place they sent their plague victims to die alone so they wouldn't infect healthy people."

"Jesus, Mary Alice. That's grim."

She shrugged again. "There's a cemetery island too. Nothing but graves. Like I said, Venice is dying. What do you think that says about Galina that she chooses to live here?"

"Maybe nothing. Maybe she just lives here because her boyfriend works here."

She shook her head slowly. "I don't think so. I think she's got that gloomy Russian thing going on."

"She's only half-Russian," I reminded her. "She's also half-Bulgarian."

"Bulgarians are gloomy too," Mary Alice said.

I couldn't argue with that. I looked again at the service door of the theatre. "A man should have the good manners to show up for his own extortion," I said. "Even if it is a surprise."

"Well, this one isn't," she said, gesturing towards the waiter for the check. She paid cash and we strolled out of the campiello.

When we got back to the house, ready to admit defeat for the day, Nat appeared from the kitchen, her hair standing on end, flour on her nose. She was wrapped in an apron that was creased and stained with what might have been blood or wine. Akiko was right behind her, also wearing an apron but looking much tidier.

"What happened to you?" Mary Alice asked Nat. "Your hair looks like it belongs on one of those shelter dogs on a humane society commercial."

"Taverner's out, so I was making dinner and the steam got to me," Nat said. "And save your insults, because I just had a brilliant idea that will get us Wolfgang tomorrow."

She retrieved her phone from the pocket of her apron and scrolled for a few minutes, jotting notes onto the back of her hand with a felt-tip pen. Then she tapped out a number before handing the phone to me. "La Fenice's personnel office. Get Wolfgang's personal cell number."

"What the hell, Natalie," I started, but just then the phone was answered with an abrupt, "Pronto."

I switched to Italian, smoothing it into the Venetian dialect. "Good evening, signora. I am calling from the office of—" I reached for a name, any name, and blurted out "Dottoressa Lidia Maradona. We must reach a patient of hers,

Wolfgang Praetorius, but the telephone number we have for him is incorrect. Please give us the correct number so that we can give him his test results."

I waited, expecting her to argue. Italians love nothing more than thwarting you with bureaucracy, but the woman I was speaking to was bored or hated her job or didn't give a shit, because she simply rattled off a series of numbers.

"Grazie mille," I said, ending the call and handing the phone back to Natalie.

Akiko stared, wide-eyed. "Do Italians not have the equivalent of HIPAA? I can't believe that worked."

I shrugged. "You'd be surprised how often people are willing to hand out personal information if you just act like you're entitled to it."

Helen came in while Nat keyed in the numbers I gave her and we brought her up to speed. Nat waited, her expression expectant, then mouthed a word at us. "Voicemail." When the greeting ended, she left a message, lapsing into her natural New York accent with a little extra nasal something thrown in. "Good evening, I'm phoning on behalf of Christine Fellowes, honorary chair of the board of directors of the Metropolitan Opera in New York. Ms. Fellowes is in Venice for a short time and has an opening in her schedule to meet with you and discuss a possible opportunity for you to sing with us next season. Please confirm your availability to meet with her at your earliest convenience at this number."

She pressed "end call" and sat back.

"There's no way," Mary Alice began. But before she could finish, the phone rang. Nat looked at the screen and grinned.

"It's him. You were saying?"

The conversation was short. They set up a rendezvous for the following morning, and Nat stressed to him the importance of discretion. "Ms. Fellowes is not authorized to formally offer a contract," we heard her tell him, "but if she likes you, well, she has great sway with the rest of the board. Naturally, we would not wish for La Fenice to get wind of this," she added. "Secrecy is of the utmost importance."

We could hear a torrent of vehement reassurances on Wolfgang's end.

"I am glad to hear it," she told him. "I will text you the address to meet Ms. Fellowes."

She ended the call while he was still talking. "I am embarrassed for him," she said. "He was so eager, he didn't even take the time to google Christine Fellowes."

"And if he had?" Helen asked.

Nat grinned. "He'd have found an honorary board member of the Metropolitan Opera. That's what I was looking up before I called."

Akiko shook her head. "No way. It cannot be that easy. Nobody is that stupid."

"It's not stupidity." I explained the basic psychology. "It's optimism. Like any other scam, we're taking advantage of his longing for something. Wolfgang Praetorius wants to sing for the Met. We dangled the possibility in front of him, and he snapped at the bait. He's willing to overlook anything suspicious because his ambition outweighs his sense of self-preservation."

"It happens all the time," Helen told Akiko. "People look beyond red flags waving right in front of their faces because they want something so desperately that they will explain away anything that might endanger that."

"You just described two of my marriages," Natalie said.

"Everybody sees what they want," Mary Alice said quietly. She got up and went into the kitchen then. Akiko didn't follow her, but stayed at the table with the rest of us.

I turned to Nat and Helen. "We need to set the meet-up with Wolfgang. Ideas?"

Nat looked up. "I've already sent him the address. Bar Foscarini." It was a small open-air restaurant at the foot of the Accademia bridge, touristy and overpriced, but by way of compensation it had planter boxes full of mandevillas and bottles of decent rosé. And the location meant if anything went south, it would be easy to get away, blending into the crowds that thronged the bridge at any hour of the day.

"Who is going?" Helen asked.

Natalie didn't even have the grace to look embarrassed. "Billie."

"Why me?" I demanded. "Did we draw straws and I missed it?"

Nat tapped on her phone some more, then turned it around. "Christine Fellowes."

The woman in the picture wasn't my doppelgänger, but she was damned close. Like me, she was on the other side of sixty—not too far, but distant enough that I figured the streaks in her blond hair were her natural grey. I kept my body tight with yoga and weightlifting, although she probably achieved the same effect with Pilates and the odd trip to the plastic surgeon's office. Our haircuts were even similar.

"Damn," I said to nobody in particular.

I went to my room after dinner to get ready for the next day. Nat had set the rendezvous for eleven AM, late enough so the bar would be open, but early enough so that there wouldn't be too many witnesses to the scene we were going to play. I laid out a linen suit, expensively rumpled, and a bag with a recognizable logo on reluctant loan from Helen. A huge pair of dark glasses would keep Wolfgang from looking too closely even if he had taken the time to google Christine Fellowes. There was nothing we could do about the hundreds of CCTV cameras around the city, but prosperous respectability is always a good disguise.

I was just stocking my bag with the things Christine Fellowes might carry—a tourist map of Venice, a folding fan, a makeup bag and hairbrush—when Taverner came in, smelling of tobacco and sea air.

"Nice evening?" I asked.

"Very," he told me, slipping out of his leather jacket. "I went on a bacari crawl." Venice was famous for its wine bars, each one offering standing-room-only service with good wine, heavy appetizers, and as much atmosphere as you could ask for. It was just the sort of evening we would have shared if I hadn't been working. I wasn't sure if I was annoyed he'd gone alone or relieved he had been out of the way while we had been plotting Wolfgang's kidnapping. Taverner was always good for an idea, but I had no intention of letting him get mixed up in this.

I waited for him to introduce the subject of why we were in Venice, but he washed up, humming "American Pie" in the shower—all eight minutes and thirty-four seconds of it—before brushing his teeth and slipping into bed. He was half-way through a Zadie Smith book and picked up where he'd left off.

I stared at him until he looked up with a warm smile. "Is there something you wanted, love?"

I bared my teeth back at him. "No, darling," I said in a sweet tone. "Nothing at all."

He patted the bed next to him, and I went to lie under his arm, tucked up against his side. His free hand stroked my hair lazily while he read, brow furrowed over his bifocals. He was being completely courteous, respectful of my boundaries, and doing exactly as I asked of him.

I didn't trust it for a goddamned minute.

CHAPTER NINETEEN

THE NEXT DAY I WAS IN PLACE WELL BEFORE ELEVEN, WATCHING THE foot traffic on the bridge. School groups, official tours, even the odd bachelorette party crowded each other as they jostled for the perfect shot of the Grand Canal. The sun was glittering off the water—good for me, since it meant my oversized sunglasses weren't suspicious. I had chosen a table near the hostess stand, and a few minutes after I arrived, Helen appeared with a bulging shopping bag from the Accademia and a large camera slung around her neck. She'd asked for a table near the water and angled herself so she could watch me discreetly. The waiter brought her a pizza, and she occupied herself by breaking off small bites and pretending to eat as she paged through a Rick Steves guidebook.

Up on the bridge, Mary Alice was snapping selfies. At the foot of the bridge, on the opposite side from the Bar Foscarini, Nat had set up an easel and was lazily sketching the canal.

I ordered a cup of black tea and studied the photograph of
Wolfgang that Nat had bookmarked on my phone. He was
exactly what you'd expect of a German opera singer—well-
padded with a blond beard. (Jonas Kaufmann being the exception, of course.) Wolfgang looked like he just stepped out
of *The Aryan Opera Lover's Guide to Wagner,* and I wondered
what his grandparents had gotten up to in World War II. I
closed out the tab on my phone just as he walked up, smiling
a wide, nervous smile.

"Frau Fellowes?"

"Ja," I said, rising and extending my hand. I greeted him
in fluent German, making a point of including a few minor
grammatical errors and flattening my accent. People are always more at ease when they think they know more than you
do. To my surprise, he didn't correct me. Instead, he gave me
an even bigger smile.

"You speak German!" he exclaimed in real delight.

I smiled. "You should not be surprised. We who love opera must have at least a passing acquaintance with German
and Italian and French." I waved him to a chair and signaled
the waiter to bring another tea. Over his shoulder I could see
Helen fighting off a seagull that had swooped in for some of
her pizza.

"I have never known a singer who didn't want something
hot to drink," I told Wolfgang with a warm smile. "Would
you like some honey?"

"No, no," he said, helping himself to four packets of sugar
as the waiter appeared with a tiny teapot. Wolfgang poured a
small cup and stirred in all four packets. He took a deep sip,

sitting back with a little sigh. "I am honored by your invitation, Fraulein," he said, putting his hand to his heart. He had obviously decided that a charm offensive was warranted, and my strategy was to pretend to be charmed. I had had plenty of time to decide how to play it and plenty of advice from Helen, the only real opera lover among us. His official biography stated his age as thirty-three, but Natalie's internet digging had turned up a few early competitions in his hometown of Erlangen. Working out the dates, it was clear he'd shaved a few years off, no doubt to give himself a little more time to make it as a pro. He was closer to thirty-seven and probably getting desperate. The role at La Fenice was his biggest one yet, and it still wasn't a lead. He'd never believe it if I hinted at a headlining spot in a major production, so I said some vague things about showcases and fundraisers and perhaps a chance to understudy *Der Rosenkavalier*. The suggestion of performing a German composer lit him up. He started to talk about the themes of the opera, gesturing expansively as he went on and on about infidelity and selflessness.

I let him chatter until he was good and warmed up. Then I touched his hand, a light, quick touch. It wasn't intended to be sexy. It was just a small bonding gesture to let him think I liked him and put him at ease for the request I was about to make. I pulled my phone out and gave him a self-deprecating smile. "I hope you don't mind," I said shyly. "But I'd love to get a selfie with you."

He preened, sliding his chair closer to mine and draping a beefy arm around my shoulders. I snapped a few, tilting my head at the last second so that my hair brushed his cheek. I sat back and pretended to study them. Instead with a couple of taps I forwarded them to the others. I got back three thumbs-up emoji, so I knew they'd gone through. Minka never stints on the international data plan, bless her.

When I was satisfied, I put the phone face-up on the table. It displayed the clearest picture I'd snapped. Wolfgang and I were grinning, looking like the best of friends.

"You will send that to me?" he asked hopefully.

"Of course." I'd saved his number so it took only a few more taps to send him the photo. "I hope that doesn't make your girlfriend jealous," I said as he looked at his incoming message.

He glanced up quickly as he pocketed the phone. "I have no girlfriend."

I tipped my head, giving him a conspiring look. "Don't you? I'm surprised you'd bother to deny it. I mean, I understand pop stars and actors not giving out that kind of information, but are B-list baritones really worried about groupies getting butthurt that they've got significant others?"

He looked confused at the transformation from patrician New York opera buff to plainspoken Texan. "I'm sorry?"

"You will be if Galina Dashkova sees that," I told him, nodding towards the phone in his hand.

His eyes widened. "You know Galina?" He looked confused but not suspicious. He was such an unsuspecting little lamb, I almost felt bad for what I was about to do.

"Let's just say she knows me," I replied. "And she doesn't like me very much."

"I don't understand—" he began.

I held up my hand. "Let me shorthand it for you. Your girlfriend wants to kill me—and a few of my friends. But I'm going to kill her first."

He gaped at me for a long minute, opening and closing his mouth several times before he found his voice again.

"This doesn't make sense," he mumbled. He rubbed his forehead. "Is this some kind of joke? It is a bad joke."

"No, my sense of humor is better than this, I promise. Look, Wolfie, can I call you Wolfie?" He nodded mutely. "Good, I think it's better to be friendly about these things. You can call me Billie."

"But your name is Christine," he corrected.

"No, it's Billie," I told him patiently.

The truth was beginning to dawn. "You are not Frau Fellowes?"

"No, I am not."

"Then you are not with the Met?" He looked crushed.

"No, sorry about that. I didn't mean to get your hopes up, but we had to get you alone for a chat."

"But the job next season—" he began.

"Wolfie, let me save you the trouble. There is no job next season. I have nothing to do with the Met in any way, shape, or form. The only opera I know is what I learned from Bugs Bunny."

"Bugs Bunny?" His confusion turned to outright bewilderment.

I hummed a few bars of *Figaro*. "Bugs Bunny," I repeated.

He stared at me without responding. "Look it up on YouTube when you get home. You'll enjoy it. But in the meantime, I need your help."

"I don't understand any of this." He dropped his face into his hands and I sighed.

"That's because you're not letting me finish. Wolfie"—I snapped my fingers and he raised his head—"focus. I need information from you. If you give it to me, you walk free. If you refuse, that photo goes to Galina. As I explained, she really, really loathes me. If she thinks you're chummy with me, well, I'd hate to be in your shoes." Of course, I didn't have Galina's number since she'd disconnected the one I'd found in Pasha's diary, but Wolfie wouldn't know that.

"Why does she hate you?" he asked. It wouldn't have been my first question in his shoes, but I was okay with satisfying his curiosity.

"Because I killed her father," I told him. "My friends helped, but I'm the one who actually did the deed. Oh, and I killed her brother too. Pasha. Did you ever meet him?"

He swung his head from side to side as if to clear it.

"Pasha was interesting," I told him. "He carried a big teddy bear around everywhere he went. Really sharp dresser. Galina didn't tell you he died?"

"She said he had a heart attack." His voice was a whisper.

"Yeah, I'm what attacked his heart," I said. "I drowned him in a bathtub. Galina has had two major losses in a week. Did she tell you about her aunt Evgenia?"

He didn't even shake his head that time. He simply stared at me, his pupils dilated in fear.

"Aunt Evgenia is dead too, but I'm not responsible for that. Galina is. She killed her own aunt, Wolfie."

"Why?" His voice was such a hoarse little croak, I really hoped he didn't have to sing that night. He'd have sounded like Michigan J. Frog.

"Because she thought Aunt Evgenia gave us information about her," I explained. I gestured towards the phone in his pocket. "And now she's going to think you did too. You're not safe unless you work with us."

"What do you want?" He licked his lips, but they didn't look any wetter. That meant his mouth had gone dry from the terror, which was good news for me.

"We need to make contact with Galina to set up a meeting."

I was about to elaborate when he bolted. One second he was there, the next he was up and gone, pelting up the steps of the bridge. Helen was too busy still fighting the seagull away from her pizza to chase him, and I got tangled with a waiter who was delivering plates of pasta to the table next to mine. It was all up to Natalie and Mary Alice.

CHAPTER TWENTY

"WHAT DO YOU MEAN YOU LOST HIM?" I DEMANDED AN HOUR LATER when we all met back up at the house in the Campo Santa Margherita.

"I mean we lost him," Mary Alice said testily.

"He's a husky blond opera singer in a city full of Italians," I reminded her.

"What can I say? He moves like Baryshnikov. Besides that, I am a sixty-two-year-old woman with bad knees," she shot back.

I glanced at Natalie. "What's your excuse?"

"Let me count them. One," she said, lifting up her middle finger, "you missed out on chasing him too, Billie."

"She knows," Helen said mildly. "That's why she's annoyed and taking it out on you."

"Don't talk about me like I'm not here," I said.

She shrugged and turned back to Natalie. "I'm not taking that personally and neither should you. She'll get over it."

I headed to my room then and I might have stomped a little as I went. It wasn't mature, but it felt damned good. I sat in the chair by the window, sulking and smoking, watching life in the campo go by. A market had been set up with stalls of lettuces and onions. A tiny section of it was devoted to fish, freshly silver and gleaming on their beds of crushed ice in the afternoon light. They'd probably been swimming that morning. I watched the housewives move from stall to stall, carefully choosing the freshest artichokes, the fattest bulbs of fennel. It was oddly peaceful watching people go about their lives.

After a few minutes, Helen joined me. She didn't say anything when she took the chair next to mine. She just sat and watched the market, clocking the comings and goings of the Venetians. The fish vendor was having a good-humored argument with a man about the state of an octopus and kept waving its little tentacles around to indicate freshness. Across the aisle, a woman was running a finger over an embroidered tablecloth.

"Those table linens are a nice color. I should pick up a set," Helen mused. She was always Wendy to our Lost Boys, sweeping up the hearth and setting a place for everyone.

"You don't have a house anymore," I reminded her. "Thanks to me."

She shrugged. "I like to nest, even in temporary accommodations," she said, waving a hand to indicate the safe house.

"You'd hang curtains in hell if the devil would let you," I replied.

She turned to me with a curious expression. "Are you happy? Just living quietly on your Greek island with Taverner."

"I was," I told her. "I am."

"What do you do with your time?"

"Mostly what I always did between missions. I have translation work, I do yoga. I run. I'm learning to sail."

"Sounds as if you keep busy," she said mildly.

"I do. I miss the job," I admitted. "And I miss all of you." I waited a beat before launching into what I really wanted to say. "Helen, about Benscombe—"

"I know." When you've been friends as long as we have, you can shorthand a lot. With those few short words, I'd apologized and she'd accepted. She knew I'd never completely forgive myself. "I'm still mad at you, though," she added.

"I would be too. It was a nice house."

She shrugged. "It was a money pit with termites and dry rot. But I loved it."

"I know," I said. "What will you do now?"

She considered that a minute before answering. "I could rebuild, I suppose. But maybe it's time for something new. Kenneth bought that house for me, and there was never a minute I spent there that I didn't think about him, about Constance. I adored it, but there were a lot of ghosts in those walls."

"Where would you go?" I asked her.

"I don't know. That's why I'm still mad at you. Not

because I lost Benscombe, but because now I have to figure out what's next. I had that all mapped out, and suddenly it's gone. There's this whole emptiness stretching out in front of me, and I'm not sure if it's terrifying or exciting."

"Maybe it's both," I suggested.

"Maybe it's both," she agreed.

We were silent a minute, still watching the market. Below us, the fish vendor was wrapping up the octopus, stuffing its tentacles gently into a bag as the customer held out a banknote.

When she finally spoke, she didn't look away from the market to face me. Sometimes it's easier to tell a truth sideways. "I want to call Benoit, but I don't know if I'm ready to take that step. What if he doesn't want a future with me?"

"Is this where you'd like me to quote a 'Live, Laugh, Love' plaque? Tell you that you'll never know unless you try? Sing you a few bars of 'I'm Every Woman'?"

She eyed me up and down. "Don't think that just because we've been friends for forty years, I won't inflict harm on you."

I smiled. "You're not afraid he'll say no, Helen. You're afraid he'll say yes. Because then you have to figure out how to build a life with him. Tell me I'm wrong."

"You're not. I'm a coward. I think of the things I've done in my life—terrible, wonderful things—and I can't even believe *I* did them. But I did, and I did them well and for a very long time. But this? Every time I think about picking up the phone to ask him to move in together, I want to be sick in my own handbag."

"Well, don't. It's Hermès," I reminded her.

213

She reached out a hand for my cigarette and I gave it to her. She took a long drag, holding the smoke inside her, then exhaling it like a prayer.

"Billie, tell me the truth. How often do you do something that scares you? I mean really, really chills you to your marrow?"

I took my cigarette back and blew a smoke ring that drifted out over the market, past the fish vendor, dissolving into a tiny cloud of nothing. And I thought of the man I lived with who could see right through me to every broken bit and who insisted on loving them anyway.

"Every damned day."

DINNER WAS TENSE. TAVERNER HAD OVERCOOKED THE ROAST CHICKEN and the rice was tough. Mary Alice carped at Natalie, and Natalie bit back which meant Akiko waded in to defend her wife. Minka sniped some just because she enjoys a good fight. That set Helen off, and I detonated in her direction on Minka's behalf. None of it was serious, but it set everybody's teeth on edge.

We'd just descended to general bickering when Taverner stood up.

"Right. I know what we need. Get your coats."

We weren't good at following orders, but whatever he had in mind was bound to be better than sitting around snarling at each other. We left the dinner dishes on the table and headed out, hats pulled low and walking almost single file through the narrow alleys. Taverner and I were in the lead since he knew where we were going. The temperature had dropped since the afternoon, and a brisk breeze was blowing in off the Grand Canal. Taverner set a quick pace until we got to a landing where a few private water taxis were idling. The price was extortionate, but Taverner paid it, giving the driver a set of instructions I couldn't quite hear. We slipped into the Grand Canal, the water black and oily in the evening light. We crossed it in a few minutes and the driver swung left at the ducal palace, heading up the narrow length of the Rio del Palazzo where he cut the speed.

A few minutes more and we were there, alighting at the Donà Palace. It was a boutique hotel, small and elegant, but we weren't there for the rooms. Canalside, the hotel had a terrace garden. It was small and secluded, bordered by high brick walls thick with creeping vines twined with tiny lights and wide planter boxes full of mandevilla. Candles glowed on each table, illuminating a scene that resembled something out of a fairy tale. The terrace was deserted, probably due to the chill. But the waiter behind the bar came over and lit the patio heaters before guiding us to a table. It was a tight fit for seven and the waiter explained they didn't serve food except to hotel guests, although he'd be happy to bring wine and bar snacks. I was just beginning to wonder why we'd even come when I saw what was lying on the table: water pistols.

I picked one up and grinned at Taverner. "Seriously?"

Pigeons are the bane of Venice, and Venetian waiters have a particular hatred for them. The birds peck and shit and generally make nuisances of themselves on every terrace and open square. Only the seagulls prey on them, and there aren't nearly enough seagulls to handle the problem. Some waiters will turn hoses on the pigeons when they get too close and scold children who try to feed them. But the Donà Palace had figured out a solution that discouraged the pigeons and amused the tourists at the same time.

"Seriously," Taverner affirmed, collecting enough pistols for everyone. The waiter reappeared with a few bottles of Valpolicella and little jars of nuts and tortilla chips. He poured out the first bottle of wine, and it wasn't long after that the first pigeon appeared.

It turned into a quick-draw contest, and soon we were formalizing it with rules, handicaps, and a spreadsheet Akiko had roughed out on the back of a napkin. Not surprisingly, Helen was the clear leader—she was our sharpshooter, after all—and Nat clawed her way to second place. I was just aiming at a particularly aggressive pigeon when my phone buzzed in my pocket. It cost me the shot, but I checked the number, waving the others to silence as I answered.

"It's him," I mouthed.

"This is Wolfgang Praetorius," said the voice on the other end. He sounded unhappy which I figured was good for us.

"Good evening, Wolfgang. I'm pleased to hear from you."

"I'm not pleased to be calling," he said. "Someone followed me to my apartment."

"Who?"

"Galina's bodyguard. A small woman named Tamara."

"You're sure it was her?"

"Her hair is very black. She wears it in a short bob. Very severe. She is difficult to mistake."

I could hear vague restaurant noises in the background.

"Where are you now?" I asked. "We could come and get you."

"Tomorrow," he said shortly. "I did not go into my apartment. When I realized I was being followed, I jumped into a water taxi and she could not follow me. I got away."

"Good thinking," I told him. "But if Galina's people are tailing you . . ."

I let my voice trail off, hoping he'd put the pieces together.

"I do not feel safe," he replied.

"Because you aren't safe, not until Galina is out of the way," I explained. "If she had you followed, she may already know that you met with me."

"She has tried to call me, but I have not answered."

"Keep it that way," I instructed. Now that Wolfgang was leaning our direction, the last thing we needed was Galina talking him around. "Tell me where I can find her."

"Not on the phone," he said in a hoarse whisper. "She is clever. Maybe even now she is tracking my phone and knows I've called you."

He sounded panicky, and I knew I had to do some damage control.

"If she were tracking your phone, she'd have found you already and she wouldn't need someone to surveil you," I said. "Where are you?" I asked again. "I can meet you."

"Tomorrow," he repeated quickly. "I will bring you the information you want. I am very tired now." He rattled off a location and a time and I agreed.

"Wolfgang, are you sure you're safe tonight?" I asked. We had manufactured the threat Galina posed to him, but if she had him under surveillance, he was in greater danger than we'd anticipated. And I didn't like the idea of him roaming loose for a night with Galina's henchwoman prowling after him.

"I will stay with a friend—someone she does not know," he said quickly. "I will see you tomorrow. Do not be late."

He ended the call then and I looked up to find the others watching me. A pigeon was edging closer to the table, eyeing a peanut that Helen had dropped.

"Tomorrow morning at six," I told the others. "The Scala Contarini del Bovolo."

The Palazzo Contarini del Bovolo was a tiny palace a stone's throw away from St. Mark's Square. The palazzo was unremarkable, but its staircase, the scala, was the most famous in Venice, beloved of filmmakers and photographers and selfie-takers. It was a good choice for a rendezvous, public but not too public, and theatrical enough to suit an opera singer.

Mary Alice grabbed the napkin Akiko had been using as a scorecard and turned it over, roughing out the plan as we discussed it. Nat pulled the scala up on her phone and Minka found us satellite maps to study from every direction. We batted around loads of possibilities before finally settling on a plan.

"You realize it's a trap," Taverner said coolly.

The pigeon was back, pecking at bits of tortilla chip. I picked up a water pistol and in one fluid motion raised it and fired, hitting it right between the eyes. It flew off in a squawk of offended feathers. I put the water pistol down and grinned at Taverner.

"I'm counting on it."

CHAPTER TWENTY-ONE

WE WERE UP LATE INTO THE NIGHT MAKING PREPARATIONS, INCLUDING a bit of reconnaissance on our rendezvous point. But we managed to snatch a few hours' sleep, rising before dawn to make our way to the scala. Well before the sun came up, we were en route. In the interest of discretion, Mary Alice had hired a private boat, a narrow little beauty with a fast engine and a low hull that she piloted herself. She handled it expertly, gliding up the Rio de Ca' Foscari to pick me up. Helen and Nat had already made their way on foot and were in position near the scala.

On the boat, Mary Alice slowly powered up the engine, easing us into the Grand Canal and hanging a left. There was already traffic on Venice's main waterway, small craft loaded with fish and ice and vegetables, a heavy barge with a crane—even an ambulance boat, making its way slowly past without lights or sirens, which seemed ominous. A light mist rose from the water, swirling around each boat as it moved through the low chop of the waves. The water in the canals is usually green, sometimes brown. But in the hour before dawn, in the last hour of the dying night, the water is black and fathomless. I didn't like the look of it, and I was happy when Mary Alice navigated us to the Rio di San Luca, the canal that ran nearest the Palazzo Contarini del Bovolo. We'd mapped out the route during our recon the previous night, planning half a dozen potential getaways if things went south. I leapt off the boat, leaving Mary Alice to secure it and assume her position. The area was quiet, full of tall, narrow houses packed closely together. The palazzo was a tourist attraction, but a modest one, with a tiny courtyard and a gate that had been unlocked and left ajar. Wolfgang must have bribed the security guard, I realized as I eased through the gate, leaving it like I found it. Just inside the front gate was a courtyard garden the size of a postage stamp with a few bits of statuary and a couple of rosebushes that weren't even thinking of blooming. It was deserted, and by the time it opened at nine-thirty AM, we planned on being long gone.

At first glance, the palazzo looked like an elaborate town house with five levels of arched galleries that ran across the front. What made it a standout was the staircase at the end, a spiral in a tower that rose to the full height of the palazzo. It was open to the elements, topped with a belvedere, a small circular pavilion that offered panoramic views over the city. The only thing separating the staircase from the courtyard was a velvet rope tacked across an arch, so I hopped over it and waited, listening to the silence. I was early, but the unlocked gate meant Wolfgang was probably already in place. I moved to the stairs, and as I started to climb, I noticed the first suggestion of morning, a softening of the black in the night sky to the east, beyond St. Mark's. Morning comes slowly in Venice, the ceiling of the sky shifting through a watercolor palette of light—grey, then blue, then purple—long before the sun shows herself, the sort of light that inspires painters and poets. I moved like a shadow up the stairs, watching as that light moved with me.

At the top of the stairs was a small wooden door that had been left unbolted. I edged it open, a few cautious inches at a time before easing past and into the short, open gallery that led to the belvedere. As expected, Wolfgang was waiting for me, standing in the center of the belvedere and looking distinctly unhappy. He eyed the door about twenty feet behind me.

"Wolfgang, if you bolt down those stairs and make me chase you, I will not be happy," I warned him.

He shook his head. "It is not that. It is"—he gestured vaguely to the arched openings of the belvedere—"heights. I do not like them." Through the arches I could see the jumble of nearby rooftops, the tiles spiked with satellite dishes and chimneys, some strung with washing lines, the laundry fluttering limply in the morning breeze.

"Then don't look down," I told him. Around the circumference of the belvedere, a stone parapet sat about waist high, the only thing between us and the ground nine stories below. He looked at it and flinched. He was pale and shaky, and I felt almost sorry for him. "It's fine," I told him. "I won't let anything happen to you."

"I wish I could say the same for you," he said with an obvious attempt at bravado.

"Dammit, Wolfgang," I said as I saw a red laser dot settle on my chest, just over my heart.

Several things happened at the same time. I dropped to a crouch, a shot rang out, and Wolfgang screamed, a hand clapped to his ear.

I crawled to the parapet and peeked over. Ninety feet below, a small group of men was assembled—private mercenary types with their identikit gear and stupid, matching haircuts. Weapons drawn, they were starting up the staircase of the scala which happened to be the only way up or down from the belvedere. Our exit was well and truly blocked.

Just behind them stood two women in dark glasses. The shorter of them had a severe black bob—Galina's bodyguard, Tamara, I guessed. Her weapon was out and from the smirk on her face, it was obvious she was the one who'd just shot Wolfgang. The other woman had to be Galina Lazarov herself. I'd seen her only in profile, but I recognized her just the same. She lifted her glasses to make eye contact with me, then drew her index finger across her throat in the universal symbol for "You're so fucked." Then she headed inside behind Tamara, the men covering her rear. Galina wanted to be in at the kill.

Still in a crouch, I charged as fast as I could back to the door, slammed it shut, and jammed the hasp of the padlock closed. It wouldn't buy us more than a few seconds, but that delay might be the difference between living and dying.

When I got back to him, Wolfgang was still screaming, blood pouring through his fingers and running down his shirt. A second shot hit the wall behind him, and he hadn't moved from where I left him, apparently finding it hard to believe he was about to be murdered. I would have been exasperated if I'd had the time. Some people just have no sense of self-preservation.

From my peripheral vision, I could see ropes dropping on either side of the belvedere which meant more goons were getting ready to abseil down from the roof. We were trapped.

"Well, shit," I muttered.

"We are going to die," Wolfgang whimpered in German.

"There is no fucking way I am getting killed by somebody who looks like Edna Mode," I told him. I made a quick assessment. It was impossible to take a stand in that situation, so I did the only thing I could under the circumstances. I spun on my heel and bent, driving my shoulder into Wolfgang's midsection, flipping him neatly over the parapet. Shots were ringing out as I followed him, diving out just as the first of Galina's henchmen rappelled down from the roof.

Wolfgang shrieked again and I couldn't blame him. One minute he was standing upright and clearly convinced he was bleeding to death, the next he was flying through the air, ass over teakettle. He landed hard on the roof next door, a drop of maybe twelve feet. I went over the parapet right after him. Wolfgang was right where he'd landed, clutching a vent stack and babbling in fear. I dropped next to him and was up before he'd even registered he wasn't dead. Honestly, I was a little surprised he made it, but I'd figured they were going to kill him anyway, so I might as well at least try to save him. I hauled him up by his collar and shoved him forward as bullets rained around us. We hit the edge and he stopped dead, blubbering a little.

"We don't have time for this," I told him as a series of shots rattled the tiles, heading towards our feet. I shoved between his shoulder blades. He flailed, windmilling his arms as he took his second dive, but this one was a shorter distance, maybe six feet. We landed on a neighbor's terrace—I rolled and ended up on my feet, Wolfgang flattened a collapsible lounge chair. He was still disentangling himself when Helen stepped out from behind a potted palm and opened fire, covering us until I got Wolfgang up and across the terrace, making it through the door. She was in good form, dropping two of Galina's men with a pair of quick shots. One of them was still attached to his abseiling harness and he swung there, gently, like a ham in a butcher shop window. Helen followed us through the door and the three of us charged down the stairs towards the street level.

It was going to be a footrace to the boat, but at least Wolfgang had finally figured out his best chance was with us. He was still screaming a little, and if I'd had time, I would have stopped to slap him.

Natalie had been posted around the corner, and she emerged from the alley, covering us as we ran. Mary Alice had stayed with the boat in case things went south. You might think that because I was in position to take the brunt of the action, I'd drawn the short straw, but you'd be wrong—I drew the longest. Whatever happened, we all wanted to be at the sharp end, and Mary Alice had been forty kinds of pissed she was going to miss it, but as the four of us charged up, bullets flying, she was in charge of the rescue.

I looked up at the scala as we ran and saw Galina, halfway up and staring at the carnage of her ambush in obvious rage. She raised her gun and aimed directly at me. I don't know what would have happened if she'd gotten the shot off, but Helen fired first, hitting the barrel of Galina's gun and sending it spinning out of her hand. Galina yelled and grabbed what was left of her hand. She'd probably broken a bone or two, but the most important thing is it bought us a few seconds to get to the boat. Heavy footsteps pounded behind us, and I realized Natalie had missed someone on her mop-up. We had arranged that she would make her own way back, and she must have miscounted when she peeled off to leave our flank exposed. We made tracks for the boat, tumbling into it together as Mary Alice stared.

"What the hell happened?" Mary Alice demanded as we untangled ourselves.

"Shut up and *go*," Helen yelled. She and Wolfgang headed for the cabin, taking cover while I brought up the rear. Mary Alice revved the engine, opening the throttle to get us out of there. Just as we pulled away from the mooring, one of Galina's goons leapt, crossing a good five feet of water in a running jump.

Before I could turn, he was on me, grabbing my shoulders as he brought all of his weight to bear me down onto the deck.

The instinct in situations like that is to fight back immediately, but it's almost always better to go limp, using the fall to position yourself. In this case, I twisted as we fell, and we landed like lovers, with his body covering mine, hands still at my shoulders. The weight of him was nearly crushing me as his chest pressed down on me. His fingers went to my throat, tightening. Mary Alice, at the front of the boat, was too busy driving to notice what was happening, and I assumed Helen was busy taking care of Wolfgang and making sure he hadn't acquired any more bullet holes. I was on my own with this one, and I didn't have much time. Black spots were starting to dance across my field of vision. I figured I had less than half a minute before I lost consciousness altogether.

Something flickered at the edge of my vision—the Ponte de la Cortesia—and I realized where we were. I closed my eyes, tracing a path on my mental map of Venice. Mary Alice was breaking all the speed limits, keeping the throttle open as we blew through the water. The goon was still on top of me, squeezing, and I knew I had one chance.

Just past the Ponte de la Cortesia is the Ponte de San Paterniàn. It's not a remarkable bridge; it's not particularly pretty, and it's not very high. It was the last fact I was counting on. I reached down and grabbed his genitals hard and gave them a twist. His reaction was to stop killing me for just an instant as he drew his pelvis back, giving me the opening I needed.

I pulled my knees up to his chest and just as we passed under the Ponte de San Paterniàn, I kicked my legs out as hard as I could, thrusting upwards and pushing his head directly into the stone bridge. I expected a hit, but the dull crunch was a bit of a surprise—kind of like the sound of tearing a head of iceberg lettuce in two. It was loud enough that Mary Alice heard it over the engine. She whirled around, taking in the situation at a glance.

"Shit!"

"I'm on it," I told her. I heaved his body over the side. What was left of his head followed.

"He's just going to bob back up to the surface," Mary Alice called.

"Good," I yelled back. "Maybe it will be a warning to the others."

Mary Alice grinned as she turned back to the wheel. She piloted us out of the small canal just as the sun rose fully over the city, turning the water of the Grand Canal to molten gold. Helen emerged from the cabin.

"Wolfgang's fine. The bullet nicked his ear is all," she told me. She looked at the deck where blood had puddled along with a few less savory bits. "Problem?"

"I handled it," I told her.

I pulled out my phone and opened the Menopaws app which Minka had updated with a tracker. I watched the little dot that represented Natalie making its way back to the house, moving fast. In spite of Galina's best efforts, the four of us had survived. I turned my face to the rising sun and smiled. We'd come out of a gunfight alive, we had kept Wolfie from getting killed, and for now the adrenaline was keeping all the aches and pains at bay. It was a good morning to be alive.

CHAPTER TWENTY-TWO

NEW YORK, 1994

"LADIES, THANK YOU FOR BEING SO PROMPT. I AM MARILYN CARSTAIRS, Provenance." The speaker stops to take a drink of water, spilling a little as she sets the glass down. She blots the tiny puddle with a tissue from her pocket and clears her throat.

"You don't have to be nervous," Helen tells her kindly.

Marilyn darts her gaze around the table at the foursome assembled for the meeting. "I've never met anyone in Exhibitions before. Actually, this is the first time I've done a briefing in person. Usually we just send the dossiers by courier," she admits. She doesn't want to say that she is nervous in a room with four killers, but she doesn't need to. Like all predators, they can smell fear.

"We don't bite," Natalie says. "Unless it's called for." She grins, baring her teeth at the hapless woman from Provenance.

"Knock it off, Nat," Billie says, but there's no heat to it.

"Marilyn? Why don't you just tell us why we're here." She tries to be encouraging, but there's an edge to her voice, an edge that says she'd rather be somewhere else. In-person briefings are rare for the Museum, reserved for extremely high-profile or complicated hits. And it's been years since she worked with the others. They've been given assignments around the world, usually solo, sometimes in a group, but not all together, and Billie has been surprised to arrive at the meeting and find the others already in attendance.

There had been no inkling of a reunion, just a postcard of the Empire State Building. A coded message scribbled in pencil gave the exact address and time, but no further information. Her plane ticket had been waiting at the airport counter, a car had collected her at the other end. The Acquisitions agent behind the wheel had driven her straight to the rendezvous on 70th, a block away from the Explorers Club. The brownstone is unremarkable except for the security system which is as discreet as it is comprehensive. The door opens before she can knock, and another Acquisitions agent shows her to the meeting room. Billie sees several closed doors on the way, and behind them all is the hushed murmur of contained power. The air smells like wax and wood fires and burnt coffee.

She is shown in, the last of the four to arrive, and after a round of greetings, they are seated at a table stacked with folders. The files are dark blue, each marked with a seal in gold, falling stars surrounded by an elegantly lettered phrase. Fiat justitia ruat caelum, the motto of the Museum. *Let justice be done though the heavens fall.* Sitting on the far side of the table is a woman in beige. It's not just her clothes. Her skin, her hair, her very aura is beige. The pin in her lapel is a ladybug, the only sign of personality in her appearance. But when she spills the water during her introduction, Billie understands she is afraid of the killers in the room. Provenance agents are information people, gathering facts from resources all over the world, harvesting data and stockpiling it, carefully sorting and arranging until the patterns emerge. From those patterns, targets are identified for either recruitment or assassination. Marilyn Carstairs doesn't know it, but they find her just as alarming as she finds them.

She clears her throat again and starts over, her voice a little firmer.

"I am here to brief you on your next assignment. I have prepared a set of files for each of you," she adds, nodding towards the pile of folders in front of them. They reach for the top one on each stack. Inside is a photograph of a man in his forties, good-looking but not ostentatiously so. He is almost smiling at the camera, one side of his mouth quirked up into a lopsided attempt at a grin. He is dressed in khaki and holding a small Egyptian figurine. It is made of alabaster and wearing a solemn expression that the man seems to be gently mocking.

As they study their files, Marilyn pulls down a white screen and turns on a slide projector. She fumbles with a remote until an image beams onto the screen, the same photograph of the man in khaki.

"This is Fermín Bosque," Marilyn tells them.

The name means nothing to them. Bosque is not famous

or even infamous. He is simply the latest link in a chain that stretches back fifty years—a link which must be broken.

Natalie focuses on the artifact in his hands. "Is that a funerary figure?"

Traditionally, royal Egyptian tombs are crammed with the little statues. They represent those who would serve their masters in the afterlife, ensuring all comforts would be present, all needs met. Originals in good condition are rare and costly; cheap reproductions flood the tourist market. They make for handy souvenirs—tiny, wide-eyed figures that will go on to collect dust on suburban bookshelves for decades to come.

"Ushabti, actually," Marilyn says, pushing her glasses up her nose. "Late Twenty-First Dynasty. And authentic, although the gentleman in question went to great lengths to pretend otherwise."

"Wait," Mary Alice says, holding up a hand. "This guy wanted people to think an original artifact was fake? Isn't it usually the other way around?"

"Not in this case," Marilyn says. "Egypt has strict laws about exporting authentic items. So this gentleman disguises real artifacts as cheap reproductions in order to get them past Customs. The paperwork that establishes the provenance always travels separately so as not to tip off the authorities that he's illegally shipping artifacts out of the country."

"How does he disguise them?" Billie asks.

Marilyn explains, speaking more quickly, with more animation in her voice as she grows comfortable with her audience. "A variety of ways, depending upon the items. They might be painted over, dipped in plastic, covered in plaster of paris. Once he has them safely back in his workshop in England, he removes the disguises and restores them to their original condition."

"That's a hell of a risk," Natalie says. "Egyptian antiquities aren't exactly sturdy stuff. He could easily ruin a valuable piece."

"That is a risk he's apparently willing to take," Marilyn replies. "After restoration, the pieces are sold to collectors, complete with the authentic Egyptian provenance. And if, for whatever reason, he cannot supply an authentic provenance, he isn't above faking one." She runs through the next few slides. There are more photographs, a few of a cluttered workshop, one of a happy collector posing with a newly acquired mummy mask.

After they've studied the picture for a moment, Marilyn switches to a fresh slide, this one with biographical data including the target's name.

"You said his workshop is in England. Fermín Bosque doesn't sound English," Billie remarks.

"German by way of Argentina," Marilyn explains.

Mary Alice looks up with a grin. "I smell a Nazi."

"Your instincts are correct, Miss Tuttle. Fermín Bosque is the grandson of Albrecht Danner." The next slide is black-and-white, taken at some sort of party function. Hanging in the background are wide banners marked with swastikas. In front of the banners is a small group, and in the center of that group is a familiar figure with a narrow toothbrush mustache and untidy hair. "Danner is standing to Hitler's right," she explains, pointing out the taller, slimmer man with a matching mustache. On the other side of the Führer is the unmistakable bulk of Hermann Göring. At the edge of the photograph are easels, each set with a painting in a heavy gilded frame.

"What do we know about Albrecht Danner?" Mary Alice asks.

"He was a wealthy industrialist from Mainz. He made his money in dog food. But Danner was keen to downplay his origins and promote his role as an art collector and amateur archaeologist. He donated several pieces to Hitler for the Führermuseum."

Marilyn clicks on another slide, this one showing a model of a massive, sprawling complex, building after building rendered in ghostly white. "The Führermuseum was Hitler's pet project, a plan to establish a sort of German national museum in Linz. It was expected to hold the greatest artworks from all of western Europe—paintings, sculpture, weapons, jewelry."

She flicks back to the group shot of the previous slide and points towards the robust figure standing next to Hitler. "To that end, he tasked this man, Hermann Göring, with acquiring the art to fill it. Göring assembled the art from a variety of sources. Some was taken from other museums, national collections seized by the Germans when they invaded. Some was looted as Germans passed through towns which held particular items of interest. That's how they got the Ghent Altarpiece," she adds with a frown. "And some was taken from Jewish families who were forced to abandon their possessions when they fled or were forced into camps."

She changes to a slide showing an enormous warehouse

stacked with paintings, clothes, beds, even shoes. They are all silent at this, but Natalie's silence is heavier than the others'. She stares at the piles of household goods, each representing hundreds, thousands of people displaced. Destroyed.

"Let's move on," Helen tells Marilyn gently.

Marilyn is momentarily confused until she remembers what she has learned about these killers from each of their files, facts clicking into place like tumblers in a lock. Natalie's grandmother. Dutch Resistance. Missing in the war.

"I'm sorry, Miss Schuyler," she stammers.

Natalie doesn't respond, and Helen repeats herself. "Let's move on." Her voice is a little firmer this time, and Marilyn presses the button on the remote.

It is a studio portrait of Albrecht Danner. The photographer who took the picture has captured the image of a prosperous man who looks pleased with himself. "Because of their mutual interest in art and Danner's generosity in donating paintings to the planned museum, he and Hitler became friendly. Besides collecting paintings, Danner had traveled extensively in Egypt and funded numerous archaeological expeditions, most of them complete failures. When Hitler needed a discreet envoy to send to Egypt in 1941, Danner was the obvious choice."

"Why did Hitler need an envoy to Egypt?" Billie asks.

"He wanted secret talks opened with King Farouk. At the time, Egypt was under British control, but Hitler believed the British would eventually be driven out. When that happened, he wanted Germany to step in to form an alliance with Egypt. The goal was to eventually control the Suez Canal."

"How did things go with Farouk?" Mary Alice asks.

"Slowly," Marilyn replies. "The negotiations were top secret, of course. Farouk couldn't afford to alienate the British since they were still in charge, and he made no official promises. In the end, he was forced to declare war on Germany, but only at the very last minutes of the war—1945 to be exact."

"Better late to the party than never get to dance, I suppose," Mary Alice remarks.

"It was nothing more than a way of saving official face, but it meant that Danner couldn't easily return to Egypt. In fact, he was forced to flee Germany ahead of the Allied invasion. He landed in Argentina where he took the name Bosque."

"I suppose he thought that was clever," Billie puts in.

"Why?" Helen asks.

"Danner and Bosque are both words related to trees," Billie explains. She turns back to Marilyn. "So why would this little Nazi even want to go back to Egypt?"

"Because he left something behind." Marilyn puts the remote down and gestures towards the files in front of them. "Each of these folders is full of photographs and notes regarding the cache of art Albrecht Danner stashed in Egypt in 1941. He may have been on a diplomatic mission for Hitler, but he also used that trip to purchase an enormous load of Egyptian antiquities—all of them incredibly cheap because, after all, there was a war on. Papyri, jewels, statues, grave goods, sarcophagi. He bought them all and left them in Egypt to be collected when the war was over. He anticipated a German victory and presumed it would be safe to retrieve them."

"Only Germany doesn't win and he's left with a load of Egyptian antiquities he can't retrieve," Billie adds. "But after a few years, the heat would have died down. He could have slipped back into the country. Why didn't he?"

"By 1950, Albrecht Danner was dead. Stomach cancer."

"Oh no. So sad," Mary Alice says in a deadpan voice.

"He left a family behind," Marilyn carries on. "A son, Maximilian, who was seven when they left Germany and whose name was changed to Maximiliano. According to our research, this son had no interest in Egypt at all. He never left Argentina. He lived quietly and did not appear to share his father's political leanings. He taught mathematics at a university in Buenos Aires and died two years ago. That brings us to his son, Albrecht Danner's grandson and your mark—Fermín Bosque."

She returns to the slide of the smiling man with the ushabti. "Fermín appears to have inherited his grandfather's interest in antiquities and has made many trips to Egypt. He runs a small business dealing in the sale of artifacts. To all appearances, he is legitimate. But we know that he has been selling authentic pieces after smuggling them out of Egypt and occasionally faking provenances when necessary."

"Since when does the Museum care about a little smuggling?" Billie asks.

"Since we discovered what else his grandfather stashed in Egypt." Marilyn gestures towards the folders. "More artwork, but these pieces are not Egyptian. They are European—paintings looted from Jewish families in Austria and Germany at the start of the war."

She skims through the next slides, each featuring a dozen images. They flick past like a carousel of extraordinary works, every piece more exquisite than the last.

"Danner was tasked with assessing the various collections seized from prominent Jewish collectors. The most famous paintings—those on Göring's personal shopping list—were immediately pulled and sent to Göring to hang in his country house at Carinhall. Others were crated up and delivered to various storage facilities in Germany and Austria. In the course of our research, we have discovered that Danner kept two sets of books. One was a meticulous record of the transactions I've just described—art procured for members of the Third Reich."

"And the other?" Mary Alice asks.

"An inventory of the pieces Danner kept for himself— pieces he brought with him to Egypt in 1941."

"He smuggled pieces *in*?" Helen stares at the images on the slides that are still changing. "But how?"

"He labeled them furniture and household goods. And nobody has ever been much concerned with what gets into Egypt, only what goes out," Marilyn tells her. "Once the shipments arrived, they were taken to a storage facility in Cairo. From there, the trail went cold, and every piece was presumed lost. Until now."

She returns the slides to the image of Fermín Bosque. "Fermín was a small-time player, dealing in the grey margins of Egyptological artifacts." She glances at Billie. "As you pointed out, Miss Webster, these are not the sort of activities which would have ordinarily drawn our attention. But a few months ago, this painting"—she pauses and brings up a black-and-white slide featuring a painting with a heavily carved frame—"was put up for auction at a small house in Sweden. It had been purchased privately only last year from Fermín Bosque. Our research has confirmed it was one of the paintings his grandfather looted from a family in Stuttgart. It is *The Rape of Atalanta* by Rubens, depicting the attempted abduction of the heroine Atalanta by the centaur Hylaeus."

"And you're sure it's authentic?" Mary Alice asks, her tone frankly skeptical.

"As sure as we can be. Everything was tested with the most up-to-date methods—canvas, wooden stretchers, pigments—and it all checks out."

"How did we get our hands on samples?" Billie asks.

Marilyn hesitates. "We don't care to divulge specifics of how we work in Provenance, but I can tell you that the purchaser of the piece at auction wished to authenticate it for insurance purposes. He used a firm with whom we have a . . . relationship."

Billie smiles. "A relationship? Or do you mean it's just an arm of the Provenance department masquerading as a legitimate firm?"

Marilyn stiffens noticeably, and when she answers it is with a mouth that is tightly pursed. "It is in the Museum's best interests to keep a finger on the pulse of whatever is happening in the art world. It has been a long time since we managed to secure a cache of art looted by Nazis."

"Thirteen years, to be exact," Billie shoots back. "I know because I was there. We all were."

"Of course," Marilyn replies, her mouth relaxing. "The Zanzibar job. That was an extremely important get for us. That's why you've been chosen for this one."

She returns to her slides, putting up a new one, a landscape so desolate it looks lunar. "The Valley of the Kings. Albrecht Danner's favorite playground and where we believe he stashed the art he smuggled into Egypt after it left Cairo. Chosen, we assume, for its remoteness as well as its suitability for storing art. The low humidity and darkness mimic the salt mines in Europe where the bulk of the Nazi loot was stored."

"Why do you think the art was stored in the Valley of the Kings?" Nat asks.

"The condition of *Atalanta*. We would have expected a piece squirreled away in a storeroom somewhere for five decades would show traces of where it has been. And there was some wear and tear, but the painting was in remarkably good shape, all things considered. That suggested it had been stored in conditions of low humidity. Coupled with what we knew of Danner's activities and travels, we formed the hypothesis that the painting had been taken to Egypt and left there for some time. With that in mind, we went looking for anything that might confirm or discount our working theory. It was a tiny blade of grass that proved it," she adds with a smile, the first she's offered them. "We found it caught in a bit of the outer wrappings, barely thicker than a thread—a variety of sedge that grows only on the banks of the Nile. In the times of the pharaohs, it was dried to make papyri. For us, it proved that this particular painting had been in Egypt."

"Damn, Carstairs, you're a regular Agatha Christie," Nat says.

Marilyn pinks again and pushes her glasses up her nose. "Well, I don't know about that, but it was a *very* satisfactory conclusion to the case."

"Why did he wait so long to retrieve his grandfather's stash?" Mary Alice asks.

"We think he only found out about it when his father died two years ago. Fermín inherited his grandfather's papers and a short while later made a few trips to Paris and Koblenz to do archival research. Following that he made two trips to Cairo with detours to the Valley of the Kings. We think he has thus far only brought back a limited number of artifacts and paintings, using them to test the waters, so to speak, for retrieving the entire cache. If we are correct—and there is no reason to think we aren't—*Atalanta* was his first major sale. He has been very, very careful."

"The Valley of the Kings isn't exactly off the beaten path," Helen says thoughtfully. "It might have been remote in Danner's time, but it's a tourist attraction now. It must be tricky for him to bring things out."

"More so after recent terror attacks on the popular tourist sites," Marilyn agrees. "Egyptian authorities have increased security enormously in order to protect the tourism business they depend on. Eluding the security forces would be just as difficult for Fermín Bosque as evading the terrorists themselves. And even more dangerous for him if he were apprehended."

Billie flicks through the catalog Provenance has compiled, an entry for each work believed to be in Bosque's cache. Besides the pages of Egyptological artifacts, there are dozens of European paintings, most of them traditional Old Masters, things chosen not just for their beauty but for their ability to hold their value. Most are small, their dimensions making it simpler to remove them from Germany as well as stash them in Egypt. She thumbs through reproductions of sketches from Leonardo and Dürer, a delicate Van Eyck, a Botticelli engraving.

The others are doing the same, each pausing on a different page.

"My god. What he stole would fill an entire museum," Helen says, gesturing towards the remaining files. Two dozen folders lie on the table in front of her, each crammed with photographs and notes.

"Not this guy," Mary Alice reminds her. "His grandfather."

"His grandfather may have stolen it, but Bosque kept it," Helen replies. "That makes him just as much of a thief."

"And he's the one planning to sell it," Billie says. She is about to say more when she turns the next page and the words stick in her throat. She is looking at an image she has never seen before, but one she feels she has always known. The setting is a garden, lush with olive trees and a pomegranate in the foreground, bursting with ripe fruit that spill their scarlet seeds to the grass. Beside the pomegranate tree is a woman whose face is familiar, and it takes Billie a minute to place her. She has the smooth dark hair of Ingres's *La Grande Odalisque*, the same luminous skin and cool stare. But there is something more in her gaze, a challenge to the viewer, a sense that the flush rising in her cheeks is due to something that is both shameful and irresistible. At the woman's side is a swan, an enormous beast with snowy wings outstretched to embrace her, one feather trailing along the bared silken thigh. At their feet is a nest with a clutch of four eggs, the result of their strange coupling.

"*Leda and the Swan,*" Billie murmurs as she skims the notes.

"What are you looking at?" Mary Alice asks idly.

"Miss Webster has identified the most important item in Bosque's collection," Marilyn says, pulling up the corresponding slide. "Raphael's *Leda and the Swan.*"

"Oh my," Nat breathes, reaching for the page to compare it to the slide. "That's where she's been."

"What's the big deal about it?" Mary Alice asks, squinting at the image. "Everybody and their cat has painted a version of this."

"And the most significant ones are missing," Billie tells her. "Raphael was one of the big three of the Renaissance along with Leonardo and Michelangelo. Those two both did versions of *Leda,* but theirs are long gone. Raphael's was the only one that survived—until it didn't."

"Until now," Marilyn corrects smoothly. She seems a little miffed to have her narrative interrupted by Billie and she hurries to fill in the blanks. "Raphael worked at the Vatican at the same time as Michaelangelo. Both were engaged to paint the papal chambers, but they were also given other commissions to carry out on behalf of the pope. This *Leda* was commissioned by His Holiness as a gift for King Francis I of France. She hung at his palace at Fontainebleau during the king's lifetime. After his death, the painting was sold out of the royal family's collection to a private owner and eventually changed hands several more times. She went up at auction through the major houses in England—Sotheby's, Christie's. Even Tollemache's. Every time she sold, she at least doubled or tripled the price she'd gotten the time before. Her last sale was to a Jewish collector in Salzburg. Then she disappeared."

"So Danner snaffled her up before Göring could get his hands on her," Billie says.

"He did," Marilyn affirms. "We have the records he kept noting where and when he acquired the painting and he was very careful not to leave any trace of her for Göring."

"So he went to all that trouble to get his hands on her and then brought her to Egypt to sit in a cave for fifty years," Mary Alice says.

"He couldn't have known that," Helen points out reasonably. "After all, he believed the Third Reich would be victorious. He expected Germany would take control of Egypt and then he'd have been free to do as he liked with his collection."

"And if they failed, he had the means to finance his getaway," Marilyn adds. "Only he never made it back to Egypt and the collection languished there for decades."

"Do you think Maximiliano knew his father had been sitting on a gold mine?" Billie asks.

Marilyn thinks a moment, then shakes her head. "No. He was careful to conceal any mention of his family's history. No one in Argentina knew where the Bosques had come from. We suspect Maximiliano never even looked at his father's papers, and if he did, he might have assumed—quite logically— that the collection had been seized after the war."

"And then Fermín inherits his grandfather's papers and sets off on a wild-goose chase," Billie says.

"Only to find an actual wild goose at the end of it," Nat says with a nod towards the painted swan. She cocks her head as she studies the painting. "How much is it worth?"

"More than all the rest combined," Marilyn answers coolly. "There is another missing Raphael. His *Portrait of a Young Man,* seized from a Polish noble family at the beginning of the war. Despite their best efforts, the Monuments Men were never able to recover it during their cleanup afterwards. Its current whereabouts are still unknown although there are suspicions it never left Poland." Nat gives her a narrow look and Marilyn sighs. "Its estimated value is in excess of a hundred million dollars U.S. The value of *Leda* would probably be more. Raphael painted several portraits, but only two others with a Greek mythological theme. That makes it exceedingly rare. I would suggest one hundred and twenty million would not be unreasonable. Perhaps even higher."

"One. Hundred. And. Twenty. Million. Dollars," Nat says flatly.

"U.S.," Marilyn says.

"Do you suppose Bosque knows that?" Mary Alice asks.

"If he does, he's going to move her fast," Billie says. "He will have used other works to test his ways of moving art out of the country. Since they were successful, he'd move the

Raphael sooner. No way he leaves her for last." She looks around the group. "How fast can we figure out a way to kill Bosque?"

Dinner reservations have been made for them at Lutèce, but they miss their table and eat take-out sandwiches instead. They do not leave the meeting room until dawn is breaking the next morning. There are details to work out, but the broad strokes are complete. It is an audacious plan, relying on timing, nerve, and only a little luck.

It is the 6th of May, 1994. Fermín Bosque has three days left to live.

CHAPTER TWENTY-THREE

IF WE'D HAD TIME, WE WOULD HAVE DEBATED THE WISDOM OF BRINGING Wolfgang to the house, but I figured the faster we got off the streets, the better. The last thing you want in our line of work is to be memorable. Venice is a city that wakes slowly, and—with no actual rush hour to speak of—there aren't many places to hide. Besides that, Wolfgang was still making a spectacle of himself, dripping gore onto his shirt and blubbering in broken German. I fished his phone out of his pocket and dumped it in a canal just in case Galina was tracking him after all. He was so busy crying he didn't even notice.

Mary Alice brought us as close as she could to the house, maneuvering the boat into a narrow channel behind the campo. From there it was a fast walk of two minutes to get into the house, and we made a point of coming from the opposite direction as the police station.

Akiko was waiting at the door, her face creased in worry

wrinkles until she saw Wolfgang covered in blood. At that point, she swayed and had to sit down.

"What happened?" she asked, her voice muffled by the fact that she had her head in her hands.

"Shootout," Helen said succinctly.

Akiko gave a low moan.

"I'm fine, honey, we're all fine," Mary Alice assured her. She knelt on the floor next to Akiko, circling her wife with an arm.

"I am not fine!" Wolfgang howled.

I shoved him towards the bathroom. "Let's get you cleaned up."

Helen looked at me. "Are you sure? It's not going to be pretty."

"I'd rather put him back together than witness whatever's coming next," I said with a nod towards the married couple in our midst. The only thing less interesting than my relationship problems is other people's.

Just then, Taverner emerged from the kitchen, wiping his hands on a dish towel. He took in the scene with a glance, assessing the situation. He looked at me long enough to realize the blood flowing freely wasn't mine and then went back to the kitchen. I knew there was going to be a conversation coming that I didn't want to be a part of, but that was a problem for later. The first priority was to mop up Wolfgang and keep him from going into shock.

Wolfgang followed me to the bathroom where I sat him down on the toilet lid and went to work. Cleaning the wound was the worst part. The bullet had clipped the bottom of the lobe, shearing a bit of it clean off. If we'd had the piece, we might have sewn it back on. As it was, I had to make do with pinning the edges together as neatly as I could and securing them with tiny stitches. When it was finished, I sprayed it with antiseptic and bandaged it, then gave him a couple of painkillers and an antibiotic shot out of the medical kit I always carried. It was basic, just the nuts and bolts, but it could handle a lot of small jobs. Luckily, in our line of work, a missing bit of earlobe was considered a small job.

"I'm not the best at this, but it'll do," I told him. "I should have asked Helen to stitch it. At least she does needlepoint."

He shrugged, looking down at his hands. His shirt was sticky with coagulated blood, and I helped him peel it off, handing him a warm washcloth to mop himself up. He was built like a toddler, pale with a sloping belly. I brought him a henley of Taverner's which was too small, but he stretched it over the curve of his stomach. He looked up as I rinsed out his shirt the best I could, soaking and wringing until the water ran pink and then clear. I hung it up. The stains would never fully come out, but at least it fit him and would be clean.

"She shot me, didn't she?"

His hands were shaking a little—delayed shock setting in. Little crescents of blood had dried under the whites of his fingernails.

"Yeah. I'm sorry." Galina herself may not have pulled the trigger, but we both knew she'd given the order.

"What happens now?" he asked in a small voice.

I took the washcloth and wiped up some blood he'd missed on his cheek. "What happens now is we eat."

249

———

NATALIE HAD ARRIVED BY THE TIME WOLFGANG AND I JOINED THE group. She was looking a little the worse for wear, but most of the blood belonged to other folks and her eyes were bright as she told the others how she took out two of Galina's hired ruffians.

"I mean, I've seen people bang two guys' heads together in movies, but I've never had the chance to try it for myself," she was saying. "It makes a fun little crack. Like coconuts."

She stopped and looked up in surprise at Wolfgang. "What happened to you?"

"They shot me," he said morosely.

"Bummer. The first time's always a bitch," she told him. "Get something to eat. You'll feel better."

The next few minutes were spent loading our plates. When the adrenaline fades after a fight, the only things you want to do are eat and have sex, and sex wasn't on the table that morning. So we filled up on eggs Benedict and sourdough cardamom cinnamon rolls, courtesy of Taverner, and when our plates were finally empty we pushed them away and looked at each other.

"Postmortem?" Helen asked. The rest of us nodded and she began. "I think it's safe to say that could have gone better."

"Well, we couldn't really anticipate that she would try to kill Wolfgang," Natalie pointed out.

"I cannot believe it," he said, still looking dazed.

"Wolfie, you realize you're not safe until we take her out," I said.

250

He nodded miserably. "She is a monster."

"Don't take it personally. She killed her own aunt, after all," Natalie reminded him soothingly.

He said a few things in German—mainly expressions of woe—and lapsed into silence, covering his face with his hands. Mary Alice gave me a look, jerking her head towards him. I sighed and patted his shoulder awkwardly.

"It's okay, Wolfgang. We'll protect you," I promised him. "And the sooner we find her, the sooner we can take care of this and you can go back to hitting those high Cs."

He pushed his bottom lip out. "I do not have a high C. That is for tenors."

"Whatever. As long as Galina is out there, you aren't safe. You can't go home, you can't work. Help us, Wolfie."

His fingers were busy, picking at a few drops of dried blood on his hands. "She tried to kill me," he said, maybe more to himself than to us.

"She did," I said gently. "Maybe next time, Galina tries herself or maybe she lets Tamara have another pop at you. And maybe she hits her bull's-eye." I pressed a fingertip to the center of his forehead and he shuddered.

I went on. "Wolfie, you didn't tell us anything when we met yesterday. You didn't betray Galina. There was no reason whatsoever for her to give the order to kill you—except that she's a sadistic bitch. And she's not going to stop until she's dead. Or you are."

I think he'd have caved then, but before he could speak, Taverner brought out another pan of cinnamon rolls dripping in cardamom cream cheese frosting. Wolfie looked up, sniffing the air like a dog. Taverner handed him the entire pan and a fork, and Wolfie gave him a worshipful look. Wolfie busied himself for a few minutes, and just when I was about to try again, he looked up, cream cheese wreathing his mouth.

"What do you want to know?"

I smiled. "Everything, Wolfie. Everything."

CHAPTER TWENTY-FOUR

ONCE WOLFIE MADE UP HIS MIND TO WORK WITH US, HE SANG LIKE the canary he was. He didn't know much about Galina's professional life, but he told us everything he'd picked up over their few months together. Taverner kept him supplied with coffee thickened with cream and plates of food, and as long as Wolfie was eating, he was talking. He chomped his way through sandwiches of mortadella and provolone, apple turnovers, a bowl of Greek yogurt with cherry compote, and a pear tart.

"Let's start with her associates," I suggested. "Who does she see? Who hangs around her?"

"Tamara," he said with a shudder. "She is the bodyguard. Very small, very mean. But I only see her once or twice. She stays outside when Galina comes to see me."

"Anyone else?"

He waved away the idea. "Nobody. Galina is private. I never meet family or friends."

"What do you know about her business? About her brother's, Pasha's, business?"

He thought for a moment as he chewed. "I heard Galina yell at him on the phone once about being too lazy, about not working hard enough. That too much was left to her. She says they must spend money to make money, but Pasha was living too well, keeping profits she wanted to put into the business."

"But you don't know what kind of business?" I pressed.

"No, but sometimes she changes phone numbers or hotels without warning. This is not the sign of someone who is doing legitimate business. Galina is a woman with many secrets."

"Are you lovers?" I asked.

He shook his head so vehemently, little crumbs of pastry went flying. "No, no! I earned my role at La Fenice," he said stoutly.

"Of course you did," Helen told him in a soothing tone. She darted a look at me and I shrugged. She was welcome to take over.

"Has she helped other protégés like you?" Helen asked.

He shrugged. "Some. But none with as good a voice as me." He thumped his chest for emphasis.

"How did you meet?" was Helen's follow-up.

"I was singing at a music festival in Nürnberg," he answered through a mouthful of mortadella. "She travels much to such places, small festivals to find undiscovered talent, she says." His eyes welled and he stopped chewing. "She says I am the find of a lifetime." He folded his hands in his lap and his expression was tragic. "She is so private, so careful of her little secrets. She never tells me where she travels but often she leaves for short trips a few days here and there, sometimes a week. She is so secretive, I tease her about bodies buried in the garden." He broke off with a shudder. "I thought it was a joke." He dropped his face into his hands and began to cry.

We let him sniffle for a few minutes before Akiko spoke to Mary Alice in a low voice. "Why don't you just ask him where she lives? She has to have a house or favorite hotel here."

"Because she won't go back there," Natalie put in. "She knows we've got Wolfie, so she'll burn her connection to any place he knew about. She'll be on the run now. All the more reason for her to kill him, actually. The sooner he's dead, the sooner she can get her life back to normal."

Wolfie moaned and dropped his hands. His face was a mess of tears and snot and a few streaks of dried blood I'd missed.

Taverner took a handkerchief from his pocket. He always carried a handkerchief, handy for makeshift tourniquets or bandages—or even a white flag of surrender, except Taverner had never given up on anything in his life. We usually used our own initials for cover identities, so he could have had them monogrammed, but his were stitched with a tiny oak leaf in one corner instead.

Taverner handed the handkerchief over and Wolfie mopped his face. When he looked up, he seemed a little calmer and about a thousand years older.

"Come on in the kitchen," Taverner urged. "I'm going to

put on a fresh pot of coffee. And I think there are some more cinnamon rolls."

Wolfie shambled after him, looking dead on his feet as he followed Taverner into the kitchen, meek as a lamb. Adrenaline takes some people like that. He'd had a massive shot of it and then an even bigger crash. He would probably be out of it for a few hours which was fine by me. Wolfie might have become another target on Galina's list, which should have made him our natural ally, but that didn't mean I completely trusted him.

Minka, who'd been notably quiet through it all as she tapped away on her screen, gave me a narrow look. "The shooting at him, it was real? Not just a ruse for getting him here so Galina could follow and ambush you?"

I shook my head, remembering all the crying and shaking he'd done as well as the expression of abject disbelief in his eyes. "Nope. He's not that good of an actor."

"And it wasn't an accident?" Natalie added.

"No. She brought a pack of mercenaries with her and the shooter had a clear line. They were after Wolfgang, and they wanted to take him out first so he couldn't talk."

"Excellent," Mary Alice said briskly. "That means he knows something worth telling."

"Exactly," I replied, pouring a cup of coffee from the dregs of the old pot.

"But he just said he didn't," Akiko pointed out.

Helen gave her a kind look. "No, dear. He doesn't *think* he does. And that's a different thing altogether."

"So what now?" Akiko asked.

It was Natalie who answered. "Now we get to practice our interrogation skills."

And she looked a little too pleased at the prospect.

"Do you travel with a torture kit?" Mary Alice asked pleasantly.

"No, but it would be easy enough to put one together out of random things lying around. The kitchen is full of useful tools."

"Like what?" Akiko demanded. I hoped for Mary Alice's sake she wasn't taking notes.

Natalie shrugged. "Off the top of my head? Meat mallet, corkscrew, cheese wire. You can do some pretty messed-up shit with a melon baller, come to think of it."

"Natalie," Mary Alice cut in sharply. "We are not going to torture an innocent man for information."

Nat rolled her eyes. "Of course not. We're just going to make him *think* we are."

"Hold off on the psy ops," I told her. "I think this is a flies-and-honey situation. He's still in shock from being shot. Any more pressure and he may crack entirely."

Just then Taverner emerged from the kitchen.

"How's our guest?" I asked him.

"Much calmer now. In fact, he remembered that Galina told him she was taking over for her brother on a very important deal, something about Montenegro. She was getting ready to travel."

I remembered what Grigory had drunkenly sniveled about not trusting Montenegrins. "Anything else?"

He shrugged. "Apparently she was involved in the deal from the start. Lots of meetings and phone calls with someone.

He said it was Pasha's baby, but since his death, she has to finish it. Galina never told Wolfie details, but she used the phrase 'pick up,' so something must be changing hands."

"Is she collecting it personally?" Helen asked.

Taverner nodded. "She gave Wolfie the impression she was more upset about traveling to the Balkans again than she was about her brother dying. He said she seemed nervous about it."

"If Galina is so secretive, how does Wolfie know so much about the deal?" Mary Alice asked.

"They had tickets to the opera—*Don Giovanni* in Paris—but she had to cancel. Reading between the lines, he threw a bit of a strop and she had to explain why it was necessary for her to be away."

I gave him a tip of an imaginary hat. "Good job getting that much out of him."

"Nothing to it," he said. "He seemed inclined to talk. I do have one question. What's a 'stern brunch daddy'?"

Natalie gave a short howl of laughter and Taverner looked at me in puzzlement.

"It means I think I know why he and Galina aren't lovers," I told him with a grin.

He might have been past sixty and a career assassin who practiced naked tai chi in the garden, but he blushed forty shades of red. "Well, it's nice to be appreciated," he murmured. He turned to head back to the kitchen but stopped, fishing in the pocket of his apron. "Oh, I almost forgot. I had him jot down Galina's email address and a few other details. Hope it helps."

He dropped the slip of paper in my lap. "Thanks."

I looked up to where he was still standing. "You've got your guilty face on. What did you do?"

"I'm going to tell you something and you're going to want to get mad. Instead, all I want to hear is 'Thank you, Taverner.' Is that clear?"

"As the proverbial crystal. Spill it."

"I tailed Galina from the scala this morning."

"God*dammit*," I started. He folded his arms over his chest, and waited. I clapped my mouth shut. "Go on," I said through tight lips.

"She went to the train station. Just her and another woman. Shorter with a black bob. They left Venice."

"They *left*?" Mary Alice was incredulous.

"They left," Taverner confirmed.

"Maybe it was a blind," Nat suggested. "Maybe they knew they were being followed and went to the train station to lay a false trail."

"Not likely," I said flatly. I might have been pissed, but I could still admit that Taverner was the best tracker I'd ever met. His idea of a fun day out was to choose someone at random and follow them for hours without being detected. He was a ghost.

Helen shook her head. "I don't get it. Why would they just leave without finishing the job? They know we're here and Venice is a small city. With the proper resources, they could find us."

The $64,000 question. Why would Galina abandon the chance to settle a blood feud with the women who killed her father and brother? It didn't make sense. Unless—

"She had to," I said suddenly. "The only reason she'd leave is if she didn't have a choice. The Balkan deal." I turned to Taverner. "Did you see which train she got on?"

"Slow train to Trieste," he said. He paused, giving me an expectant look.

"Thank you, Taverner," I said with exaggerated sweetness. He grinned and went back to the kitchen. The slip of paper was still lying in my lap. I skimmed it before handing it over to Minka. "Can you do anything with this?"

She gave me a pitying look. "Please. I am the queen of the rodeo."

Mary Alice cocked her head. "Queen of the rodeo?"

"She heard the phrase 'not my first rodeo' and decided she has been around long enough and knows so much she must be the queen," I explained. I turned back to Minka. "Just get us her emails, please."

"Not my circus, not my monkeys," she said airily.

"That isn't how you use that one," I reminded her.

She shrugged. "Whatever."

I turned back to the others. "What other threads can we pull to get to Galina?"

"I still say I can torture him. Gently," Nat suggested.

"Let's call that Plan B, dear," Helen told her.

"I'm on it," I said with a sigh. I punched in Naomi's number, prepared to eat a little crow considering how I'd hung up on her the last time. I wasn't expecting her to pick up and immediately break the connection. I redialed, and she answered, sounding harried.

"Naomi, how nice to hear your voice. I hope you're not

holding a grudge and that's why you just hung up on me," I said, slowing my Texas drawl to cold-molasses speed.

I heard a sigh puffing down the line. "Sorry about that. I am in the office, juggling three phones and somehow managed to change my calendar to Arabic, which I can't read, so I'm having a bitch of a time figuring out how to change it back."

"Where's Lyndsay?" No woman could have it all, but Naomi came damned close thanks to her husband's efforts at home and Lyndsay's at the office. One of them wiped baby butt and braided hair, the other one took dictation and kept her calendar in order. I just hoped they never got mixed up.

"Vacation," she said shortly. "Her sister's getting married and she's the maid of honor. Seafoam green taffeta," she added before I could ask.

"For a bridesmaid's dress? That's a hate crime. I won't keep you, but I need to know—the other information that was accessed besides the Lazarov file. What was the job?"

She told me and I listened, then asked a follow-up question or two. I thanked her, and just before I hung up, I asked another. "You don't think there's any possibility that Lyndsay could be your mole, do you?"

There was a taut silence on the line. "I don't like that question."

"I don't like asking it, but you have to at least consider the possibility."

"Good-bye, Billie." The phone went dead.

I turned to the others. "The security breach in Provenance that Naomi was investigating—whoever did it accessed the Lazarov file and one other. An assassination that happened two months ago."

Mary Alice looked alert. "Whose?"

"She said it was some nasty piece of work, an art collector named Jovan Murić."

Helen raised her brows. "That was us?"

I nodded. I'd seen a brief mention in the newspapers about the death. Murić's car had rolled down a mountainside and exploded into a fireball. There hadn't been any hint of foul play which meant the killer was good—really good if they were one of ours.

"That was us. But I don't think this is about the hit itself. Pasha was working a deal in Montenegro—a deal that Galina now has to finish. And Jovan Murić was Montenegrin."

"Shiiiiiiit," Nat said under her breath. Helen was nodding slowly while Mary Alice just looked grim.

Akiko glanced around. "What did I just miss? Why would the Museum kill an art collector?"

I turned to her. "Because he wasn't just an art collector. That was a front for his real job as an arms dealer. Murić was indiscriminate. He sold to the highest bidder, everything from handguns to rocket launchers."

Mary Alice picked up the thread. "The implication is that somewhere in the Museum is a mole, accessing information from secured files they shouldn't be looking at. And then it seems this source in the Museum sold information to the Lazarovs—information about the mission that took out their father so they could exact a little revenge."

"Starting with Lilian Flanders," Nat put in.

"Starting with Lilian Flanders," Mary Alice agreed.

"Why would the Lazarovs also buy information about Murić? Is it so they could avenge him too?" Akiko asked.

I shook my head. "I don't think so. As far as Provenance can tell, there's no previous connection between the Lazarovs and Murić, no reason for them to be out to settle any scores on his account." I paused, thinking. "The point of Murić's art dealing was that it provided a cover for moving paintings around without attracting undue attention."

"Why is that important?"

"In the underworld, lots of money changes hands, only it isn't always in the form of cash. You can leverage a deal with drugs, guns, jewels. And art. Anything that has intrinsic value. And accepting a painting as collateral has one huge advantage over a shipment of heroin or handguns—it's not criminal. You can hang it on your wall if you want. If it's too hot for that, too well-known, you wrap it up and put it in a storage locker or under the bed. Nobody would think twice about it."

"There are more advantages than that," Helen put in. "Art theft is a hugely underinvestigated crime. Nobody but insurance companies really care about it. The FBI didn't even have a team dedicated to it until 2004. Interpol is trying to make up for lost time, but there are thousands and thousands of pieces missing thanks to various wars and thefts with little to no hope of recovery."

"Interpol has an app now," Minka added. "I can show you later."

Akiko looked at me. "What do you think is happening?"

"I think," I said slowly, "that there was something in that file that the Lazarovs wanted—information that would help them level up in the underworld. In our briefing materials, it said they deal mostly in club drugs. They're not big-time players. They have money, but it's not oligarch money. And if Pasha dumped a few Russian gangsters out of his windows in Mayfair, he may well have burned his bridges there. From what Wolfie told us, Galina was ambitious, pushing Pasha to do more. Intercepting something of Murić's and selling it to the right buyer might just put them in that category. And I think that's why Galina is on a train to Trieste. It's on the way to Montenegro."

The others fell to arguing about how likely that was, with Mary Alice siding with me while Helen and Nat thought otherwise. Akiko kept batting back and forth like a tennis ball, agreeing with whoever was talking, usually her wife. Minka gave a whoop of triumph from behind her laptop.

"What are you doing, Minka?"

"Being ace investigator and cracking this case wide open," she said as she tapped.

"Minka, have you been watching Humphrey Bogart movies again?"

"William Powell," she corrected. "*Thin Man*. I like Myrna Loy's clothes."

A few more taps and she shared her screen with the TV.

"What are we looking at? I don't even know what language that is." Helen peered through her bifocals at the website Minka had pulled up.

"A variation on Serbo-Croatian," I told her. "Specifically, Montenegrin, I'm guessing."

Minka nodded. "It is the Montenegrin national rail site. I got into Galina's email and there was a forwarded confirmation from Pasha, confirming he had a ticket booked for the day after tomorrow from Podgorica to Athens via Belgrade and Thessaloniki." She pulled up a map with the route highlighted. Montenegro was small, tucked along the Adriatic coast between Bosnia and Herzegovina to the north and Albania to the south. Podgorica was located in the south, only a bit of countryside and Lake Shkodër separating it from the Albanian border. It would have been more direct to go south across Albania to get to Greece instead of looping northeast to Belgrade, but the little red line showing passenger routes stopped dead in the middle of Albania.

"There are no passenger trains between Tirana, Albania, and Greece," Minka said when I asked. "This is the most direct route."

"And he was booked through to Athens?" Mary Alice asked.

"He was."

"Can you see the start of the trip?" I asked. "How long was he supposed to be in Podgorica?" His planned time in the capital might give us a hint as to how far from the station he meant to travel to collect whatever he was supposed to move.

Minka clicked around. "Ten minutes. That is how long the train stops in Podgorica. He was booked straight through with no delays."

"Ten minutes?" Nat protested. "That's impossible. He couldn't get off the train to collect anything."

"Unless he intended to pick it up *on* the train," I said. "There could be a planned rendezvous with whoever has it."

"Or it could be cargo," Mary Alice suggested. "Maybe it is being loaded in Podgorica and he was supposed to supervise it being hauled to Athens."

"There is cargo on that line," Minka said. "It is possible."

"Maybe," I said with a shrug. "The trouble is, we don't know what it is. Could be as small as a microdot or big as a missile."

"And whatever it is, Galina clearly has a buyer lined up in Athens," Helen finished.

"Unless we get to her first." I turned to Minka. "How long until that train boards in Montenegro?"

She pulled up the train schedule. "Thirty-six hours."

I looked at the others. "Well?"

"Galina's not after us now," Helen pointed out.

"She will be," Nat countered. "She probably only took a break from hounding us to finish this deal that Pasha set up. What do you think is going to happen when that's over? She'll come right back to us."

"With more resources," Mary Alice said quietly. "Whatever she's selling, it has to be worth a lot if Jovan Murić owned it and Pasha wanted it."

"And it has to be worth a lot if she's willing to chase it instead of finishing us," I added.

Helen smiled. "I don't even know why I bother. Of course we're going. Minka, book the tickets. We've got a train to catch."

CHAPTER TWENTY-FIVE

EGYPT, 1994

DAWN IS BREAKING OVER LUXOR AS BILLIE STEPS FROM THE TRAIN. IT is eleven hours since she left Cairo, and she is lightheaded from lack of sleep. Through the night, the train jolted and jerked every mile, but it is the anticipation that has kept her awake, the blood fizzing in her body. Today is the day that Fermín Bosque will die.

The foursome surveilled him from his hotel in Cairo the previous afternoon, handing off to each other as he changes direction. He is cautious, discreet even, dressed in a plain djellaba in subdued grey as he emerges from his hotel. Without looking around, he dodges through the crowded alleys of the Khan el-Khalili. He ignores the calls of the vendors in the souk as they press leather goods and spices on him, waving them off with a brusque hand. He follows the narrow, twisting passageways to emerge on the far side of the bazaar. He dives into the hectic city streets to make his way on foot to the

Windsor Hotel. He does not go inside. Instead, he climbs into one of the many tuk-tuks idling outside waiting for tourists. He gives directions to a travel agency near Tahrir Square where he collects a plane ticket, taking a moment outside to tuck it into his pocket. Then he walks briskly up the street towards the Egyptian Museum. They follow him for the better part of two hours as he slowly circles the exhibits, studying Tutankhamun's grave goods.

As he comes to the end of the exhibit, he checks his watch and disappears into the men's room, emerging a moment later wearing nondescript trousers in desert khaki and a shirt to match. A hat shields his eyes, and he keeps his head down as he steps outside and hails a taxi that delivers him back to his hotel. He stops at the desk and makes conversation with the clerk for several minutes. They hear little of the discussion, but the desk clerk hands over a business card shaped like a car. Taking it with a smile, Bosque heads to his room. The four assassins, footsore and annoyed, assemble in a coffee shop across the street, watching the main door. They order coffee and pastries and plan their next steps.

"He is careful, you have to give him that," Helen says, stirring sugar into her coffee. It is thick with grounds and has to be sucked through the teeth to strain it.

"Is it paranoia if they're really out to get you?" Mary Alice asks with a grin.

"How are we doing this?" Nat asks as she reaches for a pastry. "We know he's headed for the Valley of the Kings and he has to go through Luxor to get there. He's got a plane ticket, but that could be a decoy." The others nod agreement and Nat continues. "You saw the card the desk clerk gave him. He might be renting a car. Or hiring a private driver to take him to Luxor."

"It's at least three hundred and fifty miles," Mary Alice points out. "Over really, really bad roads."

"Further than that if they've closed some of the highways," Helen says in agreement. "They're always rerouting and detouring and setting up roadblocks. I don't think our man wants anything to do with official channels and heightened security."

Mary Alice frowns. "Did you see all the police at the airport when we arrived? Every one of them carrying a semi-automatic."

"Can you blame them? People are tense," Nat says with a shrug.

Terror attacks at tourist hot spots have left everyone—visitors and law enforcement—twitching, waiting for the next explosion or outbreak of violence. Armed guards patrol pyramids and temple complexes, a sight that is both threatening and reassuring to tourists.

"What about a Nile cruise?" Mary Alice asks. "Couldn't he just sail up to Luxor?"

"Most cruises leave from Luxor to cram all the highlights into a few days," Billie tells her. "He could hire a private boat from Cairo but it might take a week to sail down to Luxor. That's a lot of wasted days when you have loot to move."

Mary Alice speaks up. "The plane is the fastest way to go. An hour wheels up to wheels down. I'll book a ticket on the evening flight in case that's the way he chooses to go. And if he chooses to sail, we'll be there waiting when he shows up. The most important thing is that we can't let him get to the valley before we do or we'll never find his little stash."

"I'll come with you," Helen says. "It might take two of us to track him."

Mary Alice turns to Billie. "You have your pensive face on. What are you thinking?"

"That this guy is all over the map," Billie says slowly. "Why slip out of his hotel in a half-assed disguise and wind through the souk to pick up a decoy plane ticket and then openly ask about a car to rent? I think he's hoping to mislead us—or anybody else who might be watching him."

"I'll ask around about a car," Nat says to Mary Alice and Helen. "Then I'll fly down on the late plane to meet up with you in Luxor. Tomorrow morning at the latest. Book me a room at the Winter Palace."

They agree and Helen turns to Billie. "Where will you be?"

She shakes her head. "I don't know yet. I need cigarettes." She gets up as Mary Alice points to the hotel across the street.

"I saw some in the gift shop," she calls. Billie gives her a wave over her head and crosses the street, nipping under the nose of a horse drawing a calèche for tourists. They don't carry Eves, but she finds a pack of Marlboros along with an assortment of pharaoh-themed tchotchkes. She grabs a Tutankhamun pocket knife as a joke for Helen along with a stack of postcards and is paying cash for her purchases when she catches something out of the corner of her eye.

Fermín Bosque is on the move. He is wearing the grey djellaba again, but this time he has shaded his eyes with dark glasses. He is carrying a small leather satchel, and as he makes his way through the lobby, she sees him slip his room key into a box on the front desk without breaking stride. He walks smoothly out the front door and steps into a waiting taxi.

There is no time to signal to the others. She follows him out of the hotel and dives into the first taxi she can find. Traffic is heavy and her taxi is able to keep pace with his, always with several cars between them. They head east to the Ramses Railway Station, where Billie loses sight of him twice, finally finding him at the ticket window. She edges into line ahead of a placid-looking woman with several children hanging around her neck.

"Hadha hu zawji," she says to the woman with an apologetic shrug. The woman nods as if to say she understands about husbands. Billie thrusts cash at the clerk.

"A ticket on the same train, please," she says, nodding to Bosque's departing back and crossing her fingers the train is not about to leave. The sleepy clerk shoves a ticket and too little change back to her, but she doesn't stop to count it.

She hurries after Bosque, but he does not move to the platforms. Instead, he goes directly to the taxi rank, climbing into a vacant cab that swings into traffic.

"Oh, this is bullshit," she mutters to herself. She shoves in front of an annoyed businessman to take the next cab in line and listens to him cursing her and her entire line of progeny, but she is still in pursuit. They plunge into the murderous Cairo traffic once more, crawling their way towards the Nile. It is not until they have crossed the river and the Great Pyramid of Cheops is in sight that she realizes where he is headed.

"The Giza railway station, please," she tells her driver. "As quickly as you can."

He floors it, nipping in and out of cars until he delivers her to the curb. She tips generously as she jumps out, blending with the crowds before Bosque's taxi arrives. She goes directly to the platform where the eight PM sleeper has just arrived.

When she approaches the train, she understands the cleverness of Bosque's tactics. While Egyptians must wait to be cleared by security, tourists are simply waved on board. The tickets they're holding were from the Ramses station, but by boarding at Giza instead, Bosque ensures he has bypassed the stringent security in the capital. She locks herself in her sleeper compartment and turns out the light, watching the platform from behind a gap in the window shade. At the last moment, Bosque passes her window and turns left, climbing aboard. She waits until they have left the station to relax. They are en route to Luxor and Bosque is on the train. She has no way to contact the others and no gear, nothing but her passport and a toothbrush and an emergency belt of gold pahlavis. But she has Fermín Bosque in her sights.

The next morning, she rises before dawn, sipping gritty coffee as they approach the Luxor station in the dark. It is not even six AM when they arrive. She hangs back, waiting to make sure Bosque gets off the train, and heaves a sigh of relief when she sees him. He's dressed in his khakis this time, wearing a fedora like half the other Indiana Jones wannabes at any other archaeological site. His leather satchel is strapped over his chest, and he keeps the hat pulled low. Behind him, Billie tugs on her khaki jacket and dark glasses, the nearest thing she has to a disguise. She has to rely on nothing more than body language and how she carries herself to seem like a different person than the woman he might have spotted in Cairo.

The bag carriers swarm the arriving passengers outside the station, but Bosque and Billie have nothing for them. They make their way through the throng, taking a direct route to the corniche, the elegant pavement lined with palms that faces the Nile. At another time, Billie might have been distracted by the restaurants and shops facing the river, but she is focused on one thing only as she follows Bosque onto the ferry dock. There are dozens of brightly painted boats to carry tourists across the river to the Valley of the Kings, but Bosque has opted for the local ferry, riding with the people on their way to work. The ferry is enormous compared to the little tourist boats, and Billie takes a seat far from Bosque, positioning herself to disembark ahead of him. The rising sun spreads across the river as they cross, sending long beams of light over the cliffs that surround the tombs. Billie heads that direction after leaving the boat, stopping long enough to purchase a ticket for the tombs. From there, she is directed to a tram, garishly painted to look like Tutankhamun's headdress. It takes the tram three minutes to cover the distance to the entrance to the valley. Armed guards patrol the area, a reminder of the violence that has been dealt here. But none of them look twice at the American woman who passes by, guidebook and map in hand as she searches for the first tomb.

It is early, but already tour groups are assembling. One group from Australia passes by, the leader holding aloft a stuffed kangaroo tied to a stick as she calls out facts about the valley. "This is one of the most important and comprehensive archaeological sites in the world. It is the resting place of pharaohs from the Eighteenth, Nineteenth, and Twentieth Dynasties of the New Kingdom. The tombs were dug out between 1539 and 1075 BC. Now, if you look directly ahead, you'll see a peak shaped almost like a pyramid. This mountain, the highest spot in the valley, is called Al-Qurn. Don't worry, folks, we're not hiking up there! But if you step this way, we will be heading first to the tomb of Ramesses V. A quick reminder about flash photography—"

Billie uses the group as a shield as she steps off the main path, pretending to study her guidebook. Other travelers pass her by, and just as she is wondering if she has somehow lost him, Fermín Bosque comes into view. She keeps her face in her book, turning away slightly as he passes. The morning is warm and damp patches are already forming on the back of his shirt. He moves quickly but without hurry, directing his steps to the west, past the tombs of Amenhotep II and Seti II. Billie is thirty yards or so behind him, keeping pace. Around them, the walls of the valley rise starkly, the barren brown of the cliffs softened only slightly by the rose gold of the rising sun.

The furthest tomb from the entrance is Thutmose III. No one else has made it this far so early, and the area is quiet. Billie can hear only her own pulse beating steadily in her ears and the soft scrape of her shoes on the stones. The walls of the valley seem to shrink together as they approach the tomb, narrowing so closely they begin to shut out the morning light.

Long shadows fall over the entrance. A low stone wall separates the rockier ground from the pathway that leads to a steep staircase up to the tomb's entrance.

Just before he reaches the bottom step, Bosque smoothly steps over the low wall and disappears. It is as quick as a conjuring trick, and Billie stops short, staring at the blank space where Bosque had stood a second before. She steps over the wall herself and pauses there for a moment, reaching down to collect three of the pebbles at her feet. She sets them atop the wall and then turns back to the sheer cliff rising above her. It is heavily shadowed and it's these shadows that have concealed the narrow gap, a fissure splitting the high wall of the valley in two. It is the smallest of wadis, the chasms that form the landscape of this part of Egypt, each cut by the merciless flash floods of the rainy season.

The rift in the rock is hardly large enough for a goat to fit, and as Billie moves into the passage, her shoulders brush the sides. The walls press so closely around her there is no other way to move but forward. Once or twice, her path is almost blocked by piles of stones, but Bosque has not come back, so she knows he must be ahead of her. She pushes through, scrambling over the piles and ducking under outcroppings until the wadi widens just a little, opening to an area perhaps six feet across. There is no sign of Bosque. She examines the ground until she finds a mark, the fresh scrape of a sole at the bottom of a cliff, and realizes there is a narrow path, maybe eight inches wide, edging upwards along the cliff face. She slings her bag to her back and sets her feet as she faces the rock wall. There are tiny handholds, nothing more than little gaps in the stone where she can put a fingertip to help her balance. She is smart enough not to look down. Some of the rock is rotten, crumbling away under her feet as she moves. She edges along the cliff until she is ten or twelve feet above the ground. The path seems to stop dead, falling away into nothingness, and Billie perches, willing her breath to slow as she takes stock. Her foothold is solid enough, but the rock wall turns sharply to the left and the path does not follow. There is a little outcropping about a foot above and two feet out. She will have to jump for it. Missing is not an option.

She pulls in one slow breath, rolling her shoulders down and back as she loosens her knees. Then she pushes up, explosively, vaulting herself across the gap and up to the outcropping. She lands sloppily, but she's safe, and she scrambles to stand, happy to find that she is on a proper path at last—three feet wide and sheltered by an overhanging bit of rock. The path winds around the face of the cliff, following the wadi, and Billie moves fast. She is filthy, smudged with dust and sweat, her hands bloody from the various slips and scrapes, but she is enjoying herself.

She even enjoys herself when she comes around a curve and finds Bosque standing in the middle of the path, revolver raised to the level of her heart.

There is no reason to pretend she doesn't know exactly who he is and exactly why he is here. A casual tourist might have gotten lost in the Valley of the Kings, but there is nothing casual about the rock climbing she has just done.

"Buenos días, señor Bosque."

"Your accent is good, but I prefer English," he tells her.

His own accent is pure Oxbridge. "I suppose you've been following me since Cairo?"

"Yep. That was a nice trick with the train. I almost missed you."

He shrugs but the gun doesn't waver. "I knew your people would get onto me eventually. I thought it was worth taking a few precautions."

"My people?"

His grin is humorless and unpleasant. "Interpol."

"Ah. Yes. Interpol," she says, nodding seriously.

His mouth thins, and she realizes her flippancy has annoyed him. "Don't try to pretend you're not Interpol."

"Okay, but I'm not, actually. People have really strange ideas about Interpol. They don't make arrests, you know. They pretty much just hang around the office. I don't even think they have guns."

"Then who are you?"

"I'm employed by a completely different organization." She holds three fingers up. "Scout's honor."

"I was hoping to do this quickly, but it might be helpful to know exactly who is tracking me. So, I'm sorry to say, you're not going to enjoy this next bit very much." He jerks the gun. "Inside."

She realizes then that they've been standing outside a narrow gap in the cliff wall, this one leading into a cave. The first few feet of the cave are tight, but it turns and widens into a full room, twenty by ten she estimates, with a ceiling eight or nine feet overhead. Not enormous, but big enough for Bosque's purposes. The turn in the passage has blocked out the morning light, but Bosque has lit a lantern. The light is battery-powered, cold and flat, and the room deserves better. It is a treasure trove, stacked with slim wooden cases she knows are filled with paintings. And one of them must be *Leda,* waiting all these years to go home. Next to the large, flat boxes are small crates that must hold the Egyptological trophies his grandfather collected, ushabti and papyri and jewels for a pharaoh's queen.

"I like what you've done with the place," she tells him cheerfully. "It's homey."

"Shut up." His tone is rough, but she can see he is sweating. Whatever he is planning for her, he is not hardened enough to take pleasure in it. He stinks of desperation, and desperation is unpredictable, dangerous. Billie knows she has to take control of the situation. She doesn't look around, but uses her peripheral vision to scan for possible weapons. There is nothing within arm's reach except a wooden case which must contain one of the paintings, and she doesn't dare use it for fear of damaging the art inside. A slender crowbar is propped against the opposite wall, but between her and the bar is Bosque, still holding his gun—a gun she has to prevent him from firing. If nothing else, the noise would deafen them both, but she is thinking about the rotten rock she has passed and wondering how safe the cave is.

"Your grandfather must have had a hell of a time finding this place," she says.

He doesn't bother to hide his surprise. "You've done your homework."

"Not me personally," she says modestly. "We have a whole

department for that. But yes. We know all about Grandpa Albrecht. Tell me, does it bother you having a Nazi in the family? Because I'd be really, really bummed about that."

"I told you to shut up," he says, moving like he means to hit her.

"I wouldn't if I were you," she says in a different voice, soft and lethal.

"I think you're forgetting who has the gun," he tells her. She doesn't believe the bravado. It feels forced, and she knows every minute she lets him hold a gun on her is another chance for him to fire it.

She gestures towards the weapon. "If you don't mind my saying so, you don't look entirely comfortable with that. You can put it down if you like. I won't take it and I'm not going anywhere."

He laughs and the gun wavers a little. "I don't think so."

She shrugs. "It was worth a try." She looks around the cave. "So, what are you going to do with me? Shoot me and leave me here? Risky. There are jackals in these hills. They'll smell the rotting meat and come in for a snack. That might attract attention. And a gunshot is risky in the first place. Did you see that seam of rotten rock outside? This valley has been falling apart for about eight thousand years. You could get caught in a rockfall and injured or killed. And again, the jackals would smell the blood, and that's not pretty. Basically, it always comes back to the jackals."

"You seem really relaxed about the possibility of dying," he tells her.

"Buddhists believe you should act as though every day

were your last," she replies. "Because one of these days you're going to be right." He doesn't have an answer for this and she continues on. "Do you think about dying, Fermín?" She gestures towards the stacked boxes. "None of this will mean anything when you're dead. These paintings didn't mean anything to your grandfather after he kicked it. Or to the people he stole them from. You know they died, right? Sent to camps while people like your grandfather picked over the carcasses. He was a Nazi vulture. You must be so proud. Do you tell people about him at parties?"

Goading a mark is dangerous, but not as dangerous as standing in the crosshairs of an amateur. Bosque's mouth thins again and he moves forward. Billie lunges to the side and forward as he pulls the trigger, the shot going wide. The noise is like a bomb going off inside the cave, reverberating painfully. Before he can squeeze the trigger again, she is on him. She wraps one hand over his, trapping his finger on the trigger as she twists sharply, breaking the finger. At the same time, her other elbow comes up hard, catching him just under the chin. He drops the gun and she kicks it aside. He is holding his wounded hand and moaning as she grabs him by the throat, forcing him backwards into the cave wall. He slams against it, knocking the breath out of his lungs. He realizes then that this is a fight to the death and the wounded animal inside him takes over.

He forgets the broken finger, the blood dripping from the back of his head. He aims his fist under her arms and up, punching her jaw with a savage undercut that snaps her head back. Momentarily stunned, she drops to the floor, blinking away the stars dancing across her field of vision. She stays there, crouched at his feet. She doesn't react when he reaches down and picks her up by her collar. He lifts her off her feet, bringing her face close to his.

"You're going to be sorry you did that," he promises.

But before he can do anything else, she moves her hand once. It takes him a moment to realize he has been stabbed. There is no pain, just a dull pressure.

Until she pulls the knife out. It is a silly thing to kill a person with, covered in photographs of Tutankhamun's burial mask. But there is something satisfying about killing Fermín Bosque with a cheap tourist souvenir. The blade isn't long, but she knows exactly how to direct it into the femoral artery. For a moment it acts as a barrier to the blood building up behind it, but as soon as she pulls the knife out, the blood gushes, pumping a flood over Bosque's shoes, splashing the floor of the cave.

He looks down at the spreading pool in shock.

"Femoral artery," she tells him. "You're not going to make it, Fermín." He scrabbles to put compression on the gushing wound, but she shakes her head. "It won't help. I mean, what's your plan? You slow the bleeding and for what? It's not like I'm going to call 911 for you. And you can't walk out of here because the exertion will just make you bleed more." She tips her head, assessing the accumulating blood. "From the looks of it, I'd guess you've got ten minutes. Maybe less. That's enough time to make your peace with God."

With a muffled roar, he lunges for her, bloody hands raised for her throat. He is hampered by his torn leg, and she simply steps back and watches him collapse.

But he isn't finished. He rises again, pushing himself up to his feet. "If I'm dying, I'm taking you with me," he says. With one last superhuman effort, he staggers forwards towards where the gun has fallen. Billie reaches for the crowbar. She doesn't know if it's kinder to let him think he has a chance, but decides it is better to put him out of his misery.

She raises the crowbar and aims carefully. It isn't even a hard blow, just a perfectly placed tap to the skull right behind the ear. He crumples instantly into unconsciousness. A second tap finishes him, and she is checking his pulse when there is a noise at the entrance of the cave. She looks up.

"It's about damned time," she says with a grin as Natalie and Helen enter. "Where's Mary Alice?"

"Still hanging on the edge of that damned cliff, trying to decide if she's going to jump," Nat tells her. She looks down at the bloody corpse and the spreading pool of blood. "Oooh, a messy one."

"As long as the art isn't damaged," Helen says as she surveys the cave. "This has to be most of Danner's hoard. I'll let Mary Alice know she doesn't need to make the jump. She can go back and notify the Acquisitions team that it's clear for them to move in."

She disappears and Billie and Natalie move to quickly survey the hoard, skimming the codes marked on the cases.

"Oh my god, the Dürer is here!" Natalie squeals. "And

the Botticelli. And look at all the Egyptological stuff—papyri, jewelry. Everything Marilyn told us he'd taken. It's all here."

"Not all of it," Billie says, her mouth suddenly dry. "I can't find her."

"Her who?" Nat doesn't look up as she reaches for a crate with a shout of joy. "Oh my god—it's the Leonardo!"

"Where's the Raphael?" Billie asks. *Leda and the Swan?*"

Nat pauses and looks around. "I haven't seen her."

"Because she isn't here," Billie says flatly.

"Bosque must have moved her when he took the Rubens," Nat replies. She turns back to the cache.

Billie feels suddenly deflated. She has tailed the mark, executed the mission, and secured a hoard of Nazi-looted art that will be restored to its owners. This job will be celebrated by the Museum, and she will receive a considerable bonus as well as a commendation. It has been a success.

She reminds herself of this as she carefully wipes her hands and steps out of the cave and back into the sunshine.

They have only a few minutes before the Acquisitions team arrives. The team will remove every trace of Bosque's find, hauling it out under the protection of the Egyptian government. In exchange for the return of their antiquities, the authorities will look the other way when the paintings are shipped back to Europe. And they will say nothing of the dead man in the cave. They will leave him for the jackals, and then the beetles will come. And whatever's left, only the desert will know.

CHAPTER TWENTY-SIX

IN THE END, IT TOOK A LOT MORE THAN A TRAIN TO GET WHERE WE
needed to be. First, we had to reach Podgorica in a hurry
which meant flying, and that was an eight-hour trip with two
changes. The phrase "you can't get there from here" was invented for Podgorica. As capitals go, it's a rough little jewel.
It's tucked into a valley at the foothills of the mountains which
give the country its name. It has a tiny pink palace and a miniature Niagara Falls, but it also has a modern millennium
bridge and a contemporary art center. You have to love a place
that blends the old with the new, and Montenegro was giving
it a go—at least in Podgorica. The port in the bay at Kotor
was home to superyachts and nightclubs catering to the 1 per-
cent, but the countryside was exactly what you think of when
you hear the word "Balkan." Mountains, hills, escarpments,
promontories—and anything else your thesaurus suggests for
"mountain." And when you weren't looking? They added a

few more mountains just for fun. Villages dotted the hillsides up and down, each paved with steep stone streets, but beyond this was countryside that seemed like it hadn't been touched for centuries. Occasionally, a farmhouse or cottage betrayed its existence by a thread of smoke rising above the pine forests, but mostly it was just trees, crowded so close to the rail line, the branches brushed the windows, leaving tiny trails of pine resin on the glass.

The train station in Podgorica is exactly what you'd expect from former Yugoslavia. It's long and low, and not even definitive enough in its style to be Brutalist. It's serviceable and so nondescript it might be any kind of structure built after WWII in just about any town. But a little bar served the most delicious grilled sausages I'd ever had, and it was just busy enough to keep us in a crowd.

Galina and her little henchwoman, Tamara, could be anywhere, in any disguise. We had the photo I'd stolen from Aunt Evgenia and the quick glimpse I'd had of the both of them at the Scala Contarini del Bovolo but not much more. Minka had been able to dig up two other photos, grainy shots from opera events where Galina was just a blurry background figure, but we had nothing on Tamara. Taverner had pressed Wolfie for details but whatever useful information he got could have been jotted on a postcard. While we were in the air somewhere between Venice and Vienna, he dropped a message into the Menopaws app which related that Galina had blue eyes, was five foot four inches tall with a slender build. Her hair was brown, and her favorite snack was mushroom and sour cream potato chips.

"She should be killed for that alone," I muttered as I clicked out of the app. Hair and eye color were useless, they were far too easy to change. Height was harder to disguise, but it could be done. Lifts, crutches, wheelchairs, platform shoes— any of those could give an impression of a few inches gained or lost. Tamara was forty, brown eyes, black hair, and five feet even which scared the bejesus out of me. I'd learned the hard way over the years—the smaller the dog, the bigger the bite.

I shoved the phone to the bottom of my bag, hiding it under essentials for the train. Minka had handled our papers, getting a fresh set prepped from her guy in Stockholm who met up with us in the Vienna airport for an obscene amount of money. We had minimal trip gear, just a small day bag each with the basics. Since we were traveling carry-on only, we couldn't even bring Swiss Army knives, so when we landed in Podgorica, we split up, both to finish our shopping and to elude any potential tails. We didn't really think Galina was still watching us—she'd broken off to take care of whatever deal was going down on the train—but we'd been trained too well to let down our guard completely. We planned to rendezvous on the train the next evening, traveling separately and ready for whatever might come.

When my bag was packed, I looked around the hotel room, a cheap single in a small hotel near the station, busy enough to be discreet, crappy enough to be overlooked. Before a hit, there's always that moment. Whether the lodgings have been a five-star hotel with hot-and-cold running butlers or a youth hostel with shared toilets and the stink of cheap weed, there's always a moment when you're packed but you haven't walked out the door. And that's when the thought comes. Not really a thought, just the briefest flicker of an impulse: *stay.* You have papers—good ones, *impeccable* ones that would pass the scrutiny of the most zealous border guards. You have some money. Nobody will hunt you down. You could just stay there, inhabiting the personality you've put on like a snail shell. You could hang pictures and put down roots. You could get a real job instead of this endless loop of make-believe, this merry-go-round of cover stories and covert assignments.

But you don't. Because the person you're supposed to kill has been chosen for a good reason. Whatever contract exists between human beings, a contract of decency and common humanity, they've broken it. If life is a chessboard, they're the players that have gone rogue, the knight riding diagonally across the board, smashing whatever is in his path, the king who refuses to stop at one space. The basic rules that apply to the rest of the world—*thou shalt not kill,* for starters—don't matter to them. They do as they please, and they don't care about the carnage they leave behind. Somebody has to put the chessboard to rights, pick up the wrecked pieces and set it back to the start. So you pick up your bag and you close the door behind you, just like you've closed a hundred other doors. And you know that every time you do, you've left another piece of you behind.

I DIDN'T MEET UP WITH THE OTHERS UNTIL WE WERE ON THE TRAIN, each of us making our way solo to the compartment Minka had booked for us. If the rolling stock had been a toy, it wouldn't exactly have been "mint in box"—more the "played with hard and sold for a quarter in a garage sale" kind of train. Our compartment was narrow and utilitarian, the sort of accommodations Spartans would have turned down as being too luxurious, but only just. The cars were clearly holdovers from the old days, back when Yugoslavia was still a country held in Tito's iron grip as he thumbed his nose at Moscow. Our compartment was a sleeper with berths three tiers high. The upper berths had been folded back to show some truly questionable art—landscapes of Montenegro done in a style I like to call "Nouveau Fascist," all stylized trees and square-jawed men with equally square-jawed women in kerchiefs marching over the hills. The lower berths served as banquettes facing each other across a narrow table. A wide window was the cleanest thing in the place. Toilets were down the corridor, and we'd been warned to bring our own toilet paper. Simple and no frills.

I arrived first, dressed neatly with no remarkable labels or accessories. Whatever the Eastern European version of Chico's is, I was wearing it. Elasticized and forgettable, which is exactly what I intended.

Helen arrived next wearing the habit of an Orthodox nun and looking distinctly rotund.

"Did you stuff your habit?" I asked as I shoved my weekender bag out of sight.

"I have it on good authority that Balkan trains are either boiling hot or freezing cold. I am gambling on the latter and came prepared. Two layers under the habit," she told me, lifting the skirt portion to show her woolen leggings.

"Where did you read that? The Museum briefing guide?" One of the lighter tasks of the Museum's Provenance department was compiling guidebooks to every conceivable destination. In their spare time, they inserted updates, but some places were too far off the beaten path to merit much attention. The last time I'd logged into the archive, I'd poked around the Argentina section just for fun. The Pampas prison where I'd been held for three months was still listed as open, but I'd burned it down when I left. I'd have to tell Naomi to make a note.

Helen shook her head. "Lonely Planet. Did you know the world's oldest olive tree is here in Montenegro? Two thousand years."

"Maybe we'll see it when we're done," I told her. But I didn't really figure we would. This job never left much time for sightseeing.

Next came Mary Alice wearing a sweatshirt that had been decorated with vacation Bible school slogans in puff paint. She wore a scrunchie in her hair and socks with her SAS shoes.

"Not a goddamned word," she said as she shoved her bag into the storage cubby.

I grinned. "Would you like to tell me about your close, personal relationship with Jesus?"

She flipped me the bird. "Did you know they don't check tickets on this train? Second-class passengers grab seats in first and nobody cares. I can't decide if that's democratic or annoying. Also, this is the only sleeper car. The others are Serbian seated carriages."

"What does that mean?" Helen inquired.

"Seats arranged like Amtrak," Mary Alice said. "Those poor bastards are going to be sitting up for the next twelve hours. And I brought snacks," she added, holding up a bag. The plan was for us to be off the train well before the final destination in Belgrade—actually, we would be long gone before the train even crossed the Serbian frontier. We'd ditch somewhere before the Montenegrin border patrol boarded the train to check papers, and make our way on foot to the nearest town to arrange transportation back to Podgorica and catch flights from there back to Venice. With any luck, we'd be safely back in Italy before the Serbian police even figured out that something worth investigating had gone down.

"What kind of snacks?" I asked just as Natalie arrived. Whatever Mary Alice was about to say died on her lips at the sight of her. Nat was dressed as a proper Montenegrin grandma with layers of peasant skirts, three separate cardigans, and a headscarf. But what really sold it for me was the live chicken under her arm.

"Natalie, what the *fuck*?" Mary Alice hissed. "You cannot bring a live chicken on this train."

"Of course I can," Nat said calmly. "She's very tame. Her name is Nula."

"That just means 'zero,'" I told her.

Nat cuddled her chicken closer. "I know. It's the first

number I found in the phrase book. You're a lovely chicken, aren't you, Nula?"

"I am having a fever dream," Mary Alice said as she flopped onto one of the banquettes. "That is the only possible explanation."

"Oh, keep your panties on," Nat replied. "I must have seen a hundred women dressed just like me roaming around Podgorica and every damned one of them had a chicken."

"A hundred?" Helen pressed gently.

"Okay, maybe one. But she looked really convincing as a peasant grandmother," Natalie said.

"She looked convincing because she *was* a peasant grand-mother." Mary Alice's teeth were gritted so hard, if she chewed coal she'd be spitting diamonds.

"I don't think we're supposed to say 'peasant,'" Helen put in primly.

"Sorry," Mary Alice said with a sincere stab at contrition. "Economically disadvantaged Montenegrin."

"Natalie," I asked politely, "have you considered where that chicken is going to shit?"

Nat stared at the chicken for a long minute. "No," she said in a small voice.

Mary Alice groaned and Natalie turned on her. "Well, ex-cuse me for attempting to introduce a little verisimilitude to my cover, Mary Alice. Posing as a missionary from Iowa will give you every opportunity to play the judgmental bitch card. I'm sure you have a full house by now."

Mary Alice turned to lambaste her, and I held up a hand.

"Not now. We're supposed to be strangers, remember? Fighting is for people who know each other."

Helen and Nat murmured noises that I decided to take as agreement. Mary Alice gave me a sullen look. "Idaho," she grumbled to Natalie.

"Pardon me?" Nat asked with exaggerated politeness.

"It's not Iowa. It's Idaho."

"And I know just where you can shove your potatoes, Mary Alice." Before Nat could get herself on a roll, the chicken started making soft clucking noises. "I hope you're happy. You have upset my chicken."

"That chicken is going to be soup before this trip is over with," Mary Alice promised her.

"Enough," I said with just enough edge in my voice to make them sit up. "No more English for you two," I said to Helen and Nat. "You're supposed to be unobtrusive—at least as unobtrusive as you can manage." I shoved a phrase book at Mary Alice. "And you're supposed to be learning. Look up how to ask people about the state of their souls and if they'll send money to your church."

"'Da li pričate Engleski?'" she read out, butchering the pronunciation. While she did that, Helen and I, nearest the window, kept a discreet lookout for anything interesting. Helen's gaze was raised just above the newspaper she held in front of her face. I pretended to study a travel guide as we surveyed the passengers still boarding. There weren't many. Trains used to make this route in seven hours, and they were always packed. But with the decline of the rolling stock, the trip had lengthened. It was scheduled for twelve hours but often took more than fourteen. Montenegrins who could afford their own cars drove them, abandoning the train for hatchbacks and minivans. Now it was mostly less affluent locals and some crunchy granola backpacker types who made the trip by rail, and carriages were never crowded. Conductors didn't much care where you sat, and dining cars were a distant memory. Instead there was a guy who boarded at Podgorica with a cooler full of beers he sold for a euro each before hopping off again. It was a pretty good hustle, I thought, although I'd have been happier to see someone with a box full of tacos.

We waved off the beer seller, focused on the people mingling on the platform. Galina and Tamara had left Venice by train, and Minka had been able to confirm for us that they'd changed a few times but kept a slow, steady progress towards Podgorica, following Pasha's original itinerary. But if we were right about their reasons for being on the train, whoever they were meeting would be boarding here.

People watching is always fascinating, and never more so than when you're assessing a crowd for a potential mark. Most of the people we kill are not very nice; they're aware of the fact that there are folks who'd like to see them dead, so they take precautions. They might travel with a pack of bodyguards which is a nuisance but never insurmountable. In fact, having bodyguards often means people *lower* their watchfulness because they're paying someone else to sniff out threats. (See: Lazarov, Pasha.) Or they might become reclusive—a complete pain in the ass because it means setting up a cover identity you have to inhabit for months in order to get close enough to kill them. Or they might take to wearing disguises—an option they choose more often than you'd expect, mostly be-cause it's fun, I think. People have always enjoyed an excuse to wear a mask—Carnevale, Halloween, costume parties. They love dressing up and trying on a new face. The problem is, most people aren't nearly as good as they think they are at test-driving a new personality. Identity isn't just your collec-tion of facial features and the clothes on your back. It's how you hold yourself, how you communicate, how you move through the world. It's a thousand little details that are so in-grained in our behavior, they might as well be etched in ca-thedral stone. It takes years of training and careful study to be able to truly inhabit a new skin, and if you know your mark well enough, you can spot them through any disguise.

With Galina, we had almost nothing to draw on, no Prov-enance dossier, no social media profile. She was less than a shadow; she was a silhouette projected on a white screen, the details completely obscured. That wasn't surprising. Lots of our marks kept a low profile and someone running a club drug operation wouldn't want to attract the wrong kind of attention—from law enforcement agencies or from criminals higher up in the food chain who might decide to take a bite out of her business. Or she might have just been so damaged from her father's assassination and her mother's death that she had kept herself aloof, clutching her privacy like a secu-rity blanket. Who am I to psychoanalyze anybody?

There was a final flurry of activity and the train began to move, although it always looks to me like it's the platform moving away from the train and not the other way around. We pulled out of the station and in a matter of minutes were out of

Podgorica proper and on our way. Podgorica was only an hour from the coast, at the foot of the mountains. The route we followed to the east climbed the Dinaric Alps, the landscape changing from canyons to forests to river gorges and everything in between. It was rugged country with no highway system, just the same narrow byways that had been cart tracks under the feet of Roman centurions. Those roads had been traveled by a lot of folks since—Greeks, Illyrians, Ottomans, Austro-Hungarians. Anybody who'd had an empire in that part of the world had crossed Montenegro at some point.

"What do you think it is?" Nat asked. The chicken had settled down politely at her feet but I still didn't trust it. Chickens have reptile eyes and my policy is never to turn my back on one.

"What do we think what is?" Helen asked.

"The thing Galina is after. Schematics for a new superweapon? Priceless statue? Only child of the kingpin of a narco-collective?"

"A child?" Mary Alice stared. "You think she is stealing a child?"

Natalie shrugged. "For ransom. Nobody thinks it's going to happen until it does."

"What even is a narco-collective? Did you just make that up?"

"Of course not. I read about it in—"

That's the point when I tuned out. Natalie and Mary Alice can spar for days, and as long as it didn't end in bloodshed, I wasn't going to put a stop to it. We were all feeling out of sorts and maybe a little friendly sniping would take the edge off.

Instead I followed my own train of thought, considering the question Nat had just posed. The possible answers were too many to count. Galina could be after just about anything. Lots of folks in the west think that since Montenegro joined NATO, it's one of us. But like most places in the Balkans, it's not that simple. Russians still kept an eagle eye on the warm-water ports of its Adriatic coast, and while Montenegro was a democracy, it was a flawed one. If that assessment sounds harsh, it isn't mine. Blame *The Economist* Intelligence Unit. They're paid to evaluate the realpolitik of various countries so other people can decide where to put their money. Stable governments make for good investments, but there's money to be had in rocky ones too. Montenegro's most prominent politicians kept power by circulating through different offices in order to circumvent term limitations. Returning to private life is a luxury you can't afford if you're afraid of being prosecuted for a little light corruption or attempting a coup or two. The last coup attempt—allegedly—had been done at the behest of the Russians and it wasn't as far in the past as you might think. And Russians sniffing around all but guaranteed Chinese interest. Beijing had been loud and proud about wanting to spend a fair bit of coin in Montenegro to build a highway system as part of their modern Silk Road project. Being meddled with by two much larger countries would have divided Montenegrins enough, but there are always the usual historical Balkan issues of Serb vs. Croat vs. Albanian vs. Greek—you get the picture. And then there were the folks who kept a candle burning in front of Tito's picture with a rheumy-eyed longing for the old days. Sure, he might have been a dictator and they didn't get to vote very often, but crime rates were low, employment was high, and there had always been a chicken in every pot when Josip was in charge, they would tell you.

So what pretty crumbs did any of that leave for Galina? Club drugs were lucrative, but pretty small potatoes, criminally speaking. It made sense that she was looking to level up in the underworld, maybe branch into something really juicy. Blackmail material on a Montenegrin politician? Something that could help her engineer a coup of her own? Plans for a secret military base? None of that seemed likely, and even if it were, so what? It didn't change our job. She was out to kill us, so our only option was to get there first.

There's a moment in every trip where the train picks up speed and everybody seems to settle in to traveling. We hit that point just outside of Podgorica. The noise lessened considerably. A conductor moved through the cars, checking tickets, but without any of the urgency you find on slicker trains. He gave our tickets the most cursory of glances and didn't even raise an eyebrow at the chicken.

"Told you," Nat muttered as he left. She craned out the compartment to watch him move to the next car. "He's gone. It's time."

We'd gone over the plan enough to know what we were doing. We'd split into teams of two to check the entire train, Nat and Helen going forward, Mary Alice and I aft. We were looking for Galina or Tamara, but failing that, anything out of the ordinary. We had our notifications set to push on the Menopaws app, our only means of communication when we were separated. Nat said good-bye to the chicken, who clucked softly to herself as we left. We'd decided not to be precious about it. Whoever found Galina got to kill her, it was that simple. We weren't going to waste time on making a full posse out of it.

With one final look, we split up. Nat and Helen moved up the corridor while Mary Alice and I turned the opposite direction. We glanced into each compartment as we went, surprising a few folks, but most just gave us curious looks and went back to what they'd been doing. There were grandmas—none with chickens though—and grubby-looking backpackers doing the Bar-to-Belgrade trip. A small group of scouts took up several compartments, shooting spitballs at each other as their troop leaders passed out sandwiches and smacked the perpetrators gently on their heads. Beyond that lay the toilet, which doesn't bear thinking about, so I won't.

Mary Alice put her mouth close to my ear. "Unless she's disguised herself as a Boy Scout, I think this car is clear."

"I wouldn't put it past her," I said. I opened the door and we stepped into the narrow no-man's-land between carriages. The next car was just as uneventful, same grandmas, same backpackers, until we got to the last compartment. We'd been peeking through windows or open doors, but this compartment had the door jammed, the window shade drawn.

I flicked up a brow at Mary Alice. She shrugged. "Could be napping. Or having sex."

"Or something else," I said. "I hope you know the Montenegrin for 'sorry to interrupt' because I'm going in."

I grabbed the handle of the sliding door and pulled. It

took three tries before it gave way, and I realized it wasn't because the door was jammed. In the track where the slider was supposed to run, something was blocking the way. Well, some*one*, to be exact. A body had fallen against the door, wedging it shut until I applied enough pressure to pop it free of the slider track. When it came loose, I was able to move the body aside easily enough but that was probably because of all the blood. Before it coagulates and gets sticky, blood is slippery, especially if there's a lot of it.

Mary Alice and I ducked in and shut the door again, putting our backs to it as we surveyed the scene.

"What the *hell*?" she breathed. The air was thick with the metallic smell of fresh butchery, and I made a quick, professional assessment. The body was wearing a business suit, stark black and good quality. Not custom, but not off a cheap rack either. His shoes were Italian, and the watch on his wrist was a low-end but perfectly decent Rolex. The nails were buffed. This wasn't a generic messenger or goon. This had been someone's number two or maybe three, the kind of guy who functions well as a cog in a criminal machine because he gives the easy impression of respectability. He wouldn't make the big decisions, but he'd have the ear of the guy who did. His body was slender, not the overblown muscles of the enforcers, and his hands looked pretty youthful—early thirties I guessed.

If you're wondering why I didn't just look at his face, it's because he didn't have one. The only sign of violence on his body was the lack of a head, and it took me a minute to realize it had rolled under a lower berth.

"I am not picking that up," Mary Alice said flatly.

"We don't have to," I said, patting him down for a wallet. I found it in his hip pocket which meant getting a little friendlier with his corpse than I would have liked. There was no phone which meant the killer had probably taken it.

I flipped the wallet open and checked the contents. Some Montenegrin currency which I left, a few family pictures—cute kids who I hoped wouldn't miss him too much—and a prayer card with a little charm dedicated to St. Harlampy. He's a Montenegrin martyr who's supposed to protect the faithful from unexpected death. "Wouldn't count this one as a win," I told the icon before I turned to the driver's license.

The name was Montenegrin and meant nothing to me, but I'd have bet my last jelly doughnut it would find a match on a list of Jovan Murić's known associates.

"Looks like Galina has already collected what she came for," Mary Alice said.

"With Tamara's help, I'd bet, because I'd be surprised if Galina likes getting her hands dirty," I replied. The head had been taken off neatly, with a good knife, recently sharpened. There were a few deep, clean cuts on the palms and fingers, defensive wounds. They weren't significant, probably because he hadn't expected to be jumped, especially by a woman who wouldn't pass the YOU MUST BE THIS HIGH TO RIDE THIS RIDE sign at Disneyland.

"Goddammit," Mary Alice said. "If she's got it—whatever it is—she might already be off the train."

"Not a chance," I said absently. I'd spotted something half-hidden under the seat—not the one with the head. The other side. In fact, it was the head that made me look there in the first place. The eyes were still open, staring across the floor towards the other side of the compartment. Rising like a little island in the lake of blood was a piece of wood. I plucked it out of the gore. It was narrow, marked with deep pits of old staples. A series of letters and numbers had been inked on it.

It was easy to see what had happened. The courier—the guy currently lying around without a head—must have opened the parcel he was carrying. Then, before he could pack it up again, Galina and her henchwoman had arrived to take it off him. In the struggle, it had been damaged a little—and only a little, I hoped. The fact that the wood had been left behind meant they'd cleared out in a hurry. They should have retrieved it. The whole thing would be more valuable intact.

"What is it?" Mary Alice asked.

"Something I never thought I'd see in this lifetime."

I took a tissue from my pocket and wrapped up the fragment of wood with the numbers on it. It stuck out from my pocket just a little, but there was no way I was leaving it behind.

Then I went into the corpse's pockets again and retrieved his keys. I stripped off his jacket and tied it awkwardly over what was left of his neck. It wasn't tidy, but at least it would sop up some of the blood. Together Mary Alice and I hefted the corpse up into the third berth. I retrieved his head and put it into a pillowcase, tucking the whole thing above the shoulders. The naked pillow went over that, and if you peeked in the compartment quickly, you'd just see a guy sleeping under his pillow. Mary Alice waited with the body while I retreated to the toilet compartment. I'd seen a bucket in there and I filled it with tepid water and some slimy soap. It took three trips to sluice the blood off the floor and we had to use Mary Alice's jacket to wipe up the last of it. I bundled the jacket out the window before Mary Alice and I left the compartment. There was no way to lock the door behind us, but at least if anyone peeked in, it wouldn't be immediately obvious that there was a corpse inside. The last thing we needed was an emergency stop with police swarming the train because somebody had stumbled over a headless body.

We hurried back to our compartment, Mary Alice messaging the others as we went. They met us a few minutes later. We closed the door and lowered the shade. The chicken was asleep, swaying gently with the movement of the train as it gathered speed on the climb to the Pannonian Plain.

"What did you find?" Helen asked.

"Headless body," Mary Alice told her.

"Holy shit," Nat replied. "Whose?"

"We think it's one of Murić's guys," I said.

"The courier," Mary Alice clarified.

"Then Galina has whatever she's after," Helen said.

"Shit, shit, shit," Nat added.

Mary Alice sighed. "Natalie, remind me to get you a thesaurus for Hanukkah next year. Just to mix things up."

"Galina's still on the train," I reminded them. "It hasn't stopped, and unless she has a death wish, she's not jumping on this trip." I nodded towards the window where a panorama of mountain scenery was unfolding. On the corridor side of the train, we were up against a wall of rock. On the other side, it was a sheer drop to the valley below, far enough that anybody who took a flyer would be in worse shape than Jovan Murić's courier. "We've got to find her before we cross into Serbia," I added.

"Sooner than that," Mary Alice said. "You forgot about passport control and it comes around twice—once leaving Montenegro and once entering Serbia. They'll check every compartment and they'll find him."

"I don't want to be questioned by Montenegrin police about a headless body, but I really, *really* don't want to be questioned by Serbian cops," I said. Montenegrin law enforcement didn't have much of a reputation internationally, but the less said about Serbian skull-breakers the better. Anybody who had anything to hide gave them a wide berth. (Train pun intended.)

"Agreed." Helen checked the map and looked at her watch. "We're running a little behind schedule, but not much. We stamp out of Montenegro at Bijelo Polje. That's where the first set of border guards will come aboard."

"How long?" Mary Alice asked.

"Best guess? At the rate we're going, I'd say maybe eleven PM. Quarter to if we're unlucky."

"There's more," I told them. "I know what Galina took."

I put the piece of wood I'd taken from the crime scene on the narrow table. The markings were faint with age and harder to see now that blood had seeped into the grain, but there was no mistaking the letters and numbers.

"It's a piece of a stretcher from a painting," Nat said quickly.

"That's a Nazi inventory code," Mary Alice said, peering closely.

"Not just any inventory code," I corrected.

Helen was the first to get it.

"Oh my god," she said, sitting back against the banquette.

Nat looked around. "What is it? What am I missing?"

"Hell if I know," Mary Alice said. "There were thousands if not millions of paintings marked with inventory codes by the Nazis when they were looting half of Europe. How do we know the significance of this one without a catalog?"

"Because we've seen it before," I told her. "Fermín Bosque."

"Holy shit," Mary Alice said. To her everlasting credit, Nat didn't say a word.

I looked at Helen who was wearing an expression like she'd just witnessed the second coming. "Do you really think she's on the train?"

"Billie just said Galina has to still be here," Nat told her.

"Not Galina," Helen said softly. "*Leda.*"

CHAPTER TWENTY-SEVEN

THERE WAS A QUIET INTAKE OF BREATH, THE SORT YOU HEAR JUST before a prayer.

"*That's* what Galina is after?" Nat asked. She turned to me. "How sure are you?"

"I memorized that code on the Bosque job, and I've never forgotten it. It's her."

"She's our white whale," Helen said. "The one that got away."

"After all this time," Mary Alice said. "I never thought she would surface again."

Truth be told, I hadn't thought so either. I could still taste the rage and regret the day we realized Fermín Bosque had removed her from his cave in the Valley of the Kings before we could get to her. God only knew where she had been since.

We were all thinking the same thing. Helen is the one who

voiced it. "Where do you think she's been? And how did Jovan Murić get his hands on her?"

I shrugged. "We know Bosque had buyers for every load he took out of Egypt. She could have gone anywhere. Who knows after that?"

"It's been *decades*," Mary Alice pointed out. "She could have been sitting in someone's vault in a free port the whole time. She could have been hanging on a wall or shoved under a bed. Or she could have been circulating in the underworld as currency. The one thing we do know is that she couldn't have been put up for legitimate sale or the Provenance department would have spotted her."

I thought for a minute. "I wonder if the Provenance agent—the one who gave the Lazarovs our names—spotted something in the files on Murić that tipped them to the fact that he had the painting."

Nat shook her head. "That doesn't wash. If Provenance knew Murić had the painting or even knew where it was, they would have retrieved it. You know the policy about looted art. It goes back to the family it was stolen from, and if there are no surviving members, it's held in the freehold."

"That's supposing the Provenance agent who discovered the whereabouts of *Leda* is clean. We already know at least one isn't. Whoever gave the Lazarovs our names is playing their own game and it's not by Museum rules."

"You think the mole found a connection between Murić and *Leda*?" Helen asked with a frown. "And then gave that information to the Lazarovs? But why?"

"Money," I suggested. "Tip off some unscrupulous folks

as to where an extremely valuable piece of stolen art is and ask for a cut when they steal it."

"Then why wouldn't the mole just take it for themselves and keep all the profit?" Nat objected.

"That's a dangerous business," Mary Alice pointed out. "You're talking about stealing from a Montenegrin gangster. It would take big fat brass ones to just stroll in and swipe the painting. Besides, Provenance traffics in information, but deals like this are done through relationships. You can't just call up a legitimate dealer and shift a missing Raphael. You'd have Interpol on your ass in two seconds flat."

"But you could use information to leverage a relationship with the Lazarovs," I added. I took a deep breath and started to paint them a picture. "Imagine you're a Provenance data nerd. You have access to some of the most dangerous and interesting secrets in the world. Maybe you're bored one day or you have a little extra time on your hands, so you go walkabout through the databases, accessing some old files. You could do this for months, years even, before you turn up a piece of the puzzle. But eventually you realize where one of the most valuable paintings in the world is—a lost painting that hasn't been seen in decades and is worth millions of dollars—*hundreds* of millions. Maybe you've been a good little Museum soldier all these years, or maybe you've just been biding your time, waiting for an opportunity like this to come along. Either way, you have extremely valuable information. But it's going to take skills and connections you don't have to pull it off. What then?"

"You'd have to hire someone," Nat said. "Someone whose name you could find in the archives."

"Exactly," I said. "But you still don't have any money, so what do you pay them with? Criminals don't work on credit."

"Information," Mary Alice replied. "You'd pay them with information—like the names of the people who killed their father. And if the painting was the original job, that would explain why Galina was willing to walk away from us in Venice in order to get here. She has to finish the job in order to get her payday. After that, she can come after us whenever she likes."

"She'd certainly have the money to do it," Helen said.

I looked around this group of women I'd known for two-thirds of my life. "This mission has changed. We still need to get Galina because if we don't, she'll just keep hunting us down."

"Not to mention, she just killed an associate of Jovan Murić's to get the painting in the first place," Helen said.

"Are we really that fussed about a Montenegrin gangster?" Mary Alice asked, making a face.

"Gangsters are people too," Helen said calmly. "Montenegro is a difficult place to make a living. I'm sure this man was simply trying to feed his family."

"Also, I'm not sure we exactly have the moral high ground when it comes to choice of occupation," Nat said to Mary Alice.

Helen continued as if she hadn't spoken. "The point is, Galina is not just after us. She's widened her scope and she is a danger to others as well." She turned to me. "Finish, please."

I waited a second to make sure I had their attention. "We need to take out Galina, but this isn't just about her anymore.

This is about the chance to finish a job we started in 1994. That painting got away from us the last time, but we have the opportunity to get her back and give her to the family she was stolen from in the first place."

"I do hate unfinished business," Nat said. "It's untidy."

Mary Alice grinned at her suddenly. "Would Marie Kondo approve? Is *this* sparking joy for you, Nat?"

Nat grinned back. "Hell, yeah. Let's go get our girl and take her home."

THE TRAIN HADN'T STOPPED, AND THE BODY HAD BEEN WARM WHEN we touched it—conclusion? Nobody had left the train and that included *Leda.* I was betting Galina wouldn't get off with her prize until Belgrade where she could switch to a train that would take her straight to Athens and the intended buyer. It was a circuitous route, but oddly it was the most direct way if you didn't want to fly—and taking a train is a much better way to move some contraband than flying. Train security, especially in the Balkans, is virtually nonexistent. The stations are not state-of-the-art, high-speed rail facilities with X-ray scanners and metal detectors. There are no sniffer dogs or intimidating soldiers with semiautomatic weapons, no gleaming concourses with massage chairs and gift shops and Subway storefronts. These stations are holdovers from a time when the Iron Curtain was fully drawn. Some look like bus stops—*stops,* not stations—while others are just concrete slabs in the middle of nowhere. If you're lucky there might be a window into a hole where you can order a pastry or a meat pie to take with you. Seasoned travelers know to stock up at the vending machines or local grocery stores, bringing their own supplies, including toilet paper and flashlights in case of power cuts on the train. And the really experienced ones bring twice as much because you never know what to expect on a Balkan train. You need small coins for the guy walking the aisle with his cooler full of beers to sell, and you need larger notes for the border patrol guards you want to bribe because shaking down tourists from affluent countries is a blood sport. Serbian officials in particular were fond of the old "your papers aren't in order, get off the train and come with us" routine. They would make up some document you needed and threaten you with police detention—all so you would shit yourself and cough up some spare euros or dollars to buy them off. Their only redeeming feature was that they weren't too expensive. Forty euros would do the trick if you were lucky. But no bribe, no matter how generous, would be enough to get us off the hook if we were found with a decapitated body and a painting that occupied the top slot of the Monuments Men's most wanted list.

In the case of our trip, the unexpected happened just before the viaduct at Mala Rijeka. It used to be the highest viaduct in the world—something for Montenegrins to brag about, but the Chinese decided to build a higher one, and nobody wants a t-shirt that says WORLD'S SECOND anything. I still thought it was an impressive sight, spanning a gorge that bottomed out almost a third of a mile below. I knew how high it was because I read about it, not because you could see anything close to the full drop. The moon and some stingy little spotlights gave enough light to show the bones of the viaduct, crouching like a skeleton over the black emptiness of the gorge. The last thousand feet or so were in complete darkness, an abyss that was probably carpeted in pine and spruce forests and punctuated with rock outcroppings, but I couldn't see, so who knows?

In spite of what happened on the scala in Venice, I'm not actually a fan of heights, and even looking at the viaduct from a short distance across the gorge and thinking about what lay below was enough to make my knees go a little rubbery. We were pulling through a tunnel—one of more than two hundred and fifty, as Helen had informed us courtesy of Lonely Planet—when there was a sudden shriek of brakes—a full-throated scream, not a squeal—and a hard stop. We had just left our compartment to start searching for Galina and *Leda* when it happened, and the four of us were thrown hard into each other.

"What the actual hell?" Nat said as she disentangled herself from Mary Alice.

Helen peered through the smudged window. "I can't see anything from this angle. And it's almost pitch-black out there."

"We'd better check it out," I said. I didn't really think Galina had caused the train to stop—her best move was to slip away quietly and there was nothing subtle about this stop. But the possibility that she meant to leave the train here needed investigating. I didn't wait to draw straws. I headed down the corridor and into the no-man's-land of the ante-carriage. A push of the button and the door opened, letting in a rush of cool spring air. It smelled green and fresh, but as I stepped from the carriage, I caught something else, something sharp and metallic. The smell of fresh blood.

Outside the tunnel, a single large security light was helping the moon illuminate the scene. There was something that looked like blood on the tracks, patches that shone dark and wet. An engineer from the train had jumped down from his perch and was arguing loudly with a local farmer. The engineer spoke pretty standard Serbo-Croat, but the farmer was shouting in a regional accent. Still, I could make out the gist of what he was saying. Swearing is easy to translate in any language. He was telling the engineer he was the son of a shit; the engineer was telling him he should know because he smelled like he'd been screwing his own goats. By this time a few other passengers had left the train to join in the discussion, adding their own pithy comments. Opinion seemed to be going against the farmer and it was making him madder by the minute. He pointed to the track in front of where I stood and I could just make out a lump of flesh that had been something living only a few minutes before.

The discussion up front was getting more heated as passengers were demanding to know when we'd be on our way again. I listened to the answer which came with lots of gesticulating, then returned to the train to give the others the news. "It's goats. Or a horse. The words are really similar and my Serbian is pretty rusty."

"Oh god," Nat said, turning pale.

"It's not pretty, but at least it looks like it was quick," I told her. It didn't look anything of the sort—trains will pretty much mangle whatever's in their path—but Nat could be squeamish where animals were concerned.

"How long are we going to be here?" Mary Alice asked.

I shrugged. "They have to clear the tracks and apparently one of the goats is wedged under the engine. Or a piece of horse is. Like I said, the words are similar."

"Couldn't you tell?"

"Well, there wasn't much left," I told Mary Alice as Natalie horked quietly. "But we'll be here for a few minutes at least, and it looks like the entire train has emptied out to stretch their legs and look at the carnage." The Boy Scouts had seemed particularly keen.

I didn't have to spell it out further for Mary Alice. This was our best chance to find Galina and Tamara and the painting. With the passengers outside rubbernecking and walking the kinks out of travel-stiffened legs, there was no need to be discreet while we searched. We could do the whole train in a matter of minutes, far less time than it would take them to dismember the livestock under the train and clear the track.

We split up, Helen and Nat going forward again while Mary Alice and I headed back. The rest of the compartments were empty, doors left wide open or enough ajar that we could sweep them at a glance. We checked the Serbian compartment with its upright seats, but it was completely empty—those passengers were probably the first ones off, and I didn't blame them. Fourteen hours sitting up was a lot to ask. Any chance to move around freely was probably welcome. I opened the door of the compartment where we'd left the dead man and took a quick peek in. Still dead and right where we'd left him up in the third berth.

We passed only one closed door in the sleeper carriage. I tapped and a gruff voice called out a response in Spanish. "Ocupado!"

"Perdona," I called back.

"No es importa."

We went back the way we came, meeting up with Helen and Nat outside our sleeper.

"No sign," Helen said.

"Oh, we found her," I replied.

Mary Alice blinked. "We did?"

I grinned. "Galina Dashkova went to boarding school in the Pyrenees. The Spanish part."

Mary Alice let loose a stream of profanity that had even Natalie staring at her in admiration.

"How do we get her to open the door?" Helen asked. "Half the locks don't work, but Galina and Tamara will have barricaded themselves inside."

"Smoke?" Mary Alice suggested.

"On it," I said, grabbing a bag of Nat's snacks.

"What's to stop them going out the window with the painting?" Helen asked.

"I'll go around and cover it," Nat said. "Give me a head start and take care of Nula," she added, thrusting her chicken at Mary Alice before she headed out.

"I am not babysitting a goddamned chicken," Mary Alice said, shoving the bird at me. It squawked a bit and I backed up.

"Not it," I said.

Helen sighed. "Give her to me." She took the chicken and opened one of the sleeper berths, tossing the bird inside. She slammed the berth closed and dusted off her hands. "Problem solved." I could hear the chicken fussing which was a good sign.

"Natalie is going to *kill* you if anything happens to that chicken," Mary Alice said.

Helen shrugged. "That's a later problem. The now problem is how to smoke Galina and Tamara out of that compartment."

I waved the bag of snacks I'd purloined from Nat. "I told you, I'm on it."

They followed me to the compartment where we'd heard the Spanish reply. There was a slim chance that there actually were Spanish tourists on the train which is why I didn't just set fire to the door itself. (That, and it was Soviet-era steel.) Instead, I knelt in front of the door and studied the space between the door and the floor. When the compartment was built, it would have fit snugly, but after five or six decades of hard wear, a gap of a good half an inch had opened—plenty for my purposes.

I opened a bag of tortilla chips and took out my lighter.

Mary Alice pantomimed at me, and I understood she was asking if that would really work. I didn't feel like pantomiming back an explanation about the relative flammability of hydrocarbons and fat, so I clicked the lighter and blazed up a chip instead.

It caught instantly, and I shoved it under the door. There

was an immediate shriek, and some stamping of feet. More important, there was an exclamation that definitely wasn't Spanish. I lit a few more chips and shoved them where I'd sent the first, just to add to the confusion. At the same moment, I heard a thud and Nat's voice. Banking on the fact that they would have turned to the window, I grabbed the door handle and wrenched it hard. Whatever they'd secured it with snapped under the strain, and we were in.

It took a long second to work out exactly what we were looking at. Two women sat on one of the lower berths—one was Galina and the other her murderous little friend, Tamara. Across from them was a crunchy-looking older traveler wearing Birkenstocks, thick glasses, and a crocheted vest. There was more crochet in the form of a floppy hat she wore over a long, grey ponytail. She turned to look at me, fear lighting up the dull complexion.

It took me just a second to place her, but when I did, every puzzle piece that hadn't fit before slotted neatly into place.

My first thought was that I was going to have to send Lyndsay the P.A. a muffin basket for suspecting her. My second thought was—

"Marilyn Carstairs," I said. "You utter and absolute bitch."

CHAPTER TWENTY-EIGHT

IF MARILYN WAS UPSET THAT I CALLED HER NAMES, SHE DIDN'T SHOW it—she couldn't. She seemed to be plenty upset already about everything else going on in her life at that moment. Next to her was a backpack—not a small knapsack, but one of the monsters meant for trekking up Everest or something equally torturous. On the floor, the pile of tortilla chips still smoldered, but nobody was looking at that. They were staring at us—except for Marilyn who was looking at the window in horror. Nat was clinging to the open panel like a monkey, her hands curled tightly over the frame. When she offered to cover the window exit, I figured she meant to wait discreetly outside in case anybody made a break for it. I should have known better. Natalie would never choose discretion over making an entrance. So she hung there like a spider monkey, face pressed to the glass as Marilyn recoiled in horror.

Tamara leapt to her feet—honestly she was so short, it

didn't make much of a difference. (Generally, I don't make a habit of poking fun at things people can't choose, but Tamara frankly scared the bejesus out of me, and thinking of her as a pocket person helped make her less intimidating. Or I'm just not a very nice person. Maybe both.) She kept her knees loose and her hands up, curled into fists. She was ready for a fight and wanted us to know it. Marilyn kept shrinking further back into her seat, but Galina was composed, sitting quietly with a little smile playing over her mouth, as if she'd arranged a very nice tea party and her guests of honor had just arrived. She was dressed in nondescript black, the fingers of her right hand buddy-taped.

"Hola," I said.

To her credit, she laughed. "I didn't think that would fool you for long." Her voice was surprisingly friendly. "How nice to see you again. I trust Wolfie is well?"

"No thanks to you," Helen put in.

Galina shrugged. "I did not shoot him. Personally, I don't much like guns," she added in the same confidential tone women use to discuss yeast infections.

"Neither do I," I told her. "But I don't need one to get what I came for. Where is she?"

Galina widened her eyes. "Whoever do you mean?"

"Oh god, she's a talker," Mary Alice muttered. "Why can't they ever just answer a question the first time."

"She likes the feeling of power it gives her," Helen answered. "Like she's calling the shots. She's outnumbered two to four, but she thinks Tamara can take at least two of us which evens things up. And she probably thinks having a hostage gives her a leg up."

"It's rude to talk about people as if they weren't here," Galina murmured, grinning.

I jerked my chin at Marilyn. "Oh, she's not a hostage." As the others turned to her, she drew back even further, darting eyes around the compartment. She gnawed on her lip, and judging from the blood there, it wasn't the first time. I took a step closer.

"She's a conspirator, aren't you, Marilyn?"

Marilyn's mouth went tight. "I'm surprised you even remember me. Nobody remembers Provenance agents," she replied sourly. "We're just the data grunts, chasing down information and filing it away, day after day, year after year." The last thirty years hadn't been particularly kind to her. She'd been colorless and drab in 1994, but at least then she'd been neatly put together. Now her glasses were smudged and her jeans grubby. Her fingernails were as gnawed as her lip, and I almost felt sorry for her. Almost.

"Is this where you explain your motive for betraying us is always being overlooked and how you're just a tiny cog in a huge machine and selling us out was the only way you could take care of your poor elderly mother? Does she need an operation?" Mary Alice's voice was so sharp with sarcasm, Swiss Army could have used it as an attachment instead of a corkscrew.

Marilyn blushed. Usually when you say that about someone, it means a pretty rose flush rising in the cheeks. On

Marilyn it was a blotchy mess of bright red patches that made her look as if she were about to have a small stroke. She was breathing heavily, and her eyes were dilated. She was scared shitless, and the contrast between her obvious panic and Galina's calm menace couldn't have been more pointed.

"Let me guess," I said. "She"—I jerked my chin towards Galina—"has been terrifying you just a bit. Because when all of this started, you were probably sitting in your little cubicle, getting one day closer to retirement and thinking how unfair it is that everyone else is out doing interesting things in the world. Then what? Did you stumble onto the information that Jovan Murić had a lost Raphael masterpiece in his possession when he died? How did that happen?"

Marilyn licked at her lips, her tongue darting nervously. "It was my job to monitor the situation after his death, to see who took over his organization, if there were any loose ends we'd need to tie up. And then to write the final reports. I discovered Murić's widow was trying to move the painting. She was discreet, she never named the painting or the artist, but since I had prepared the dossier during the Bosque job, I knew exactly what she was talking about. And I realized I was the only person who would make that connection."

"That connection was a potential gold mine. What then? You had the details of when it would be on the move and who would have it, all you needed was the muscle to help you take it, right?"

"Something like that," she said through stiff lips.

I went on, laying out my pet theory. "But you're not exactly the type to tangle with a Montenegrin gangster by yourself, are you? So you went trawling through the archives to find someone who could help." I jerked my head towards Galina, who was listening with a little half smile on her face.

"And in the archives, you found the perfect accomplices in the Lazarovs, a brother and sister who had underworld connections, experience in dealing with art if you weren't too fussy about the provenance, and who didn't mind getting their hands bloody—just the right sort of people to help you in this little job. How am I doing so far?"

Marilyn turned even blotchier, but Galina laughed. "Full marks, Miss Webster."

"But people like the Lazarovs wouldn't take a job like this without a sweetener," Mary Alice added. "So you gave them our names—and Lilian Flanders's—so they could get a little revenge for their father's death at the same time."

"Working it out on paper is a little different than real life," Helen said in a soothing tone. "Isn't it, Marilyn? You've thrown in with people who would kill you without hesitating, and you have only just now realized how dangerous that is."

Marilyn rubbed a cuff over her face and it came away damp. Sweat or tears, or possibly both. "I knew they were dangerous," she said with a touch of defiance. I actually did feel sorry for her then. She really thought she could play in this particular sandbox and not get hurt.

"You know," Nat said from the open window, "that's a good point, Helen." She looked at Galina. "Why haven't you killed her yet? You have the painting. What do you need her for?"

Marilyn's show of bravado was brief. She gave a little choked scream and clutched at her backpack.

"Because I'm betting that Marilyn is the only one who knows where the drop is," I said. "She intercepted the information about who Murić's man was meeting in Athens. If she's smart, she's set up an account for the purchase money to be wired directly—I'm guessing Switzerland? The Caymans?" Marilyn didn't confirm it, but she didn't deny it either. I went on. "If she has any sense of self-preservation, she'll leave the second the money hits her account, putting as much distance as she can between herself and Galina. Then Galina will get her share once Marilyn calls the buyer from a place of safety."

Marilyn's expression told me I'd hit a bull's-eye. It wasn't hard to figure out; it's what anybody would have done in the situation. "Of course," I added, turning to Galina, "she's probably got the information in her phone, and phone security can easily be hacked. You don't even need to keep her alive. Basic biometrics like Face ID and fingerprint scanners work for a bit after death."

"It's not on my phone!" Marilyn said, just in case anybody got the bright idea of murdering her in the next few minutes, I supposed. "I memorized the details of the drop. If I die, nobody gets the sale."

"The buyer will be expecting Murić's man," I said thoughtfully. "Why would he buy a painting from somebody he doesn't know?"

"I contacted him from the courier's phone and told him there was a change of personnel for the job."

That accounted for why the courier's phone was missing from his jacket. I gave her a skeptical look. "And he bought that?"

"He wants the painting," she snapped. "He is buying it under the table. He isn't exactly in a position to make demands. But if anything happens to me, he will not do a deal with anyone else. You need me," she added to Galina. "Or you'll never see that money."

Her gaze darted from Galina to where Tamara still stood, springy as a cat. Her muscles were so tightly coiled, it was clear she was *dying* to take a pop at Marilyn and only Galina's instructions were keeping her in line. Nat still hung at the window, and I realized she must be standing with her toes on a ledge, watching it all with interest from her perch.

"I do not care for threats," Galina said politely.

"Especially when she can't back them up," I said. I turned back to Marilyn, keeping my voice kinder than I felt. She was already spooked enough. There was no point in making her more nervous because nervous people are unpredictable at best, and I didn't need her doing something stupid. "Galina has her own contacts. She doesn't actually need you to sell the painting. She can take it off you by force and move it herself. You've got to see it's hopeless, Marilyn. You tried, and full marks for a hell of a ballsy move. But you're swinging in the majors with a Nerf bat. You're in over your head. We can give you a way out. Just hand over the painting."

Her expression hardened. "You think I can't do this? I orchestrated this entire deal. I'm the one who found the information, who put all the pieces together. I did this," she said, puffing her chest a little and finding her confidence at last. "*I* did this."

I shrugged, palms out to show her I wasn't picking a fight. "Okay. You did this. Fair play. But what's your next move?"

She darted her eyes around again, assessing, before she turned to me. "I'll cut you in. The four of you," she clarified, gathering Mary Alice, Helen, and Nat in with a glance. "There's plenty of money. Just act as my bodyguards, protect me until we get the deal finished. Make sure I get safely on a plane to wherever I want to go when it's finished, and you can have a share of the proceeds."

Looking back, I'm sure Galina would have had something scathing to say about that. She might have even unleashed Tamara to do her worst. I was about to laugh in Marilyn's face, but just then the train gave another sudden lurch, throwing us all off-balance. Helen fell backwards into the corridor while Mary Alice landed at Galina's feet. The train bucked again, and suddenly we were moving, and not just moving, moving fast, picking up speed as we headed towards the viaduct.

"Jesus Christ, Natalie!" I sprang towards the window where Nat was still hanging on, eyes wide and knuckles white to the bone as she gripped for dear life. As I leapt, Galina grabbed my leg, yanking me down. I fell across her and we landed on the berth, close enough I could smell her breath—black coffee and mouthwash—and powerless to do anything but watch what happened next. It was over in a matter of seconds. We hit the viaduct bridge with a thunderous roar, and Tamara went for Nat. She kicked out, once for each hand, landing the heel of her boot squarely on Nat's fingers.

Nat screamed, but she held on.

Until she didn't.

One second she was there, the next she was gone.

And that's when all hell broke loose.

CHAPTER TWENTY-NINE

IT SHOULD HAVE BEEN ME, GOING AFTER TAMARA, BUT BEFORE I COULD even fix my fingers to gouge her eyes, Mary Alice launched herself, scrambling to her feet and vaulting clean over the tangle of the rest of us. She grabbed Tamara by the throat and shoved her up against the window.

"That was my *friend,* you bitch," she snarled. I'd never seen Mary Alice like that. Sure, she could be cranky as a grizzly on meth if she got up on the wrong side of the bed, and Nat was usually the one who caught the brunt of it. (Because she was usually the one to provoke it, which Nat herself would be the first to tell you.) Everybody knew Mary Alice was really all bark and no bite.

But something about seeing Tamara go after Natalie meant Mary Alice found her fangs. She had a good thirty pounds on Tamara and she used every one of them, lifting the smaller woman clean off the floor and slamming her so hard into the window, the glass cracked into a pattern like a spiderweb. One of Tamara's hands clutched at Mary Alice's, trying to loosen her grip. The other went into her pocket and came out with a knife. A quick slash and she was free, Mary Alice's wrist dripping blood.

"Oh, *now* I'm mad," Mary Alice told her. She reached out and slapped Tamara so hard Tamara's head cracked the glass a second time. The spiderweb spread to the corners of the window where pockets of rust seemed to be the only thing holding it together. Tamara slashed again with the knife, but Mary Alice threw up her left arm, blocking the blow as she hit fast with the edge of her right hand, aiming for Tamara's throat. Tamara jammed her knee up into Mary Alice's pubic bone and went for her again with the knife, slashing back and forth wildly.

With the rest of us distracted by the fight between Mary Alice and Tamara, Marilyn took the opportunity to bolt, grabbing the enormous backpack in both arms and scurrying out the door. Helen, looking a little dazed, shoved herself up from the floor and went after her. Galina tried to do the same, getting as far as the corridor before I grabbed her by the hair, yanking hard.

She twisted, slippery as an eel, and shoved a stiff index finger towards my eye. I turned at the last second, letting her hand go past me so I could grab her wrist. I pulled her forward to wrap my free hand around her broken fingers. I squeezed hard and she dropped to her knees, howling in pain. I circled her and looped my arm under her chin, locking it as I pulled her against me.

"It didn't have to be like this," I told her as I held her steady. "You could have just walked away. You killed Lilian Flanders. We killed Pasha. The score is even."

Galina had three basic options the way I had her pinned. She could have gone for my diaphragm, my foot, or my nose, any of which could cause an attacker to loosen their grip, and all of which I was prepared for. But Galina surprised me and went for the trifecta. She jammed a well-placed elbow in my solar plexus as she stomped hard on my foot. It was basic self-defense class stuff, but they teach it for a reason. When you combine it with a backwards slam of the head to the attacker's nose, that's three explosions of pain at once, and that's two too many.

I let her go, blood streaming from my nose as I gasped for breath. She'd gotten lucky, and I figured at least one rib was properly cracked, but my boots had protected my feet. I'd have a bruise there but nothing worse. She staggered to her feet, and when she looked at me, there was nothing but pure hatred in her eyes.

"Even? I don't think so. Did you forget that you killed my father too?" she asked.

I spat out a mouthful of blood before I answered. "Your father had it coming. You know what he did for a living, right? He was former Bulgarian secret service and his favorite thing was interrogations. He tortured people, Galina. And when that got boring, he graduated to freelance assassination. He worked for some of the worst dictators on earth, did you know that? And he killed really good people. Academics, activists, anybody working for freedom, your father had a pop at them."

"So that gave you the right to kill him?"

"The world is a better place without him." I didn't really want to debate the ethics of my profession with her, but the conversation was giving me a chance to catch my breath and I didn't hate that.

"You even killed my dog," she went on.

"The poodle that was on the plane?" I remembered the dog. It had been a pampered little asshole, and a complication we hadn't expected or needed at the time. And I remembered Natalie's almost hysterical insistence that she couldn't kill the dog. In the end, Helen had parachuted out of the plane we crashed with the dog strapped to her chest. To my surprise, it survived the jump with nothing more than a few bruises. Helen had kept it for the next twelve years.

"We didn't kill the dog," I told Galina, not really expecting her to believe me. It was the least of the crimes she could lay at our door, but it was important to me to tell her the truth. "I admit we killed your father, and I'm not sorry for that. Not even a little. It was one of the best day's work I ever did. But we really do draw the line at pets."

Her nostrils were wide as she pulled in heavy breaths. "And when my mother died, I had to go live with that old bitch. She hated me because I was like my father," she told me.

"Is that why you killed her?" I asked. I wasn't actually playing for time, but I was enjoying the breather.

"She tried to beat the Bulgarian out of me," she said darkly. "She loved Pasha, he was her darling. But me? She had no use for me."

"We all had shitty childhoods, Galina," I said. "But we don't all kill the people who raised us."

I was feeling stronger—the bleeding from my nose had slowed to a trickle—but giving Galina that much time to recover was a mistake. She feinted and when I went to grab her, she slipped around me, arms coming up fast and locking me into the same position I'd used on her. We were pretty well matched in height and weight, and she was a few years younger, but I had the advantage of experience. Whatever underworld skills Galina had, street fighting wasn't one of them. Somebody had trained her—Tamara, maybe? She had the basics down. She knew to keep her core tight and her face protected. But I'd been doing this a long time, and unfortunately for her, follow-through is my specialty.

I waited a beat as she choked me, letting her tire herself out a little more. Keeping a tight choke hold is exhausting if you aren't used to it. The forearms really start to burn. When I finally felt my air running out, I slipped my hand into my pocket and pulled out my lighter. It was the only thing I had of my mother's, a vintage piece of heavy silver, engraved with flowers set with turquoises. She'd left it behind the day she took off without me, and I'd kept it ever since. Unlike her, it never let me down.

I flicked it once, holding it to Galina's arm. It took a second for the flame to catch, but when it did, it flared fast, catching the fabric of her shirt and licking upwards. She shrieked and let me go, grabbing at her smoldering sleeve to slap out the fire. That was all the chance I needed. I clamped a hand around her broken fingers again, twisting her arm at the wrist until I heard the bone pop out of the joint. She screamed and her knees buckled, but I kept her on her feet by grabbing the back of her collar as I propelled her towards the open door. She flailed and kicked, landing several good shots to my legs, and one to my knee that sent me straight to the floor again.

I scrambled to my knees, curling the lighter into my fist. As weapons go, it wasn't as good as a roll of quarters, but it helped add a little heft to the right cross I delivered to her jaw. Her head snapped back and she howled like a dog in rage and pain. That's the problem with amateurs, I reflected as I backed towards the door. They always take things personally.

I glanced behind me. There were maybe six inches of train left under my feet and then nothing. We were still on the viaduct, crossing the gorge on a narrow track, more than a thousand feet above the valley below. I could see the supports of the viaduct, and some of the brickwork. Below that was just an endless blackness, and I turned back to Galina.

She pushed herself to her feet. I had to give her credit, she had guts if nothing else. Her sleeve was burned away, her arm was hanging at a funny angle, and her jaw was a different color than the rest of her. But still she didn't quit. Her father would have been proud.

She didn't bother to answer me. She reached into her pocket with her left hand, fumbling a little. It was awkward but also inevitable. I suspected she'd been lying about not having a gun. She might not like them, but there was no way Boris Lazarov's daughter wouldn't be prepared.

I'd felt the gun during our tussle and figured it would make an appearance at some point. She pointed it at me and smiled—her father's smile, incidentally. I remembered it well. Maybe it was stupid to let her have that moment. I could have disarmed her before she even got the gun raised. But maybe I felt sorry for her, sorry for the kid she'd been when we had killed her father. Or maybe I wanted her to have that one moment of hope when she thought she was going to win. Because that made what I did next all the more devastating.

There was a split second before she pulled the trigger, and in that space of time, I stepped aside, grabbing the gun and pulling hard. The shot went through the floor of the train, and she didn't have time to get off a second. The momentum of my pull dragged her straight out the door. I dodged back as she went by me, an expression of surprise on her face. For an instant, she seemed to hang in midair. Our eyes met, then she closed hers, as if she didn't want to see what was coming. That was probably for the best.

It was a long way down.

CHAPTER THIRTY

I CAUGHT MY BREATH AND WENT TO FIND MARY ALICE. I WAS MOVING a little slower than I used to, and she was wincing as she emerged from the compartment where we'd found Galina and Tamara with Marilyn. She was bleeding from a few new places, and a chunk of hair just over her ear was missing. I glanced over her shoulder to see a hole where the window had been.

"Tamara?"

Mary Alice wrapped a scarf around her wrist to stanch the bleeding from her knife wound. She finished, then jerked her chin towards the rust-edged opening in the train. "She needed some fresh air. Galina?"

"Same. We should find Helen."

"Not so fast," Mary Alice said. She rummaged in her fanny pack and brought out a handful of pills, tiny and bright red. "Take these."

"Why?"

"Because you're already limping and I can barely hold myself vertical. We're too old to have days like this without a little pharmaceutical assistance." She dropped some of the pills into my hand.

"What kind of pharmaceutical assistance?"

Mary Alice shrugged as she palmed her pills into her mouth. "Hell if I know. Nat gave them to me. Said to take them if I needed a boost."

Knowing Natalie, the pills were probably some unholy cocktail of uppers and painkillers, but I wasn't fussy. I'd learned a long time ago to do whatever I had to in order to finish a job. I dry-swallowed three of the pills and stuffed another two in my pocket for later.

We headed down the corridor in the direction Marilyn had run. We found Helen at the far end of the carriage, outside the compartment where we'd left Jovan Murić's henchman. She was carrying Marilyn's backpack, and looked almost entirely unruffled. Only a single lock of hair was out of place, and she tucked that neatly behind one ear as she looked us up and down.

"My god," she began.

"Don't start with me, Helen," Mary Alice warned. "I've had a challenging few minutes."

I gestured towards the backpack. "I take it you found Marilyn?"

She nodded to the door she'd just closed. "I left her in there with a broken arm. I thought we could lock her in and let her figure out how to explain to the Montenegrin police what she's doing with a dead man."

333

"Elegant," I said. "But we need something to hold it closed."

Helen took off her wimple and—with a little help from the knock-off Swiss Army knife Mary Alice was carrying—cut it into strips. We used a handful of these to tie the door handle to the grille of the air vent in the wall.

"Will that hold her?" Mary Alice asked. "A broken arm might not be enough to slow her down."

"Oh, she's not going anywhere," Helen assured her. "It's a compound fracture."

Mary Alice went a little green around the gills and held up a hand. "No details, Helen. You know I cannot handle bones sticking out of flesh."

She shuddered and Helen turned to me. "What about Galina and Tamara?"

"Gone," I told her.

"Well, that simplifies matters," Helen replied. "No other bodies to worry about."

"We need to get off this train," I said, glancing down the corridor to where the conductor had just shuffled into the toilet compartment. "Before he finishes zipping up."

We didn't discuss it further; there was no need. Three women had gone flying off the train and another one was locked in a compartment with a dead man without a head. And somehow we had managed all of that without being detected. It was a minor miracle, and I made a note to drop a few euros as an offering to St. Harlampy should the opportunity arise.

"Wait a minute," Mary Alice said. She darted back to the

compartment we'd started in as Helen and I headed for the open door. I leaned out, squinting into the darkness to survey the track.

"It looks like there's a slowdown coming. It's our best chance for getting off," I told Helen. "Mary Alice better hurry her ass up."

We'd left the viaduct behind, climbing away from it into the stony mountains. I couldn't see it then, but I knew from Helen's Lonely Planet that those grey peaks were melting off the last of their winter snows, the lower slopes studded with scrubby-looking pines and bushes. The train track itself had a few safety lights which meant I could see a little distance. For most of the next stretch, the ground fell straight away, and jumping off the train would mean plunging into the valley below. But coming up was another tunnel—there were 254 altogether which was another thing I learned courtesy of Helen's guidebook—and the train would slow down going in. And right where it slowed, the ground leveled up a bit, forming a shelf with a gentle slope instead of a dead drop. At the edge, where the shelf broke into the gorge, a few thorny bushes huddled together—all that would stand between us and a messy end to a truly shitty day.

I tried not to think about Nat as I calculated what would happen if we missed our window of opportunity. I glanced back. Mary Alice still wasn't out yet, and we had seconds left. I pushed Helen in front of me. "When I count to three, jump out as far as you can," I instructed her. "Then tuck and roll and pray to Jesus."

She didn't argue. She gently tossed the backpack out the

door, wincing as it landed and rolled away, but that was better than it being crushed under her as she somersaulted down the slope. She gave me one last look—her lips pressed together grimly, then nodded, more to herself than me, I think. The last I saw of her was her nun's habit fluttering out behind as she threw herself off the train. I held on as long as I could, waiting for Mary Alice, but she wasn't showing.

"Goddammit," I muttered. But we were out of time. I went at a run, hoping to get as much distance from the train as I could when I launched. I had a moment of weightlessness as I flew out over the little slope, then a landing on ground so fast it knocked the wind flat out of me. I would have taken a minute to get my breath back, but I was rolling, falling towards the line of brittle little bushes that marked the end of the slope. I threw out my hands, scrabbling at anything that would give me a handhold. The rocky ground slid through my fingers, pebbles tumbling and falling all around me as I rolled. Finally, my hands brushed something that wasn't rock. I grabbed wildly at something thin and twiggy, and I held on for dear life. I was happy not to be falling anymore, but I also knew one wrong move could hurtle me through the thin wall of bushes and over the cliff. I lay perfectly still, whooping air back into my lungs.

"Billie?" From a little distance away I heard Helen's voice, muffled and wheezing.

"I'm here," I managed after a minute. I sounded even worse than she did.

"You alright?"

"Well, if I'm dead, I didn't get into heaven, that much is

for damned sure," I said. I already had a few cracked ribs thanks to Galina, but with the fall, I was pretty sure they were fully broken. I tested my position carefully. Moving dislodged a few pebbles which rolled straight over the edge. It was maybe a foot away, and I eased slowly out of the bush I'd been caught in. "I have about a hundred thorns in my ass," I called as I pushed myself to my knees. I tried not to hear the hollow sound that underscored each breath. I sounded like an old-fashioned squeeze-box.

"Same," she called back. "But the vest cushioned the fall. What about Mary Alice?"

I was just about to tell her Mary Alice hadn't jumped when she made a liar out of me. The only warning I had was the squawking of the chicken as Mary Alice rolled over it when the pair of them came flying down the slope, tail over teakettle. They bowled straight into another cluster of bushes, even thornier than mine, and they stopped even closer to the edge.

Mary Alice was white as new milk when we got to her, and the chicken didn't look much better. It was standing a few feet away, as if embarrassed by Mary Alice's predicament. Helen and I hurried the best we could to pull her out. It took both of us—she was stuck fast—and a lot of swearing on Mary Alice's part before she was free.

She sat on the slope, puffing hard and resting her head on her knees while Helen and I did the same.

"You okay?" I asked Mary Alice.

She nodded. "Nat's goodies are kicking in. I'll be fine—at least for six hours or so. That's when they'll wear off."

"What goodies?" Helen asked.

I handed over my last two pills. "Take these and don't ask questions."

"Are you going to roofie me? Am I being roofied?"

"I said not to ask questions," I reminded her. She gulped down the pills like a cranky cat, complete with gacking noises.

"You're being the opposite of roofied," Mary Alice assured her. "Give it a few minutes to kick in and you'll feel like you could lift a building."

"Can't wait," Helen said brightly. Her voice was shaking a little with fatigue, and she didn't look great—none of us did. This job was hard enough when we were twenty, but at sixty-two? It took a hell of a lot more recovery time than it had forty years before.

"Did you get the backpack?" Mary Alice asked.

Helen swung the backpack around for us to see. It was covered in dust and had collected a few thorns, but otherwise it was in decent shape. I suppose it had been designed to withstand extreme temperatures, avalanches, and yeti attacks, after all.

She worked the buckles with stiff, bloody fingers. The inside had been specially fitted to hold a padded case, not quite two feet by three. She took it out, and we held our breath as she opened it.

We couldn't see the colors exactly; the moonlight wasn't strong enough for that. But something about that shifting, silvery light made it even more magical. We had just missed meeting her thirty years before, and here she was, turning up again. She had been pulled from her stretcher bars and there were nail holes in the margins. I couldn't see any other major damage, and something in my chest that had tightened when we lost her thirty years before began to ease.

We didn't speak—you don't speak on hallowed ground, and *Leda* made that rocky Montenegrin mountainside holy. She gazed serenely out at us, as unbothered as the moon by anything lesser than she was. We were grubby and human and small, and she was so much more.

I put out a fingertip to touch her. It was an unconscious urge, something about connecting with beauty, I think. But I stopped myself. She was untouchable. The centuries hadn't diminished her. The skin was as luminous, the stare just as challenging. She'd been stolen, hidden, coveted, treasured, captured as spoils of war, and yet none of it had touched her. She endured, eternal as a goddess but vulnerable as a child. A single spark, an errant slip of the knife, could destroy her.

And it was up to us to protect her.

Helen packed her back up into her case. Wordlessly, we fitted the case back into the backpack, the spell broken.

"Where are we?" Helen asked, squinting at the moon.

I shrugged. "Somewhere past the viaduct." I assessed what I could of the terrain in the fitful light. There was a narrow path, a goat track, that led past the edge of the bushes, switchbacking around boulders before disappearing into a pocket of trees.

"That way," I said, pointing.

Mary Alice jerked her thumb a different direction. "Podgorica is that way."

"So let's just follow the railway track," Helen suggested.

I gave them both a level look. "I'm not headed to Pod-gorica."

I didn't say her name. I didn't have to. They knew I was going to find her. I started down the track, moving slowly. Behind me, I heard Helen hoist the backpack with a grunt and follow me.

I paused, looking up at Mary Alice. She had turned to where the chicken was staring at her with baleful, dinosaur eyes. "You coming?" Mary Alice asked.

The chicken didn't make a move. Mary Alice started in our direction, and after a second, with a loud cluck of annoyance, the chicken came too.

We made a sorry little band, working our way down the mountain, sometimes dropping to our hands and knees where the track was too steep or the rock too rotten. There were places where the path was level and wide, carpeted with pine needles and smelling like Christmas. And there were other places where it plunged straight down like it had a death wish, nothing but slippery scree you could almost surf. And sometimes it disappeared altogether and we had to guess the best route, occasionally causing us to backtrack for a mile or so to choose a different way.

There were a few streams, running fast and clean from winter snow melting off the mountaintops. We stopped at each, drinking deeply. Helen rooted around in the pockets of her habit until she found some jerky she'd stashed. She shared it out, but it didn't do much to fill us up. Of course, as Mary Alice pointed out more than once, we had a chicken if things got desperate, but that was just bravado talking. I knew from the way she'd gone back for the chicken, she'd never harm a feather on its head. Nat had brought the bird on board, and since she was gone, Mary Alice had taken on its care like a sacred trust.

That night stretched on, forever it seemed. We'd gone off the train before midnight, and it was a long, cold slog until the first rays of the sun crept over the mountain above us. It would be hours before the light made its way down into the valley where we were headed, but knowing it was there, rising up the other side of that relentless mountain, somehow made it bearable. We walked on, one stumbling footstep at a time, until we emerged from the last black pine thicket into the valley floor. A narrow road wound between wooded patches, and we turned to walk along it. The level grass was a miracle after hours of falling and sliding. The pills had worn off a few hours in, and we pushed through on sheer willpower after that. I was hungry, thirsty again, and numb from pushing away thoughts of Natalie. I didn't think about her any more than I thought about my broken ribs. Sometimes pain just gets in the way of what you have to do. So you put it down until you can stand to carry it again.

After a mile or so of trudging along the road, we heard a distant rumble of engines slowly approaching. We stopped, taking stock of our situation and weighing our options.

"Hitchhike?" Helen asked.

"Who'd pick us up?" I asked. We were filthy and tattered, to say nothing of bloodstained and sporting various injuries.

"I don't care," Mary Alice said. "I will give them this chicken if they will give us a ride. I will give them all the money in my pockets. I will give them any sexual favors they might require. Just as long as they let us get off this road."

I looked her over from her torn vacation Bible school sweatshirt to her face, both streaked with blood, and shook my head. "I'm not sure you could give it away, looking like that," I told her.

"I'll do it," Helen said. "As long as I can just lie there."

Before I could point out to her that she looked even worse—and was dressed like a nun—the rumble of the engines increased to a roar. There was a bend in the road, and one second they were hidden, the next they were in front of us, rolling to a stop. A group of motorcycles, the riders all dressed in heavy leathers, faces hidden by helmets.

They braked, and for just a moment, nothing happened. We looked at them, and they looked at us. The lead motorcycle had someone riding pillion, and the passenger climbed down, tugging at the helmet strap. The helmet popped off, freeing a familiar tangle of wild curls. Behind her the morning sun shone like a nimbus, haloing her head in gold. She had a face full of bruises and one arm was strapped up in a sling. She grinned in spite of her busted lip.

"You girls want a ride?" Nat asked.

CHAPTER THIRTY-ONE

MARY ALICE FLUNG HERSELF AT NAT, NEARLY KNOCKING HER OFF HER feet.

Nat winced. "Easy, girl. I've got a dislocated shoulder and about seventeen other injuries."

"We thought you were dead," Mary Alice said through snotty tears.

"Hell, I almost was. That bitch knocked me straight into a metal panel on the edge of the viaduct. If it hadn't held, I'd have gone all the way over." The rest of us hugged her tight, ignoring her protests. We were all hurting, and I felt old as something from the Pleistocene. But Nat was there, bruised and bothered and alive.

"You saved Nula!" she exclaimed, cuddling her chicken with her good arm.

"You are not getting that thing home," Mary Alice warned her.

"Watch me."

They fell to bickering gently as somebody behind us cleared her throat.

"Naomi! What the hell are you doing in Montenegro?" I demanded.

"Following my mole," she said. She was dressed in a moto suit of padded black leather, sleek and chic, like she meant business.

I gestured towards her outfit. "You should wear that to the office. Biker Fridays."

"Office nothing. I'm keeping this to wear at home," she said. "Dennis won't know what hit him." She pointed up the mountain to the nearest railway bridge, so small it looked like a toy. "You came from up there?"

"After we bailed out of a moving train," Mary Alice told her.

"Galina?"

"Handled," I told her. "Along with her bodyguard."

"Good," Naomi said. "Now I just have to find our mole." She reached for her phone and pulled up a picture of a dark-haired young woman wearing a seafoam green taffeta dress and an expression that said she'd rather be anywhere else. "Lynd-say really was at her sister's wedding. I felt so bad for suspecting her, I had to give her a raise. And a better benefits package."

Maybe I wouldn't send her a muffin basket, after all. Some extra PTO was a lot better than pastries.

"The mole is Marilyn Carstairs," I told her.

She grinned, the kind of grin a cobra shows a mouse. "Oh, I know. I've got some plans for her."

"We handled her too," Helen put in.

Naomi's brows rose. "Permanently?"

"We locked her in a compartment with a man who was missing his head," Mary Alice said. "Murić's courier. Marilyn will be sitting in a cell by now, trying to explain that to the Montenegrin police."

Naomi gave a soundless whistle. "Permanent enough."

"Will you get her out?" I asked.

Naomi made her expression carefully blank. "Get who out? I'm afraid I don't know anybody in Montenegro."

Chapter closed on Marilyn Carstairs, then. She had set us up to die and had been perfectly content with the murders of Lilian Flanders and Jovan Murić's henchman. I was okay with her being tossed into a Montenegrin jail. If the conditions didn't kill her, Murić's connections probably would. Word travels fast in the Balkans. There was always a chance I might feel bad about it later, but I was pretty sure I wouldn't.

I reached into the pocket of my jacket and pulled out a small navy blue Smythson notebook. I held it out to Naomi.

"Pasha Lazarov's planner. I know we've wrapped everything up here, but maybe your department can find something useful in his business contacts. It belongs in Provenance."

She took it and dropped it into her bag. "Thank you. But we haven't wrapped everything up here. I still don't know exactly what Marilyn and Galina were doing on this train. If they were in business together, we've got to clean that up. No loose ends."

"I think we can help with that," I told Naomi. I gestured towards Helen and she dropped the backpack gently at my feet. She held it open while Mary Alice pulled out the case. She handed it to me, and I opened it. I didn't have to say a word. Naomi had been in Provenance all of her career. She knew everything about the ones that had gotten away.

"Oh my god," she whispered. She put out a hand to touch *Leda,* just as I had. And just as I had, she drew back reverently. "Where has she been?"

I shrugged. "With Jovan Murić, most recently. Before that, who knows?"

"We're officially handing her over to you for repatriation," Mary Alice said.

Naomi nodded. "The family she was looted from is in Stockholm now. I'll see to it they get her back before I go back stateside."

"What about us?" Nat asked.

"What about you?"

"Marilyn Carstairs gets a heaping helping of Montenegrin justice. The family in Sweden gets their painting back. What do we get? I mean, I just got flung off a train and nearly killed. Mary Alice and Helen are bleeding all over the place, and the way Billie is holding her side, I'm guessing she's got broken ribs—"

Naomi held up a hand. "Point taken. What do you want?"

"Bonuses," Mary Alice said quickly.

"Housing stipend," Helen added. "I've got to find somewhere to live while I rebuild Benscombe."

I looked at her and grinned. "Maybe a flat in Brussels?"

She grinned back. "Maybe for a little while."

"And pensions," Nat piped up.

Naomi turned to me, clearly getting impatient. "Anything else, since I'm apparently taking orders like a Hardee's drive-thru?"

"I agree about the pensions," I said. "But it needs to be official. I want us on the books as having retired from the Museum. In good standing."

Her expression softened. "I can do that. I'll push through everything you've asked for. And I'll arrange for your return home as well—first class. On the company's dime, of course."

"Not straightaway," Mary Alice said quickly. "We need to head back to Venice first."

"Akiko is fine," Naomi assured her. "I saw her on my way here. But Wolfie is still there," she warned us.

"We'll take care of him," Helen promised.

Naomi hadn't put the painting away yet. The morning sun fell across the canvas, illuminating it. "Raphael painted her in oils more than five hundred years ago," Naomi said quietly. "And she still looks like she could talk to you if she wanted." The four of us stood next to Naomi, looking at *Leda* as she looked back at us. I knew we'd probably never see *Leda* again. She'd be sent to the family that had lost her and they would hang her on their walls or stick her in a vault somewhere. They might even auction her off—anyone would be at least tempted by the kind of money *Leda* would bring in. She had once hung on the walls of a king's palace; maybe her next home would be an apartment in Stockholm or a penthouse in Shanghai. Wherever she ended up, I hoped she would be with people who loved her. She deserved it.

As Naomi zipped up the backpack, the rider who had been

carrying Nat pillion lowered the kickstand of his bike and dismounted, pulling off his helmet. He set it on his seat and came to me. My broken ribs ached and every square inch of my body felt bruised and lacerated, but a gleaming sun was coming up over the mountain. Another day was dawning and I was there to see it. He opened his arms and I went into them, resting my head in the crook of his neck.

"You good?" His voice rumbled in his chest and I nodded, thinking of the day I'd left Greece, the day he'd promised me that when the job was finished, he'd be there. Well, the job was done, Naomi had been briefed, and here he was.

"You've got good timing, English."

He tipped his head. "Do I?"

I looked at his bike and grinned as I raised my face for him to kiss me.

"Yeah. I think maybe I needed a little rescuing this time."

I couldn't lift my arms high enough to hug him back, but he did the job well enough for both of us. When he'd finished, he strapped a spare helmet on me and helped me onto the bike. The others were all settled behind the rest of the riders Taverner and Naomi had brought—Museum contacts from around the Balkans, I found out later.

I leaned back and Taverner climbed onto the bike, shielding me with his body. I looped a few fingers through his belt loop and rested my head on his back.

"Ready?" he shouted.

"Take me home, English."

CHAPTER THIRTY-TWO

WE STOPPED IN PODGORICA FOR A BIT OF MEDICAL TREATMENT, FOOD, and rest. Naomi got us a hotel suite and a doctor who made house calls. Once he'd patched us up—mostly cleaning and taping things and setting a few stitches—Naomi ordered two of everything on the room service menu and found us some new clothes. After that, we napped and ate again, and then boarded a plane for Venice. We touched down near midnight, coming in over the waters of the lagoon that rippled black as a widow's skirt. The moon rose, a little lopsided now, with a sliver pared off the edge. Taverner held my hand as we climbed into a private launch. We rode it as near as we could get to the Campo Santa Margherita where the house with the rose-colored walls waited for us.

And it wasn't just the house that waited. The door was flung open before Taverner even punched in the first number on the code. Akiko threw herself at Mary Alice while Minka looked me over to assess the damage and Wolfie gave Taverner a hearty hug.

"You are all okay?" Wolfie asked anxiously as we gathered in the salon. There were snacks and drinks laid out, but nobody touched anything. There were stories to tell, questions to answer, and a few secrets to keep. They didn't need to know *everything*. But still the talking went on for hours. It was nearly dawn before anybody moved towards bed.

"So, what now?" Wolfie asked.

"You're free to go back to your apartment," Helen told him. "You can start rehearsing again at La Fenice, go out in public. Galina is gone, Wolfie. Nobody is going to come after you."

His shoulders sagged a bit. He seemed relieved and deflated, and I wasn't sure which emotion was stronger. "This has been an interesting time," he said slowly. "I do not know what to think about it all."

Mary Alice jotted a number on a card. "Call if you like."

He looked touched. "This is your number?"

"No. It's a psychologist our organization keeps on retainer for dealing with post-traumatic stress. Free of charge, but you might want to speak with a professional," she said kindly.

He nodded. "I think this is good."

"And you can come visit us in Greece," Taverner said. I resisted the urge to kick him. Taverner was always inviting people to come stay and I was always finding reasons not to let them.

"Maybe when your time at La Fenice is over," I suggested. A lot could happen between then and June.

There was no reason for him to linger after that. He shook

hands awkwardly, hugged Taverner again, and left with a box of Malvestio pastries tucked under his arm.

"I think I'm going to miss that kid," Helen said as she closed the door behind him. We sat quietly for a while, listening to the sounds of the campo stirring to life outside. Eventually, Helen turned to the rest of us. "What now? Sleep?"

"I'm too restless," Mary Alice said. Akiko had curled herself into a corner of the sofa with one of the cats and was snoring gently. The other cat was using Minka for a cushion as they dozed together on the floor. Taverner was in an armchair, legs stretched out on an ottoman, face relaxed in sleep.

"I have an idea," I said. I grabbed a bottle of champagne from the fridge and jotted a note to Taverner, tucking it in his shirt so he'd find it when he woke up.

We eased out of the house and made our way slowly through the alleyways of the Dorsoduro. Shopkeepers were hosing off the stones in front of their stores, taking deliveries, raising metal shutters. Mothers—and a few fathers—walked their children to school, quizzing them about alphabets and times tables. Early-bird tourists were also starting their days, emerging from albergos with cameras looped around their necks and maps flapping. We climbed half a dozen bridges, pausing at each to watch the morning traffic picking up on the canals. Even first thing in the morning, Venice doesn't buzz; it shimmers, the heart of it beating with its own rhythm unlike anywhere else in the world. That morning, I like to think it was beating for us.

We were early, of course. The museum didn't open until ten AM, but we'd bought pastries and we sat on a step outside and shared the box, stuffing ourselves with maritozzi, each one bursting with cream we licked off our fingers.

As Nat and Mary Alice scrapped over the last pastry, Helen's phone rang. She glanced at the name on the screen and smiled as she sent it to voicemail.

"I really am sorry about your house burning down," I said after a minute.

"Don't be. I've been thinking of a few improvements I could make if I rebuilt it from the ground up—without any ghosts this time." Her expression was serene, like a woman who'd finished a good book and was ready to leave that particular story behind.

"Oh?"

She nodded. "It's time to let them go, I think—Kenneth, Constance. They may be gone, but I'm still here. I'd forgotten that for too long, but I'm ready for some changes. For starters, I'm going to put in heated floors and a plunge pool in the basement."

"That sounds expensive," I noted.

"Naomi and I had a comprehensive discussion on the subject of money before she left," Helen told me in a silky voice. "I think she understands what it will take to do right by us."

I liked the sound of that. "Rebuilding Benscombe will take a while. Where will you stay in the meantime?" I asked innocently.

"I'm sure I can find a spare bed," she said, blushing like a teenager.

I bumped her shoulder with mine. A thrust of pain in my ribs reminded me of what I'd put my body through in the last few days, and I thought of our little house in Greece with a longing I'd never felt before. It was time for a good, long rest on an island of herb-scented breezes set in seas once sailed by the sons of the gods.

Helen bumped me back. "You should make an honest man of him," she said. "Does Taverner ever propose?"

"He knows better," I told her. "We're good. We're forever. Just as we are."

Just then the guard approached the gate and I took Helen's hand to help me get to my feet. "Worry about your own love life," I said with a grin. "And send me a postcard of the *Mannekin Pis*."

When the guard finally opened the gate, we went inside and paid our admission, the first visitors of the day. He looked appalled at the bottle of champagne—probably because it wasn't good Italian prosecco—but a fifty-euro note bought his approval. I didn't need to look at the map to know where to go. I'd been there before.

The Peggy Guggenheim Collection is housed in a small palazzo right on the Grand Canal. It's the kind of place that makes you think being stupidly wealthy is maybe not a bad thing at all. It's a little jewel, full of modern art that old Peggy herself chose with a meticulous eye. Masterpiece after masterpiece in room after room, each one selected for its power, its unexpectedness. You could lose yourself for hours in front of any of them.

But we ignored them all. Instead, we walked straight through the dining room to where she hung. Leonor Fini's *Shepherdess of the Sphinxes*. It had been painted in 1941, when the second world war was gouging fresh scars into the landscaped face of

Europe. The painting showed a similar setting, a bleak and featureless expanse painted in deep, rich colors to contrast with the emptiness. It presented a herd of sphinxes—not the Egyptian kind with lion faces. These were the Greek sort, with the torsos of beautiful women grafted onto the bodies of lionesses. They were wild in their ferocity, absolutely untamable.

And in the center stood the shepherdess herself, a fantastical figure striding through the field with her crook. She had the kind of big hair a 1980s supermodel would have envied, and a taut, muscular body in a silvery garment shaped like a strappy bathing suit. Around the sphinxes were scattered the remains of the men they had devoured, nothing but assorted bones and scraps of humanity. The leftovers reduced to litter. But they weren't ashamed, those sphinxes. They arched their backs and tossed their manes, and above them all, their shepherdess looked at them fondly, with pride. She didn't despise them for what they were. She knew they were simply being true to their nature. Some creatures are born to destroy.

The cork made a gentle hiss as I eased it out of the bottle. Helen had packed a cluster of plastic cups into her Birkin and I poured out a bit of fizz for each of us. The champagne foamed like the tide of the Adriatic, then ebbed.

I raised my cup. "To Constance Halliday. The original shepherdess. For teaching her sphinxes that we are all necessary monsters."

"To Constance and the necessary monsters," the others said.

We touched our cups together and drank.

The champagne wasn't icy and the cups weren't crystal, but it was enough.

ACKNOWLEDGMENTS

When I wrote *Killers of a Certain Age*, I never expected the response this book received. I'm still overwhelmed, to be honest—and immensely, immensely grateful. In no particular order, here's where I'm aiming that gratitude:

The people who take care of me personally. My parents, my child, my friends, and beyond everything, my husband. Honorable mention to the dogs.

The people who take care of me professionally. The Berkley team, which includes every single person in Editorial, Marketing, PR, Sales, Production, and Art, with particular and heartfelt appreciation for my editor, Michelle Vega, who inherited *Killers* and launched it with flawless dedication. Ivan Held, Jeanne-Marie Hudson, Craig Burke, Tom Colgan, Claire Zion, Loren Jaggers, Jessica Mangicaro, Annie Odders, Tara O'Connor, Tawanna Sullivan, Anthony Ramondo, Colleen Reinhart—fervent thanks for all that you do. My literary agent, Pam Hopkins, for literal decades of devotion. My entertainment agents, Sanjana Seelam and Nicole Weinroth, at

William Morris, for helping us navigate new territory. My Writerspace team for keeping things tidy online.

The people who love books. Readers, writers, booksellers, librarians, reviewers, bookstagrammers, and anyone who hands a book to a friend and says, "I think you'll like this." Thank you.